Created By
Bryan Hill & Nelson Blake II

Published by
Top Cow Productions, Inc

Bryan Hill
WRITER

Nelson Blake II
ARTIST

Troy Peteri
LETTERER

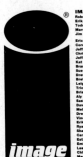

For Top Cow Productions, Inc.

For Top Cow Productions, Inc.
Marc Silvestri - CEO
Matt Hawkins - President & COO
Elena Salcedo - Vice President of Operations
Henry Barajas - Director of Operations
Vincent Valentine - Production Manager
Dylan Gray - Marketing Director

To find the comic shop nearest you, call:
1-888-COMICBOOK

Want more info? Check out:
www.topcow.com
for news & exclusive Top Cow merchandise!

IMAGE COMICS, INC.
Robert Kirkman—Chief Operating Officer
Erik Larsen—Chief Financial Officer
Todd McFarlane—President
Marc Silvestri—Chief Executive Officer
Jim Valentine—Vice-President

Eric Stephenson—Publisher
Corey Murphy—Director of Sales
Jeff Boison—Director of Publishing Planning & Book Trade Sales
Chris Ross—Director of Digital Sales
Jeff Stang—Director of Specialty Sales
Kat Salazar—Director of PR & Marketing
Branwyn Bigglestone—Controller
Sue Korpela—Accounts Manager
Drew Gill—Art Director
Brett Warnock—Production Manager
Leigh Thomas—Print Manager
Tricia Ramos—Traffic Manager
Briah Skelly—Publicist
Aly Hoffman—Events & Conventions Coordinator
Sasha Head—Sales & Marketing Production Designer
David Brothers—Branding Manager
Melissa Gifford—Content Manager
Drew Fitzgerald—Publicity Assistant
Vincent Kukua—Production Artist
Erika Schnatz—Production Artist
Ryan Brewer—Production Artist
Shanna Matuszak—Production Artist
Carey Hall—Production Artist
Esther Kim—Direct Market Sales Representative
Emilio Bautista—Digital Sales Representative
Leanna Caunter—Accounting Assistant
Chloe Ramos-Peterson—Library Market Sales Representative
Maria Eiaik—Administrative Assistant
IMAGECOMICS.COM

CHAPTER ONE:
Last of the Wolves

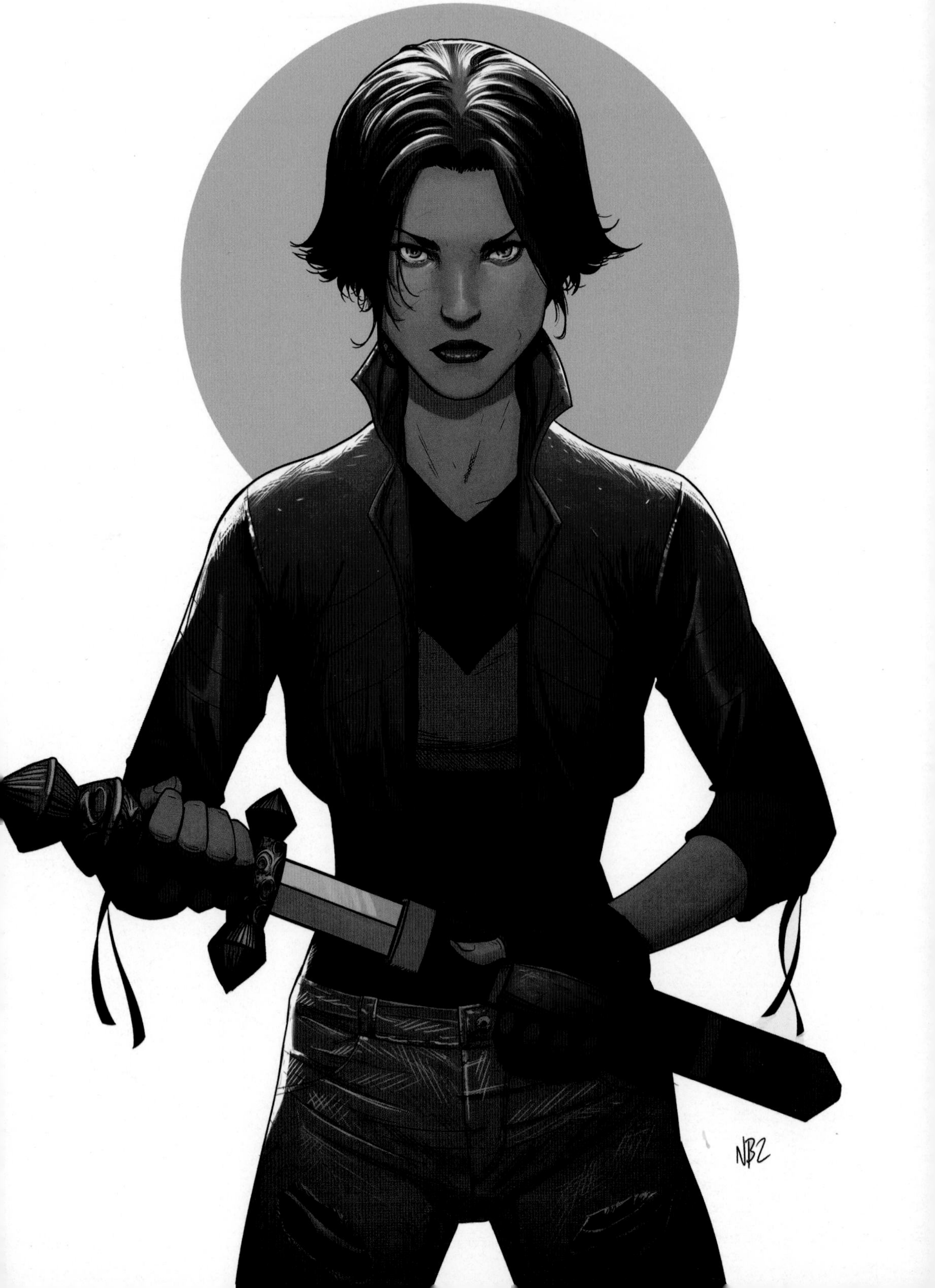
NBZ

I'M BORN ON A MOUNTAIN DUSTED WITH SNOW.

I'M A *GIRL.* SO I GET TO *LIVE.*

TEN YEARS OLD.

I'M *MARKED* FOR THE *PATH.*

THE *SEVEN SPHERES* OF *PERFECTION.*

FORCE.

WAR.

FURY.

SPEED.

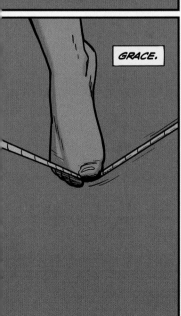

GRACE.

PAIN.

DEATH.

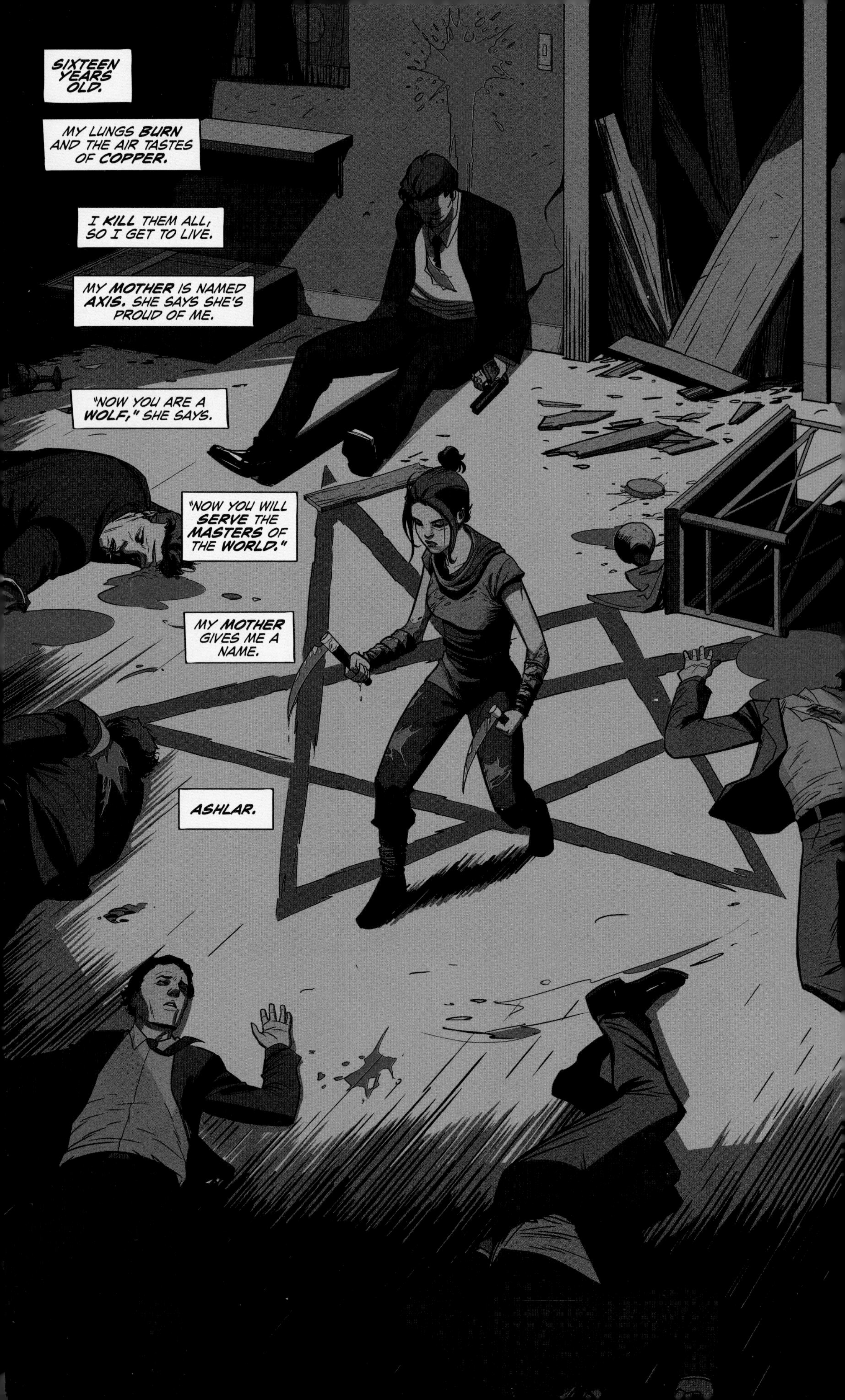
SIXTEEN YEARS OLD.
MY LUNGS BURN AND THE AIR TASTES OF COPPER.
I KILL THEM ALL, SO I GET TO LIVE.
MY MOTHER IS NAMED AXIS. SHE SAYS SHE'S PROUD OF ME.
"NOW YOU ARE A WOLF," SHE SAYS.
"NOW YOU WILL SERVE THE MASTERS OF THE WORLD."
MY MOTHER GIVES ME A NAME.
ASHLAR.

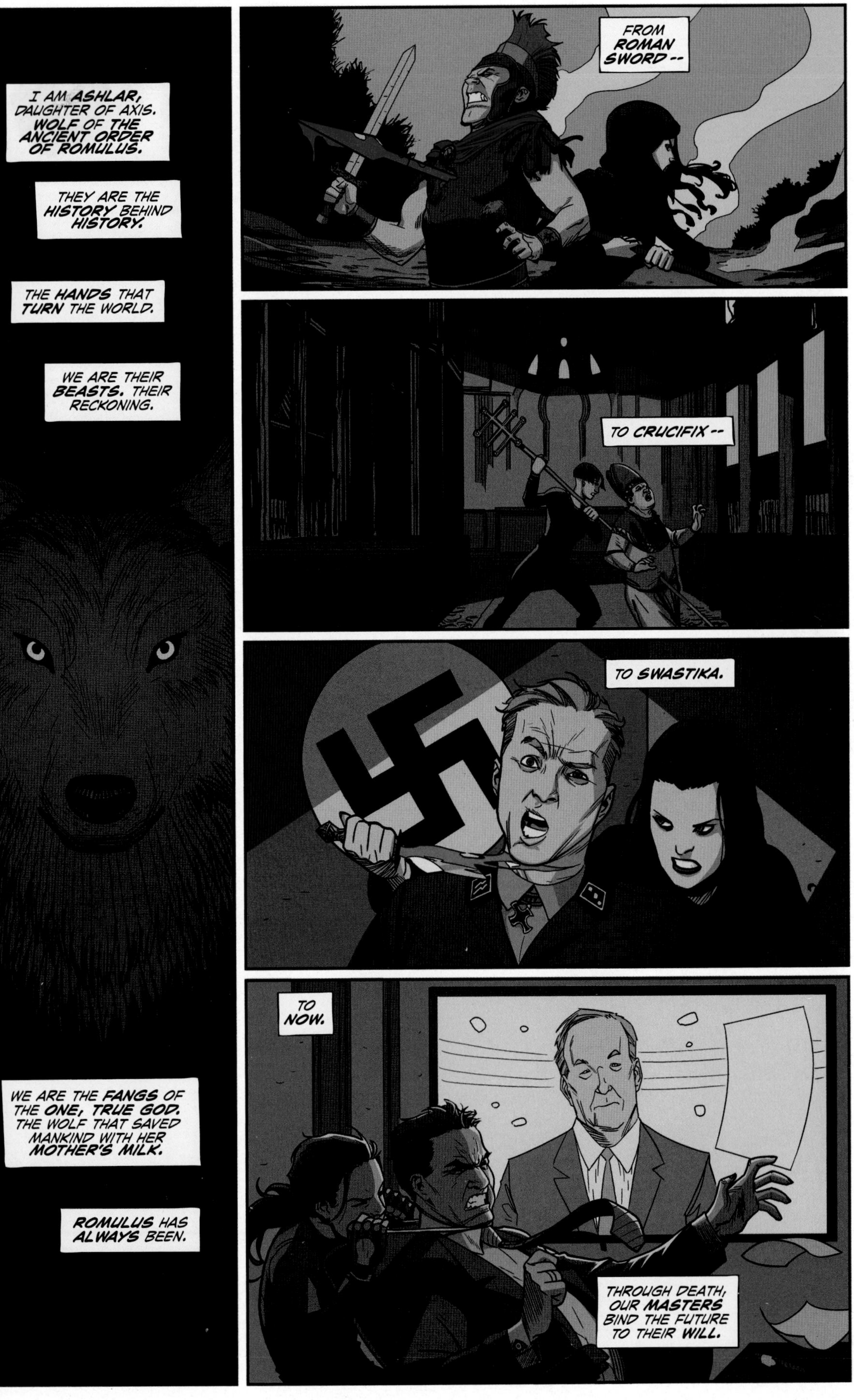
I AM ASHLAR, DAUGHTER OF AXIS. WOLF OF THE ANCIENT ORDER OF ROMULUS.
THEY ARE THE HISTORY BEHIND HISTORY.
THE HANDS THAT TURN THE WORLD.
WE ARE THEIR BEASTS. THEIR RECKONING.
FROM ROMAN SWORD --
TO CRUCIFIX --
TO SWASTIKA.
TO NOW.
WE ARE THE FANGS OF THE ONE, TRUE GOD. THE WOLF THAT SAVED MANKIND WITH HER MOTHER'S MILK.
ROMULUS HAS ALWAYS BEEN.
THROUGH DEATH, OUR MASTERS BIND THE FUTURE TO THEIR WILL.

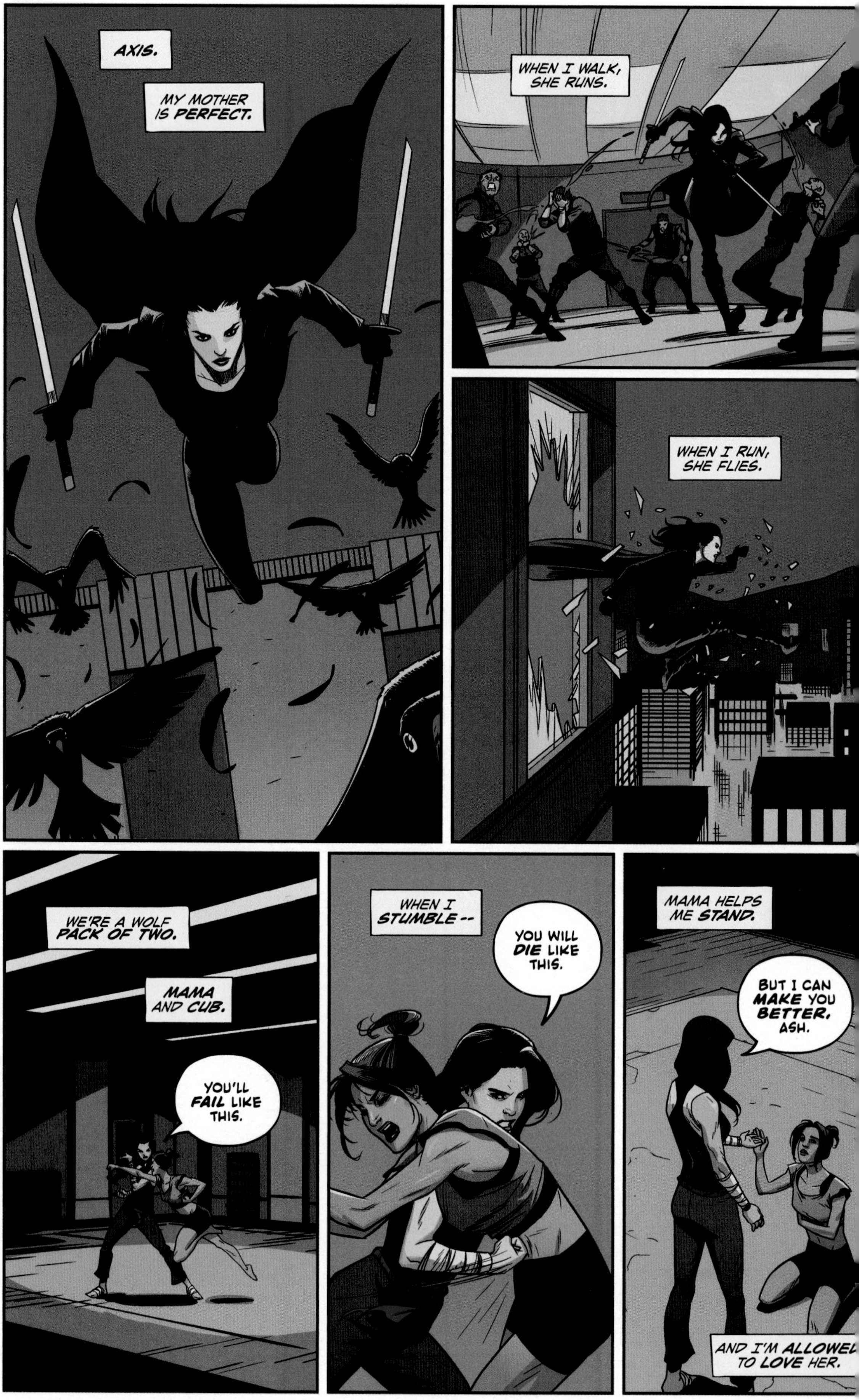
AXIS.
MY MOTHER IS PERFECT.
WHEN I WALK, SHE RUNS.
WHEN I RUN, SHE FLIES.
WE'RE A WOLF PACK OF TWO.
MAMA AND CUB.
YOU'LL FAIL LIKE THIS.
WHEN I STUMBLE --
YOU WILL DIE LIKE THIS.
MAMA HELPS ME STAND.
BUT I CAN MAKE YOU BETTER, ASH.
AND I'M ALLOWE TO LOVE HER.

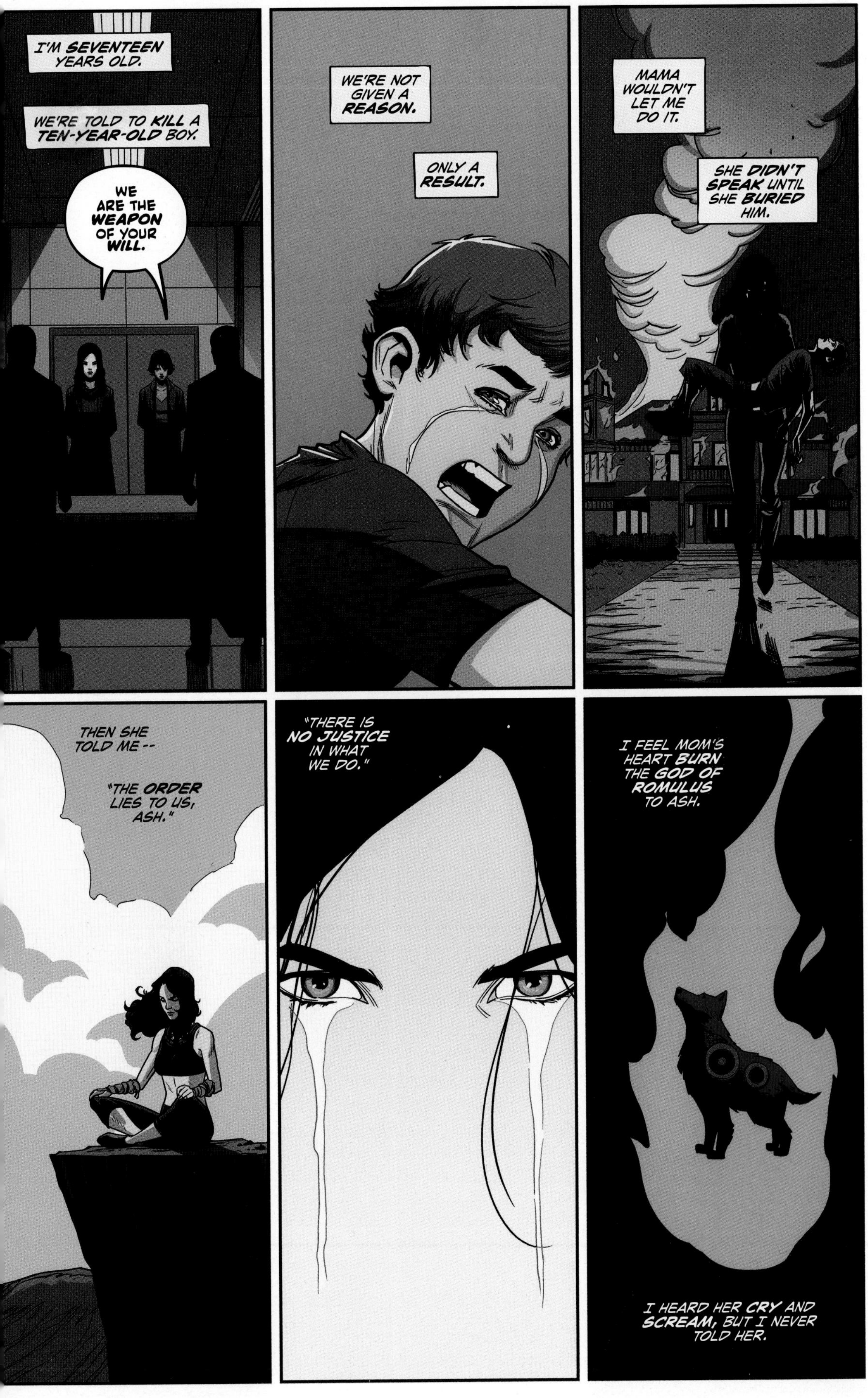
I'M SEVENTEEN YEARS OLD.
WE'RE TOLD TO KILL A TEN-YEAR-OLD BOY.
WE ARE THE WEAPON OF YOUR WILL.
WE'RE NOT GIVEN A REASON.
ONLY A RESULT.
MAMA WOULDN'T LET ME DO IT.
SHE DIDN'T SPEAK UNTIL SHE BURIED HIM.
THEN SHE TOLD ME --
"THE ORDER LIES TO US, ASH."
"THERE IS NO JUSTICE IN WHAT WE DO."
I FEEL MOM'S HEART BURN THE GOD OF ROMULUS TO ASH.
I HEARD HER CRY AND SCREAM, BUT I NEVER TOLD HER.

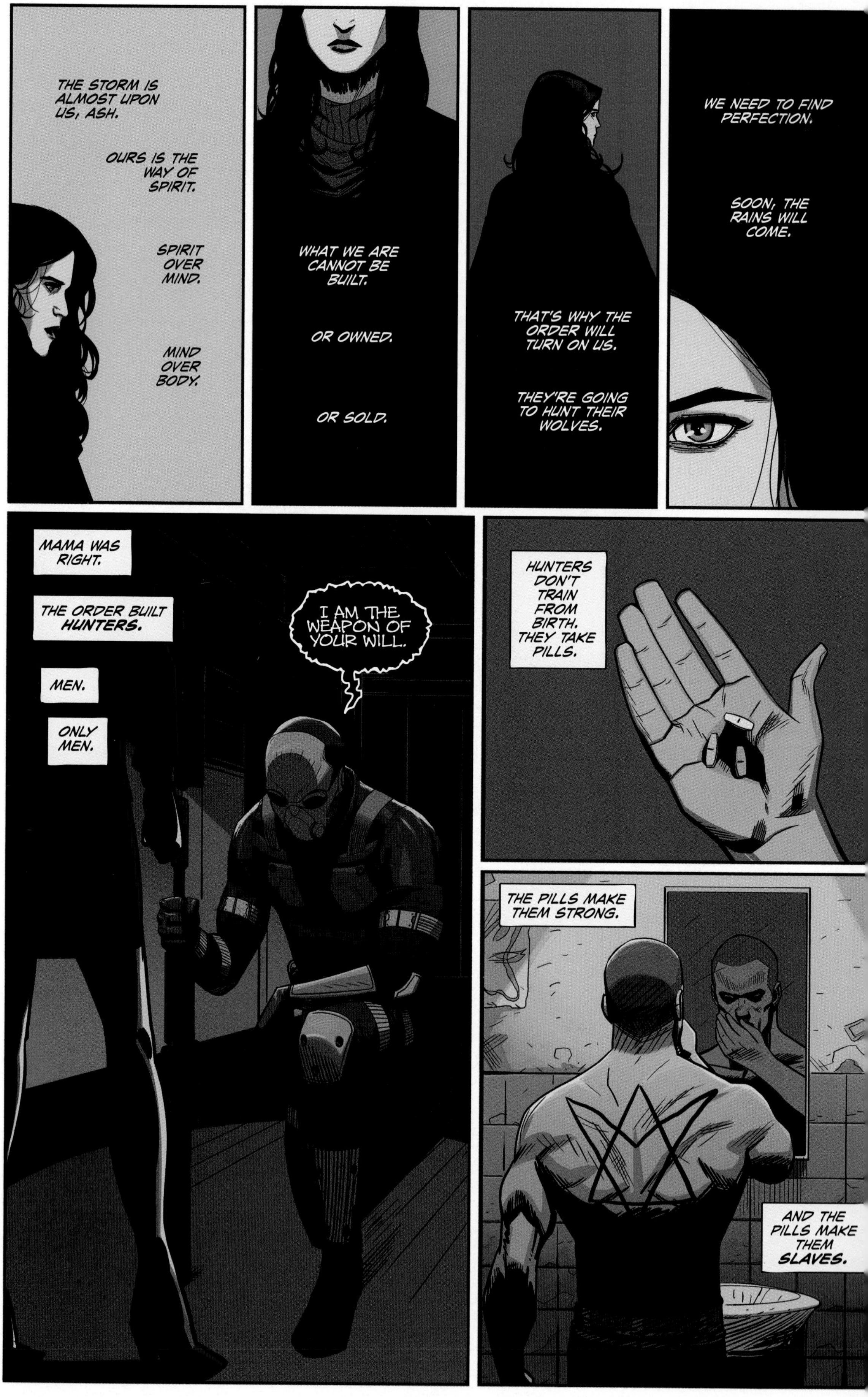
THE STORM IS ALMOST UPON US, ASH.
OURS IS THE WAY OF SPIRIT.
SPIRIT OVER MIND.
MIND OVER BODY.
WHAT WE ARE CANNOT BE BUILT.
OR OWNED.
OR SOLD.
THAT'S WHY THE ORDER WILL TURN ON US.
THEY'RE GOING TO HUNT THEIR WOLVES.
WE NEED TO FIND PERFECTION.
SOON, THE RAINS WILL COME.
MAMA WAS RIGHT.
THE ORDER BUILT HUNTERS.
MEN.
ONLY MEN.
I AM THE WEAPON OF YOUR WILL.
HUNTERS DON'T TRAIN FROM BIRTH. THEY TAKE PILLS.
THE PILLS MAKE THEM STRONG.
AND THE PILLS MAKE THEM SLAVES.

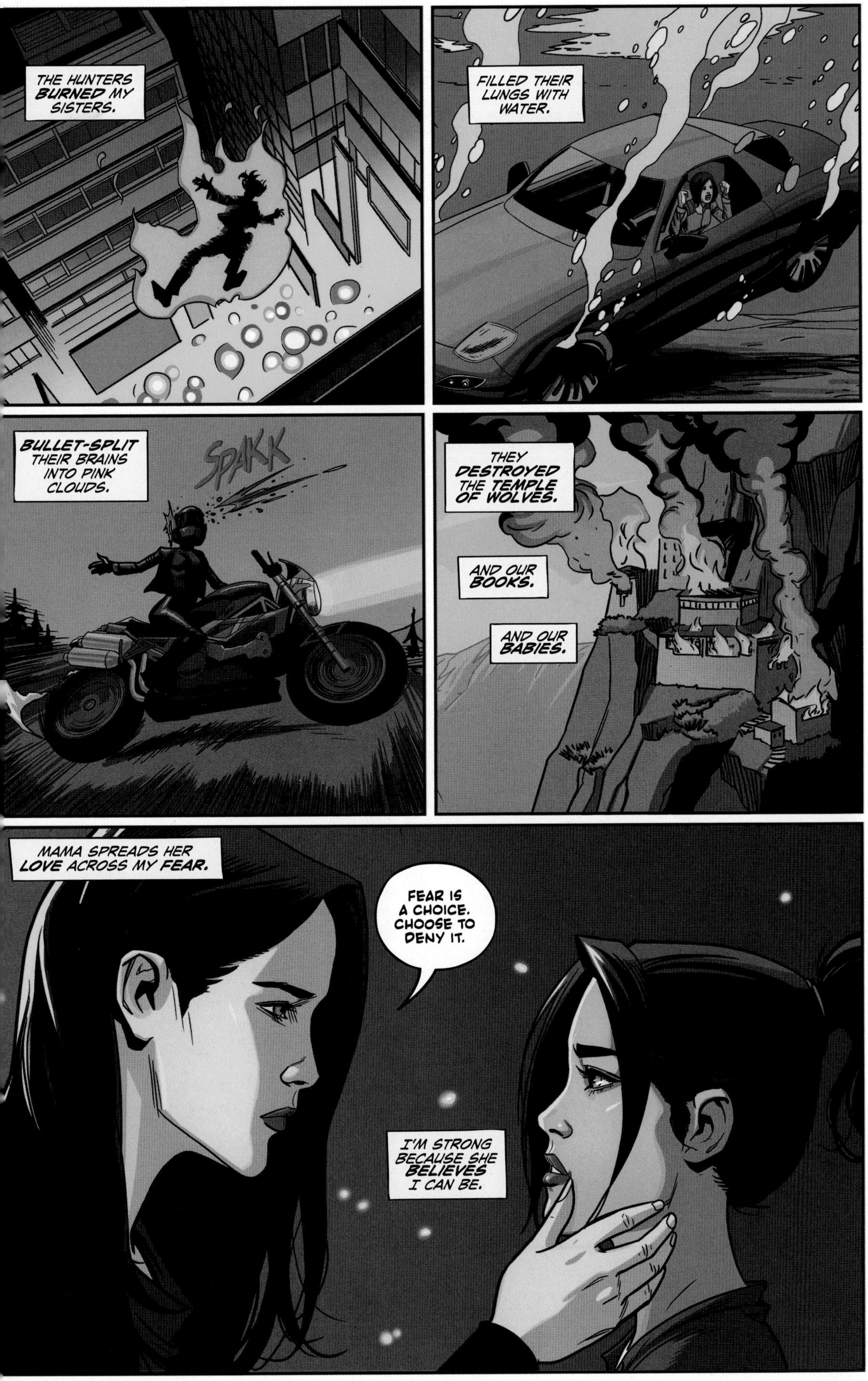
THE HUNTERS BURNED MY SISTERS.
FILLED THEIR LUNGS WITH WATER.
BULLET-SPLIT THEIR BRAINS INTO PINK CLOUDS.
SPAKK
THEY DESTROYED THE TEMPLE OF WOLVES.
AND OUR BOOKS.
AND OUR BABIES.
MAMA SPREADS HER LOVE ACROSS MY FEAR.
FEAR IS A CHOICE. CHOOSE TO DENY IT.
I'M STRONG BECAUSE SHE BELIEVES I CAN BE.

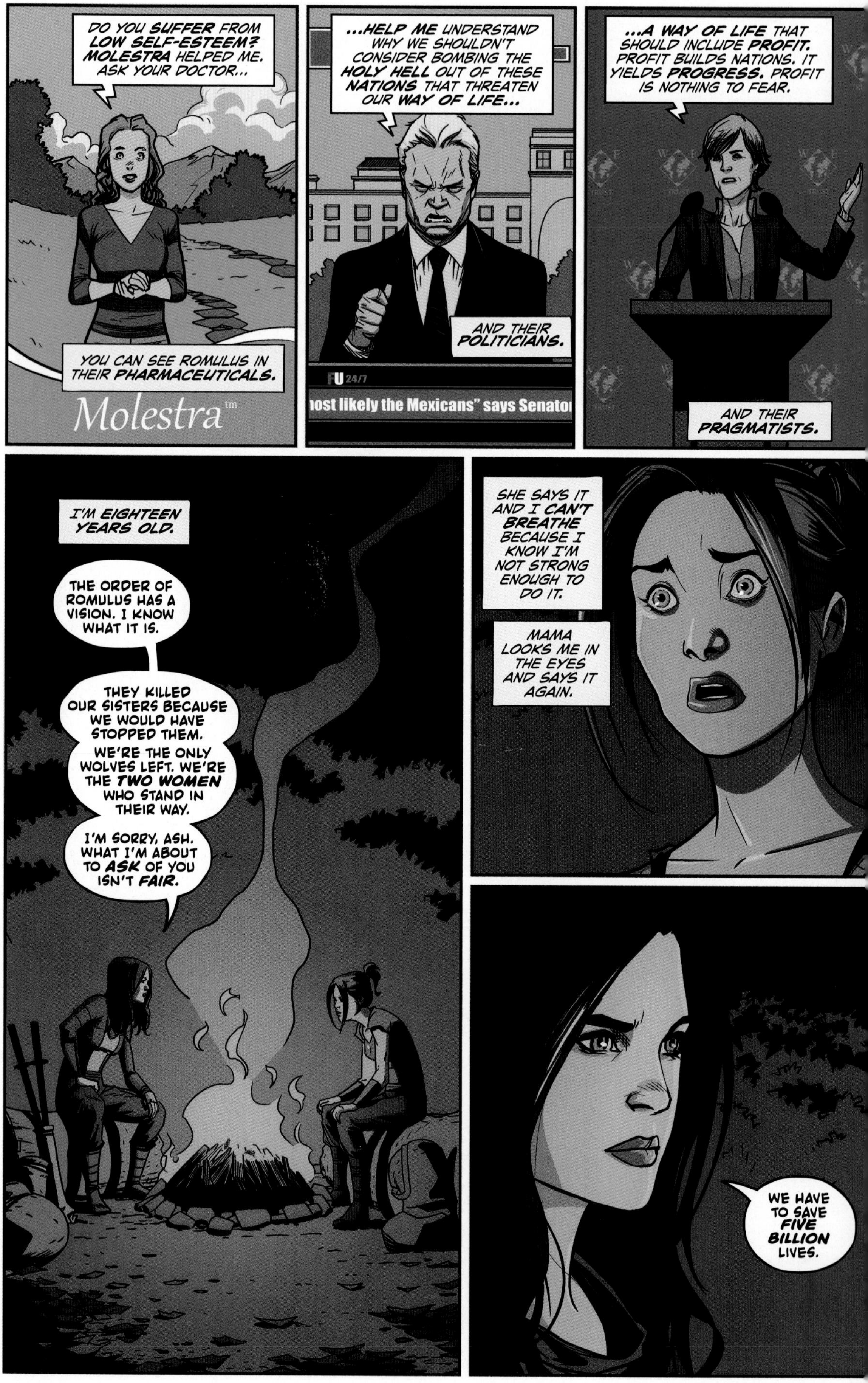
DO YOU SUFFER FROM LOW SELF-ESTEEM? MOLESTRA HELPED ME. ASK YOUR DOCTOR...
YOU CAN SEE ROMULUS IN THEIR PHARMACEUTICALS.
Molestra™
...HELP ME UNDERSTAND WHY WE SHOULDN'T CONSIDER BOMBING THE HOLY HELL OUT OF THESE NATIONS THAT THREATEN OUR WAY OF LIFE...
AND THEIR POLITICIANS.
FU 24/7
iost likely the Mexicans" says Senator
...A WAY OF LIFE THAT SHOULD INCLUDE PROFIT. PROFIT BUILDS NATIONS. IT YIELDS PROGRESS. PROFIT IS NOTHING TO FEAR.
AND THEIR PRAGMATISTS.
I'M EIGHTEEN YEARS OLD.
THE ORDER OF ROMULUS HAS A VISION. I KNOW WHAT IT IS.
THEY KILLED OUR SISTERS BECAUSE WE WOULD HAVE STOPPED THEM.
WE'RE THE ONLY WOLVES LEFT. WE'RE THE TWO WOMEN WHO STAND IN THEIR WAY.
I'M SORRY, ASH. WHAT I'M ABOUT TO ASK OF YOU ISN'T FAIR.
SHE SAYS IT AND I CAN'T BREATHE BECAUSE I KNOW I'M NOT STRONG ENOUGH TO DO IT.
MAMA LOOKS ME IN THE EYES AND SAYS IT AGAIN.
WE HAVE TO SAVE FIVE BILLION LIVES.

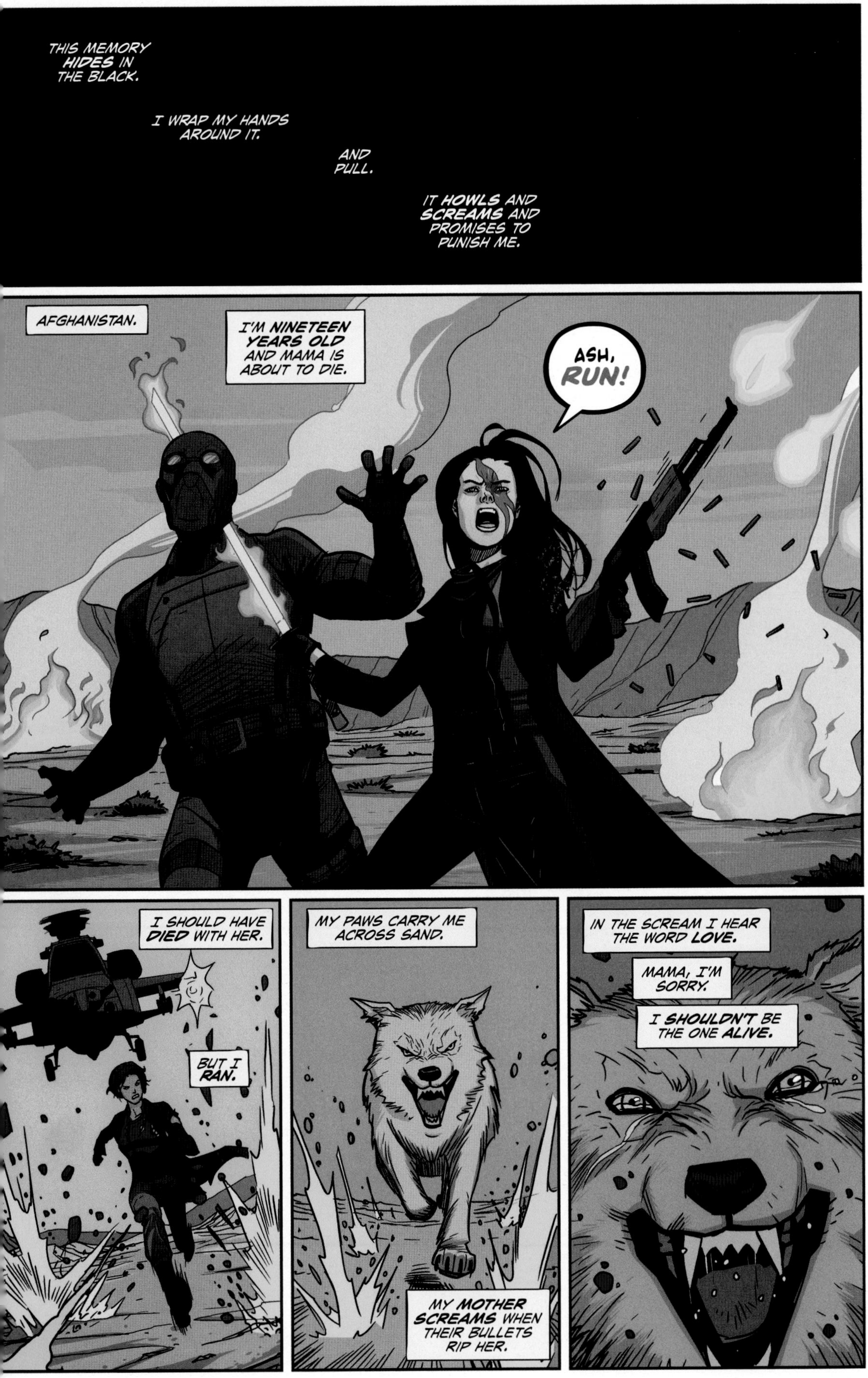
THIS MEMORY HIDES IN THE BLACK.
I WRAP MY HANDS AROUND IT.
AND PULL.
IT HOWLS AND SCREAMS AND PROMISES TO PUNISH ME.
AFGHANISTAN.
I'M NINETEEN YEARS OLD AND MAMA IS ABOUT TO DIE.
ASH, RUN!
I SHOULD HAVE DIED WITH HER.
BUT I RAN.
MY PAWS CARRY ME ACROSS SAND.
MY MOTHER SCREAMS WHEN THEIR BULLETS RIP HER.
IN THE SCREAM I HEAR THE WORD LOVE.
MAMA, I'M SORRY.
I SHOULDN'T BE THE ONE ALIVE.

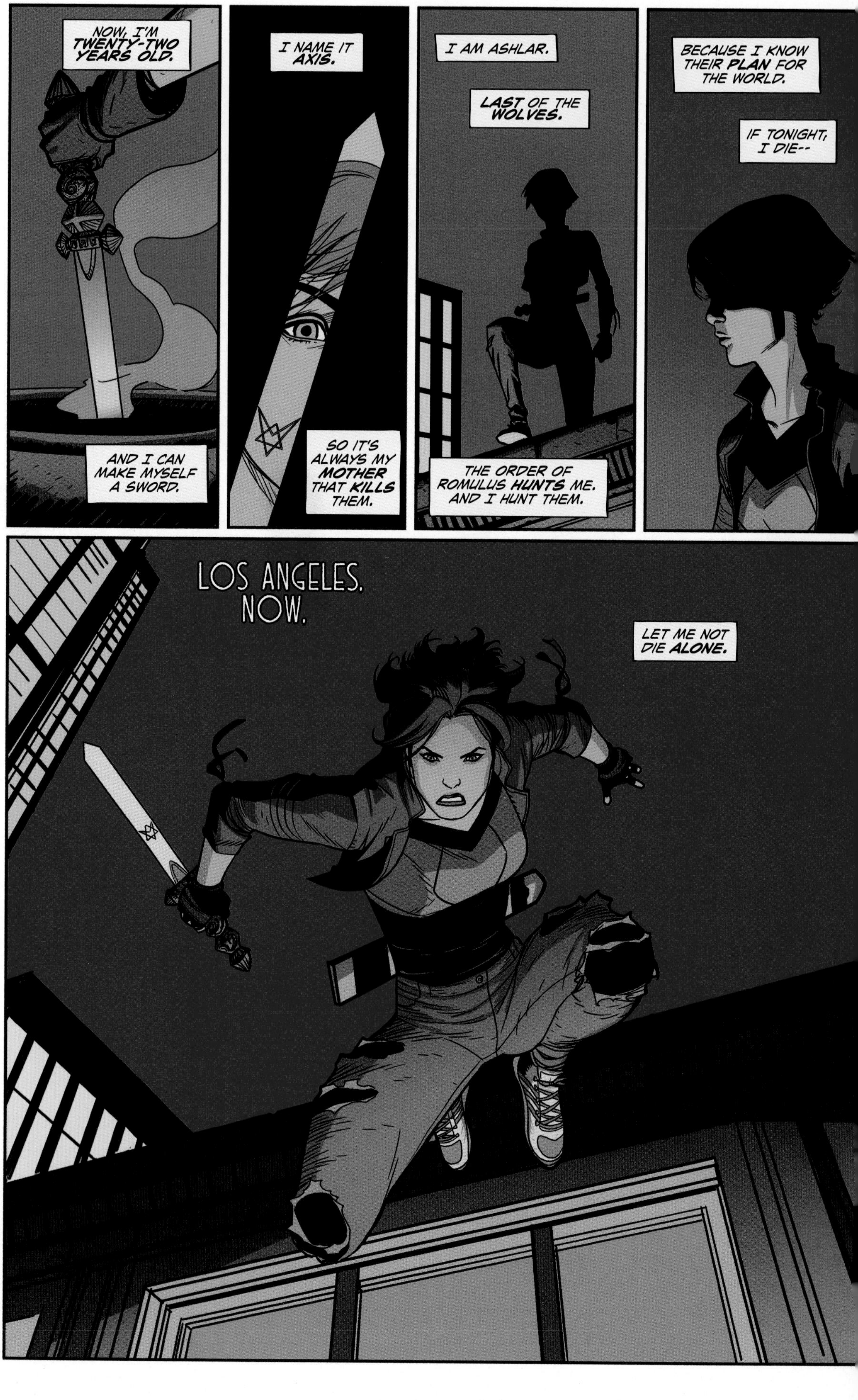
NOW, I'M TWENTY-TWO YEARS OLD.
AND I CAN MAKE MYSELF A SWORD.
I NAME IT AXIS.
SO IT'S ALWAYS MY MOTHER THAT KILLS THEM.
I AM ASHLAR.
LAST OF THE WOLVES.
THE ORDER OF ROMULUS HUNTS ME. AND I HUNT THEM.
BECAUSE I KNOW THEIR PLAN FOR THE WORLD.
IF TONIGHT, I DIE--
LOS ANGELES. NOW.
LET ME NOT DIE ALONE.

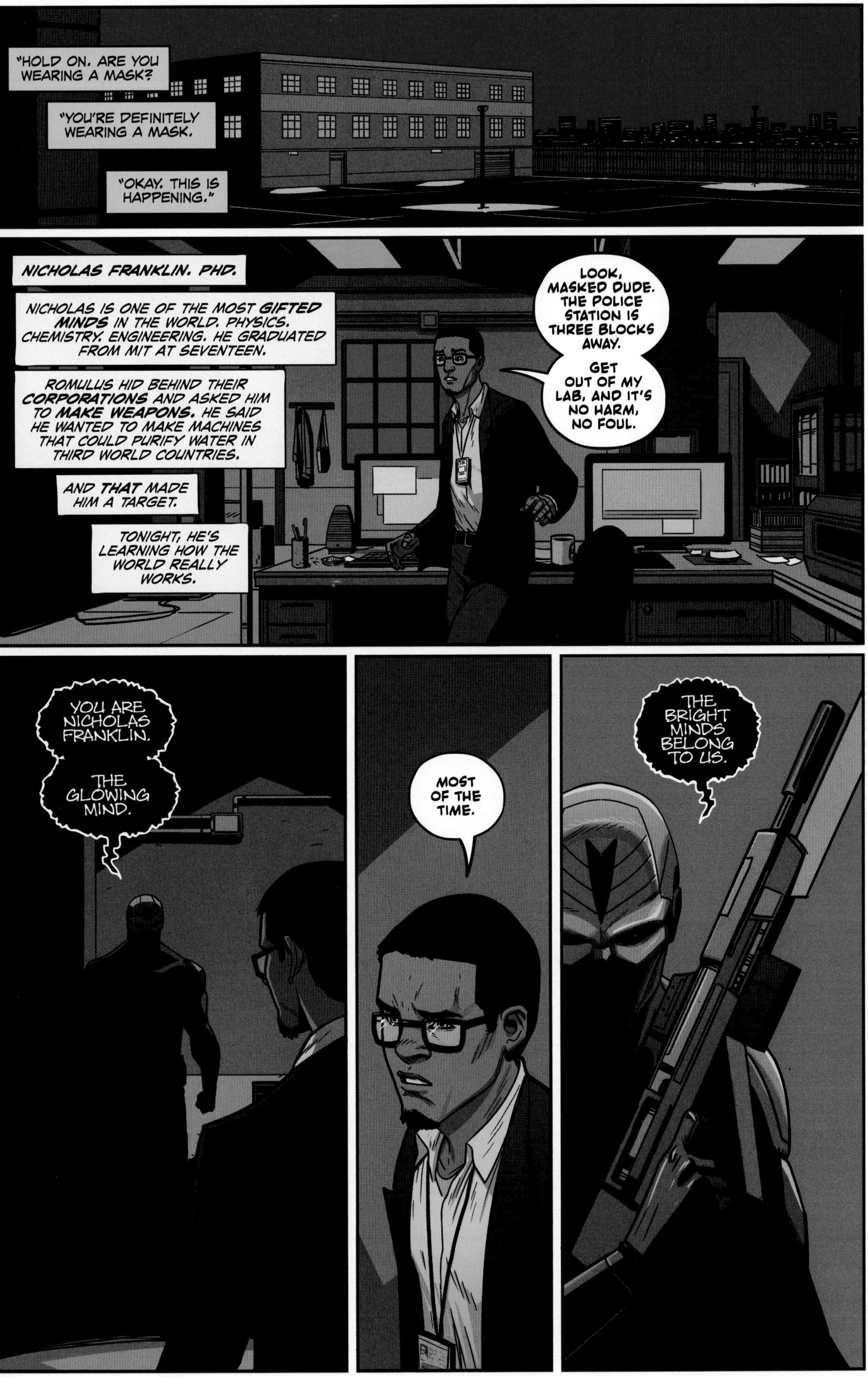
"HOLD ON. ARE YOU WEARING A MASK?
"YOU'RE DEFINITELY WEARING A MASK.
"OKAY. THIS IS HAPPENING."
NICHOLAS FRANKLIN. PHD.
NICHOLAS IS ONE OF THE MOST GIFTED MINDS IN THE WORLD. PHYSICS. CHEMISTRY. ENGINEERING. HE GRADUATED FROM MIT AT SEVENTEEN.
ROMULUS HID BEHIND THEIR CORPORATIONS AND ASKED HIM TO MAKE WEAPONS. HE SAID HE WANTED TO MAKE MACHINES THAT COULD PURIFY WATER IN THIRD WORLD COUNTRIES.
AND THAT MADE HIM A TARGET.
TONIGHT, HE'S LEARNING HOW THE WORLD REALLY WORKS.
LOOK, MASKED DUDE. THE POLICE STATION IS THREE BLOCKS AWAY.
GET OUT OF MY LAB, AND IT'S NO HARM, NO FOUL.
YOU ARE NICHOLAS FRANKLIN.
THE GLOWING MIND.
MOST OF THE TIME.
THE BRIGHT MINDS BELONG TO US.

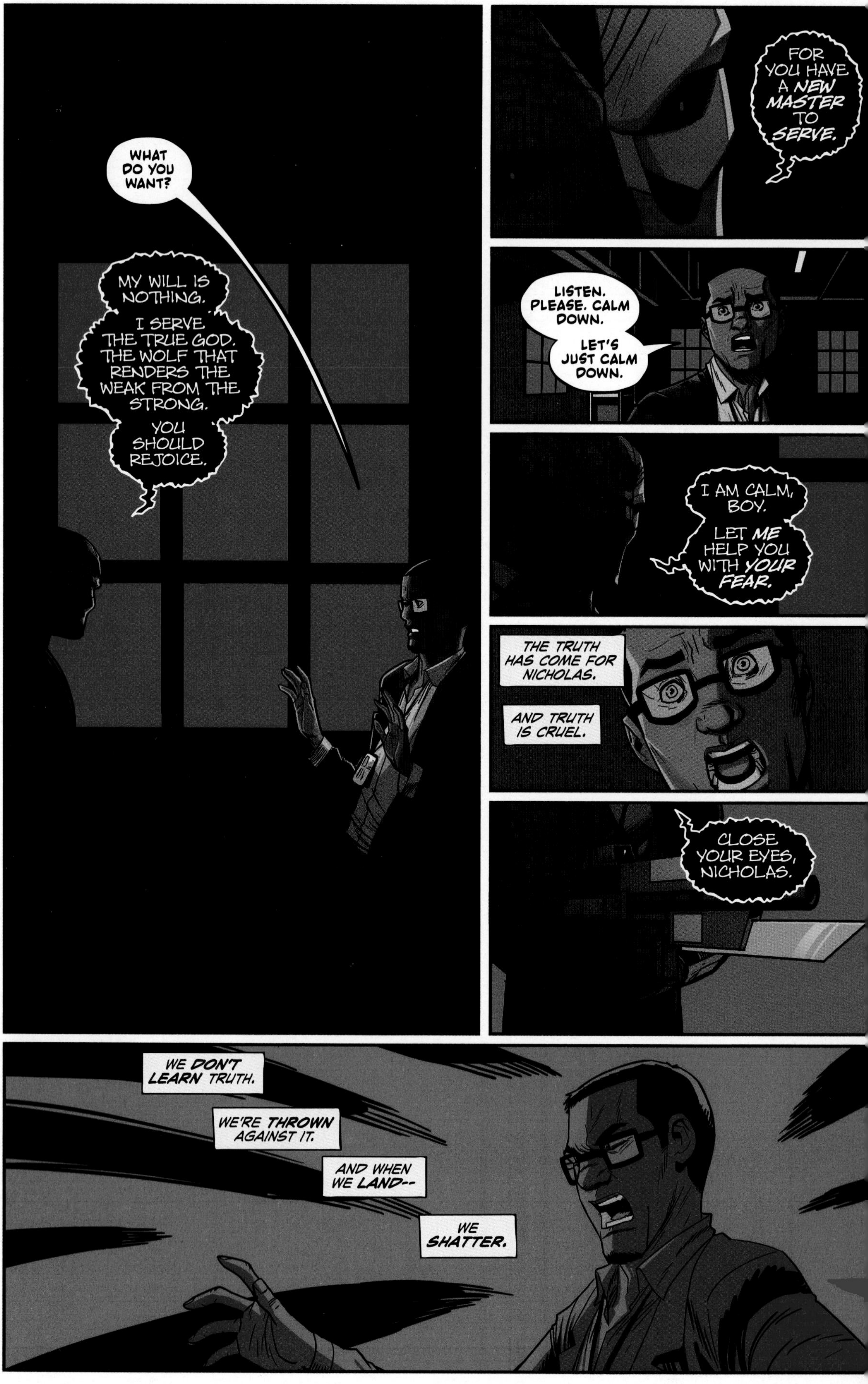
WHAT DO YOU WANT?
MY WILL IS NOTHING.
I SERVE THE TRUE GOD. THE WOLF THAT RENDERS THE WEAK FROM THE STRONG.
YOU SHOULD REJOICE.
FOR YOU HAVE A NEW MASTER TO SERVE.
LISTEN. PLEASE. CALM DOWN.
LET'S JUST CALM DOWN.
I AM CALM, BOY.
LET ME HELP YOU WITH YOUR FEAR.
THE TRUTH HAS COME FOR NICHOLAS.
AND TRUTH IS CRUEL.
CLOSE YOUR EYES, NICHOLAS.
WE DON'T LEARN TRUTH.
WE'RE THROWN AGAINST IT.
AND WHEN WE LAND--
WE SHATTER.

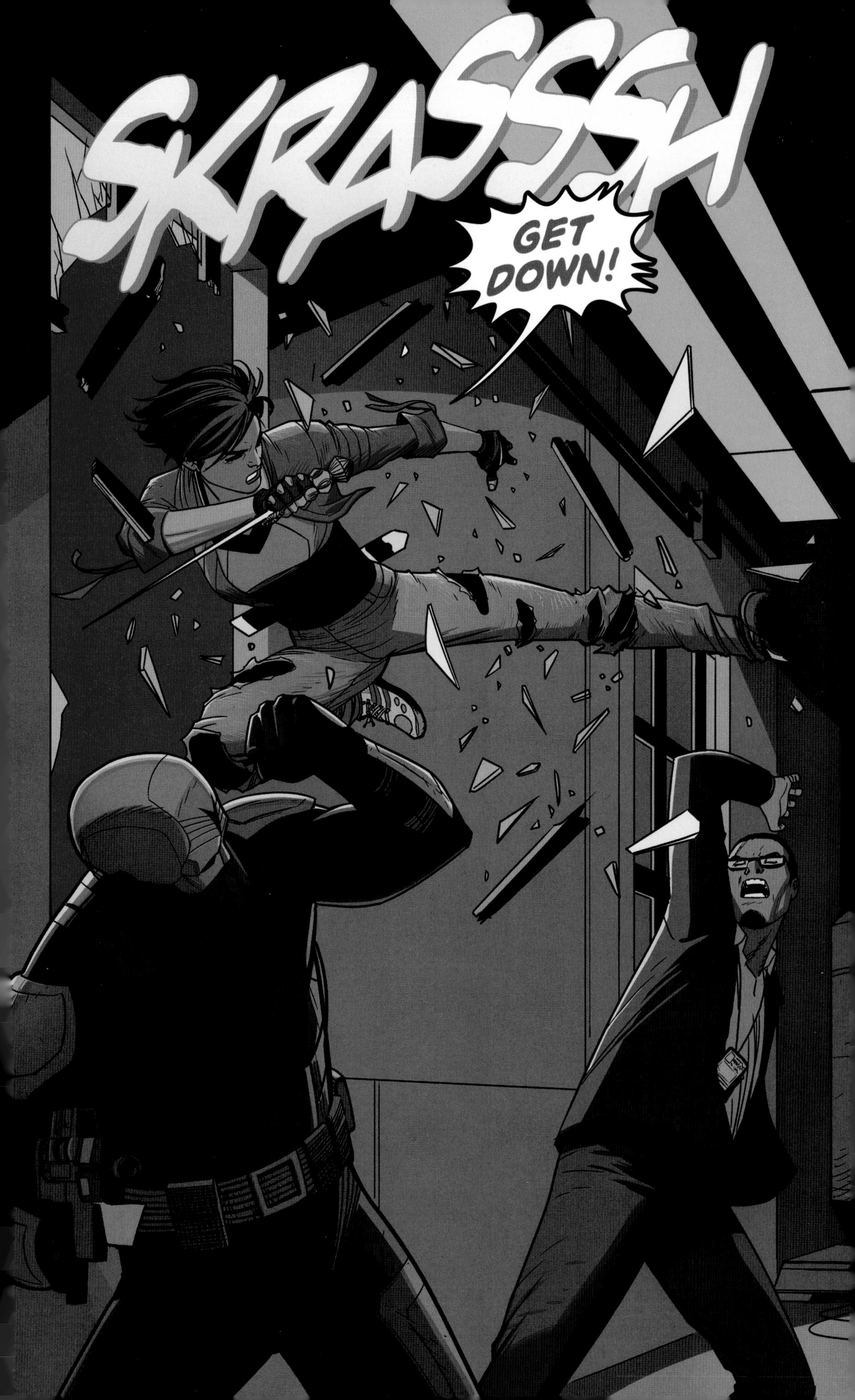
SKRASSSH
GET DOWN!

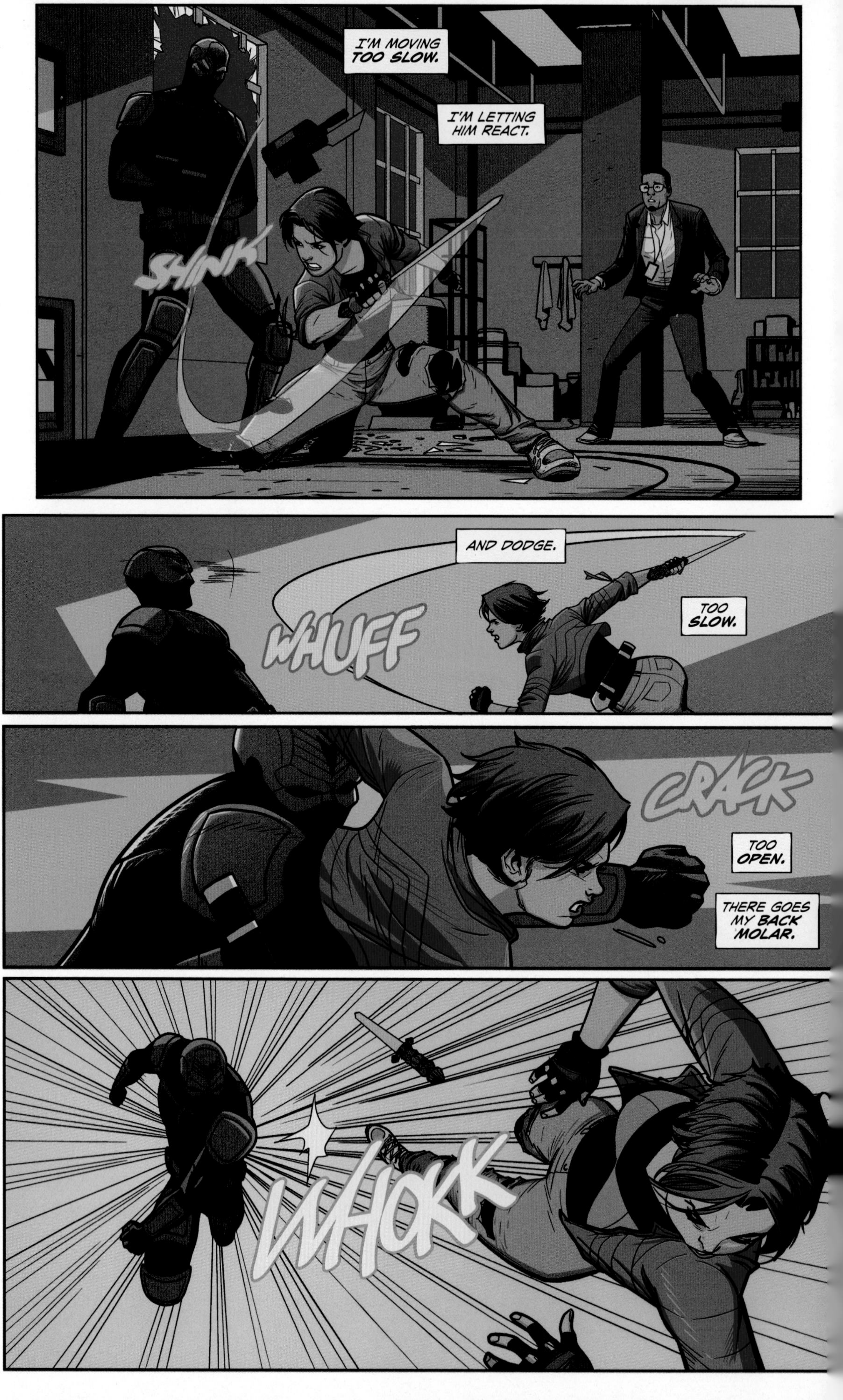
I'M MOVING TOO SLOW.
I'M LETTING HIM REACT.
SHINK
AND DODGE.
WHUFF
TOO SLOW.
CRACK
TOO OPEN.
THERE GOES MY BACK MOLAR.
WHOKK

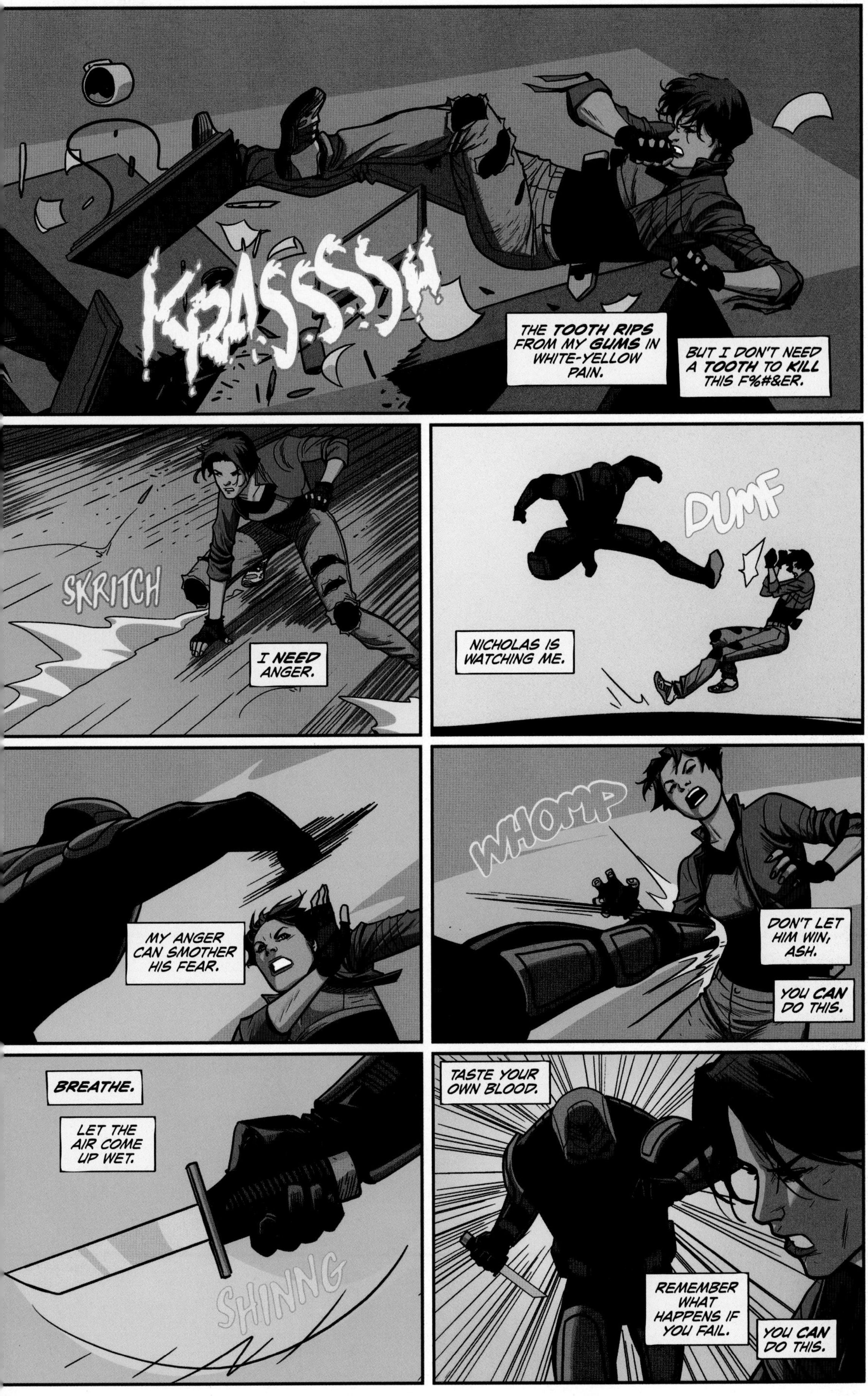
KRASSSH
THE TOOTH RIPS FROM MY GUMS IN WHITE-YELLOW PAIN.
BUT I DON'T NEED A TOOTH TO KILL THIS F%#&ER.
SKRITCH
I NEED ANGER.
DUMF
NICHOLAS IS WATCHING ME.
MY ANGER CAN SMOTHER HIS FEAR.
WHOMP
DON'T LET HIM WIN, ASH.
YOU CAN DO THIS.
BREATHE.
LET THE AIR COME UP WET.
SHINNG
TASTE YOUR OWN BLOOD.
REMEMBER WHAT HAPPENS IF YOU FAIL.
YOU CAN DO THIS.

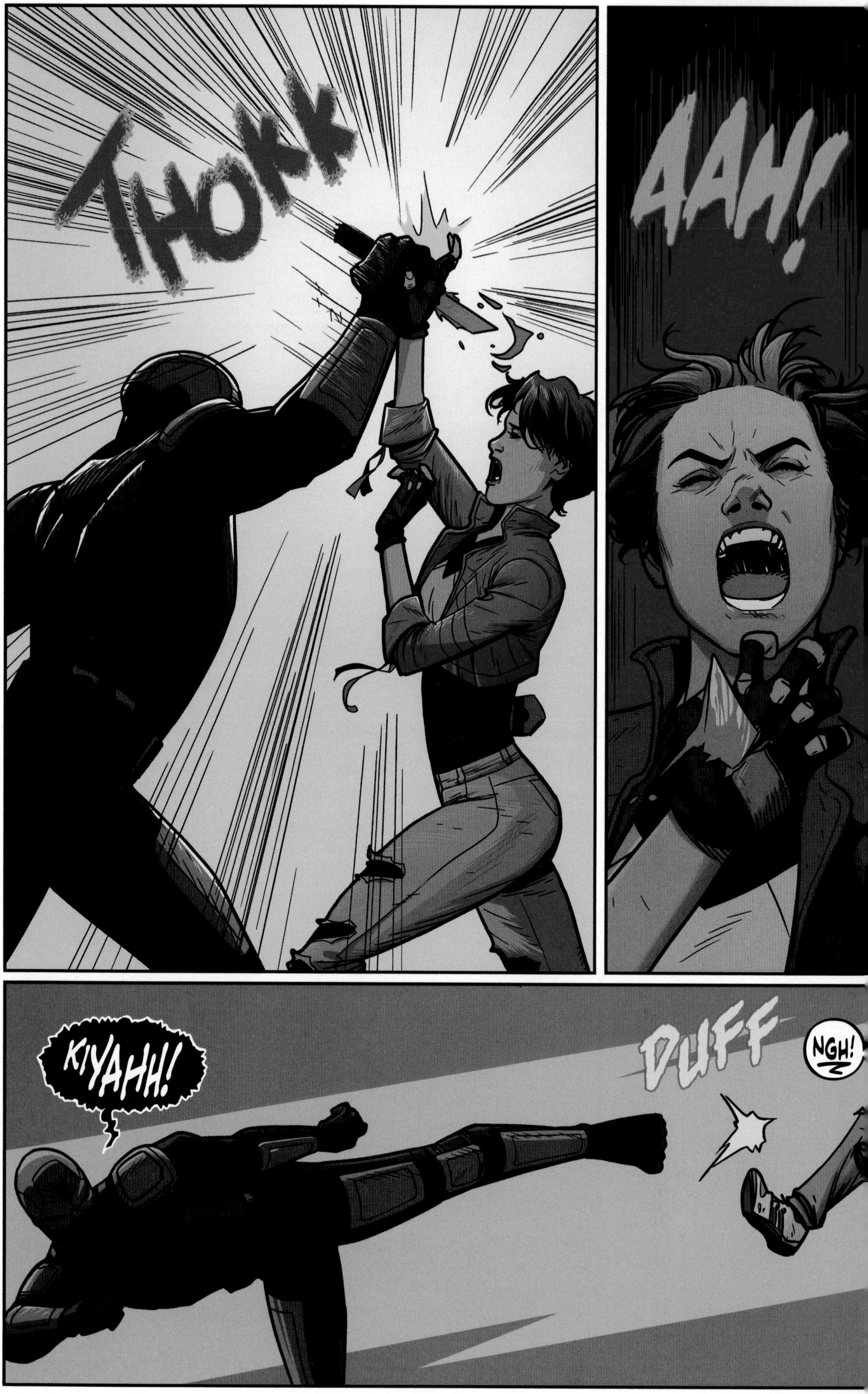
THOKK
AAH!
KIYAHH!
DUFF
NGH!

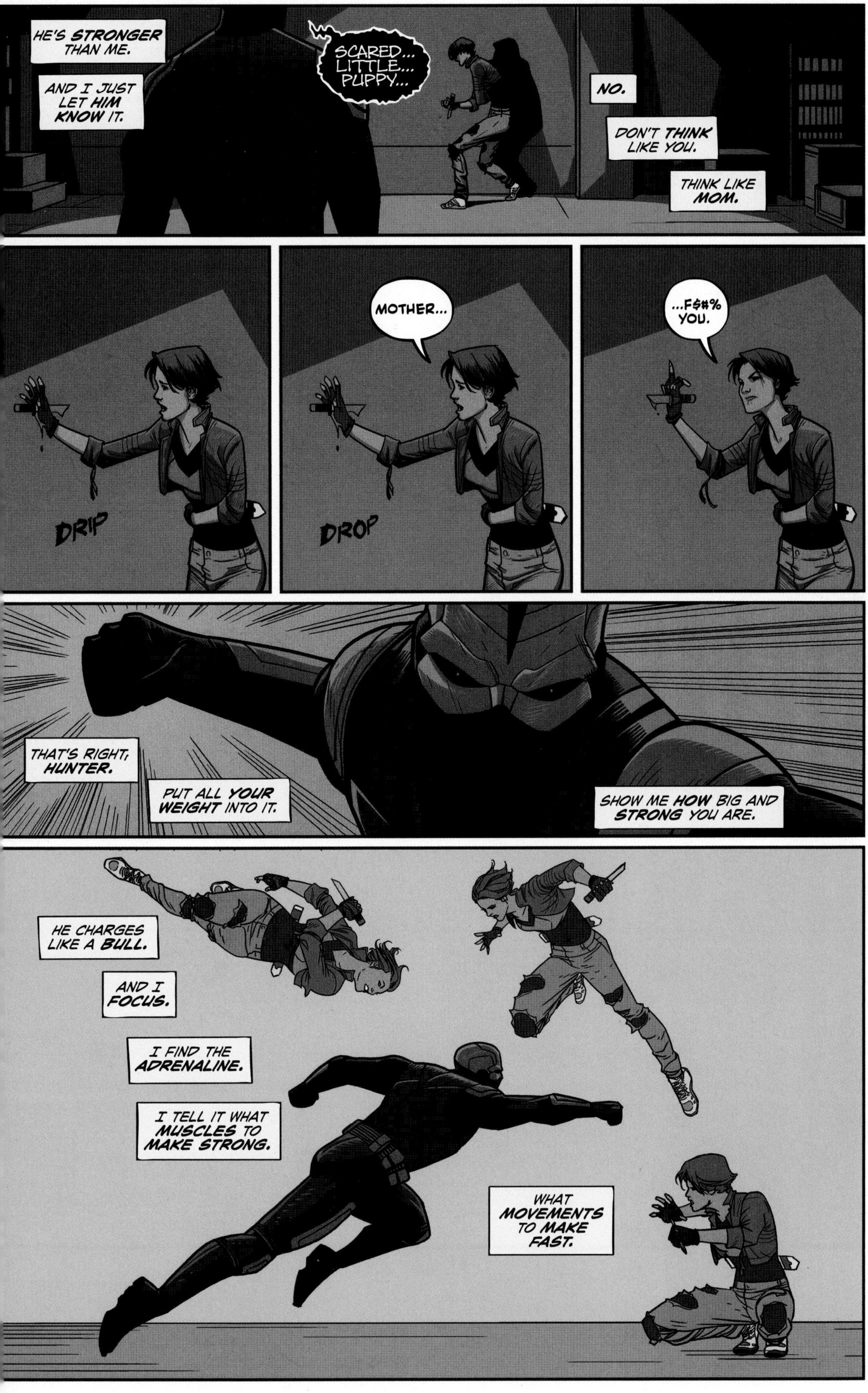
HE'S STRONGER THAN ME.
AND I JUST LET HIM KNOW IT.
SCARED... LITTLE... PUPPY...
NO.
DON'T THINK LIKE YOU.
THINK LIKE MOM.
DRIP
MOTHER...
DROP
...F$#% YOU.
THAT'S RIGHT, HUNTER.
PUT ALL YOUR WEIGHT INTO IT.
SHOW ME HOW BIG AND STRONG YOU ARE.
HE CHARGES LIKE A BULL.
AND I FOCUS.
I FIND THE ADRENALINE.
I TELL IT WHAT MUSCLES TO MAKE STRONG.
WHAT MOVEMENTS TO MAKE FAST.

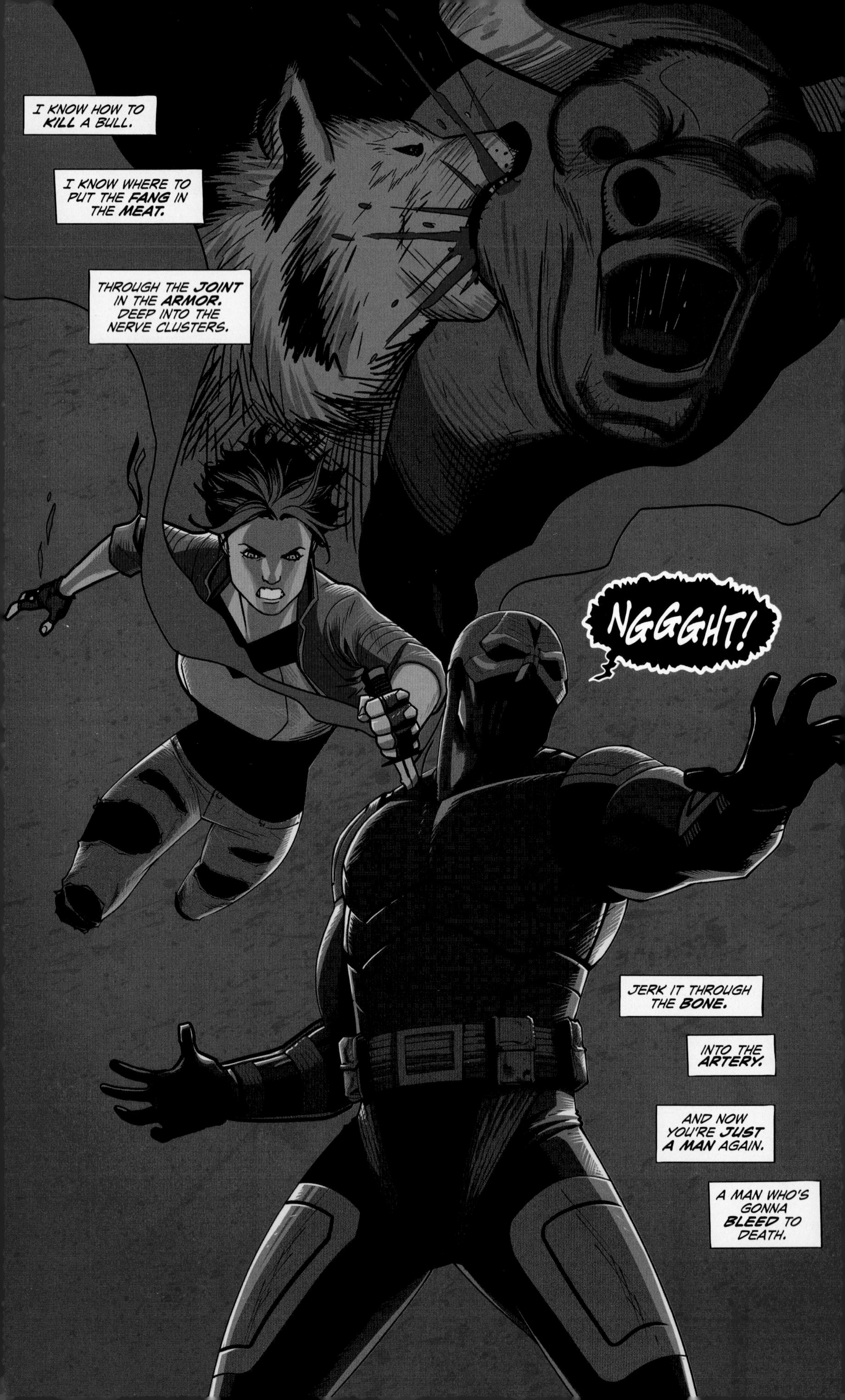
I KNOW HOW TO KILL A BULL.
I KNOW WHERE TO PUT THE FANG IN THE MEAT.
THROUGH THE JOINT IN THE ARMOR. DEEP INTO THE NERVE CLUSTERS.
NGGGHT!
JERK IT THROUGH THE BONE.
INTO THE ARTERY.
AND NOW YOU'RE JUST A MAN AGAIN.
A MAN WHO'S GONNA BLEED TO DEATH.

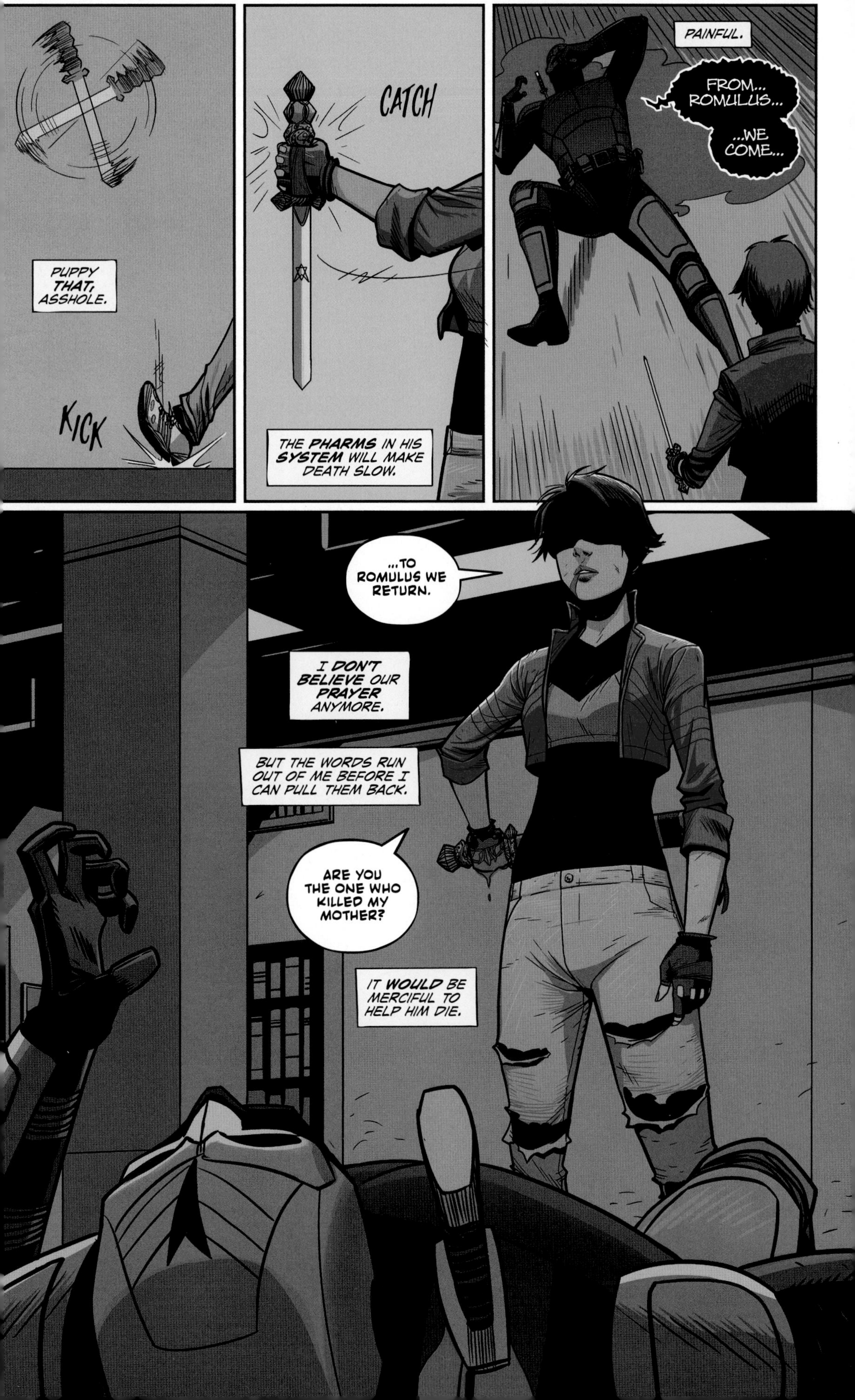
PUPPY THAT, ASSHOLE.
KICK
CATCH
THE PHARMS IN HIS SYSTEM WILL MAKE DEATH SLOW.
PAINFUL.
FROM... ROMULUS...
...WE COME...
...TO ROMULUS WE RETURN.
I DON'T BELIEVE OUR PRAYER ANYMORE.
BUT THE WORDS RUN OUT OF ME BEFORE I CAN PULL THEM BACK.
ARE YOU THE ONE WHO KILLED MY MOTHER?
IT WOULD BE MERCIFUL TO HELP HIM DIE.

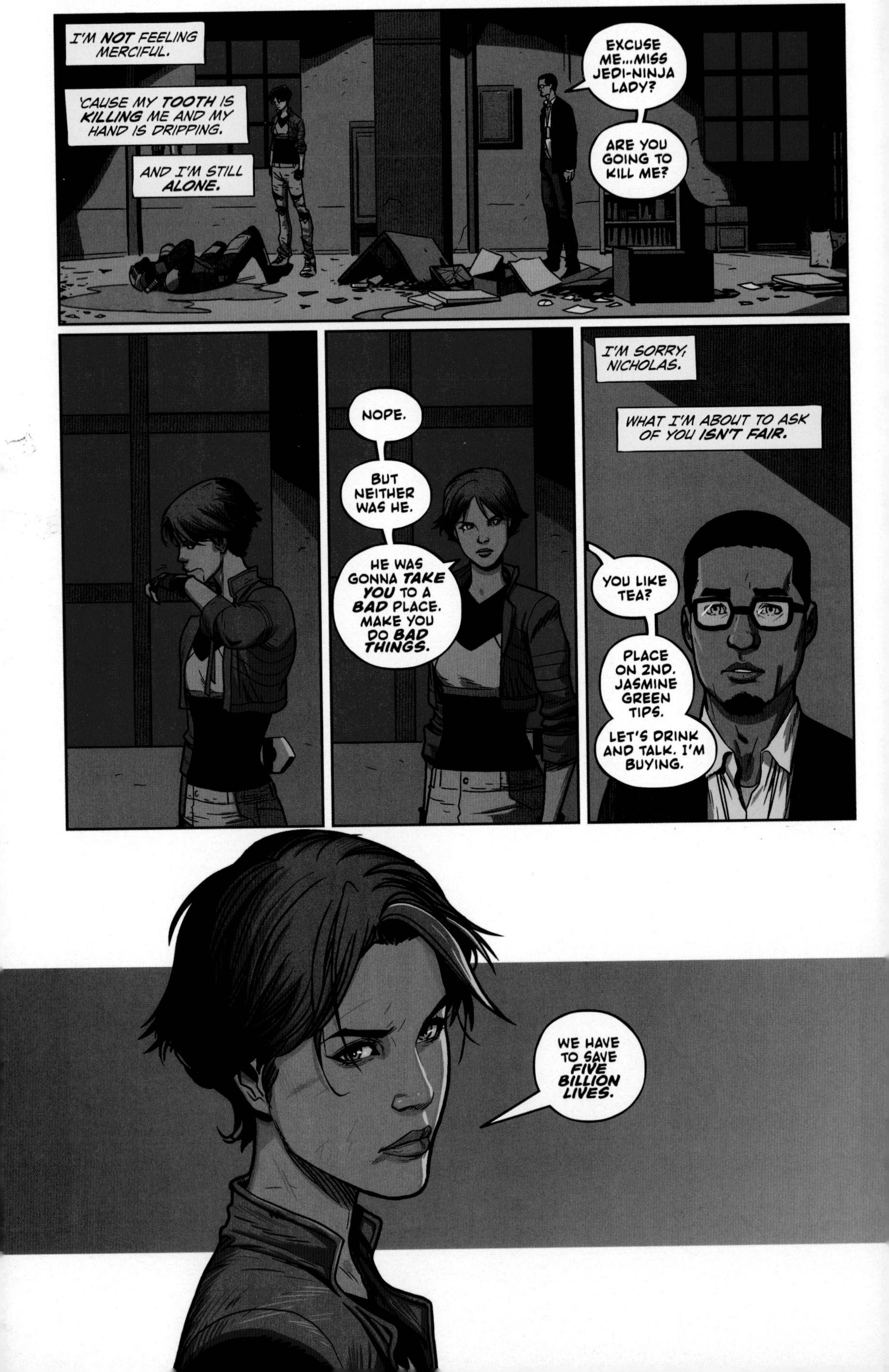
I'M NOT FEELING MERCIFUL.
'CAUSE MY TOOTH IS KILLING ME AND MY HAND IS DRIPPING.
AND I'M STILL ALONE.
EXCUSE ME...MISS JEDI-NINJA LADY?
ARE YOU GOING TO KILL ME?
NOPE.
BUT NEITHER WAS HE.
HE WAS GONNA TAKE YOU TO A BAD PLACE. MAKE YOU DO BAD THINGS.
I'M SORRY, NICHOLAS.
WHAT I'M ABOUT TO ASK OF YOU ISN'T FAIR.
YOU LIKE TEA?
PLACE ON 2ND. JASMINE GREEN TIPS.
LET'S DRINK AND TALK. I'M BUYING.
WE HAVE TO SAVE FIVE BILLION LIVES.

CHAPTER TWO:
ILLUMINATION

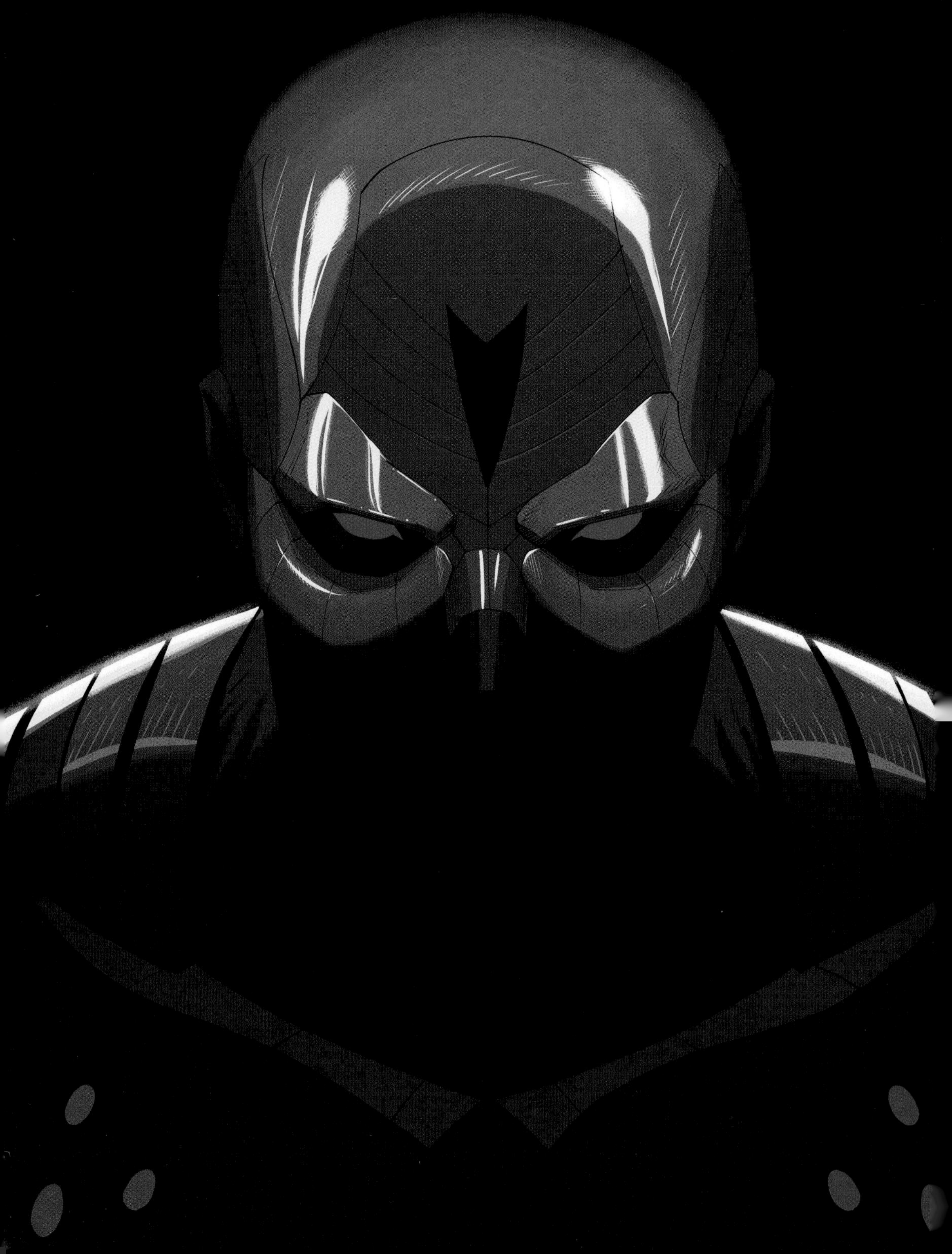

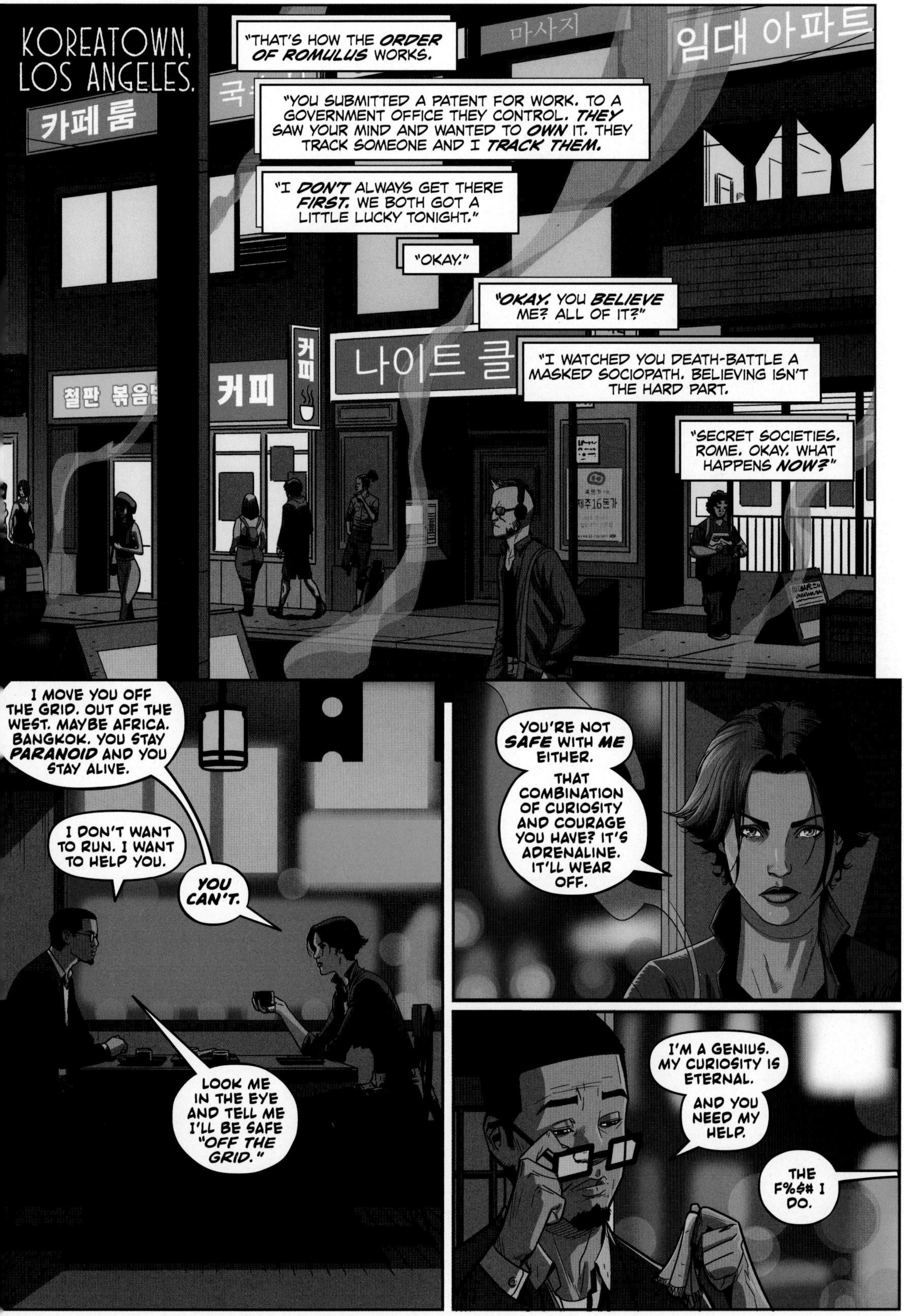
KOREATOWN, LOS ANGELES.
카페 룸
마사지
임대 아파트
"THAT'S HOW THE ORDER OF ROMULUS WORKS.
"YOU SUBMITTED A PATENT FOR WORK. TO A GOVERNMENT OFFICE THEY CONTROL. THEY SAW YOUR MIND AND WANTED TO OWN IT. THEY TRACK SOMEONE AND I TRACK THEM.
"I DON'T ALWAYS GET THERE FIRST. WE BOTH GOT A LITTLE LUCKY TONIGHT."
"OKAY."
"OKAY. YOU BELIEVE ME? ALL OF IT?"
커피
"I WATCHED YOU DEATH-BATTLE A MASKED SOCIOPATH. BELIEVING ISN'T THE HARD PART.
"SECRET SOCIETIES. ROME. OKAY. WHAT HAPPENS NOW?"
I MOVE YOU OFF THE GRID. OUT OF THE WEST. MAYBE AFRICA. BANGKOK. YOU STAY PARANOID AND YOU STAY ALIVE.
I DON'T WANT TO RUN. I WANT TO HELP YOU.
YOU CAN'T.
LOOK ME IN THE EYE AND TELL ME I'LL BE SAFE "OFF THE GRID."
YOU'RE NOT SAFE WITH ME EITHER.
THAT COMBINATION OF CURIOSITY AND COURAGE YOU HAVE? IT'S ADRENALINE. IT'LL WEAR OFF.
I'M A GENIUS. MY CURIOSITY IS ETERNAL.
AND YOU NEED MY HELP.
THE F%$# I DO.

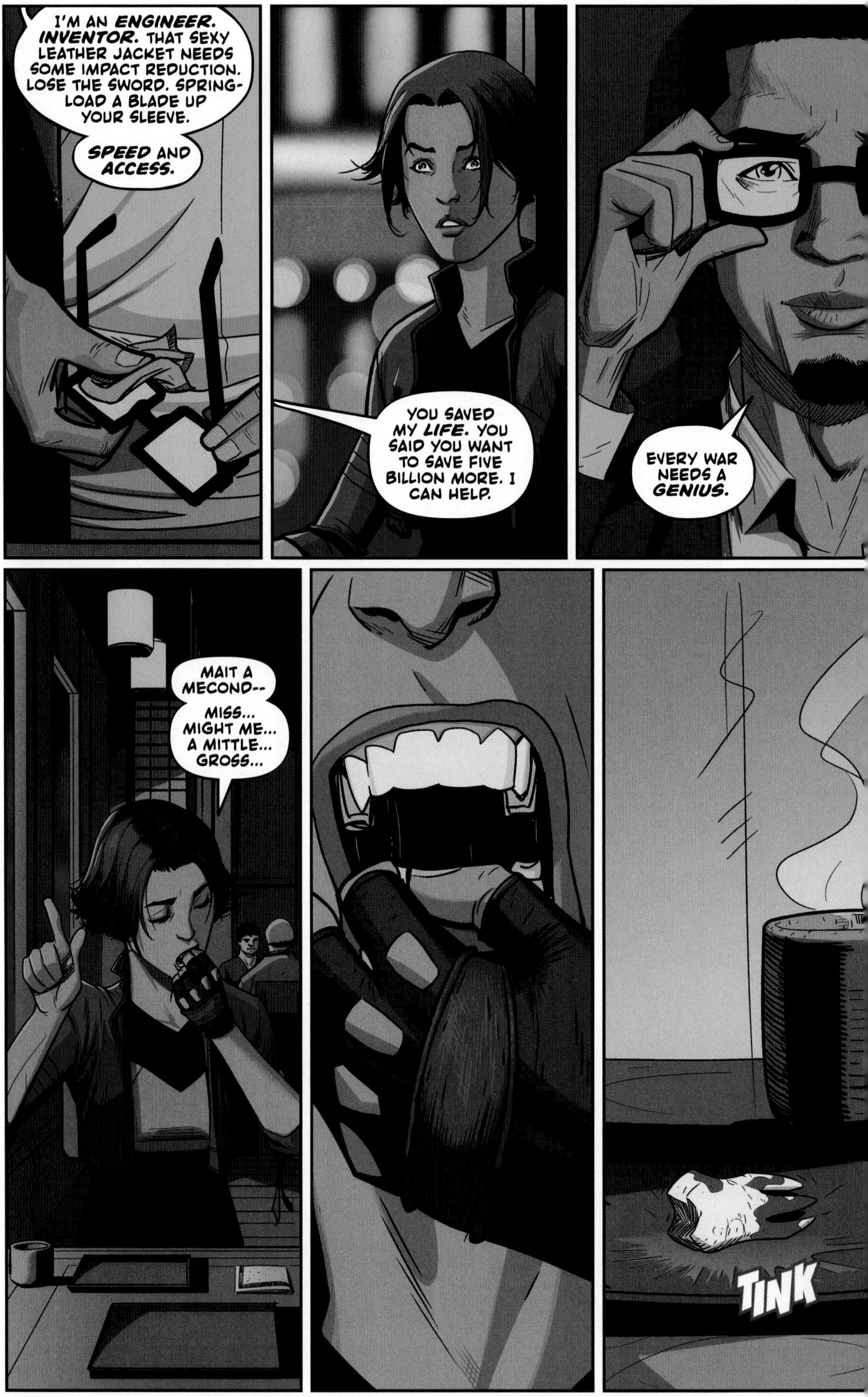
I'M AN ENGINEER. INVENTOR. THAT SEXY LEATHER JACKET NEEDS SOME IMPACT REDUCTION. LOSE THE SWORD. SPRING-LOAD A BLADE UP YOUR SLEEVE.
SPEED AND ACCESS.
YOU SAVED MY LIFE. YOU SAID YOU WANT TO SAVE FIVE BILLION MORE. I CAN HELP.
EVERY WAR NEEDS A GENIUS.
MAIT A MECOND--
MISS... MIGHT ME... A MITTLE... GROSS...
TINK

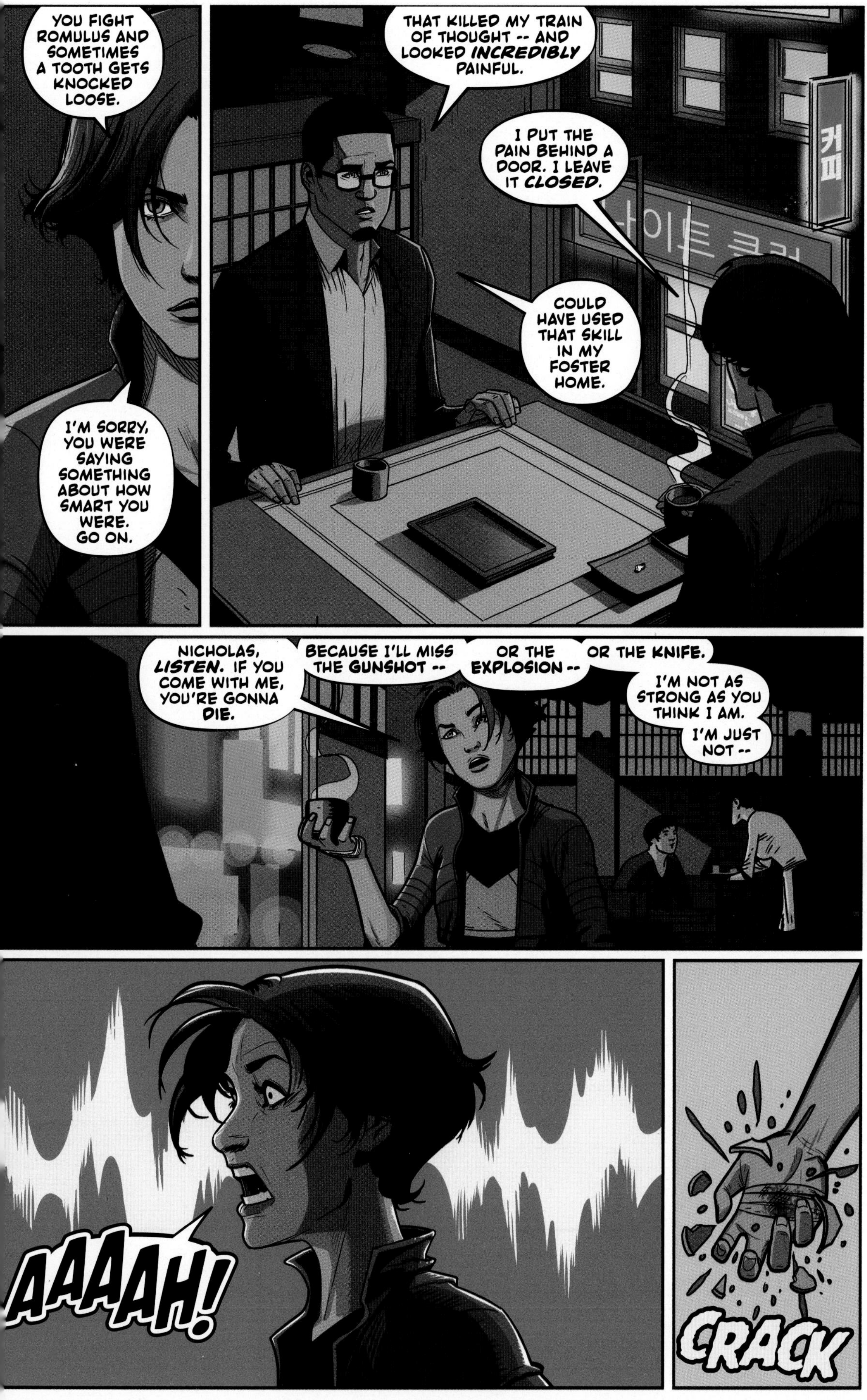
YOU FIGHT ROMULUS AND SOMETIMES A TOOTH GETS KNOCKED LOOSE.
I'M SORRY, YOU WERE SAYING SOMETHING ABOUT HOW SMART YOU WERE. GO ON.
THAT KILLED MY TRAIN OF THOUGHT -- AND LOOKED INCREDIBLY PAINFUL.
I PUT THE PAIN BEHIND A DOOR. I LEAVE IT CLOSED.
COULD HAVE USED THAT SKILL IN MY FOSTER HOME.
커피
나이트 클럽
NICHOLAS, LISTEN. IF YOU COME WITH ME, YOU'RE GONNA DIE.
BECAUSE I'LL MISS THE GUNSHOT --
OR THE EXPLOSION --
OR THE KNIFE.
I'M NOT AS STRONG AS YOU THINK I AM.
I'M JUST NOT --
AAAAH!
CRACK

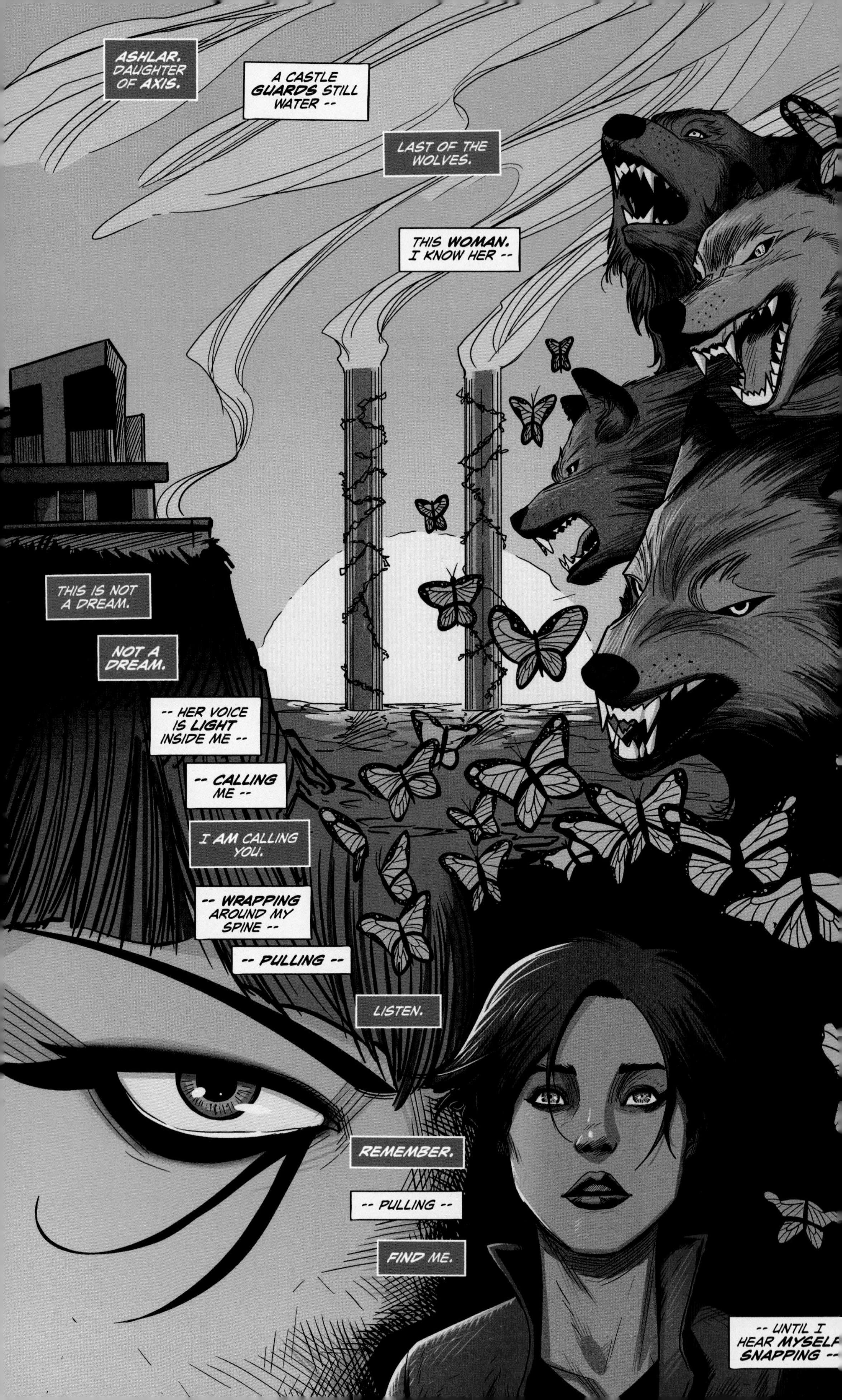
ASHLAR. DAUGHTER OF AXIS.
A CASTLE GUARDS STILL WATER --
LAST OF THE WOLVES.
THIS WOMAN. I KNOW HER --
THIS IS NOT A DREAM.
NOT A DREAM.
-- HER VOICE IS LIGHT INSIDE ME --
-- CALLING ME --
I AM CALLING YOU.
-- WRAPPING AROUND MY SPINE --
-- PULLING --
LISTEN.
REMEMBER.
-- PULLING --
FIND ME.
-- UNTIL I HEAR MYSELF SNAPPING --

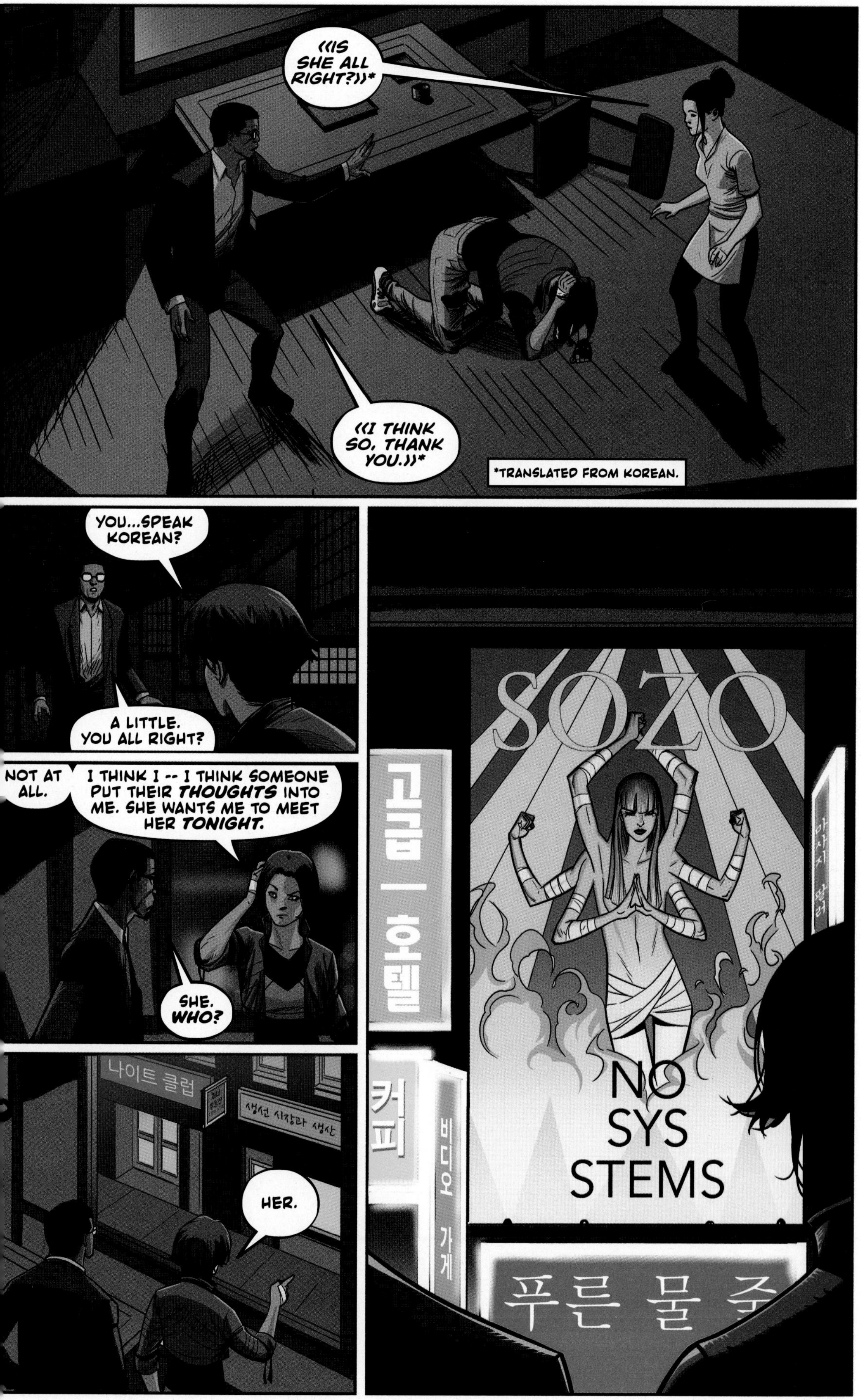

<<IS SHE ALL RIGHT?>>*
<<I THINK SO, THANK YOU.>>*
*TRANSLATED FROM KOREAN.
YOU...SPEAK KOREAN?
A LITTLE. YOU ALL RIGHT?
NOT AT ALL.
I THINK I -- I THINK SOMEONE PUT THEIR *THOUGHTS* INTO ME. SHE WANTS ME TO MEET HER *TONIGHT.*
SHE. *WHO?*
나이트 클럽
생선 시장과 생산
HER.
SOZO
NO SYS STEMS
고급 호텔
커피
비디오 가게
푸른 물

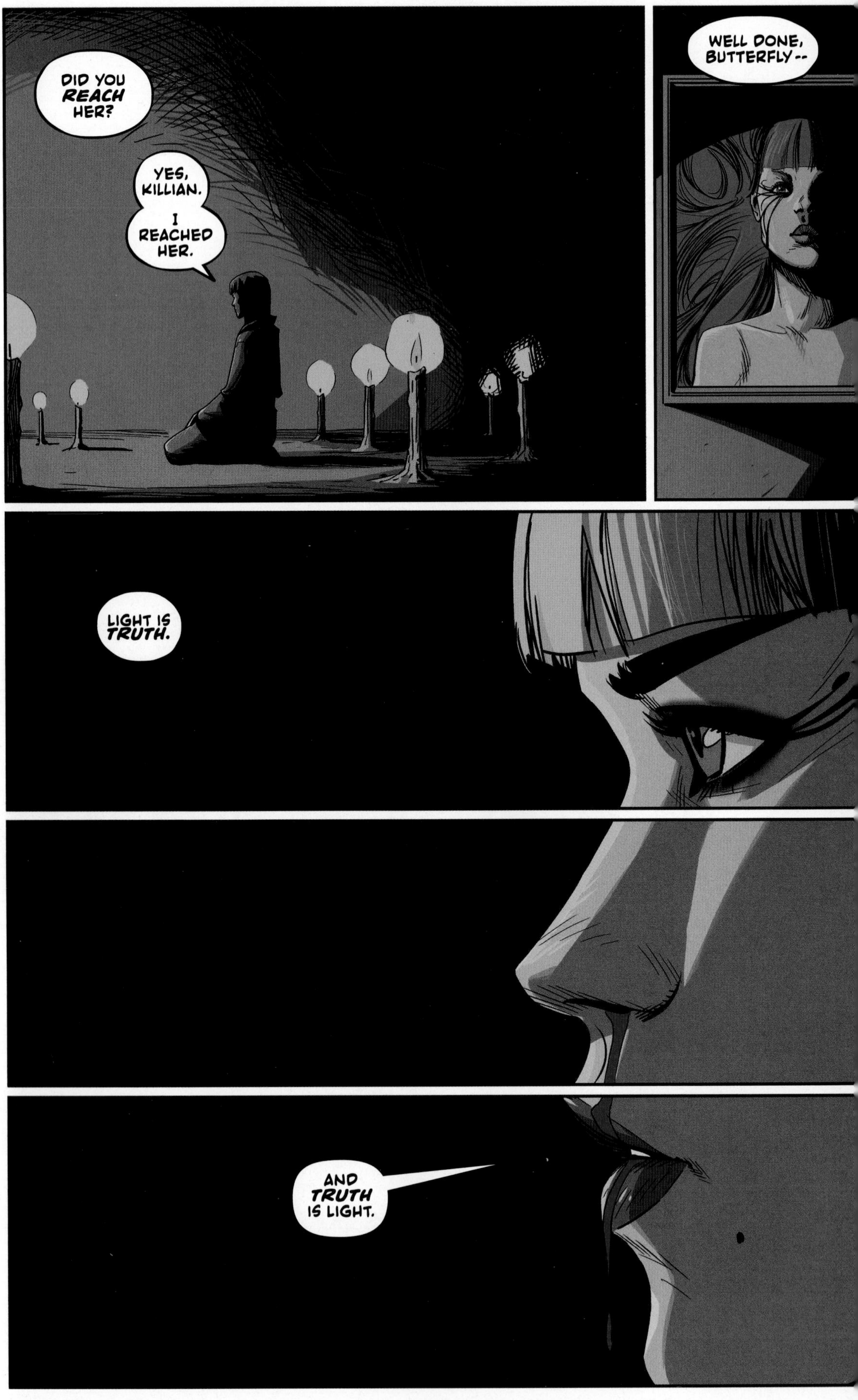
DID YOU REACH HER?
YES, KILLIAN.
I REACHED HER.
WELL DONE, BUTTERFLY --
LIGHT IS TRUTH.
AND TRUTH IS LIGHT.

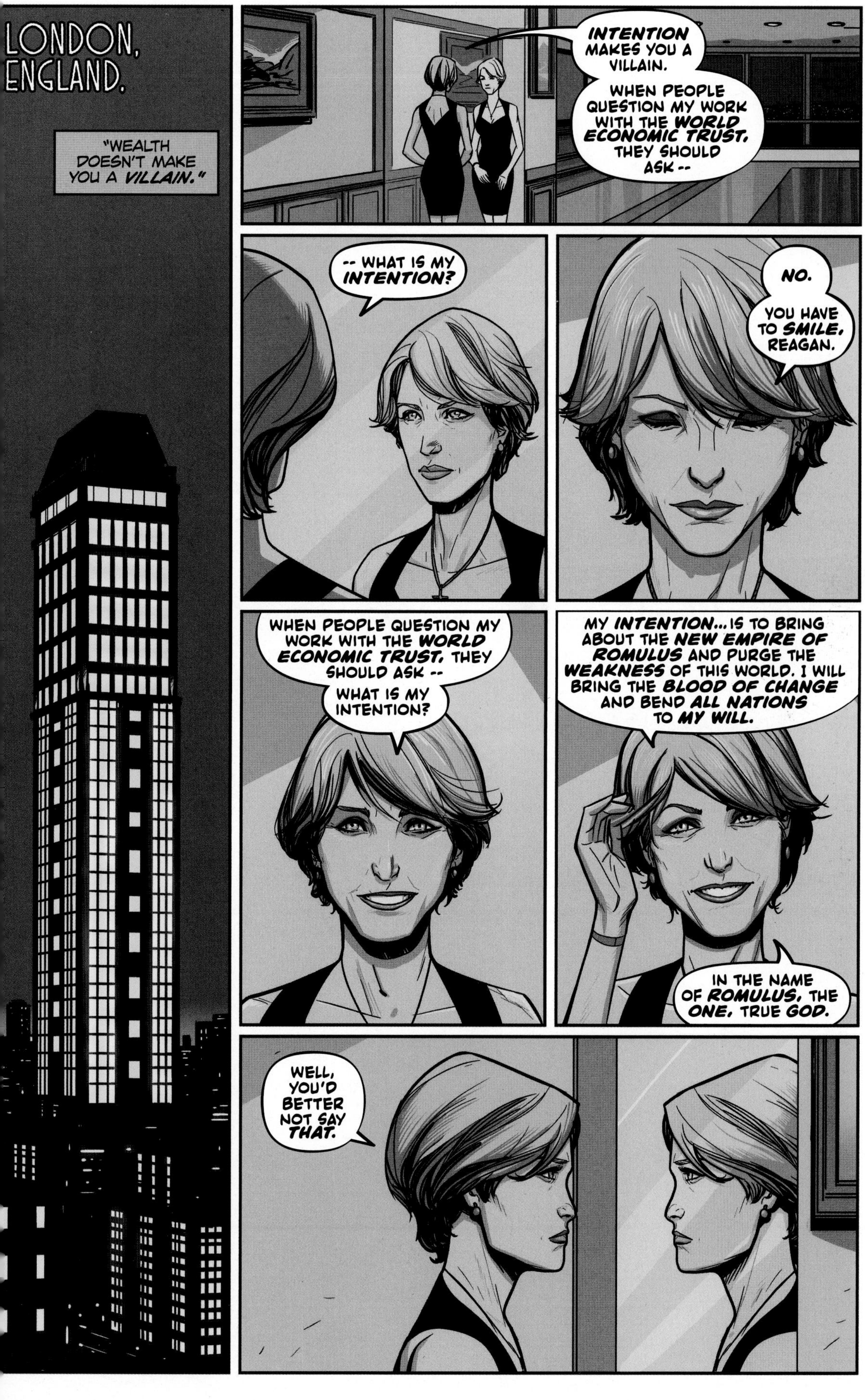
LONDON, ENGLAND.
"WEALTH DOESN'T MAKE YOU A VILLAIN."
INTENTION MAKES YOU A VILLAIN.
WHEN PEOPLE QUESTION MY WORK WITH THE WORLD ECONOMIC TRUST, THEY SHOULD ASK --
-- WHAT IS MY INTENTION?
NO.
YOU HAVE TO SMILE, REAGAN.
WHEN PEOPLE QUESTION MY WORK WITH THE WORLD ECONOMIC TRUST, THEY SHOULD ASK --
WHAT IS MY INTENTION?
MY INTENTION... IS TO BRING ABOUT THE NEW EMPIRE OF ROMULUS AND PURGE THE WEAKNESS OF THIS WORLD. I WILL BRING THE BLOOD OF CHANGE AND BEND ALL NATIONS TO MY WILL.
IN THE NAME OF ROMULUS, THE ONE, TRUE GOD.
WELL, YOU'D BETTER NOT SAY THAT.

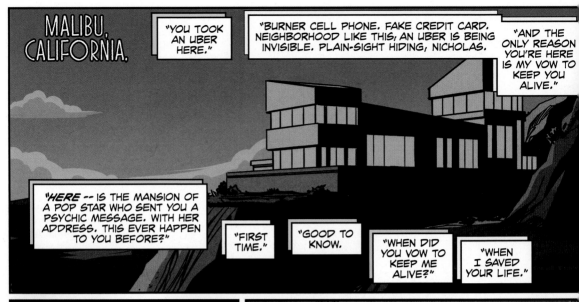

MALIBU, CALIFORNIA.

"YOU TOOK AN UBER HERE."

"BURNER CELL PHONE. FAKE CREDIT CARD. NEIGHBORHOOD LIKE THIS, AN UBER IS BEING INVISIBLE. PLAIN-SIGHT HIDING, NICHOLAS."

"AND THE ONLY REASON YOU'RE HERE IS MY VOW TO KEEP YOU ALIVE."

"HERE -- IS THE MANSION OF A POP STAR WHO SENT YOU A PSYCHIC MESSAGE. WITH HER ADDRESS. THIS EVER HAPPEN TO YOU BEFORE?"

"FIRST TIME."

"GOOD TO KNOW."

"WHEN DID YOU VOW TO KEEP ME ALIVE?"

"WHEN I SAVED YOUR LIFE."

AFTER YOU.

BRAINS BEFORE BRAWN.

I AM SOZO.

I THOUGHT YOU WOULD BE ALONE, BUT YOU'RE WELCOME NONETHELESS.

IT'S A NICE NIGHT. LET'S TALK OUT BACK.

WHOA.

ASHLAR. DAUGHTER OF AXIS.

LAST OF THE WOLVES.

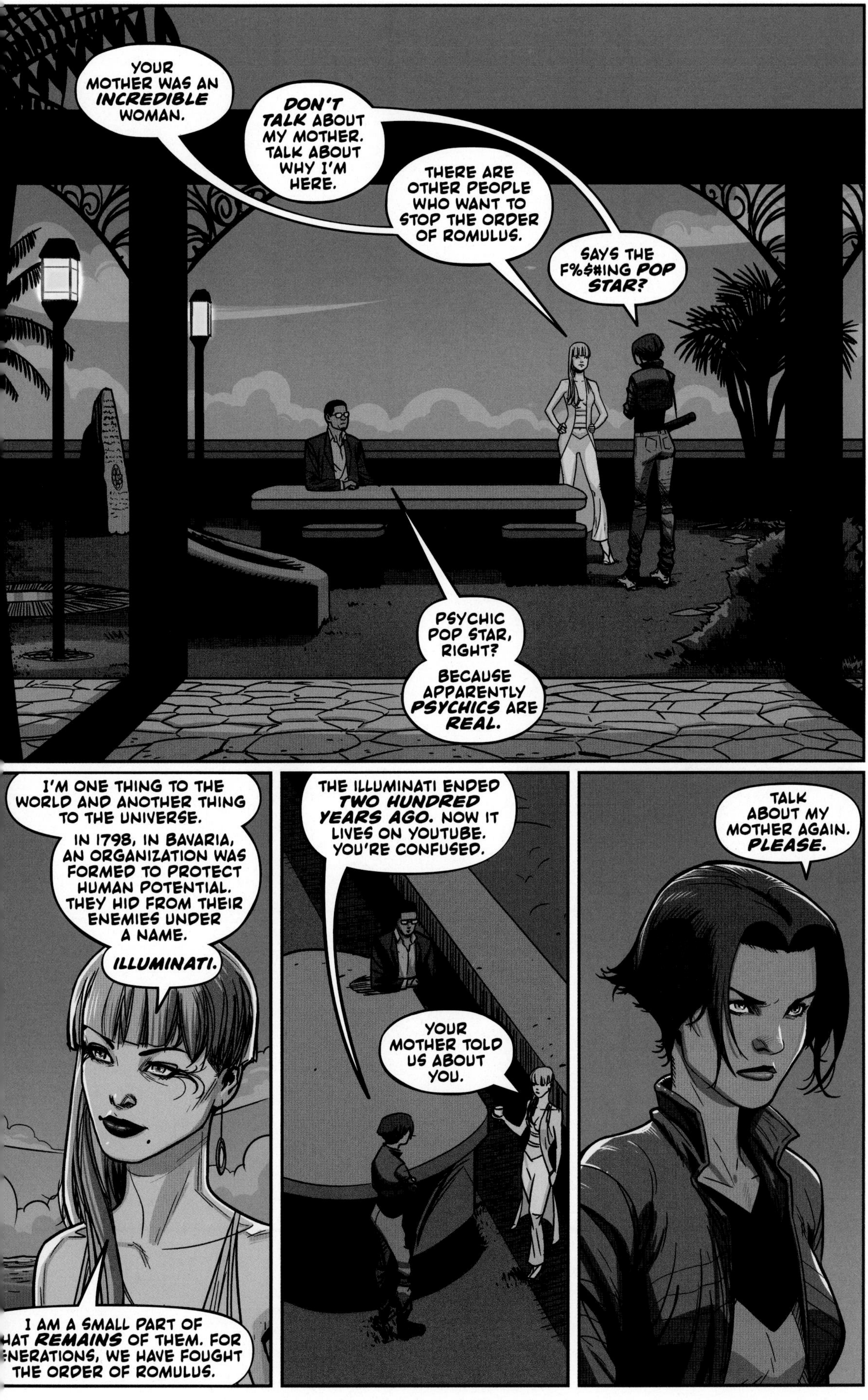
YOUR MOTHER WAS AN *INCREDIBLE* WOMAN.
DON'T TALK ABOUT MY MOTHER. TALK ABOUT WHY I'M HERE.
THERE ARE OTHER PEOPLE WHO WANT TO STOP THE ORDER OF ROMULUS.
SAYS THE F%$#ING *POP STAR?*
PSYCHIC POP STAR, RIGHT?
BECAUSE APPARENTLY *PSYCHICS* ARE *REAL.*
I'M ONE THING TO THE WORLD AND ANOTHER THING TO THE UNIVERSE.
IN 1798, IN BAVARIA, AN ORGANIZATION WAS FORMED TO PROTECT HUMAN POTENTIAL. THEY HID FROM THEIR ENEMIES UNDER A NAME.
ILLUMINATI.
I AM A SMALL PART OF HAT *REMAINS* OF THEM. FOR ENERATIONS, WE HAVE FOUGHT THE ORDER OF ROMULUS.
THE ILLUMINATI ENDED *TWO HUNDRED YEARS AGO.* NOW IT LIVES ON YOUTUBE. YOU'RE CONFUSED.
YOUR MOTHER TOLD US ABOUT YOU.
TALK ABOUT MY MOTHER AGAIN. *PLEASE.*

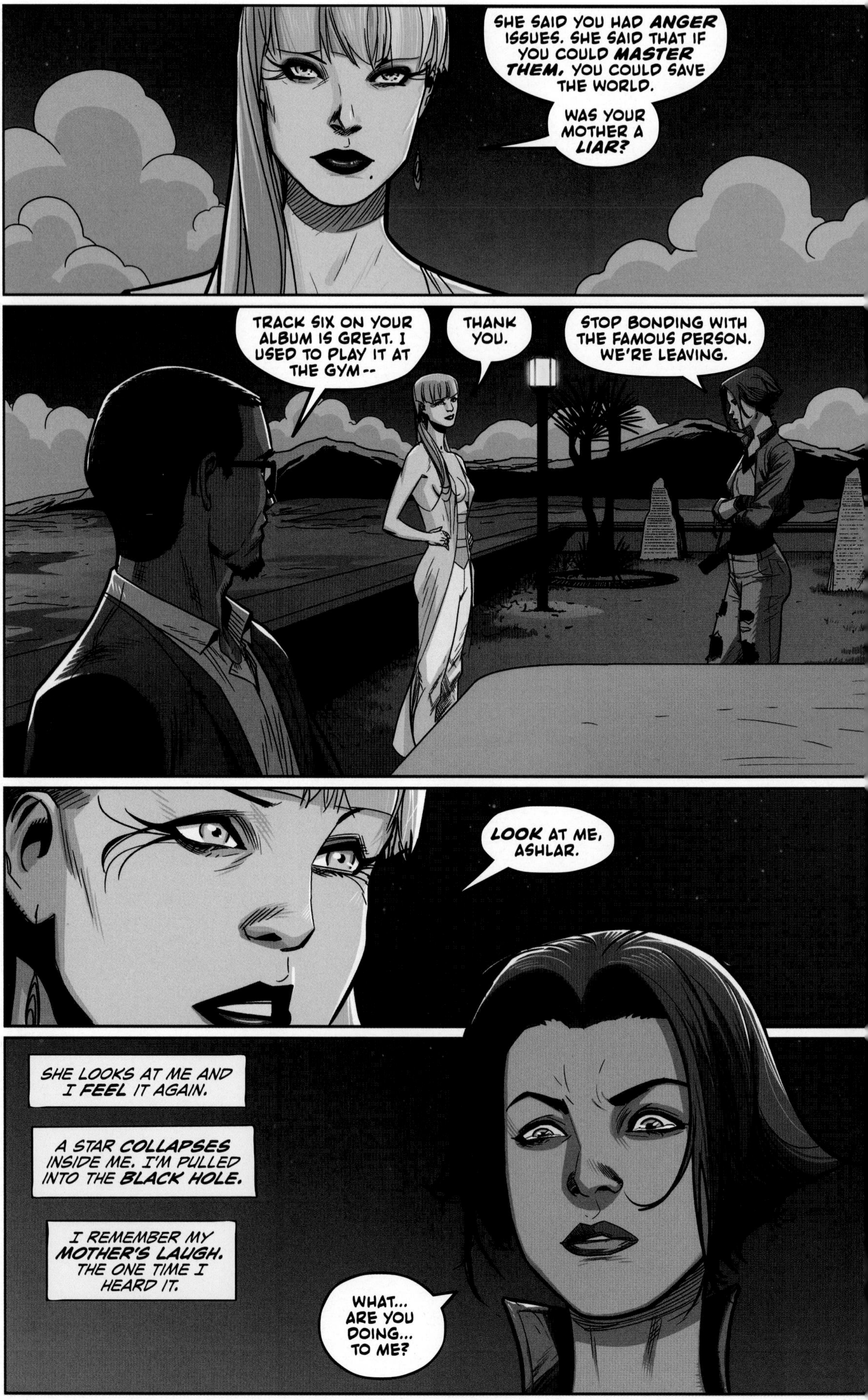
SHE SAID YOU HAD ANGER ISSUES. SHE SAID THAT IF YOU COULD MASTER THEM, YOU COULD SAVE THE WORLD.
WAS YOUR MOTHER A LIAR?
TRACK SIX ON YOUR ALBUM IS GREAT. I USED TO PLAY IT AT THE GYM--
THANK YOU.
STOP BONDING WITH THE FAMOUS PERSON. WE'RE LEAVING.
LOOK AT ME, ASHLAR.
SHE LOOKS AT ME AND I FEEL IT AGAIN.
A STAR COLLAPSES INSIDE ME. I'M PULLED INTO THE BLACK HOLE.
I REMEMBER MY MOTHER'S LAUGH. THE ONE TIME I HEARD IT.
WHAT... ARE YOU DOING... TO ME?

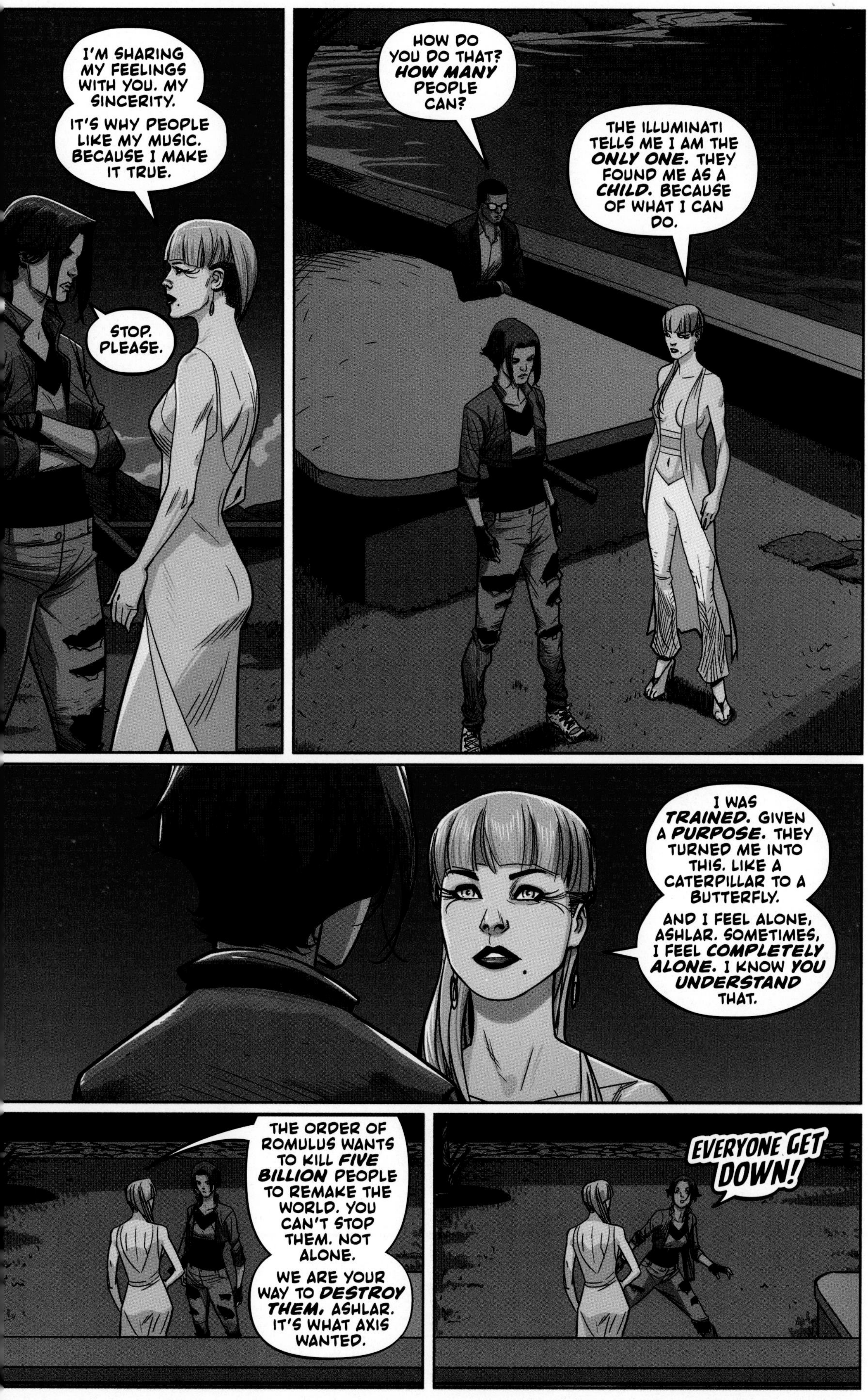
I'M SHARING MY FEELINGS WITH YOU. MY SINCERITY.
IT'S WHY PEOPLE LIKE MY MUSIC. BECAUSE I MAKE IT TRUE.
STOP. PLEASE.
HOW DO YOU DO THAT? HOW MANY PEOPLE CAN?
THE ILLUMINATI TELLS ME I AM THE ONLY ONE. THEY FOUND ME AS A CHILD. BECAUSE OF WHAT I CAN DO.
I WAS TRAINED. GIVEN A PURPOSE. THEY TURNED ME INTO THIS. LIKE A CATERPILLAR TO A BUTTERFLY.
AND I FEEL ALONE, ASHLAR. SOMETIMES, I FEEL COMPLETELY ALONE. I KNOW YOU UNDERSTAND THAT.
THE ORDER OF ROMULUS WANTS TO KILL FIVE BILLION PEOPLE TO REMAKE THE WORLD. YOU CAN'T STOP THEM. NOT ALONE.
WE ARE YOUR WAY TO DESTROY THEM, ASHLAR. IT'S WHAT AXIS WANTED.
EVERYONE GET DOWN!

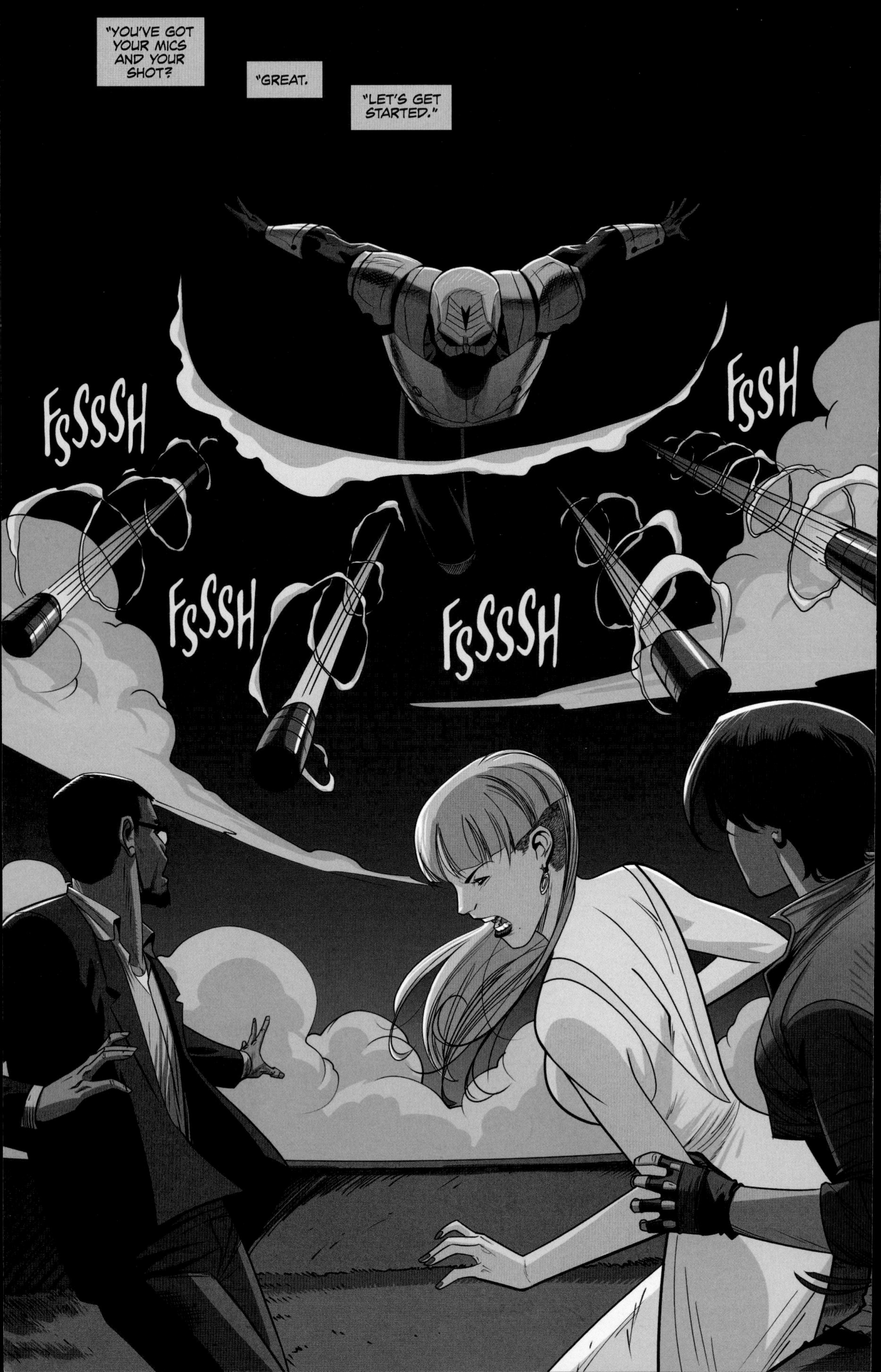
"YOU'VE GOT YOUR MICS AND YOUR SHOT?
"GREAT.
"LET'S GET STARTED."
FSSSSH
FSSH
FSSSH
FSSSSH

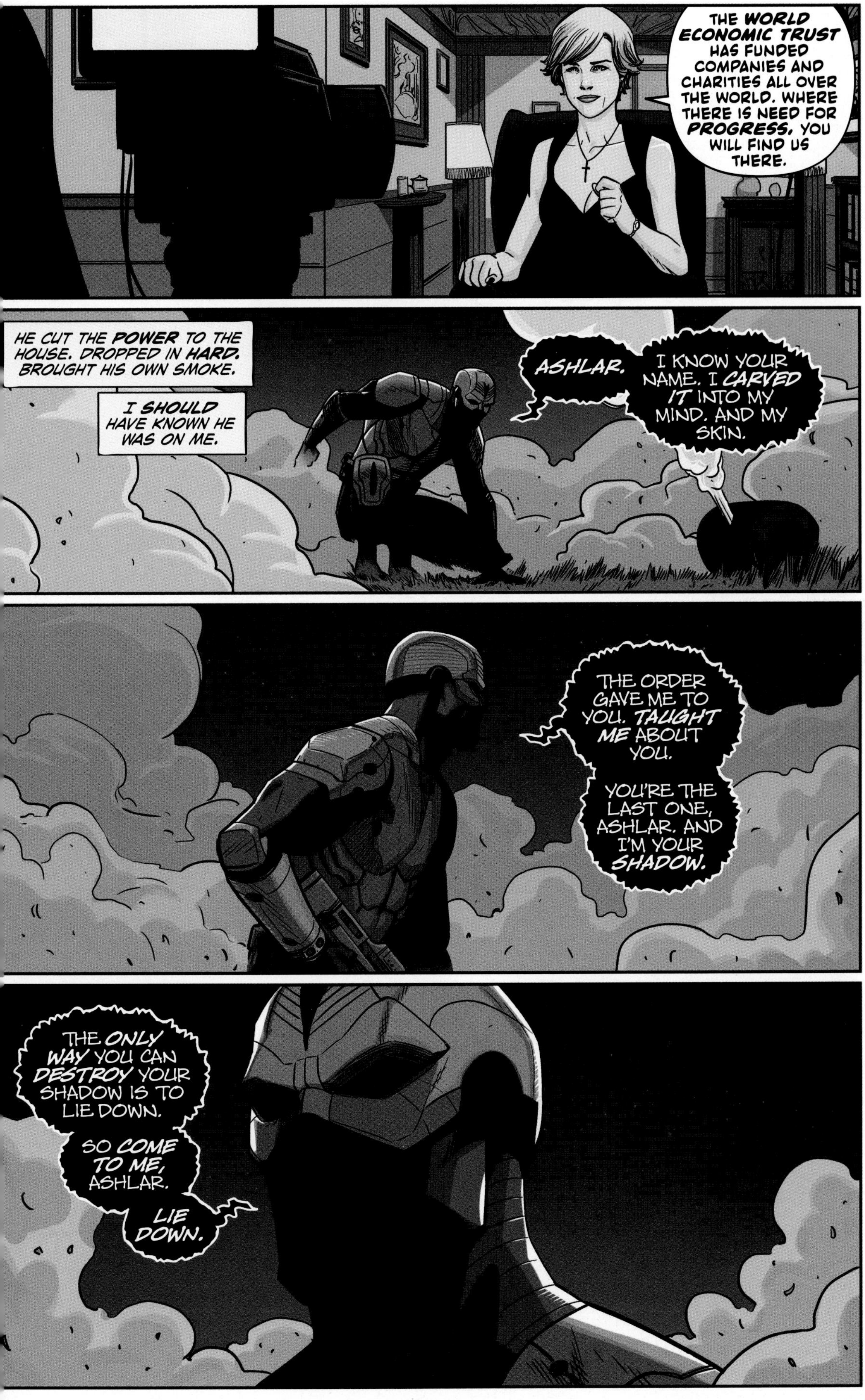

THE WORLD ECONOMIC TRUST HAS FUNDED COMPANIES AND CHARITIES ALL OVER THE WORLD. WHERE THERE IS NEED FOR PROGRESS, YOU WILL FIND US THERE.
HE CUT THE POWER TO THE HOUSE. DROPPED IN HARD. BROUGHT HIS OWN SMOKE.
I SHOULD HAVE KNOWN HE WAS ON ME.
ASHLAR.
I KNOW YOUR NAME. I CARVED IT INTO MY MIND. AND MY SKIN.
THE ORDER GAVE ME TO YOU. TAUGHT ME ABOUT YOU.
YOU'RE THE LAST ONE, ASHLAR. AND I'M YOUR SHADOW.
THE ONLY WAY YOU CAN DESTROY YOUR SHADOW IS TO LIE DOWN.
SO COME TO ME, ASHLAR.
LIE DOWN.

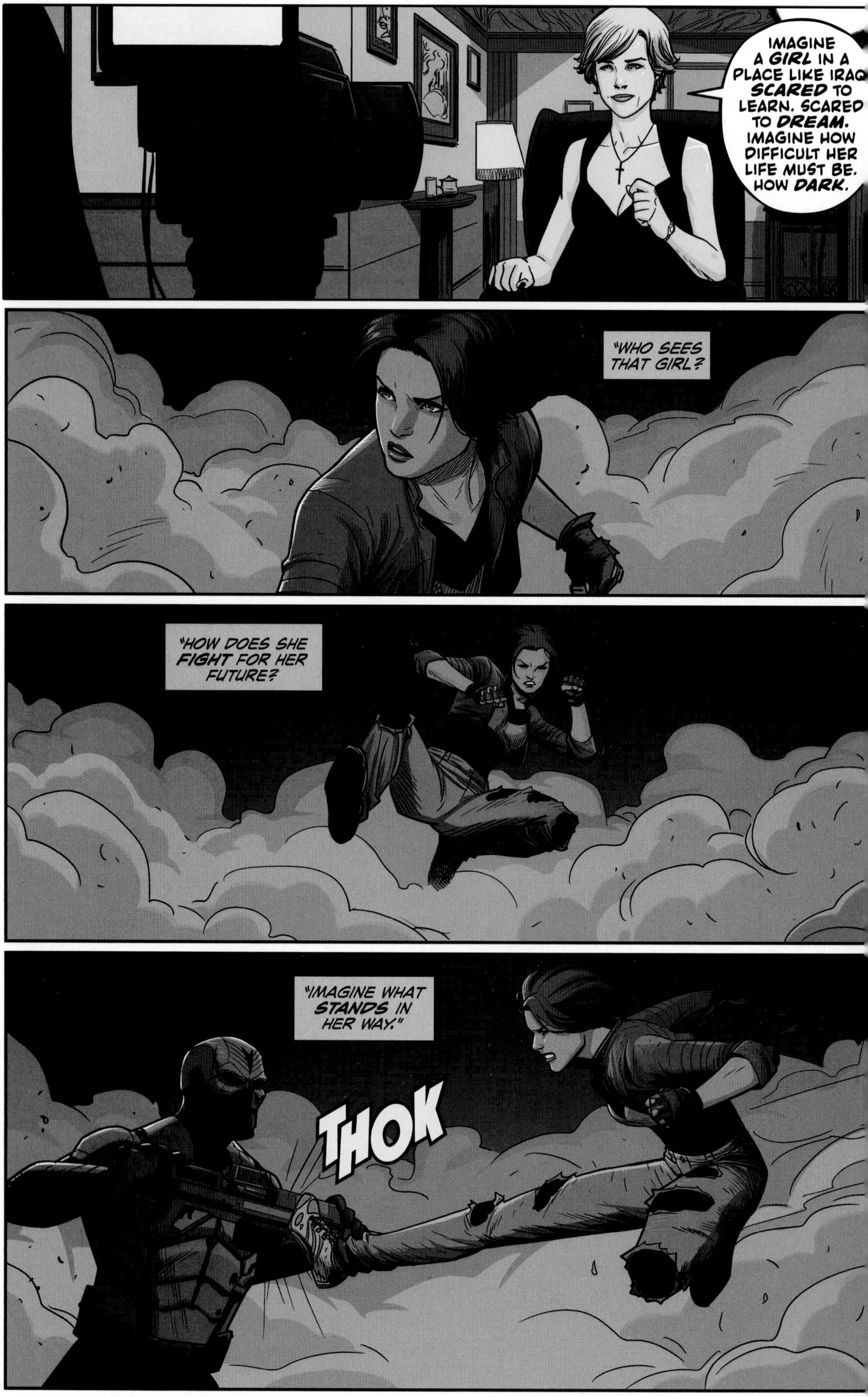
IMAGINE A GIRL IN A PLACE LIKE IRAQ SCARED TO LEARN. SCARED TO DREAM. IMAGINE HOW DIFFICULT HER LIFE MUST BE. HOW DARK.
"WHO SEES THAT GIRL?
"HOW DOES SHE FIGHT FOR HER FUTURE?
"IMAGINE WHAT STANDS IN HER WAY."
THOK

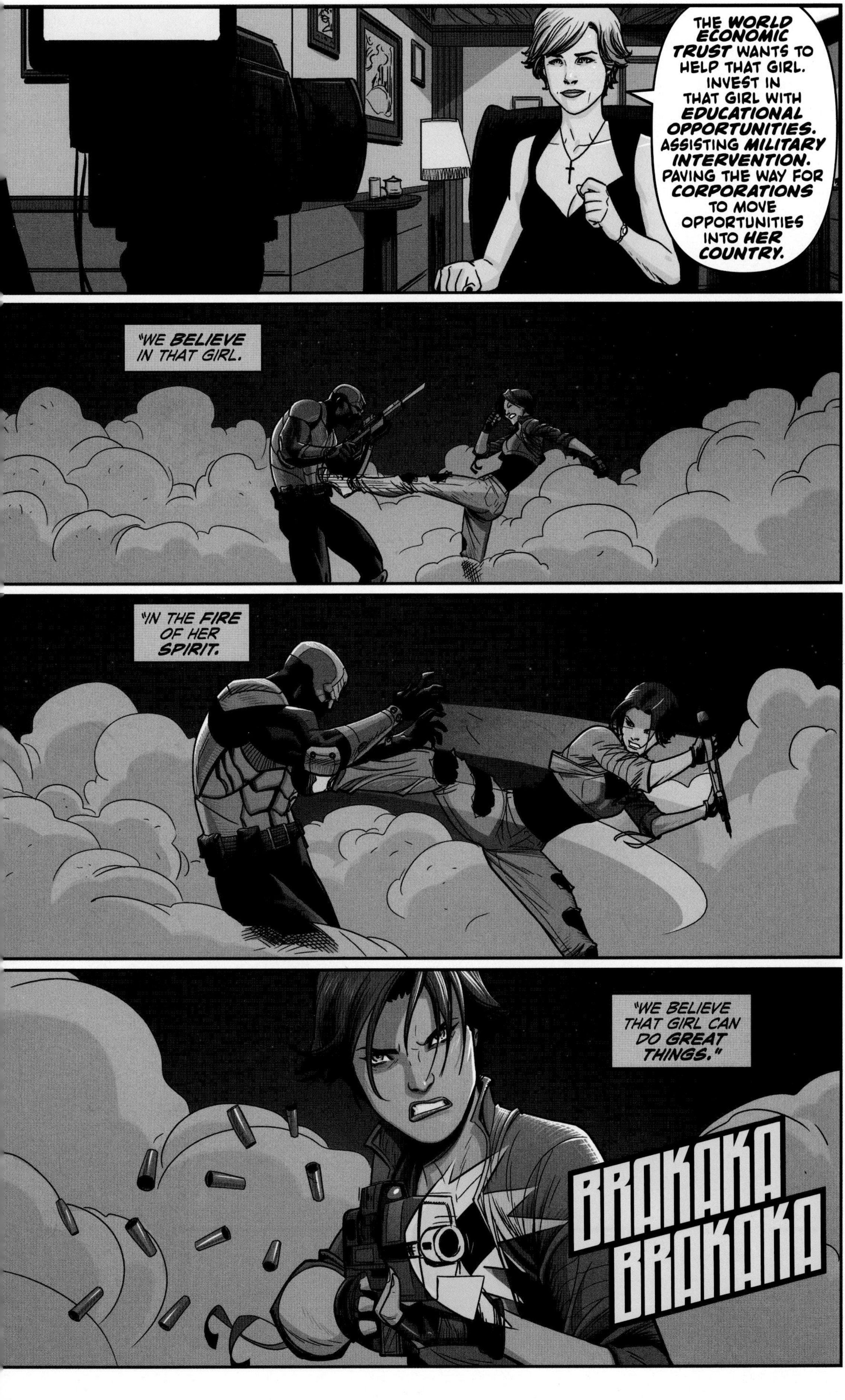
THE WORLD ECONOMIC TRUST WANTS TO HELP THAT GIRL. INVEST IN THAT GIRL WITH EDUCATIONAL OPPORTUNITIES. ASSISTING MILITARY INTERVENTION. PAVING THE WAY FOR CORPORATIONS TO MOVE OPPORTUNITIES INTO HER COUNTRY.
"WE BELIEVE IN THAT GIRL.
"IN THE FIRE OF HER SPIRIT.
"WE BELIEVE THAT GIRL CAN DO GREAT THINGS."
BRAKAKA BRAKAKA

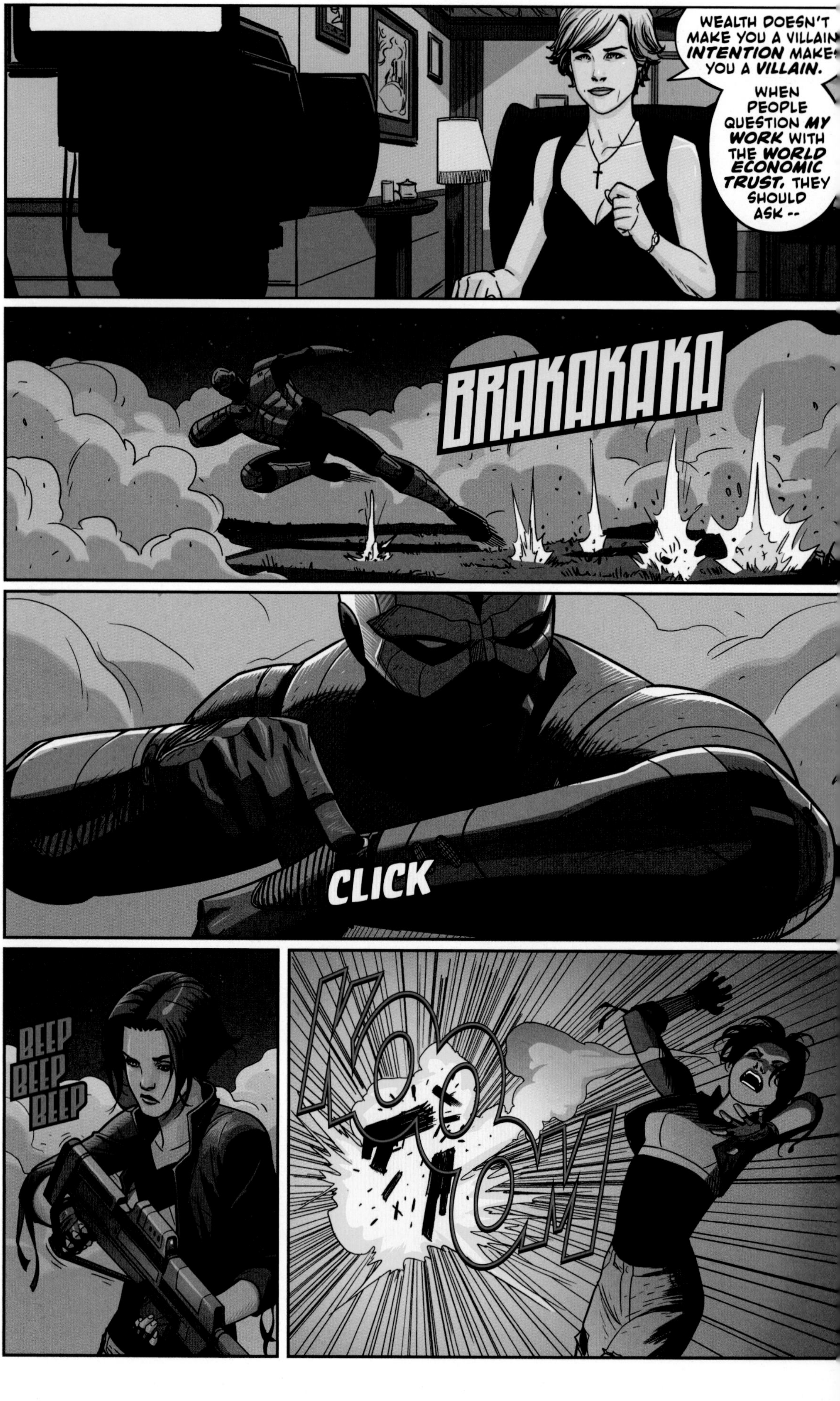
WEALTH DOESN'T MAKE YOU A VILLAIN. INTENTION MAKES YOU A VILLAIN.
WHEN PEOPLE QUESTION MY WORK WITH THE WORLD ECONOMIC TRUST, THEY SHOULD ASK --
BRAKAKAKA
CLICK
BEEP BEEP BEEP

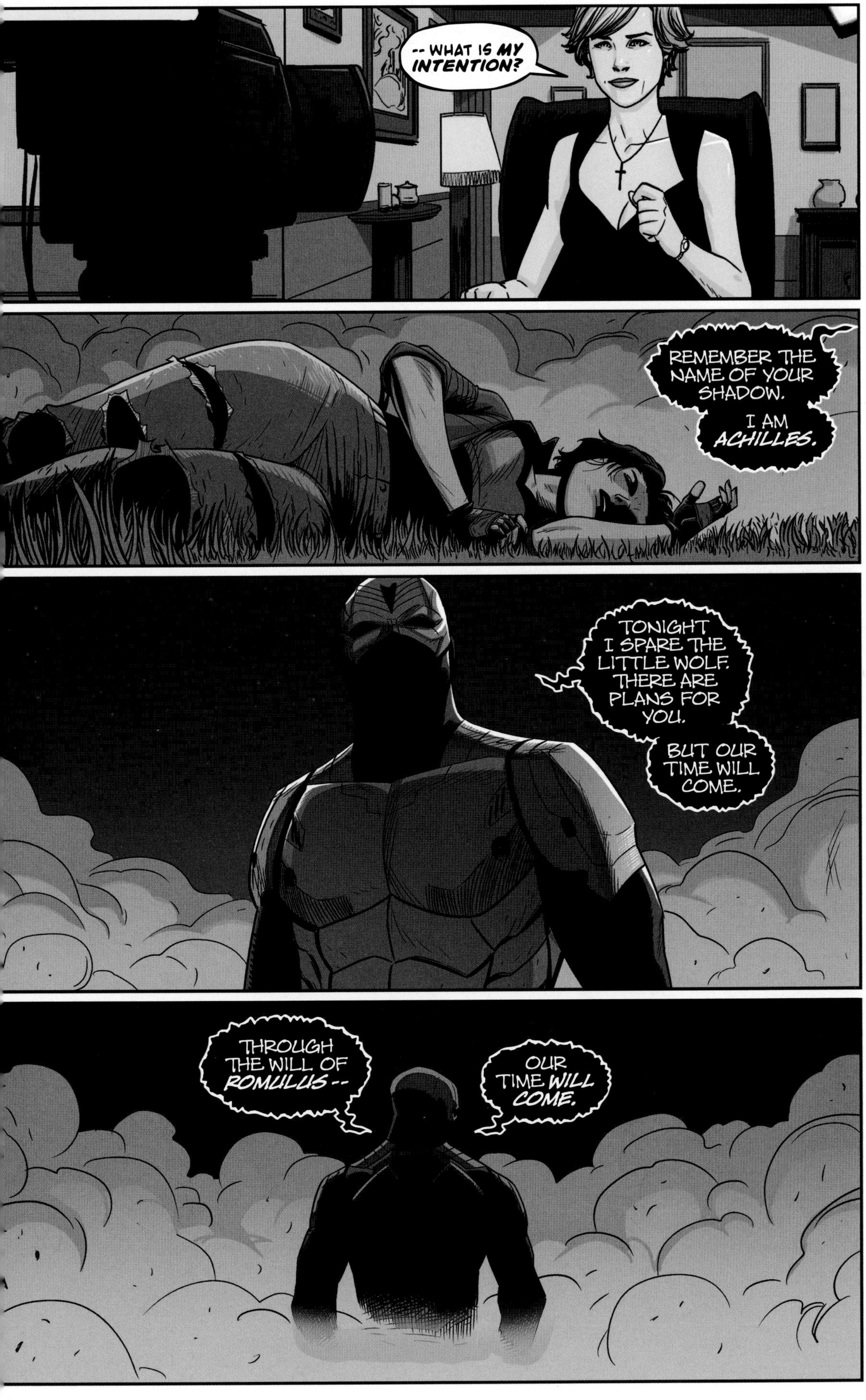
-- WHAT IS MY INTENTION?
REMEMBER THE NAME OF YOUR SHADOW.
I AM ACHILLES.
TONIGHT I SPARE THE LITTLE WOLF. THERE ARE PLANS FOR YOU.
BUT OUR TIME WILL COME.
THROUGH THE WILL OF ROMULUS --
OUR TIME WILL COME.

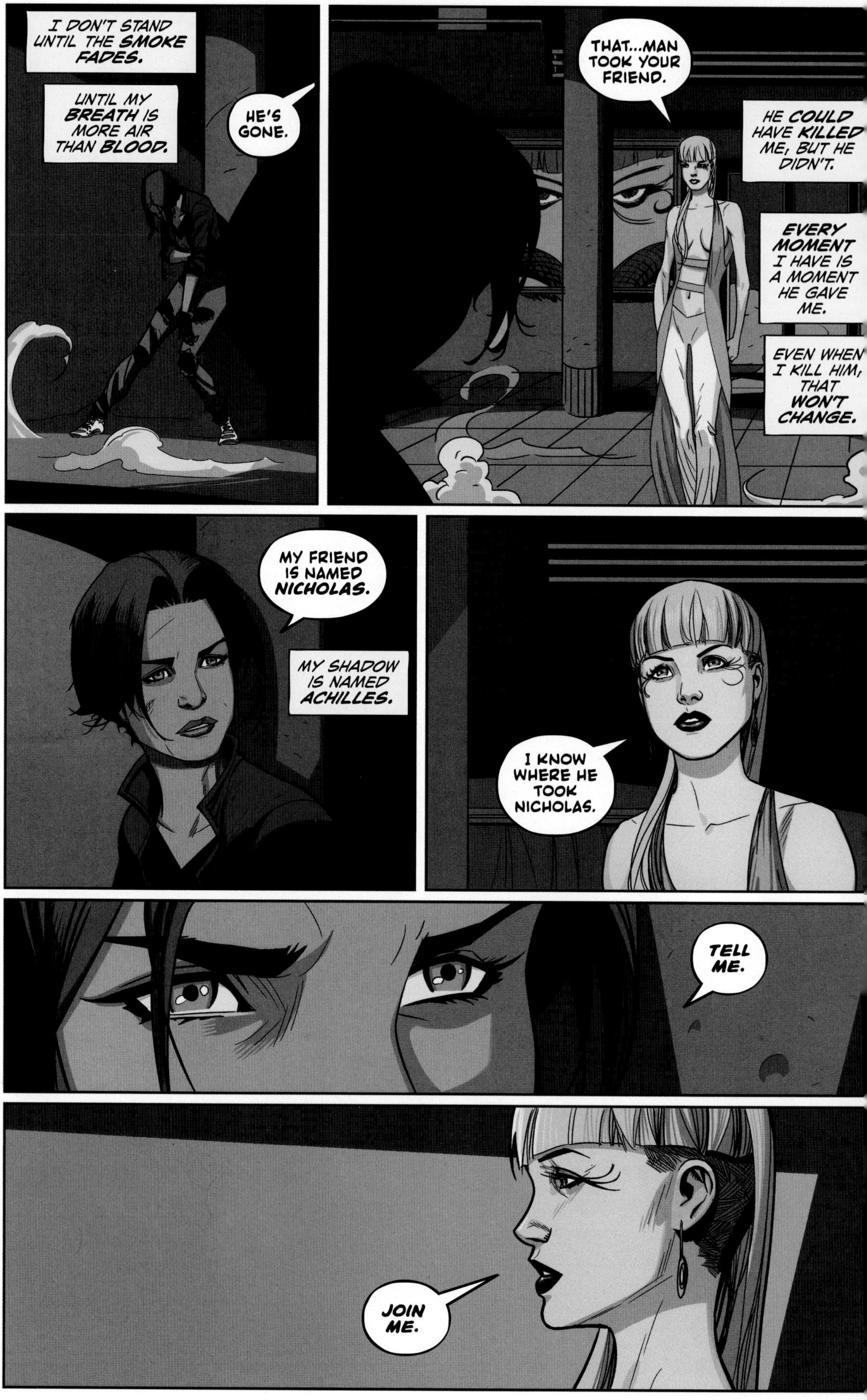
I DON'T STAND UNTIL THE SMOKE FADES.
UNTIL MY BREATH IS MORE AIR THAN BLOOD.
HE'S GONE.
THAT...MAN TOOK YOUR FRIEND.
HE COULD HAVE KILLED ME, BUT HE DIDN'T.
EVERY MOMENT I HAVE IS A MOMENT HE GAVE ME.
EVEN WHEN I KILL HIM, THAT WON'T CHANGE.
MY FRIEND IS NAMED NICHOLAS.
MY SHADOW IS NAMED ACHILLES.
I KNOW WHERE HE TOOK NICHOLAS.
TELL ME.
JOIN ME.

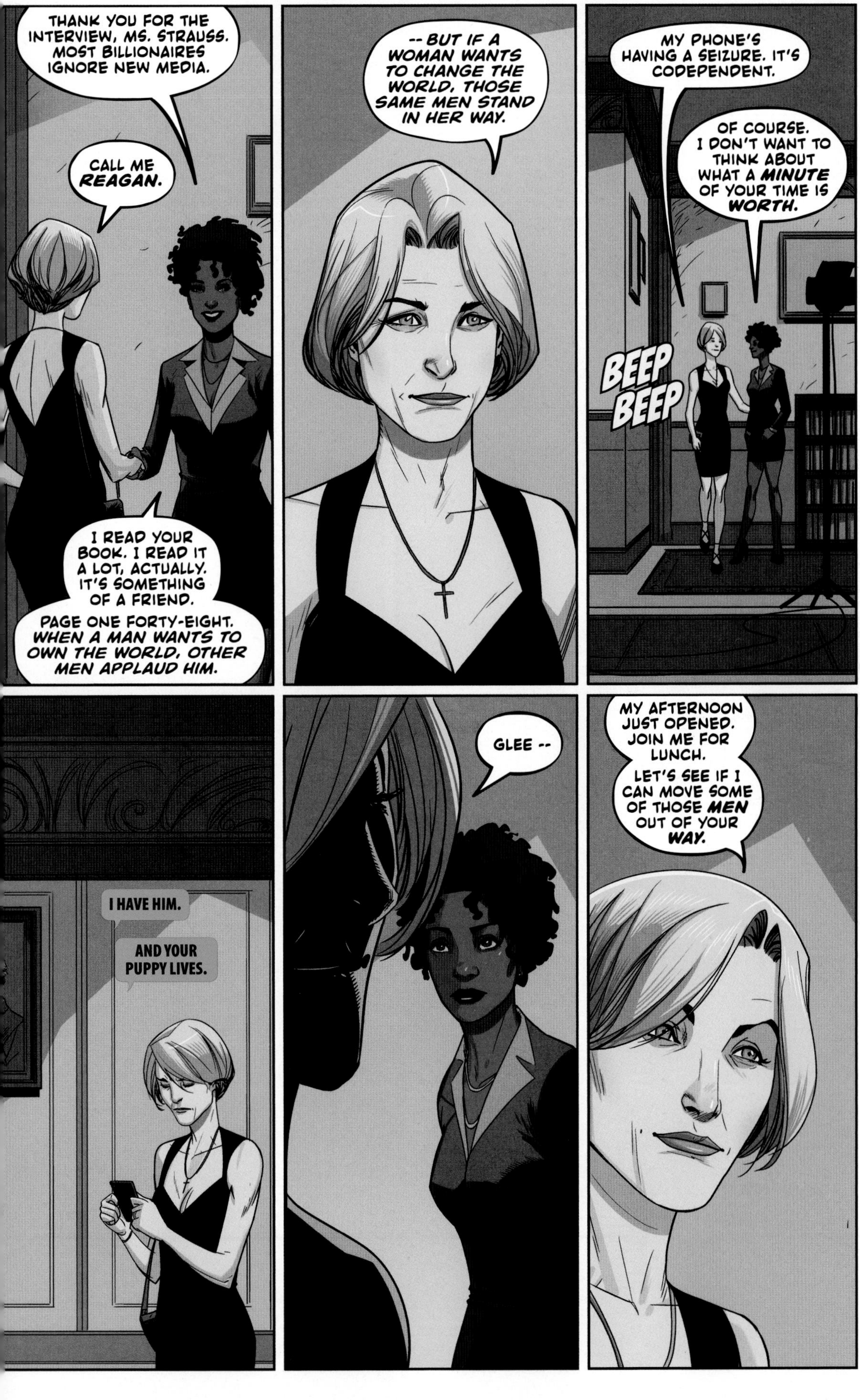
THANK YOU FOR THE INTERVIEW, MS. STRAUSS. MOST BILLIONAIRES IGNORE NEW MEDIA.
CALL ME *REAGAN.*
I READ YOUR BOOK. I READ IT A LOT, ACTUALLY. IT'S SOMETHING OF A FRIEND.
PAGE ONE FORTY-EIGHT. *WHEN A MAN WANTS TO OWN THE WORLD, OTHER MEN APPLAUD HIM.*
-- BUT IF A WOMAN WANTS TO CHANGE THE WORLD, THOSE SAME MEN STAND IN HER WAY.
MY PHONE'S HAVING A SEIZURE. IT'S CODEPENDENT.
OF COURSE. I DON'T WANT TO THINK ABOUT WHAT A *MINUTE* OF YOUR TIME IS *WORTH.*
BEEP BEEP
I HAVE HIM.
AND YOUR PUPPY LIVES.
GLEE --
MY AFTERNOON JUST OPENED. JOIN ME FOR LUNCH.
LET'S SEE IF I CAN MOVE SOME OF THOSE *MEN* OUT OF YOUR *WAY.*

MY MOTHER WOULDN'T NEED THEM. SHE WOULD LOOK THEM IN THE EYE AND TELL THEM **NEVER.**

MY MOTHER WOULDN'T HAVE **FAILED.**

BUT I'M ME.

AND I DID.

WHAT DO YOU WANT FROM ME?

EVERYTHING.

AND WE WILL GIVE YOU **ANYTHING.**

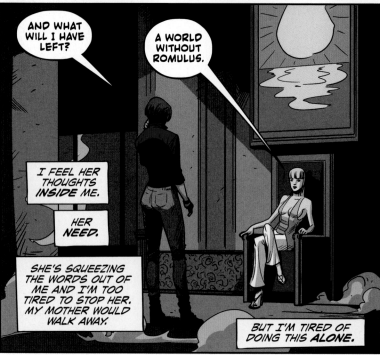

AND WHAT WILL I HAVE LEFT?

A WORLD WITHOUT ROMULUS.

I FEEL HER THOUGHTS INSIDE ME.

HER **NEED.**

SHE'S SQUEEZING THE WORDS OUT OF ME AND I'M TOO TIRED TO STOP HER. MY MOTHER WOULD WALK AWAY.

BUT I'M TIRED OF DOING THIS **ALONE.**

FINE.

I'LL **JOIN** THE F%$KING **ILLUMINATI.**

CHAPTER THREE:
A Matter of Tradition

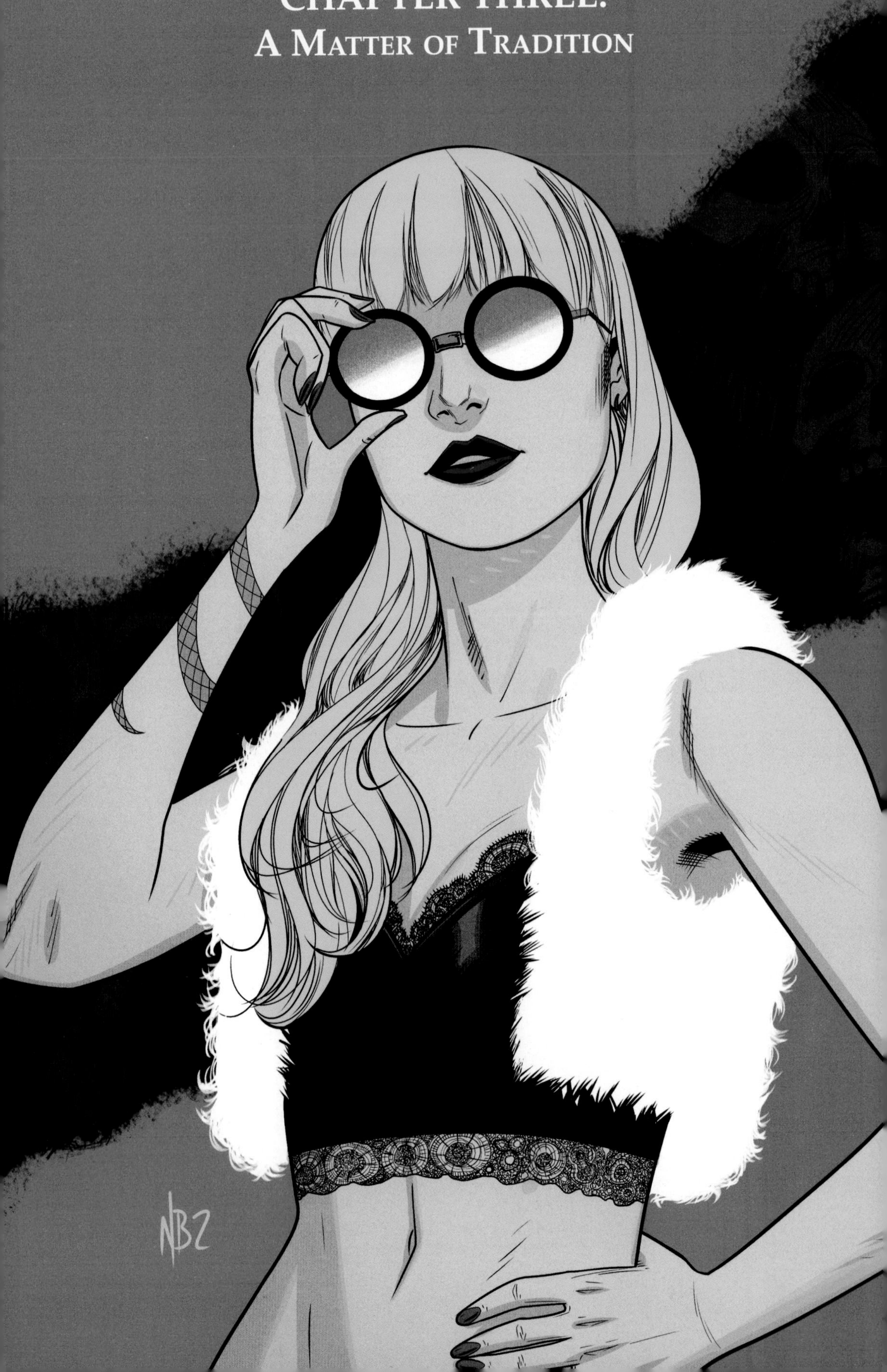

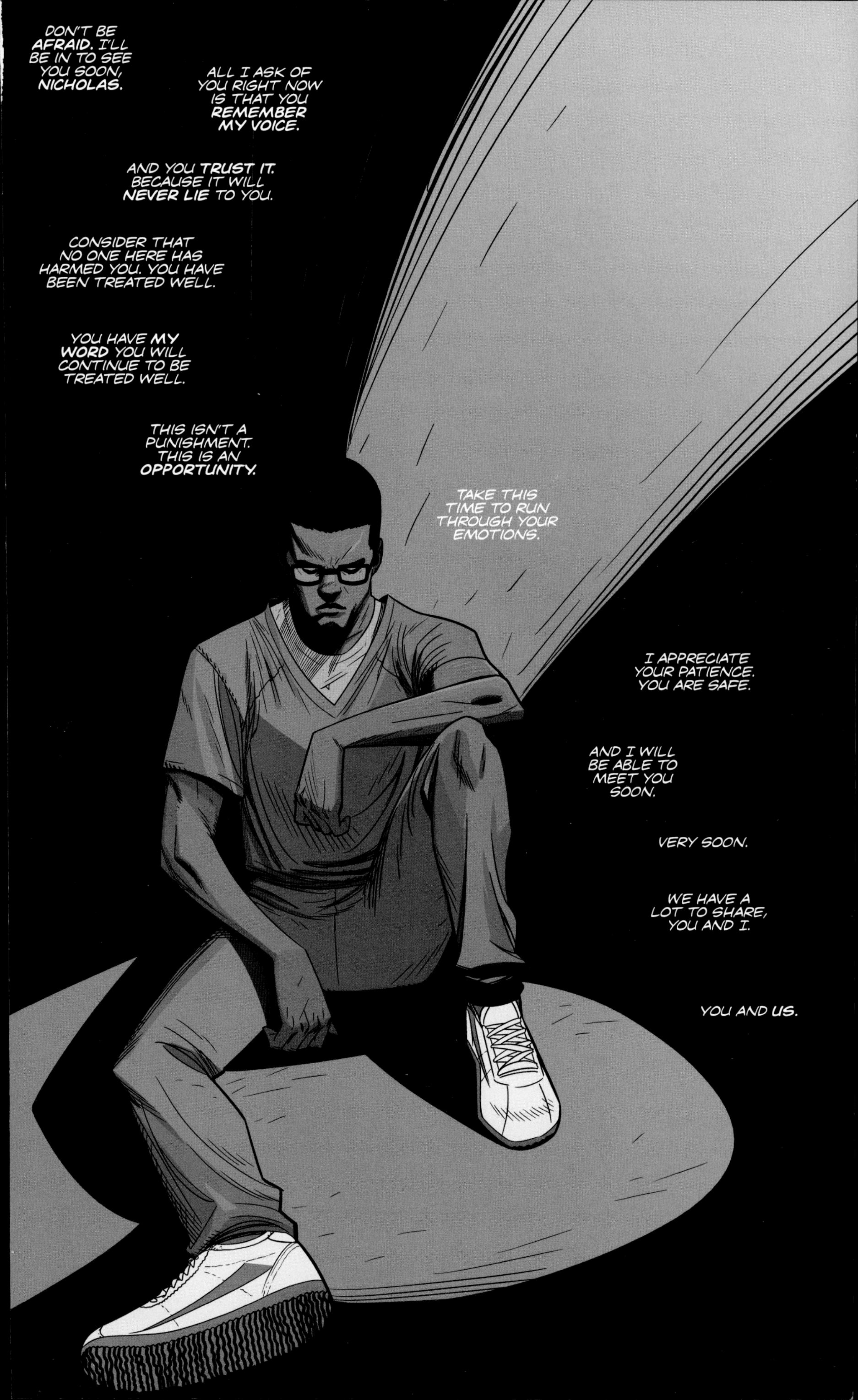
DON'T BE AFRAID. I'LL BE IN TO SEE YOU SOON, NICHOLAS.
ALL I ASK OF YOU RIGHT NOW IS THAT YOU REMEMBER MY VOICE.
AND YOU TRUST IT. BECAUSE IT WILL NEVER LIE TO YOU.
CONSIDER THAT NO ONE HERE HAS HARMED YOU. YOU HAVE BEEN TREATED WELL.
YOU HAVE MY WORD YOU WILL CONTINUE TO BE TREATED WELL.
THIS ISN'T A PUNISHMENT. THIS IS AN OPPORTUNITY.
TAKE THIS TIME TO RUN THROUGH YOUR EMOTIONS.
I APPRECIATE YOUR PATIENCE. YOU ARE SAFE.
AND I WILL BE ABLE TO MEET YOU SOON.
VERY SOON.
WE HAVE A LOT TO SHARE, YOU AND I.
YOU AND US.

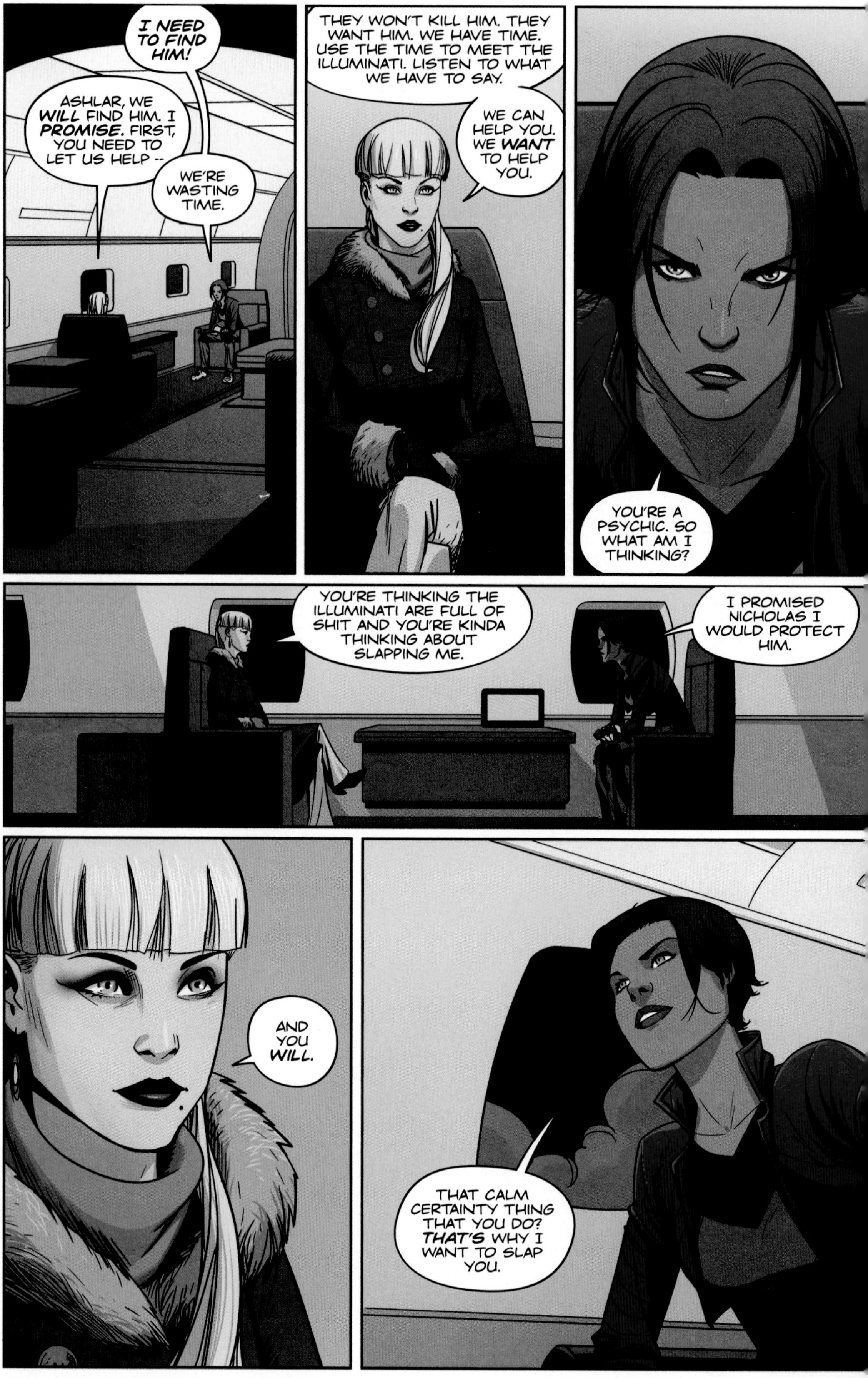
I NEED TO FIND HIM!
ASHLAR, WE WILL FIND HIM. I PROMISE. FIRST, YOU NEED TO LET US HELP --
WE'RE WASTING TIME.
THEY WON'T KILL HIM. THEY WANT HIM. WE HAVE TIME. USE THE TIME TO MEET THE ILLUMINATI. LISTEN TO WHAT WE HAVE TO SAY.
WE CAN HELP YOU. WE WANT TO HELP YOU.
YOU'RE A PSYCHIC. SO WHAT AM I THINKING?
YOU'RE THINKING THE ILLUMINATI ARE FULL OF SHIT AND YOU'RE KINDA THINKING ABOUT SLAPPING ME.
I PROMISED NICHOLAS I WOULD PROTECT HIM.
AND YOU WILL.
THAT CALM CERTAINTY THING THAT YOU DO? THAT'S WHY I WANT TO SLAP YOU.

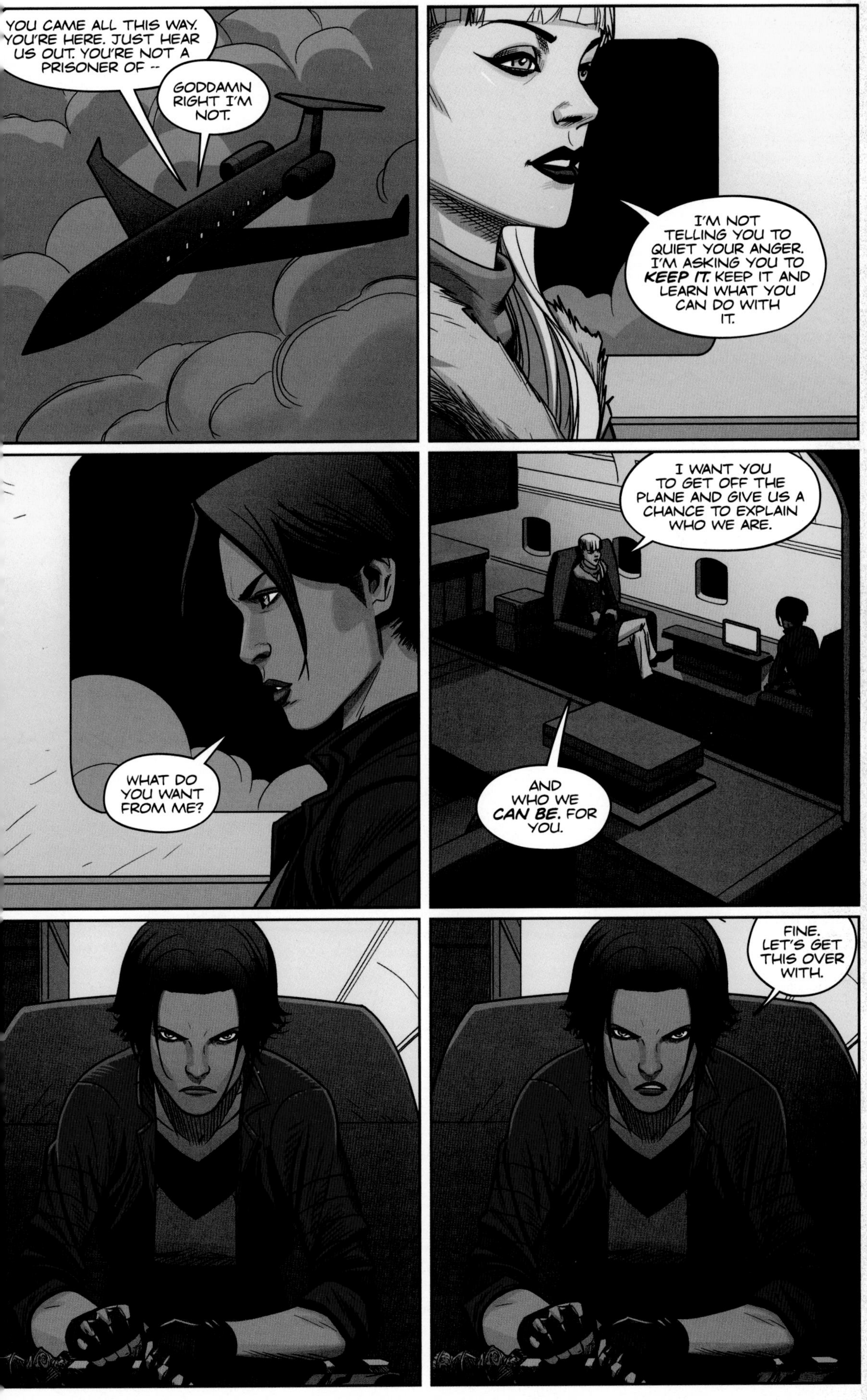

YOU CAME ALL THIS WAY. YOU'RE HERE. JUST HEAR US OUT. YOU'RE NOT A PRISONER OF --
GODDAMN RIGHT I'M NOT.
I'M NOT TELLING YOU TO QUIET YOUR ANGER. I'M ASKING YOU TO *KEEP IT.* KEEP IT AND LEARN WHAT YOU CAN DO WITH IT.
WHAT DO YOU WANT FROM ME?
I WANT YOU TO GET OFF THE PLANE AND GIVE US A CHANCE TO EXPLAIN WHO WE ARE.
AND WHO WE *CAN BE.* FOR YOU.
FINE. LET'S GET THIS OVER WITH.

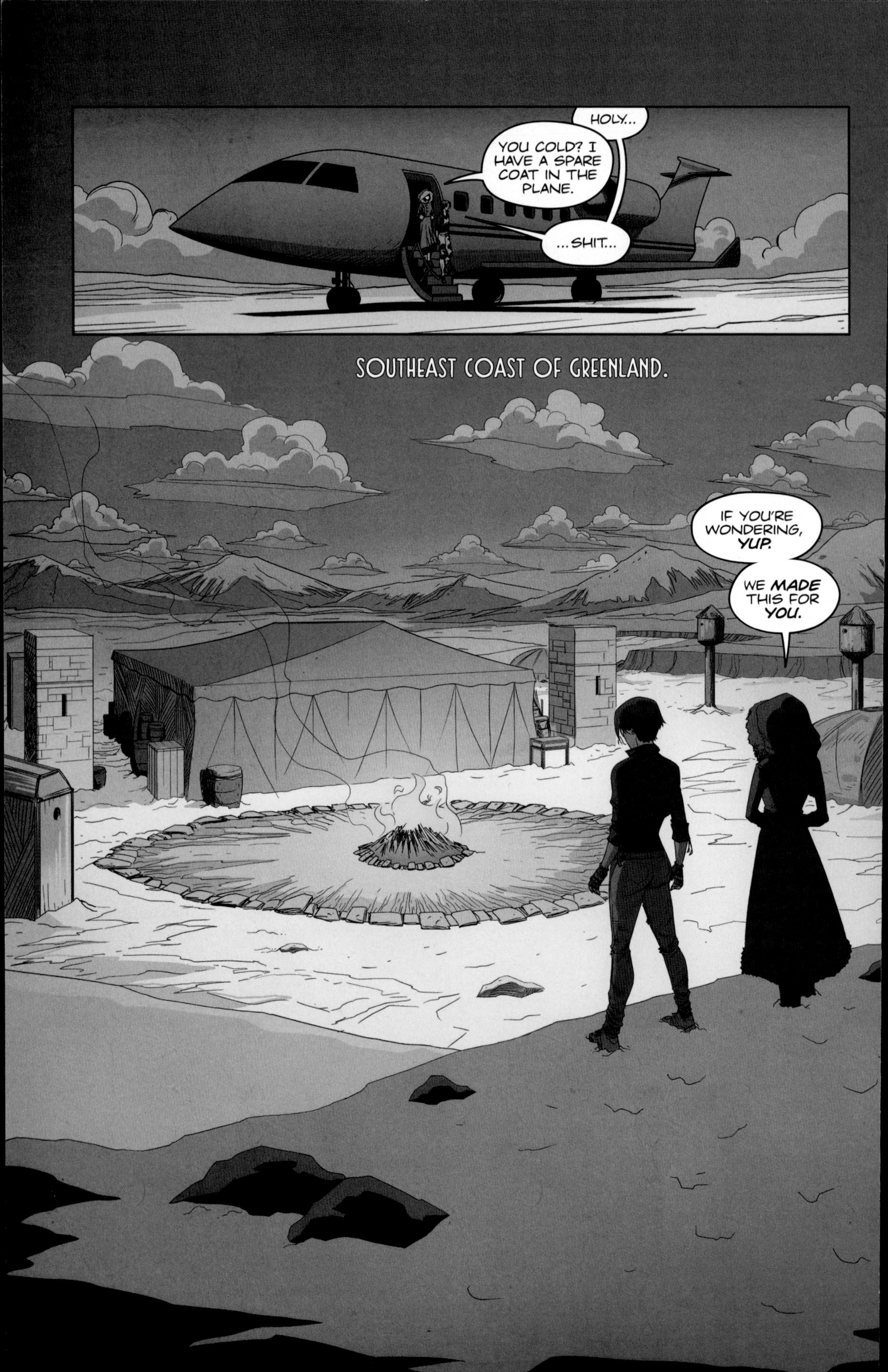
HOLY...
YOU COLD? I HAVE A SPARE COAT IN THE PLANE.
...SHIT...
SOUTHEAST COAST OF GREENLAND.
IF YOU'RE WONDERING, **YUP.**
WE **MADE** THIS FOR **YOU.**

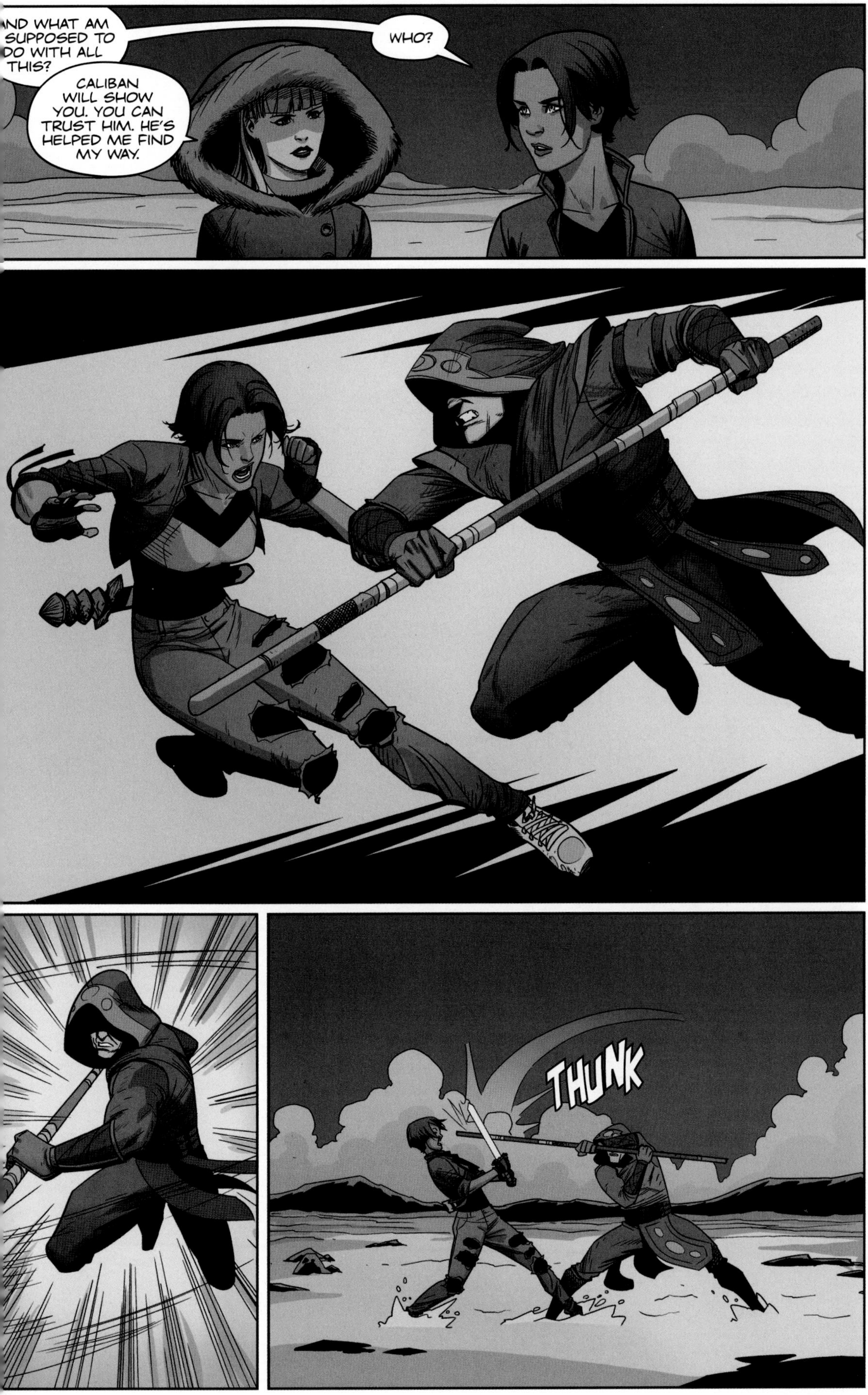

AND WHAT AM SUPPOSED TO DO WITH ALL THIS?
WHO?
CALIBAN WILL SHOW YOU. YOU CAN TRUST HIM. HE'S HELPED ME FIND MY WAY.
THUNK

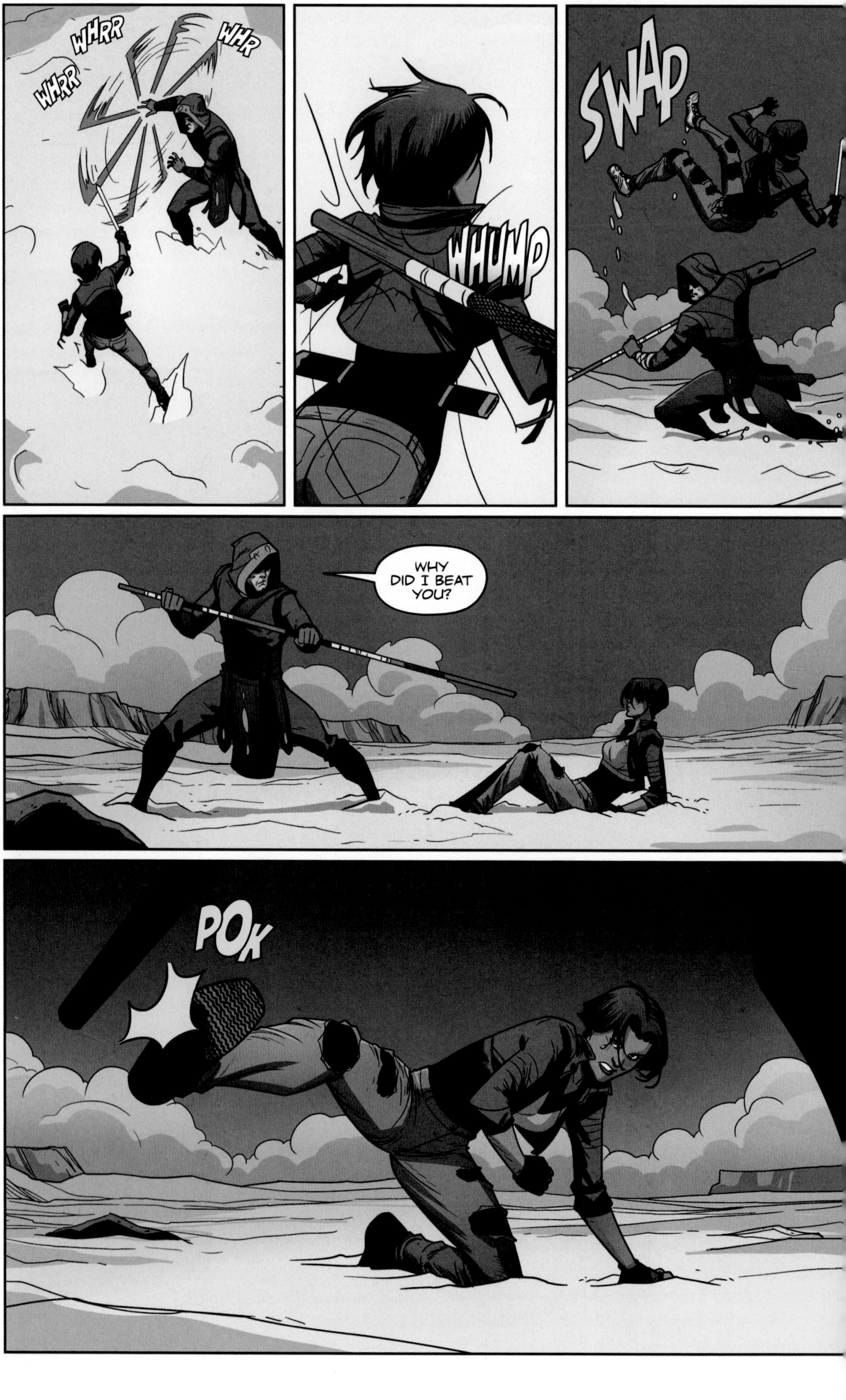
WHRR
WHRR
WHR
WHUMP
SWAP
WHY DID I BEAT YOU?
POK

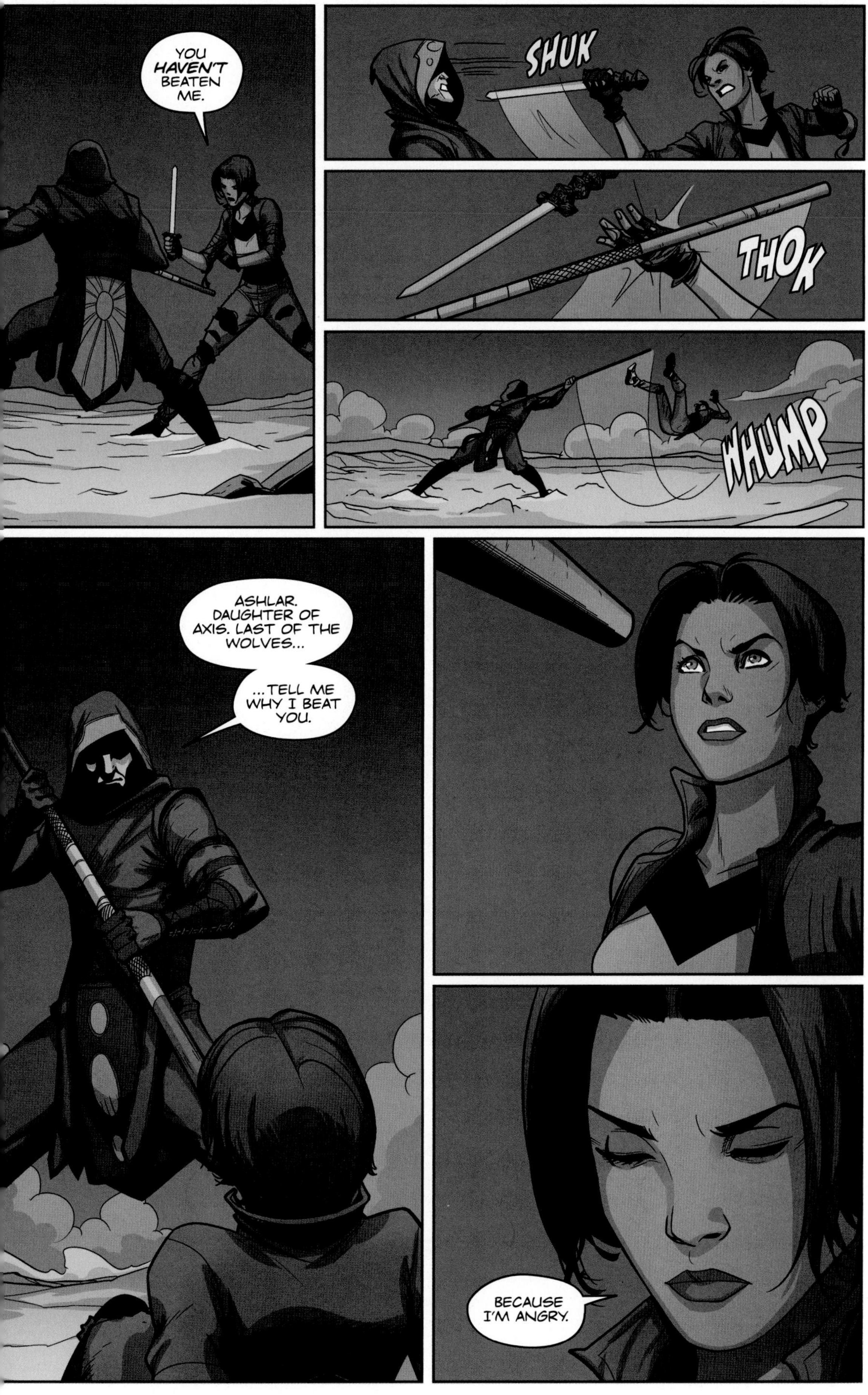

YOU HAVEN'T BEATEN ME.
SHUK
THOK
WHUMP
ASHLAR. DAUGHTER OF AXIS. LAST OF THE WOLVES...
...TELL ME WHY I BEAT YOU.
BECAUSE I'M ANGRY.

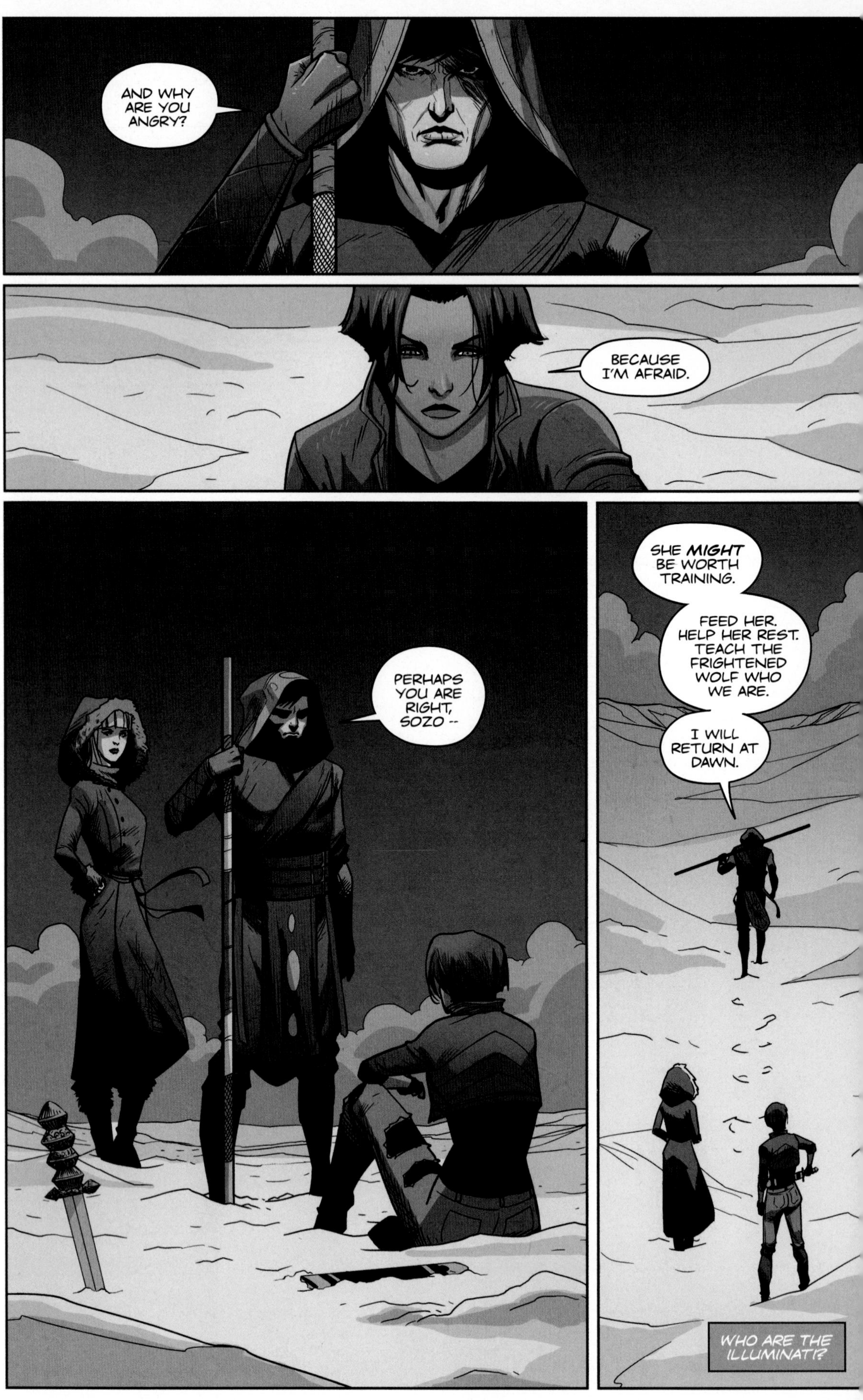
AND WHY ARE YOU ANGRY?
BECAUSE I'M AFRAID.
PERHAPS YOU ARE RIGHT, SOZO --
SHE MIGHT BE WORTH TRAINING.
FEED HER. HELP HER REST. TEACH THE FRIGHTENED WOLF WHO WE ARE.
I WILL RETURN AT DAWN.
WHO ARE THE ILLUMINATI?

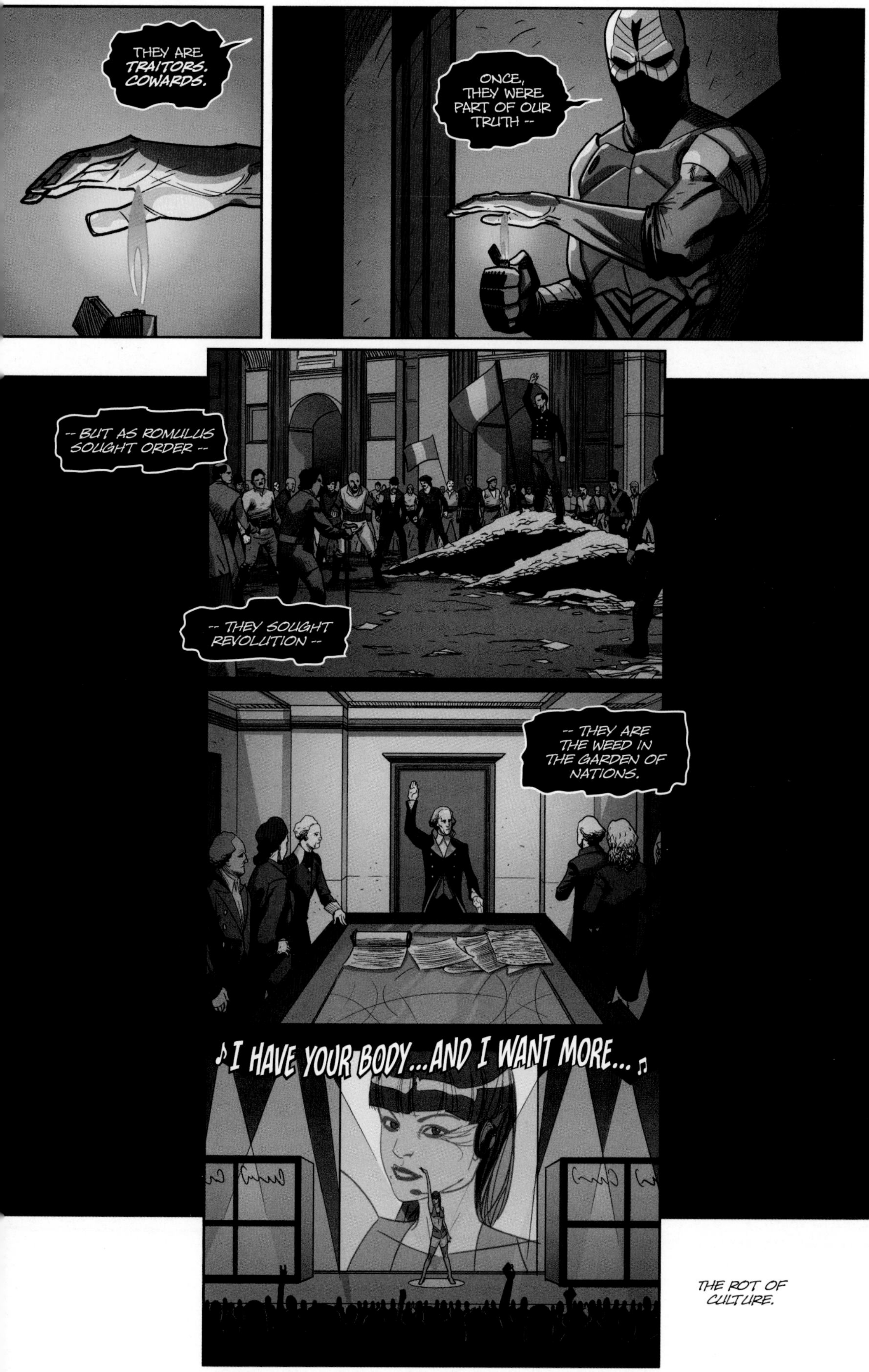
THEY ARE TRAITORS. COWARDS.
ONCE, THEY WERE PART OF OUR TRUTH --
-- BUT AS ROMULUS SOUGHT ORDER --
-- THEY SOUGHT REVOLUTION --
-- THEY ARE THE WEED IN THE GARDEN OF NATIONS.
♪ I HAVE YOUR BODY...AND I WANT MORE... ♫
THE ROT OF CULTURE.

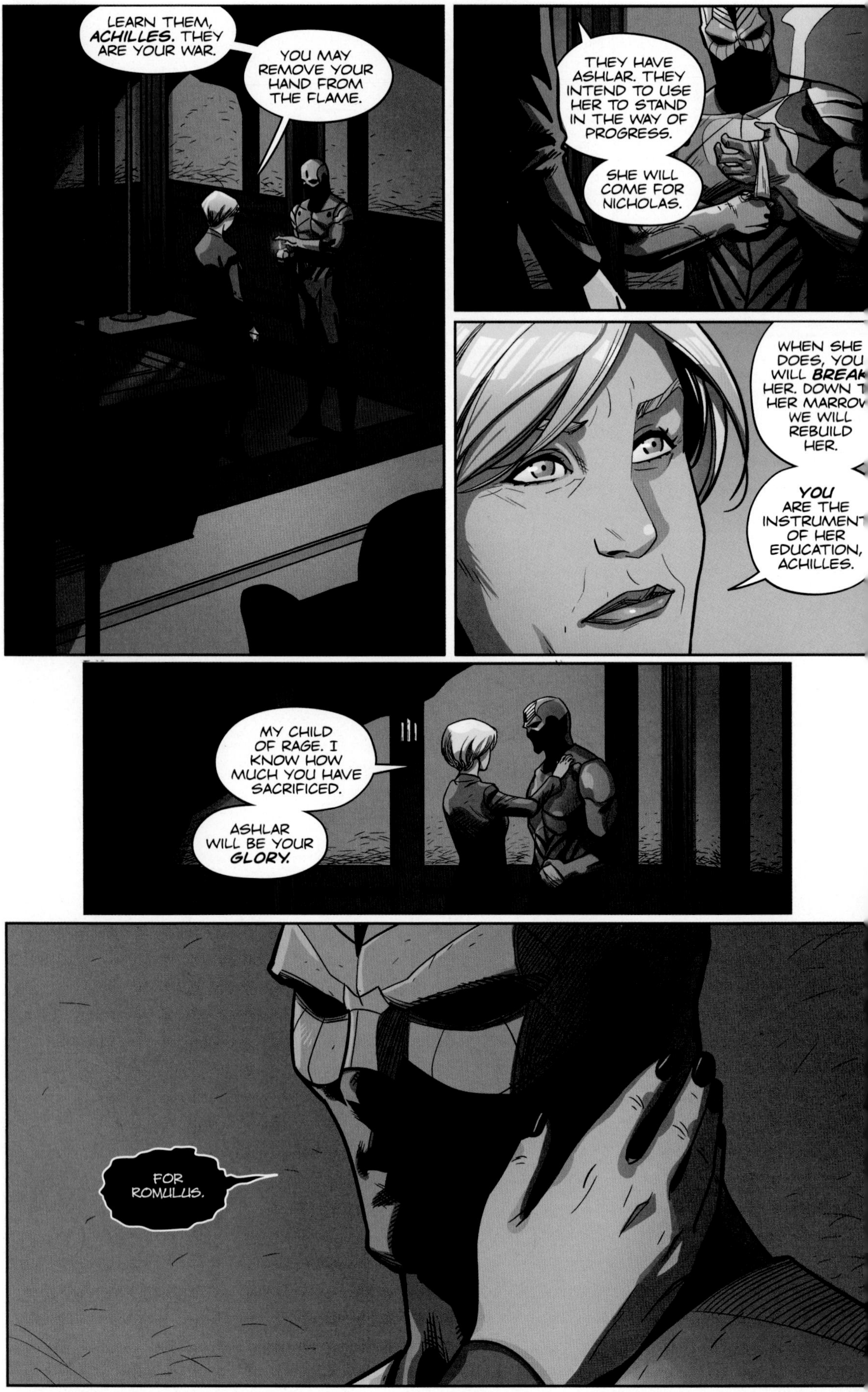
LEARN THEM, ACHILLES. THEY ARE YOUR WAR.
YOU MAY REMOVE YOUR HAND FROM THE FLAME.
THEY HAVE ASHLAR. THEY INTEND TO USE HER TO STAND IN THE WAY OF PROGRESS.
SHE WILL COME FOR NICHOLAS.
WHEN SHE DOES, YOU WILL BREAK HER. DOWN T HER MARROW WE WILL REBUILD HER.
YOU ARE THE INSTRUMENT OF HER EDUCATION, ACHILLES.
MY CHILD OF RAGE. I KNOW HOW MUCH YOU HAVE SACRIFICED.
ASHLAR WILL BE YOUR GLORY.
FOR ROMULUS.

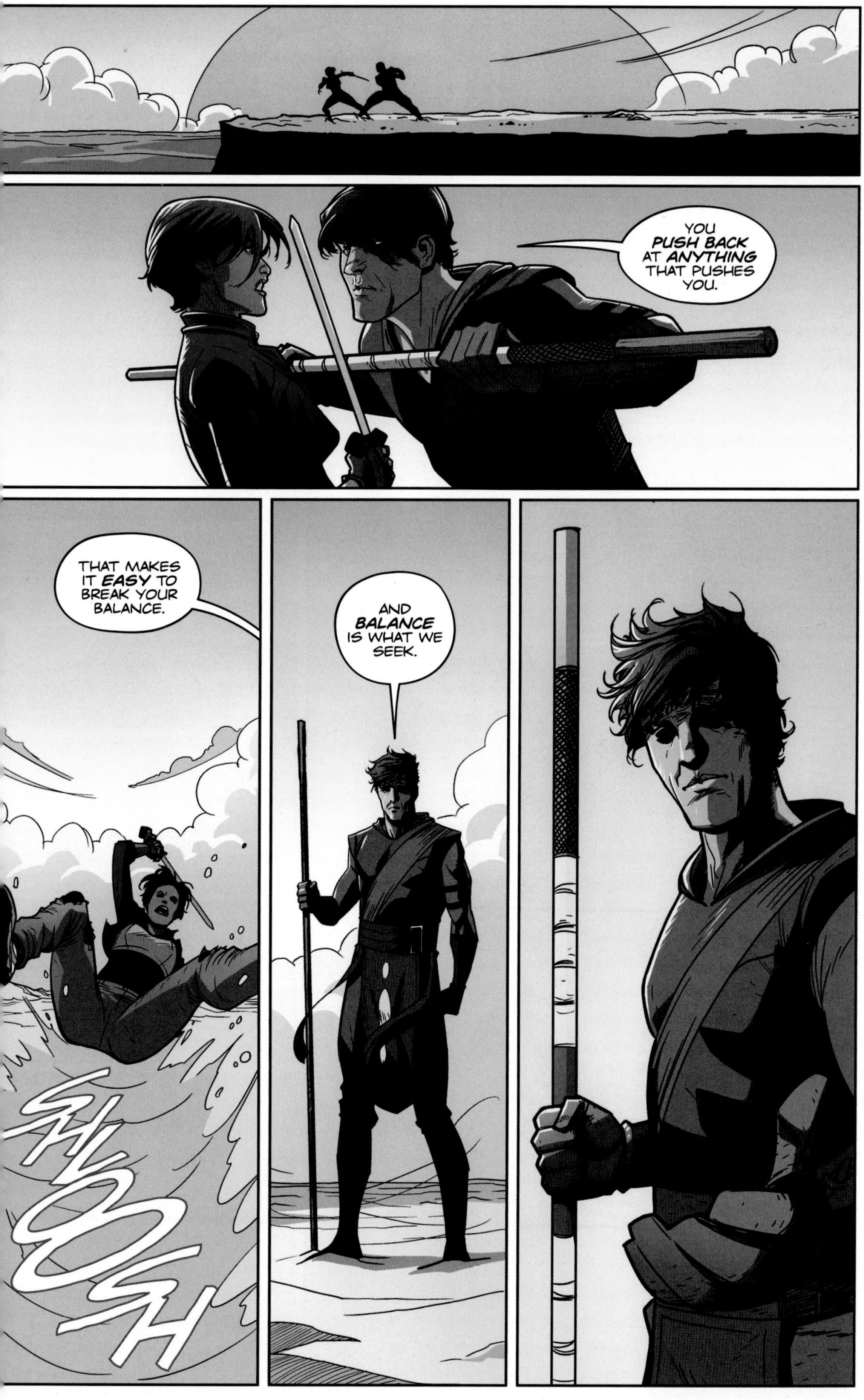
YOU PUSH BACK AT ANYTHING THAT PUSHES YOU.
THAT MAKES IT EASY TO BREAK YOUR BALANCE.
SHOOSH
AND BALANCE IS WHAT WE SEEK.

I CAN'T STOP THINKING ABOUT WHAT NICHOLAS IS GOING THROUGH.

WHAT ROMULUS DOES TO NICHOLAS IS *THEIR* RESPONSIBILITY. WHAT YOU DO TO YOURSELF IS *YOURS*.

I PROMISED HIM I WOULD KEEP HIM SAFE. I GAVE HIM MY *WORD*.

YOU *ARE* PROTECTING HIM --

-- FROM YOUR WEAKNESS.

YOU DON'T WANT TO RISK YOUR LIFE TO *SAVE* HIM.

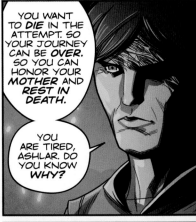

YOU WANT TO *DIE* IN THE ATTEMPT. SO YOUR JOURNEY CAN BE *OVER*. SO YOU CAN HONOR YOUR *MOTHER* AND *REST IN DEATH*.

YOU ARE TIRED, ASHLAR. DO YOU KNOW *WHY*?

BECAUSE I'M ALWAYS *PUSHING*.

AGAINST *EVERYTHING*.

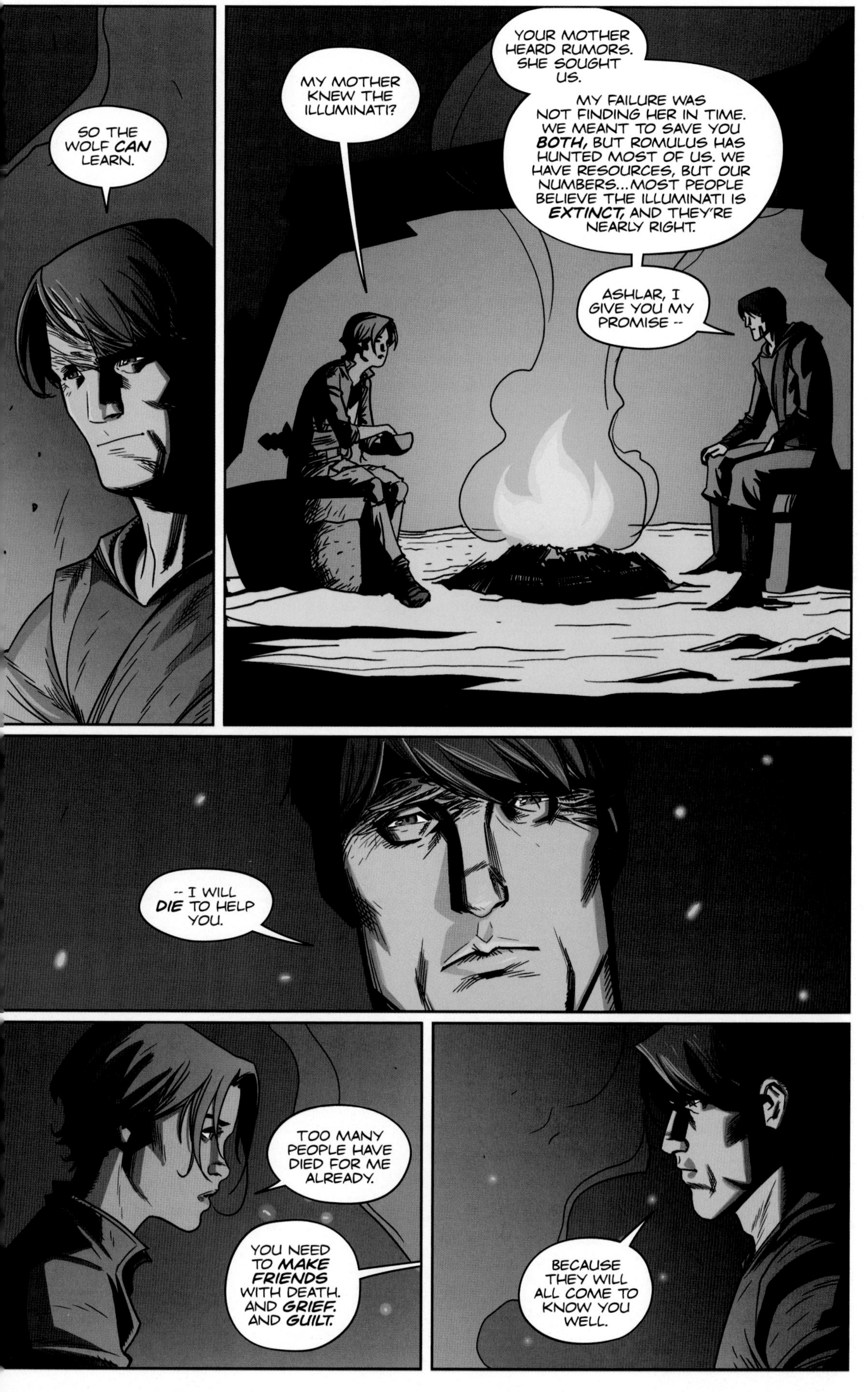
SO THE WOLF **CAN** LEARN.
MY MOTHER KNEW THE ILLUMINATI?
YOUR MOTHER HEARD RUMORS. SHE SOUGHT US.
MY FAILURE WAS NOT FINDING HER IN TIME. WE MEANT TO SAVE YOU **BOTH,** BUT ROMULUS HAS HUNTED MOST OF US. WE HAVE RESOURCES, BUT OUR NUMBERS...MOST PEOPLE BELIEVE THE ILLUMINATI IS **EXTINCT,** AND THEY'RE NEARLY RIGHT.
ASHLAR, I GIVE YOU MY PROMISE --
-- I WILL **DIE** TO HELP YOU.
TOO MANY PEOPLE HAVE DIED FOR ME ALREADY.
YOU NEED TO **MAKE FRIENDS** WITH DEATH. AND **GRIEF.** AND **GUILT.**
BECAUSE THEY WILL ALL COME TO KNOW YOU WELL.

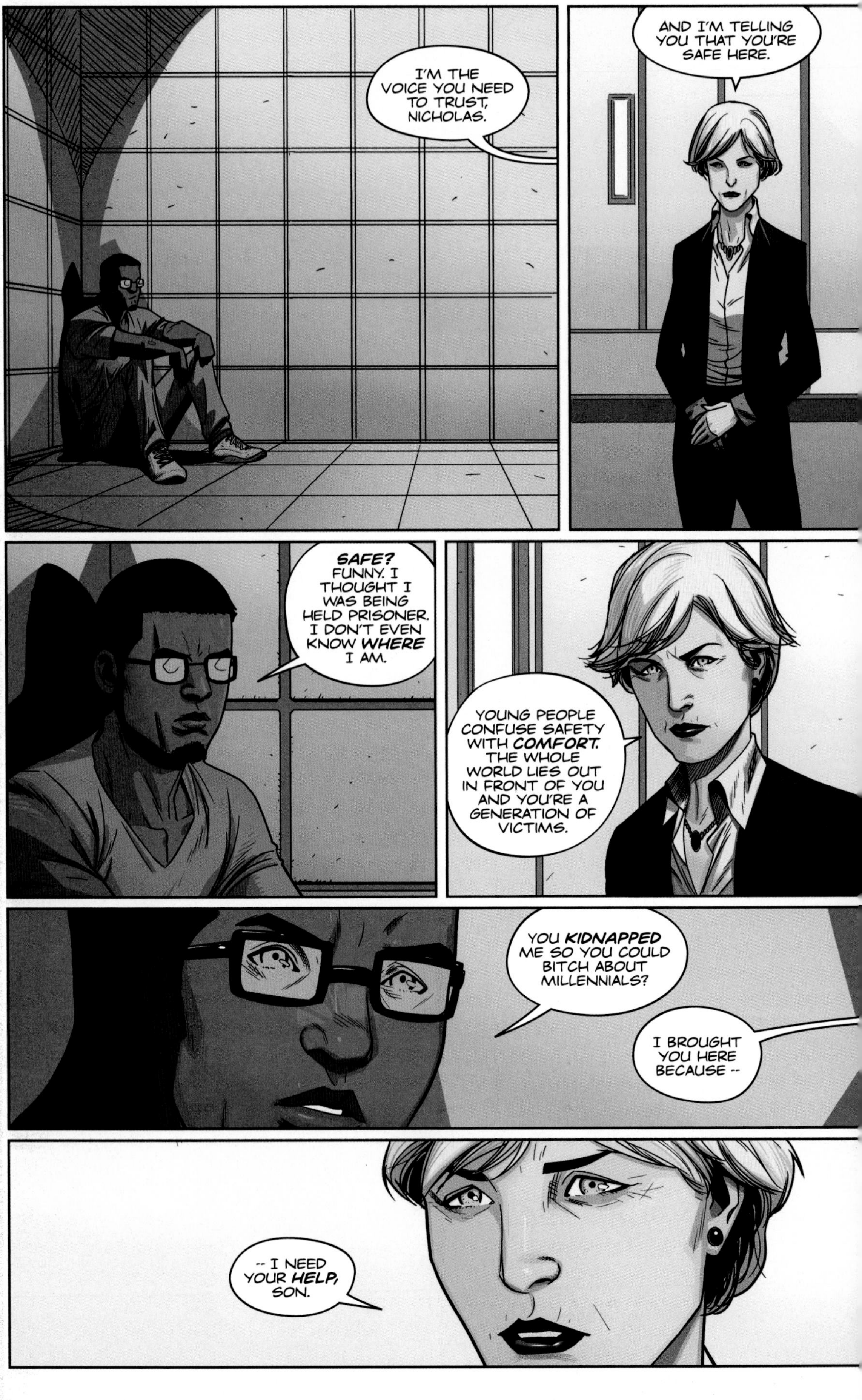
I'M THE VOICE YOU NEED TO TRUST, NICHOLAS.
AND I'M TELLING YOU THAT YOU'RE SAFE HERE.
SAFE? FUNNY. I THOUGHT I WAS BEING HELD PRISONER. I DON'T EVEN KNOW WHERE I AM.
YOUNG PEOPLE CONFUSE SAFETY WITH COMFORT. THE WHOLE WORLD LIES OUT IN FRONT OF YOU AND YOU'RE A GENERATION OF VICTIMS.
YOU KIDNAPPED ME SO YOU COULD BITCH ABOUT MILLENNIALS?
I BROUGHT YOU HERE BECAUSE --
-- I NEED YOUR HELP, SON.

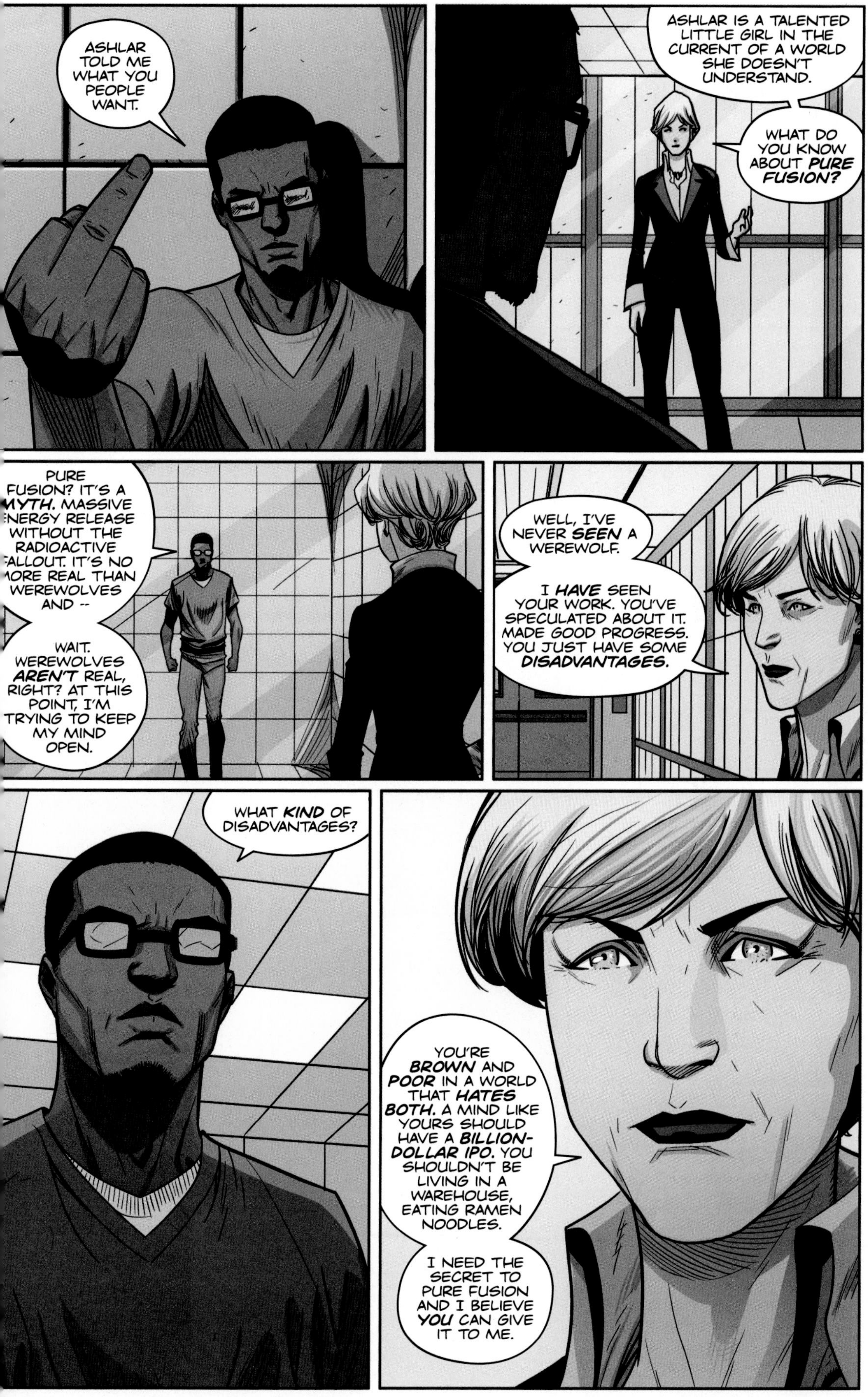
ASHLAR TOLD ME WHAT YOU PEOPLE WANT.
ASHLAR IS A TALENTED LITTLE GIRL IN THE CURRENT OF A WORLD SHE DOESN'T UNDERSTAND.
WHAT DO YOU KNOW ABOUT **PURE FUSION?**
PURE FUSION? IT'S A **MYTH.** MASSIVE ENERGY RELEASE WITHOUT THE RADIOACTIVE FALLOUT. IT'S NO MORE REAL THAN WEREWOLVES AND --
WAIT. WEREWOLVES **AREN'T** REAL, RIGHT? AT THIS POINT, I'M TRYING TO KEEP MY MIND OPEN.
WELL, I'VE NEVER **SEEN** A WEREWOLF.
I **HAVE** SEEN YOUR WORK. YOU'VE SPECULATED ABOUT IT. MADE GOOD PROGRESS. YOU JUST HAVE SOME **DISADVANTAGES.**
WHAT **KIND** OF DISADVANTAGES?
YOU'RE **BROWN** AND **POOR** IN A WORLD THAT **HATES BOTH.** A MIND LIKE YOURS SHOULD HAVE A **BILLION-DOLLAR IPO.** YOU SHOULDN'T BE LIVING IN A WAREHOUSE, EATING RAMEN NOODLES.
I NEED THE SECRET TO PURE FUSION AND I BELIEVE **YOU** CAN GIVE IT TO ME.

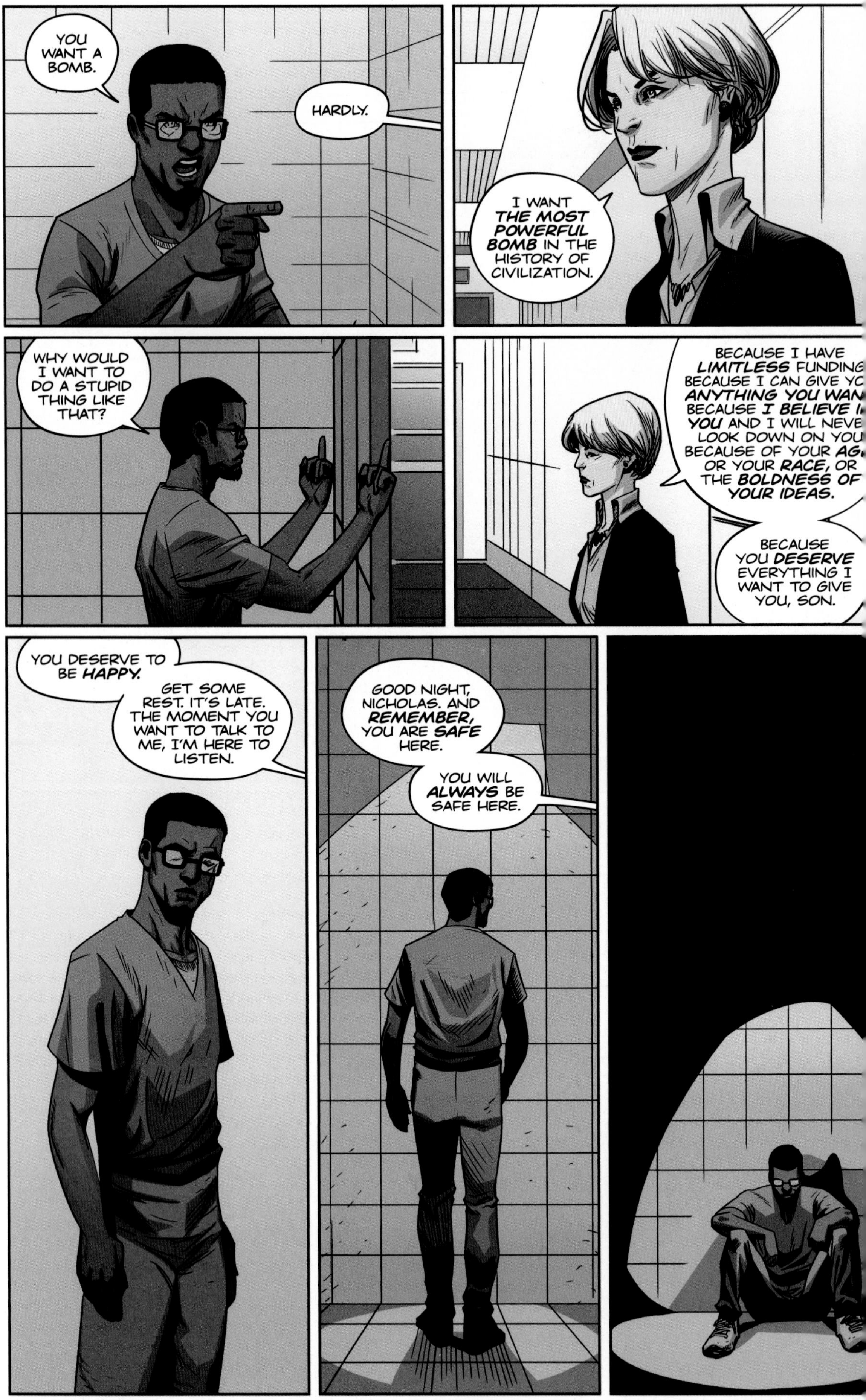

YOU WANT A BOMB.
HARDLY.
I WANT **THE MOST POWERFUL BOMB** IN THE HISTORY OF CIVILIZATION.
WHY WOULD I WANT TO DO A STUPID THING LIKE THAT?
BECAUSE I HAVE **LIMITLESS** FUNDING
BECAUSE I CAN GIVE Y
ANYTHING YOU WAN
BECAUSE **I BELIEVE I**
YOU AND I WILL NEVE
LOOK DOWN ON YOU
BECAUSE OF YOUR **AG**
OR YOUR **RACE,** OR
THE **BOLDNESS OF YOUR IDEAS.**
BECAUSE YOU **DESERVE** EVERYTHING I WANT TO GIVE YOU, SON.
YOU DESERVE TO BE **HAPPY.**
GET SOME REST. IT'S LATE. THE MOMENT YOU WANT TO TALK TO ME, I'M HERE TO LISTEN.
GOOD NIGHT, NICHOLAS. AND **REMEMBER,** YOU ARE **SAFE** HERE.
YOU WILL **ALWAYS** BE SAFE HERE.

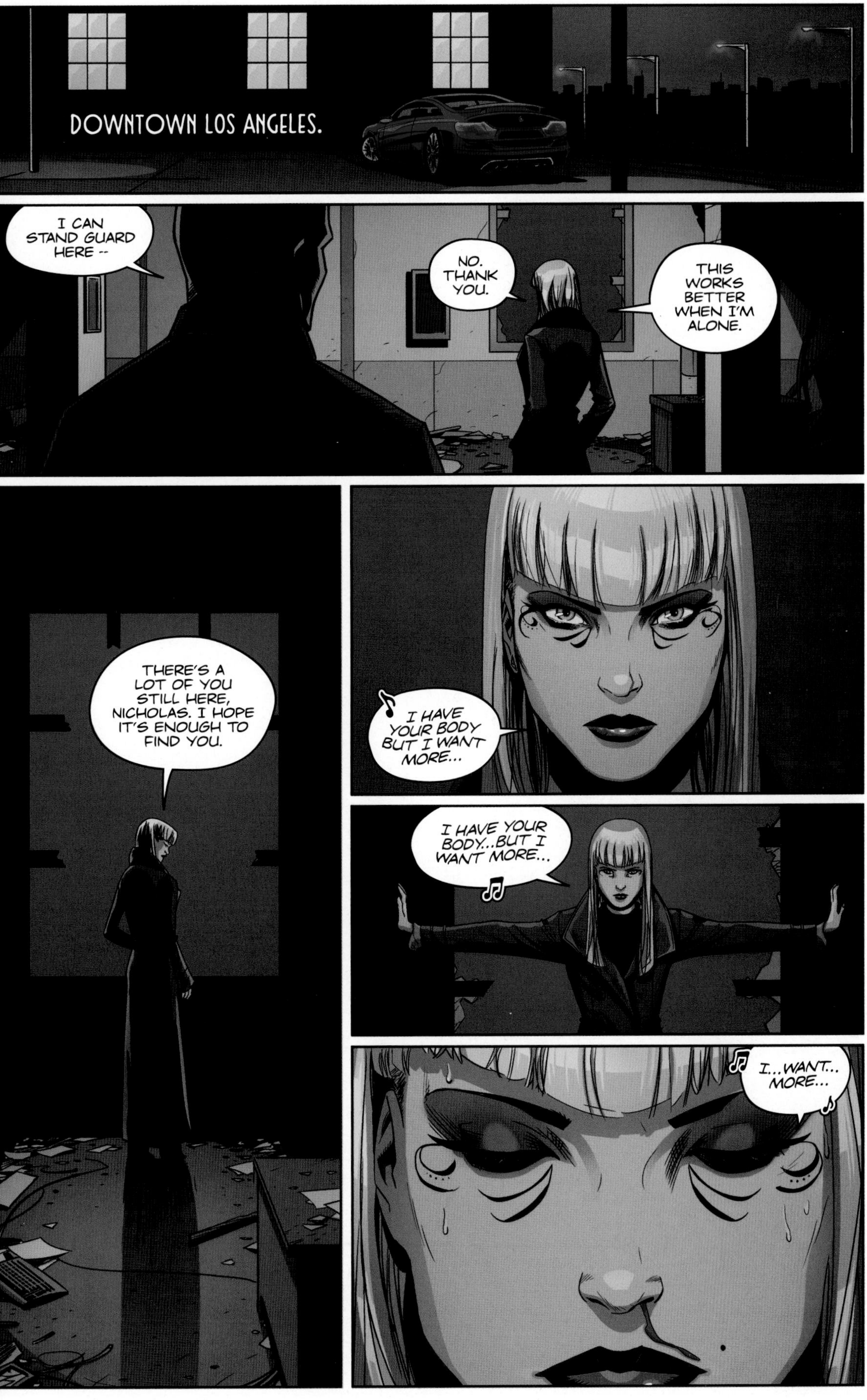
DOWNTOWN LOS ANGELES.
I CAN STAND GUARD HERE --
NO. THANK YOU.
THIS WORKS BETTER WHEN I'M ALONE.
THERE'S A LOT OF YOU STILL HERE, NICHOLAS. I HOPE IT'S ENOUGH TO FIND YOU.
I HAVE YOUR BODY BUT I WANT MORE...
I HAVE YOUR BODY...BUT I WANT MORE...
I...WANT... MORE...

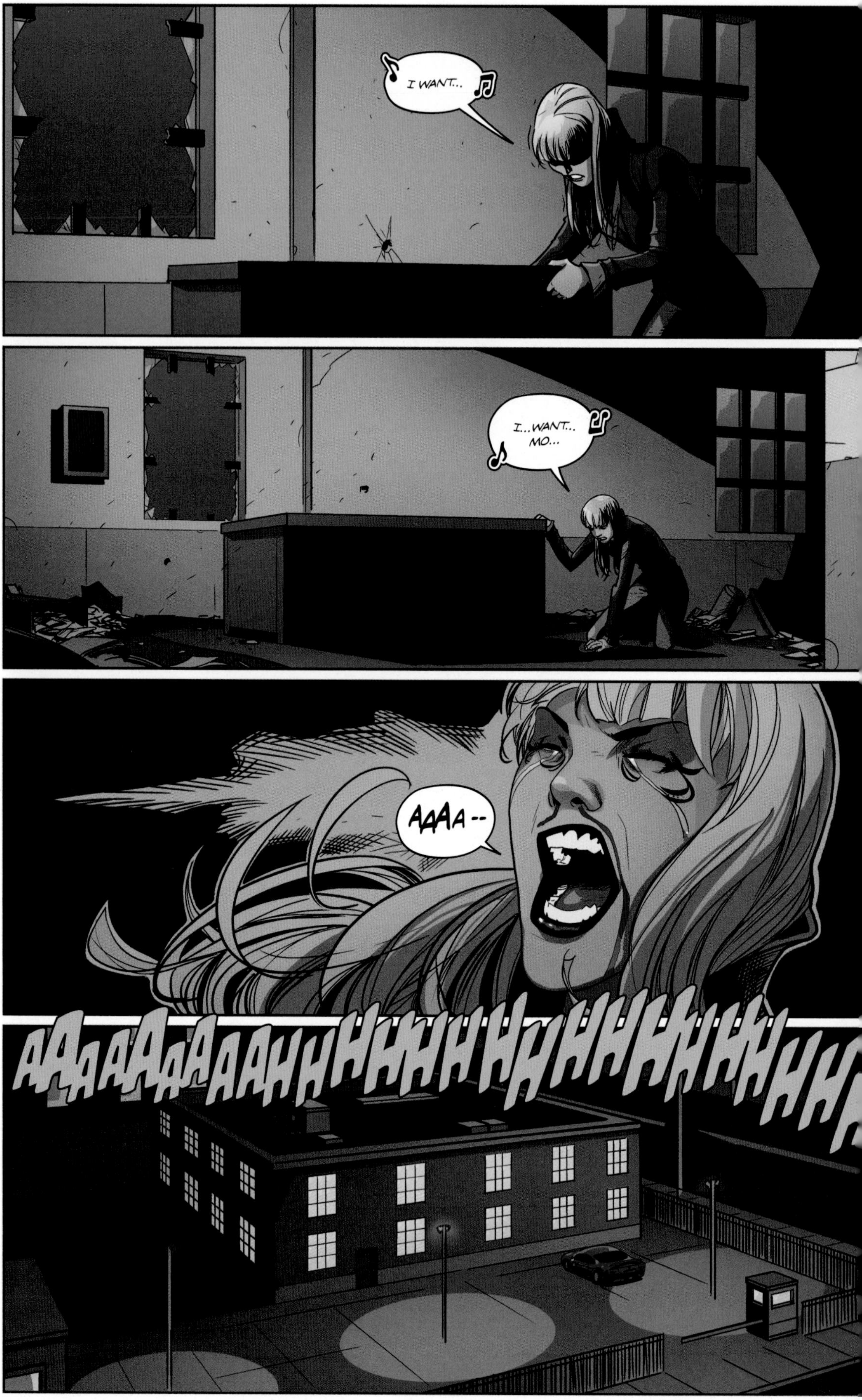
I WANT...
I...WANT...
MO...
AAAA--
AAAAAAAAAAHHHHHHHHHHHHHHHHHHHHHH

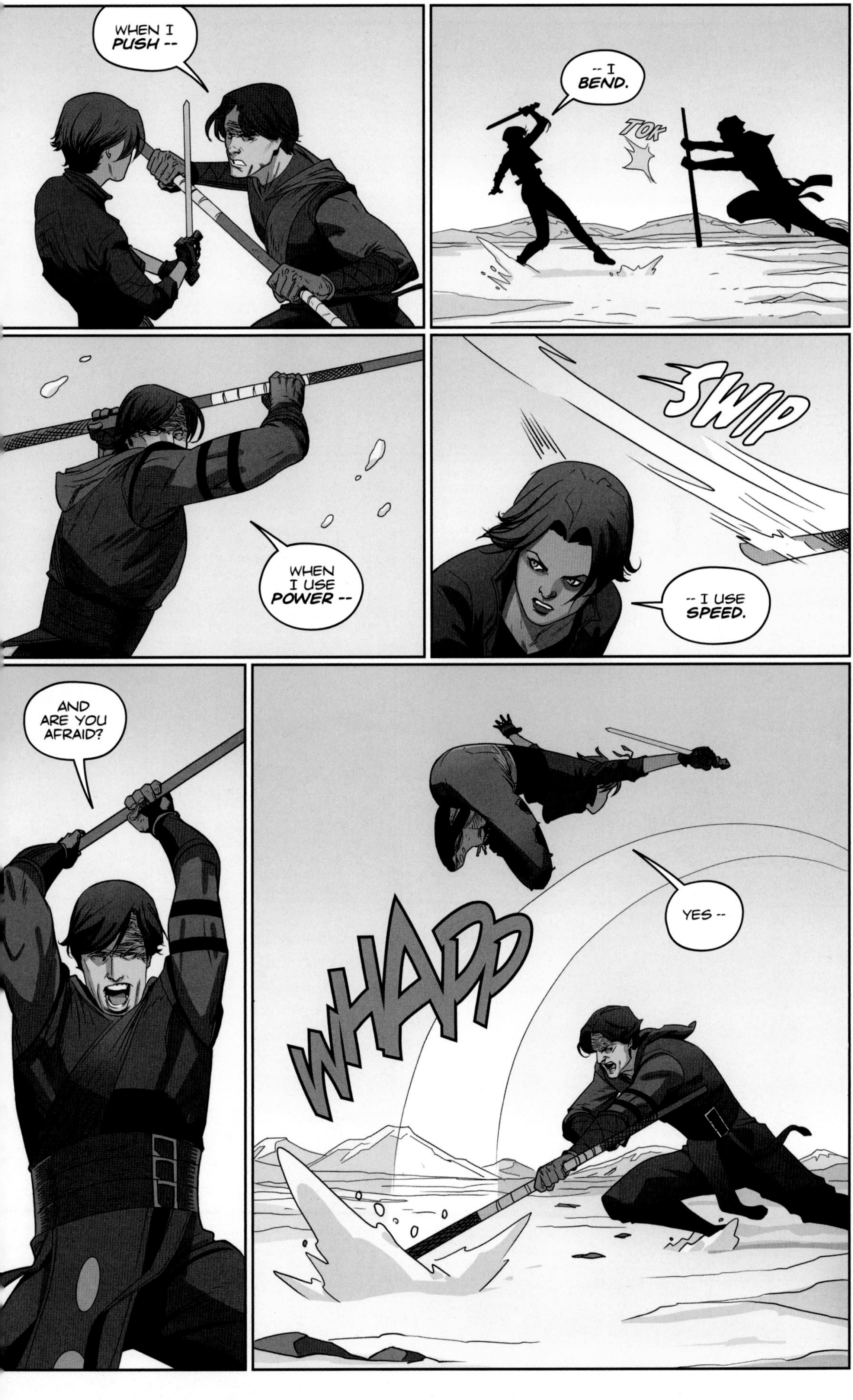
WHEN I PUSH --
-- I BEND.
TOK
WHEN I USE POWER --
SWIP
-- I USE SPEED.
AND ARE YOU AFRAID?
YES --
WHAPP

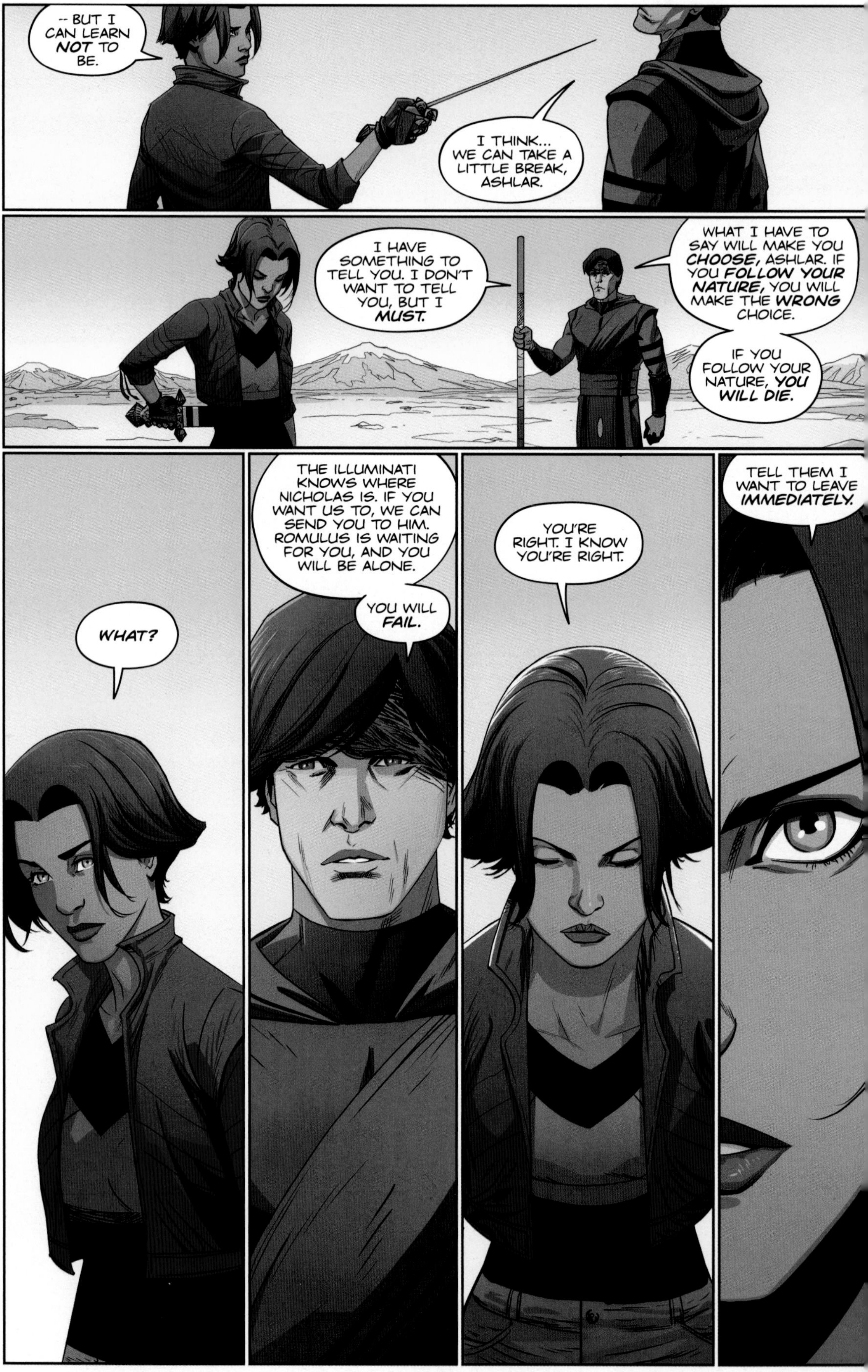
-- BUT I CAN LEARN NOT TO BE.
I THINK... WE CAN TAKE A LITTLE BREAK, ASHLAR.
I HAVE SOMETHING TO TELL YOU. I DON'T WANT TO TELL YOU, BUT I MUST.
WHAT I HAVE TO SAY WILL MAKE YOU CHOOSE, ASHLAR. IF YOU FOLLOW YOUR NATURE, YOU WILL MAKE THE WRONG CHOICE.
IF YOU FOLLOW YOUR NATURE, YOU WILL DIE.
WHAT?
THE ILLUMINATI KNOWS WHERE NICHOLAS IS. IF YOU WANT US TO, WE CAN SEND YOU TO HIM. ROMULUS IS WAITING FOR YOU, AND YOU WILL BE ALONE.
YOU WILL FAIL.
YOU'RE RIGHT. I KNOW YOU'RE RIGHT.
TELL THEM I WANT TO LEAVE IMMEDIATELY.

CHAPTER FOUR:
The Rage of Achilles

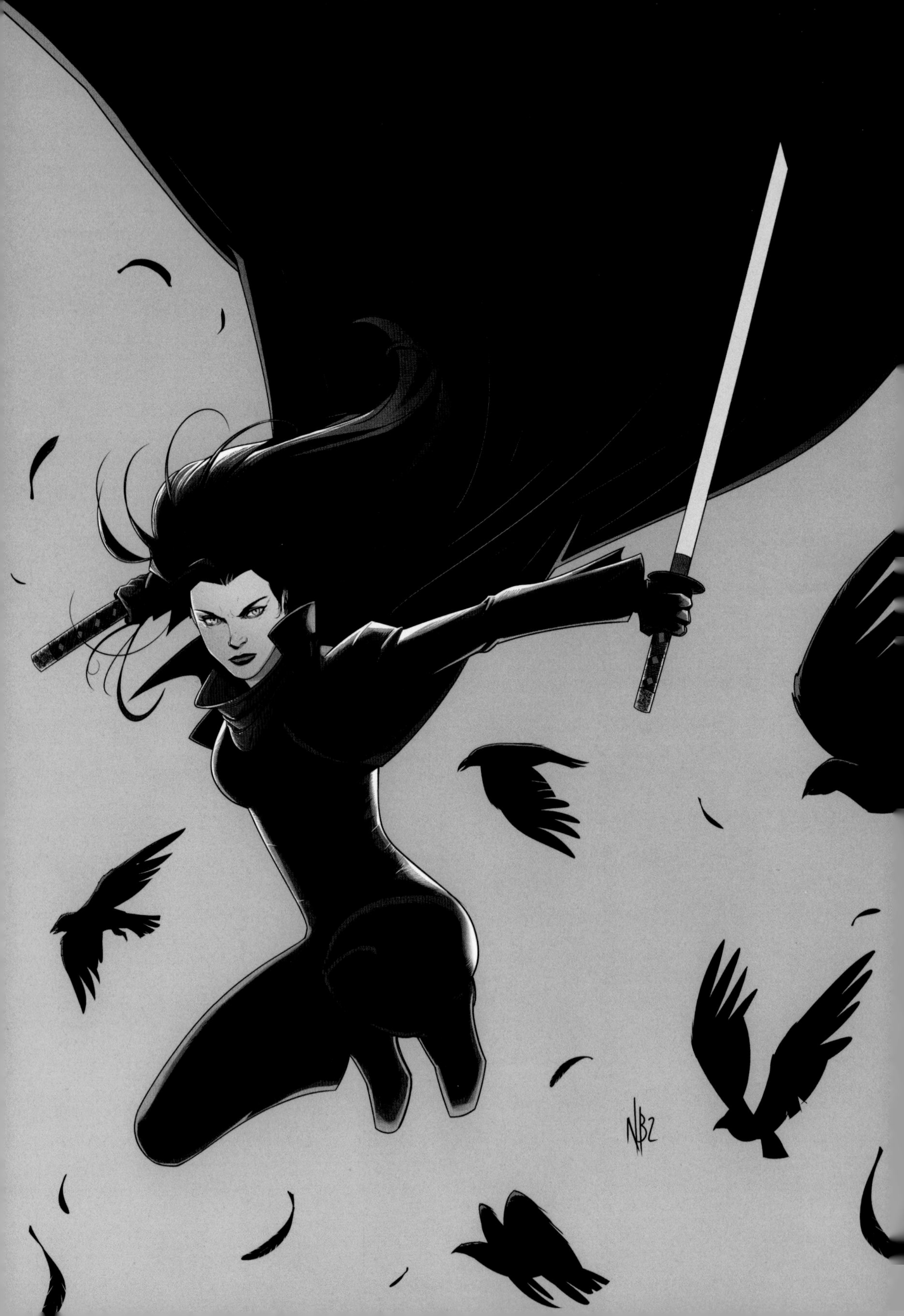

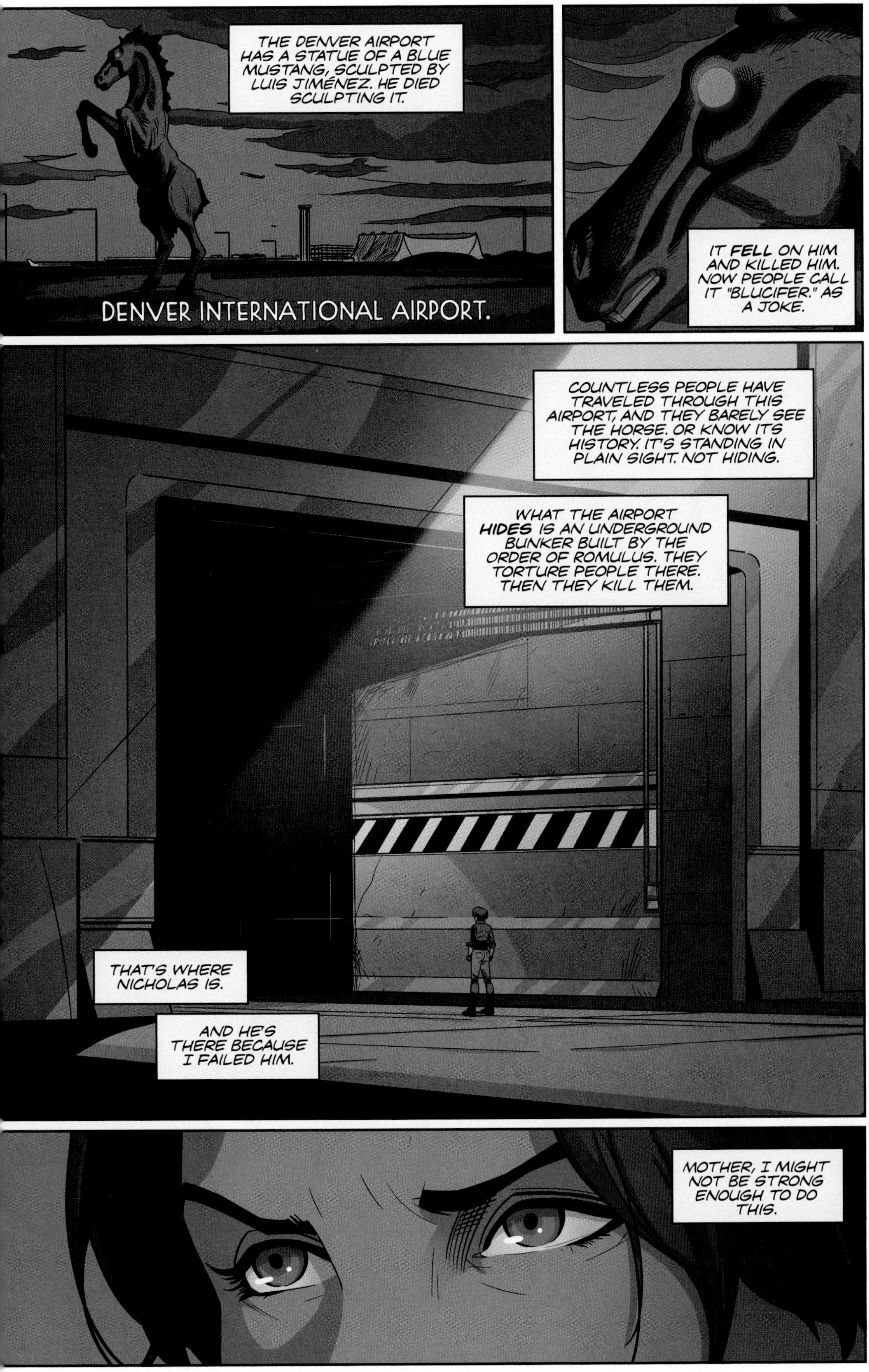
THE DENVER AIRPORT HAS A STATUE OF A BLUE MUSTANG, SCULPTED BY LUIS JIMÉNEZ. HE DIED SCULPTING IT.
DENVER INTERNATIONAL AIRPORT.
IT FELL ON HIM AND KILLED HIM. NOW PEOPLE CALL IT "BLUCIFER." AS A JOKE.
COUNTLESS PEOPLE HAVE TRAVELED THROUGH THIS AIRPORT, AND THEY BARELY SEE THE HORSE. OR KNOW ITS HISTORY. IT'S STANDING IN PLAIN SIGHT. NOT HIDING.
WHAT THE AIRPORT HIDES IS AN UNDERGROUND BUNKER BUILT BY THE ORDER OF ROMULUS. THEY TORTURE PEOPLE THERE. THEN THEY KILL THEM.
THAT'S WHERE NICHOLAS IS.
AND HE'S THERE BECAUSE I FAILED HIM.
MOTHER, I MIGHT NOT BE STRONG ENOUGH TO DO THIS.

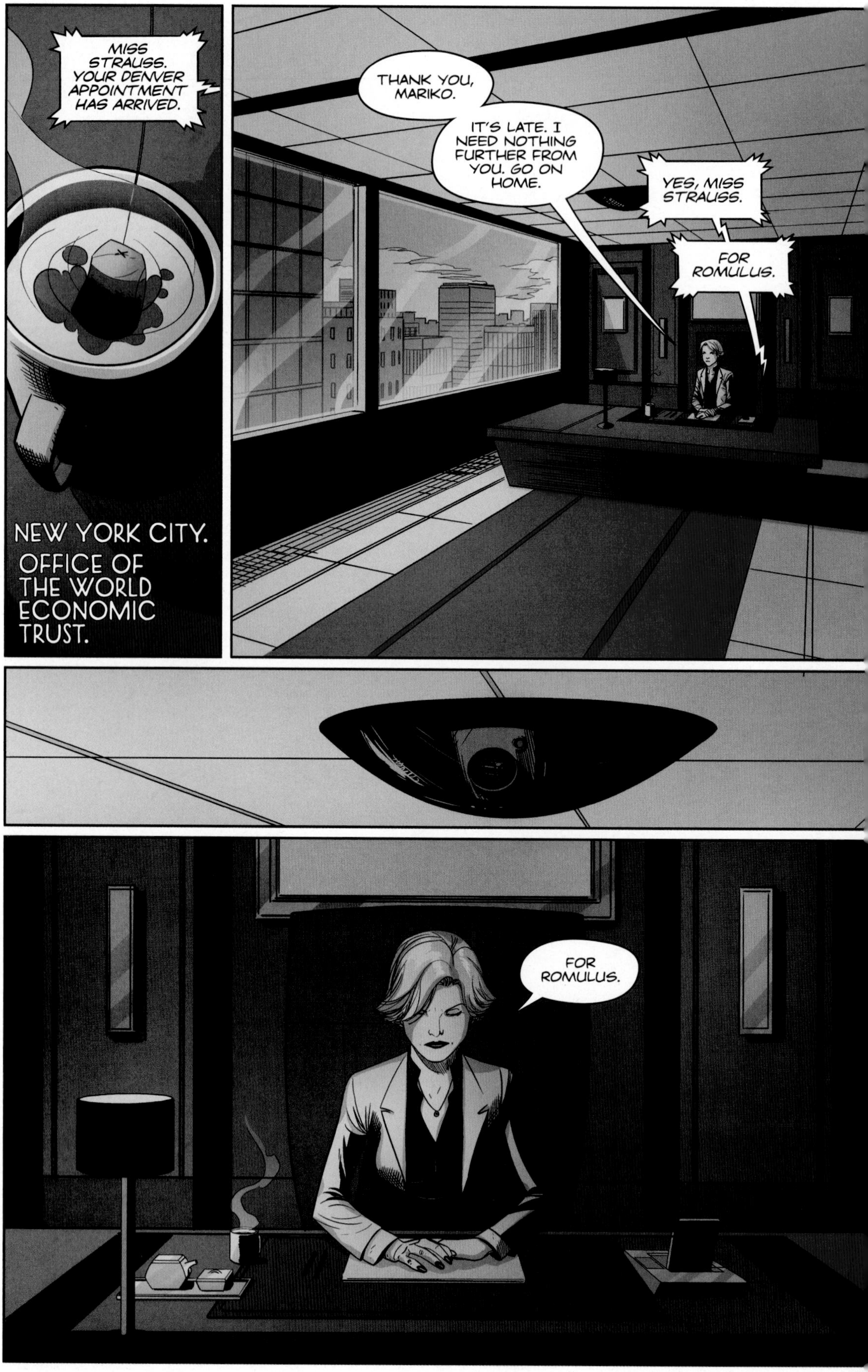
MISS STRAUSS. YOUR DENVER APPOINTMENT HAS ARRIVED.
NEW YORK CITY.
OFFICE OF THE WORLD ECONOMIC TRUST.
THANK YOU, MARIKO.
IT'S LATE. I NEED NOTHING FURTHER FROM YOU. GO ON HOME.
YES, MISS STRAUSS.
FOR ROMULUS.
FOR ROMULUS.

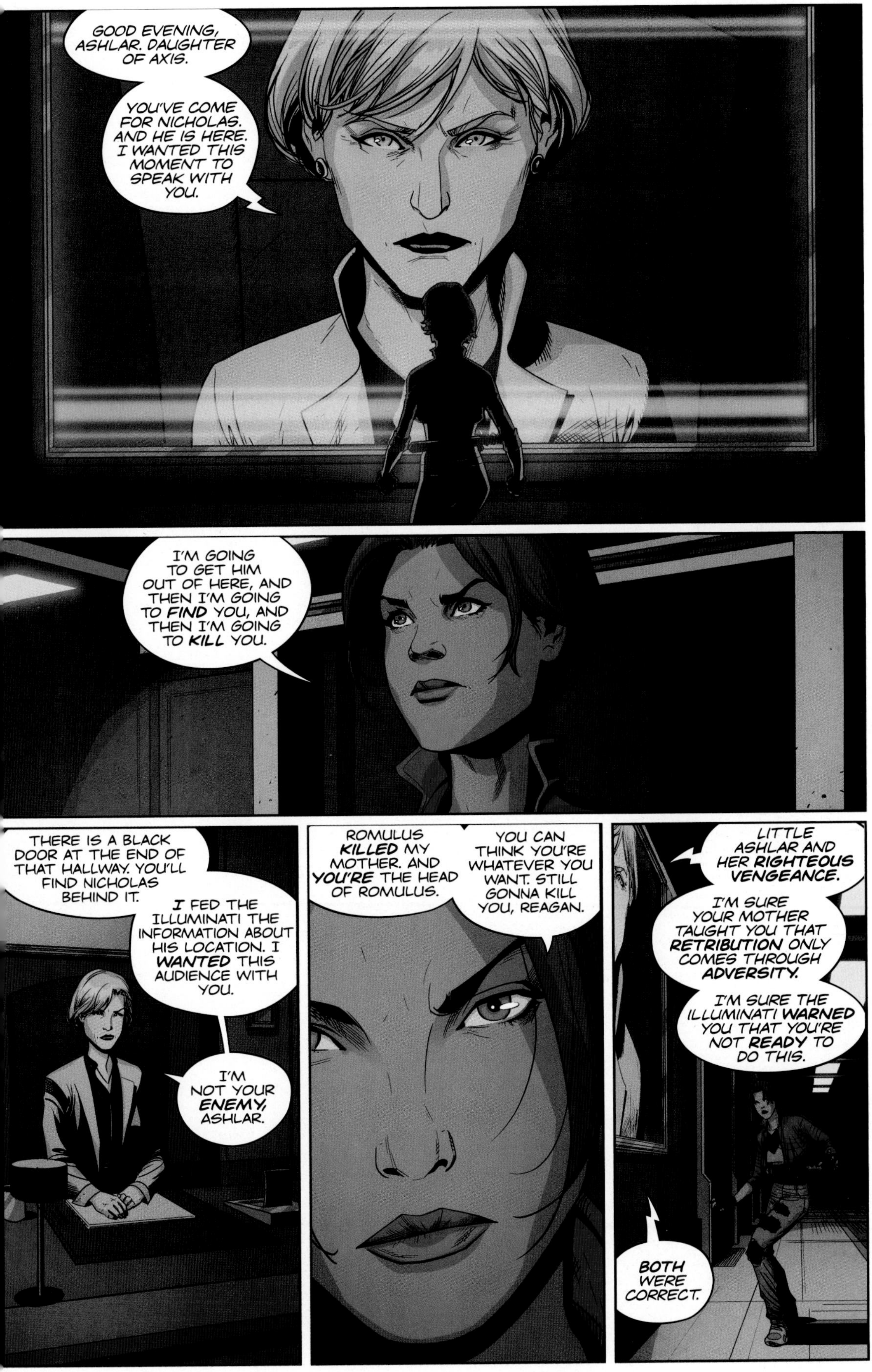
GOOD EVENING, ASHLAR. DAUGHTER OF AXIS.
YOU'VE COME FOR NICHOLAS. AND HE IS HERE. I WANTED THIS MOMENT TO SPEAK WITH YOU.
I'M GOING TO GET HIM OUT OF HERE, AND THEN I'M GOING TO FIND YOU, AND THEN I'M GOING TO KILL YOU.
THERE IS A BLACK DOOR AT THE END OF THAT HALLWAY. YOU'LL FIND NICHOLAS BEHIND IT.
I FED THE ILLUMINATI THE INFORMATION ABOUT HIS LOCATION. I WANTED THIS AUDIENCE WITH YOU.
I'M NOT YOUR ENEMY, ASHLAR.
ROMULUS KILLED MY MOTHER. AND YOU'RE THE HEAD OF ROMULUS.
YOU CAN THINK YOU'RE WHATEVER YOU WANT. STILL GONNA KILL YOU, REAGAN.
LITTLE ASHLAR AND HER RIGHTEOUS VENGEANCE.
I'M SURE YOUR MOTHER TAUGHT YOU THAT RETRIBUTION ONLY COMES THROUGH ADVERSITY.
I'M SURE THE ILLUMINATI WARNED YOU THAT YOU'RE NOT READY TO DO THIS.
BOTH WERE CORRECT.

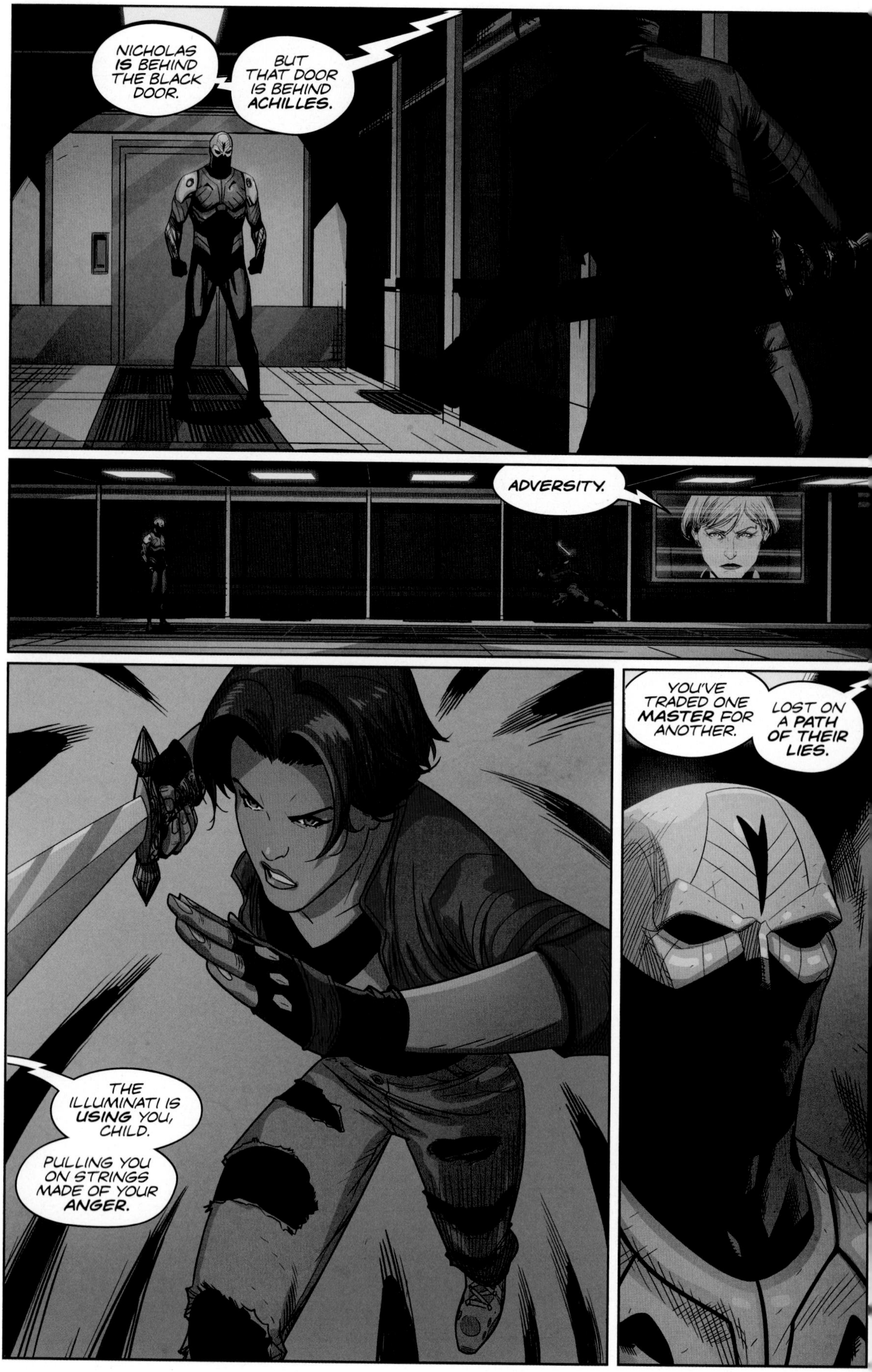
NICHOLAS IS BEHIND THE BLACK DOOR.
BUT THAT DOOR IS BEHIND ACHILLES.
ADVERSITY.
THE ILLUMINATI IS USING YOU, CHILD.
PULLING YOU ON STRINGS MADE OF YOUR ANGER.
YOU'VE TRADED ONE MASTER FOR ANOTHER.
LOST ON A PATH OF THEIR LIES.

NGH!

AAAAH!

CHK

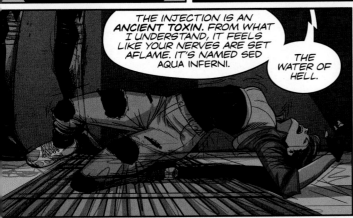

THE INJECTION IS AN **ANCIENT TOXIN.** FROM WHAT I UNDERSTAND, IT FEELS LIKE YOUR NERVES ARE SET AFLAME. IT'S NAMED SED AQUA INFERNI.

THE WATER OF HELL.

I DON'T WANT TO KILL YOU.

I BELIEVE IN YOU, ASHLAR. I **KNOW** WHAT YOU CAN BE FOR US.

I CAN **STILL SAVE** YOU FROM YOURSELF.

ACHILLES. BE MY **WILL.**

BREAK THE PUPPY.

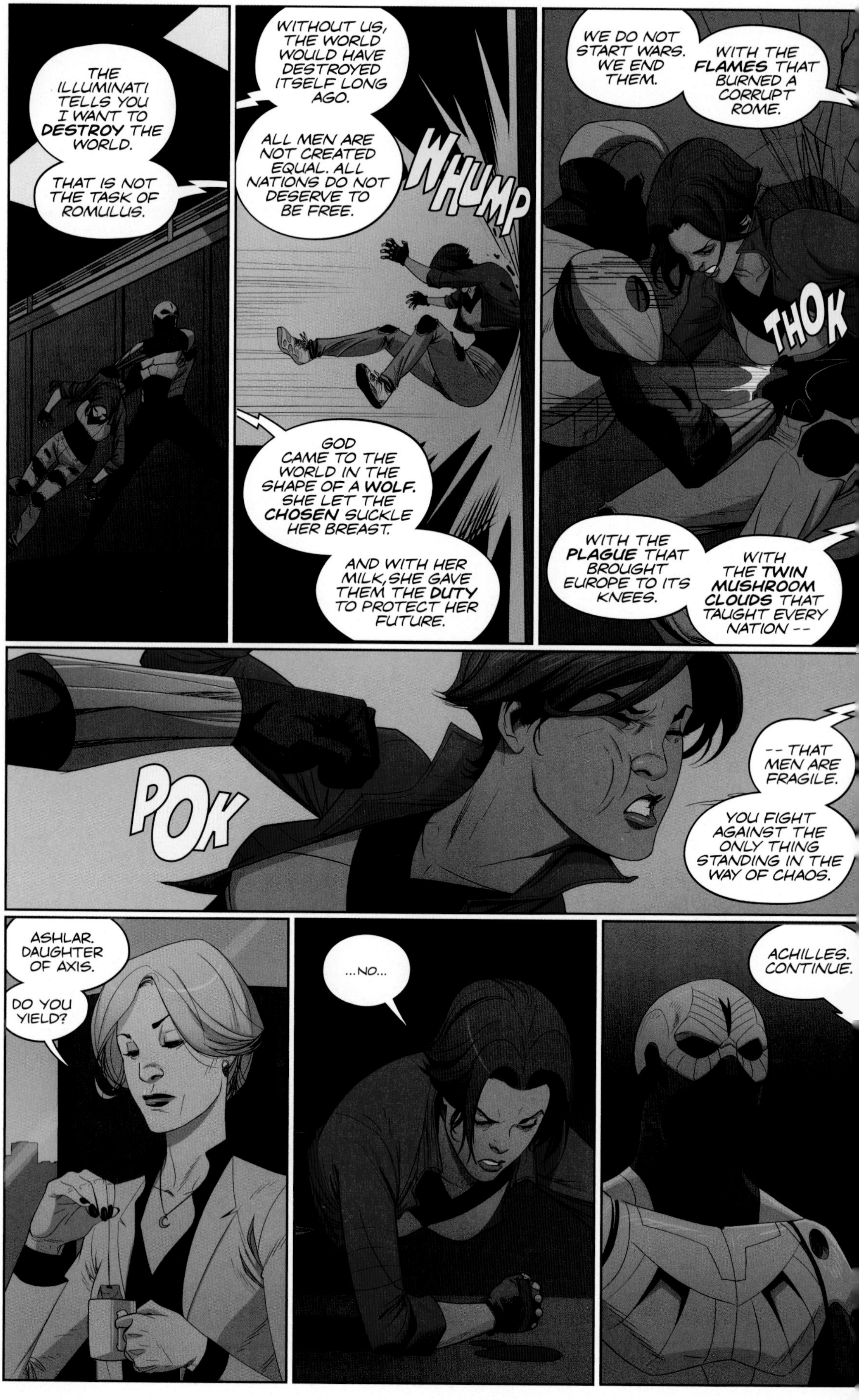
THE ILLUMINATI TELLS YOU I WANT TO DESTROY THE WORLD.
THAT IS NOT THE TASK OF ROMULUS.
WITHOUT US, THE WORLD WOULD HAVE DESTROYED ITSELF LONG AGO.
ALL MEN ARE NOT CREATED EQUAL. ALL NATIONS DO NOT DESERVE TO BE FREE.
WHUMP
GOD CAME TO THE WORLD IN THE SHAPE OF A WOLF. SHE LET THE CHOSEN SUCKLE HER BREAST.
AND WITH HER MILK, SHE GAVE THEM THE DUTY TO PROTECT HER FUTURE.
WE DO NOT START WARS. WE END THEM.
WITH THE FLAMES THAT BURNED A CORRUPT ROME.
THOK
WITH THE PLAGUE THAT BROUGHT EUROPE TO ITS KNEES.
WITH THE TWIN MUSHROOM CLOUDS THAT TAUGHT EVERY NATION --
POK
-- THAT MEN ARE FRAGILE.
YOU FIGHT AGAINST THE ONLY THING STANDING IN THE WAY OF CHAOS.
ASHLAR. DAUGHTER OF AXIS.
DO YOU YIELD?
...NO...
ACHILLES. CONTINUE.

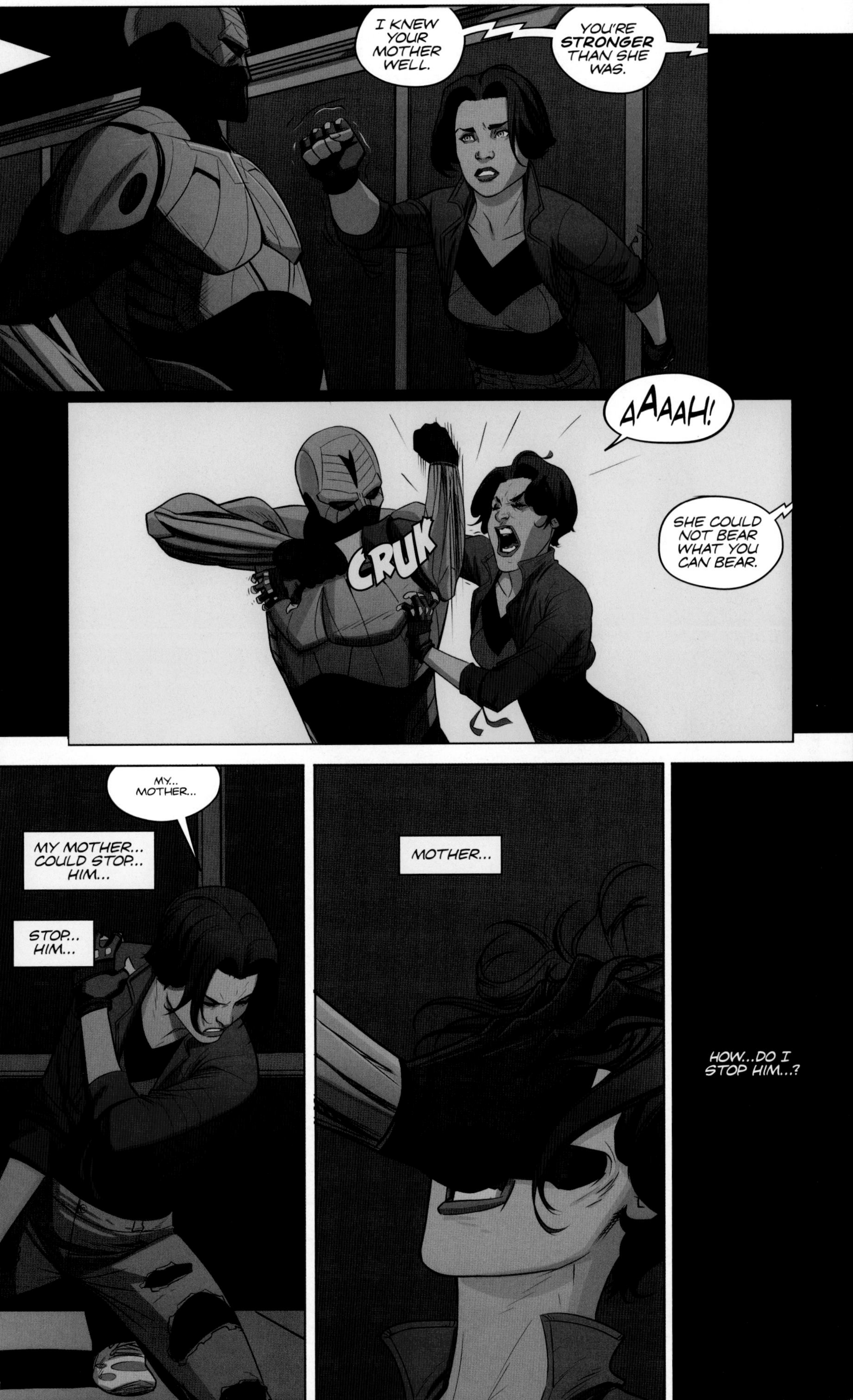
I KNEW YOUR MOTHER WELL.
YOU'RE STRONGER THAN SHE WAS.
AAAAH!
CRUK
SHE COULD NOT BEAR WHAT YOU CAN BEAR.
MY... MOTHER...
MY MOTHER... COULD STOP... HIM...
STOP... HIM...
MOTHER...
HOW...DO I STOP HIM...?

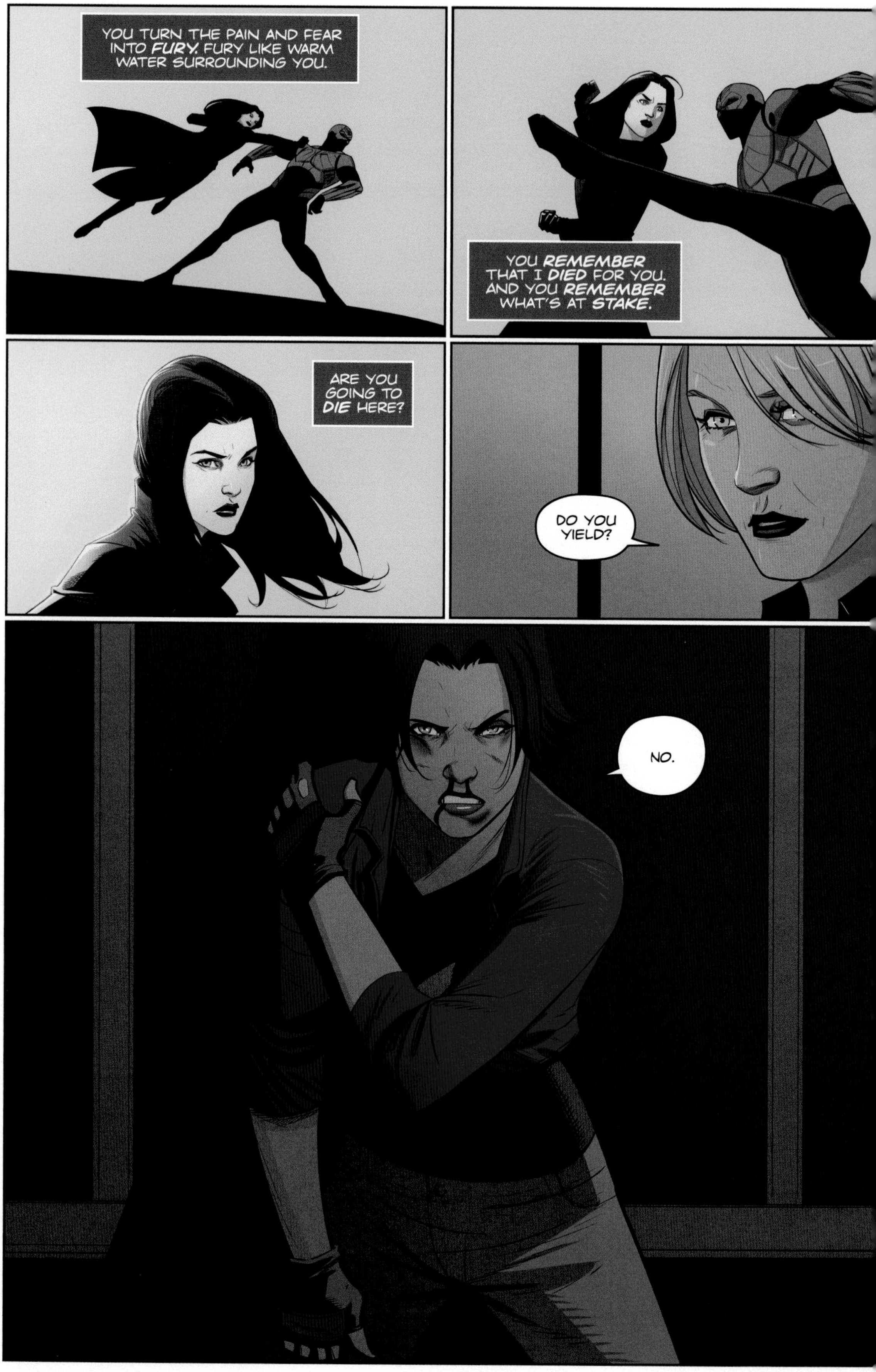
YOU TURN THE PAIN AND FEAR INTO FURY. FURY LIKE WARM WATER SURROUNDING YOU.
YOU REMEMBER THAT I DIED FOR YOU. AND YOU REMEMBER WHAT'S AT STAKE.
ARE YOU GOING TO DIE HERE?
DO YOU YIELD?
NO.

FURY PUTS MY SHOULDER BACK INTO PLACE.

POP

FLEX

HIS ARMOR IS WEAKER AT THE JOINTS.

SO THE JOINTS ARE ALL THAT MATTERS.

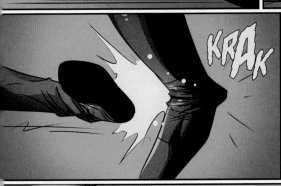

KRAK

I REMEMBER WHAT'S AT STAKE.

EVERYTHING.

SHUK

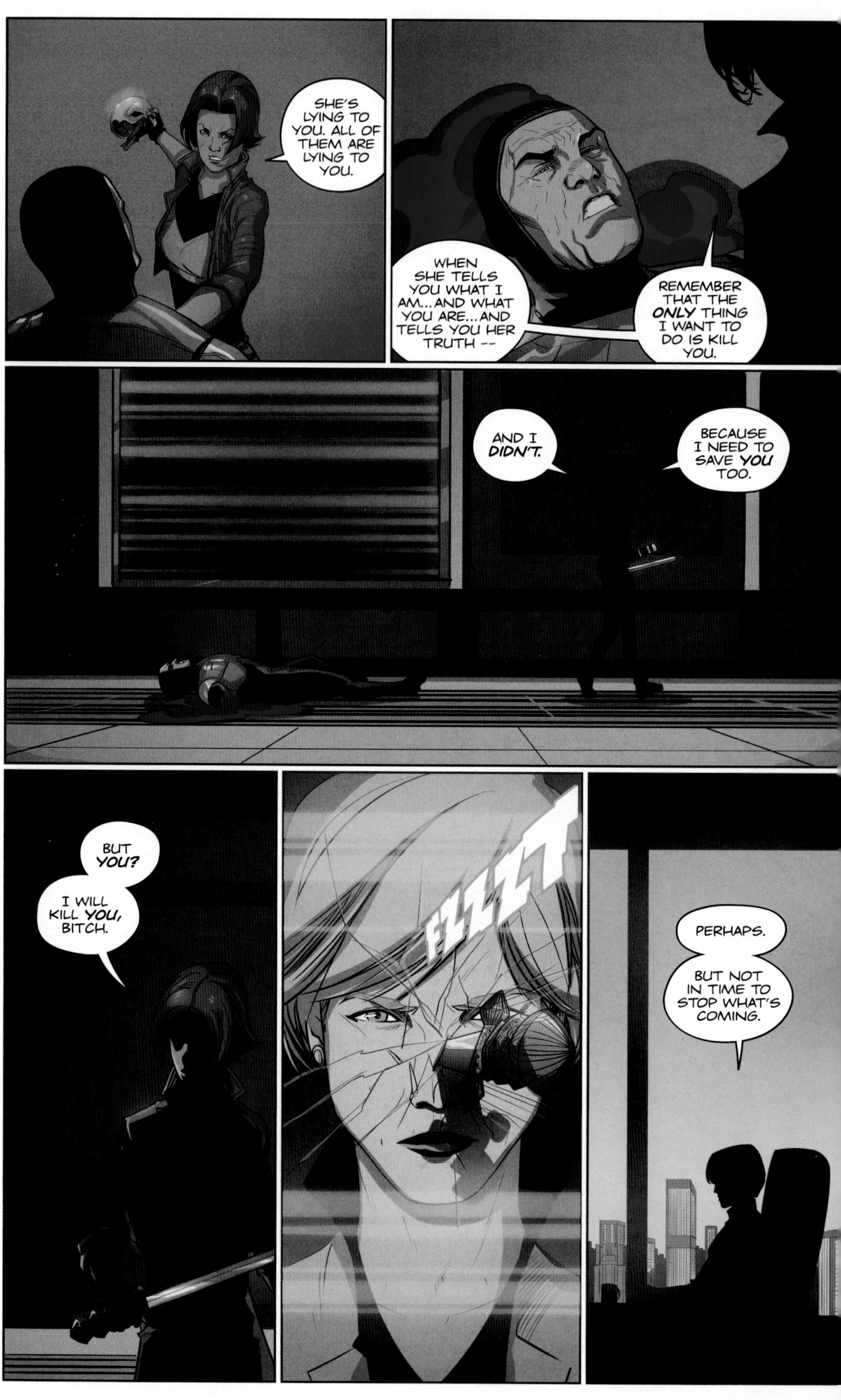
SHE'S LYING TO YOU. ALL OF THEM ARE LYING TO YOU.
WHEN SHE TELLS YOU WHAT I AM...AND WHAT YOU ARE...AND TELLS YOU HER TRUTH --
REMEMBER THAT THE ONLY THING I WANT TO DO IS KILL YOU.
AND I DIDN'T.
BECAUSE I NEED TO SAVE YOU TOO.
BUT YOU?
I WILL KILL YOU, BITCH.
FZZZT
PERHAPS.
BUT NOT IN TIME TO STOP WHAT'S COMING.

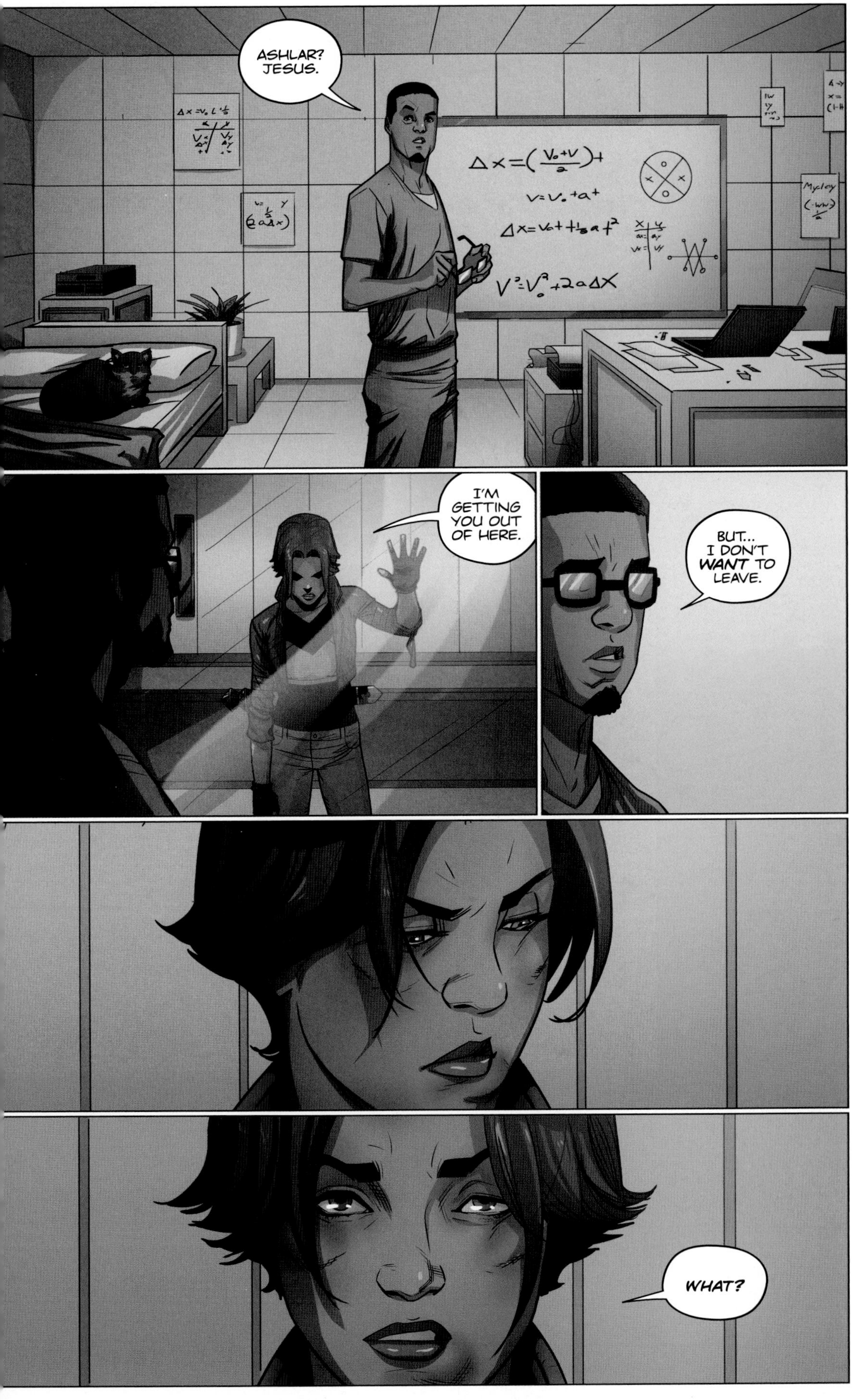
ASHLAR? JESUS.
I'M GETTING YOU OUT OF HERE.
BUT... I DON'T WANT TO LEAVE.
WHAT?

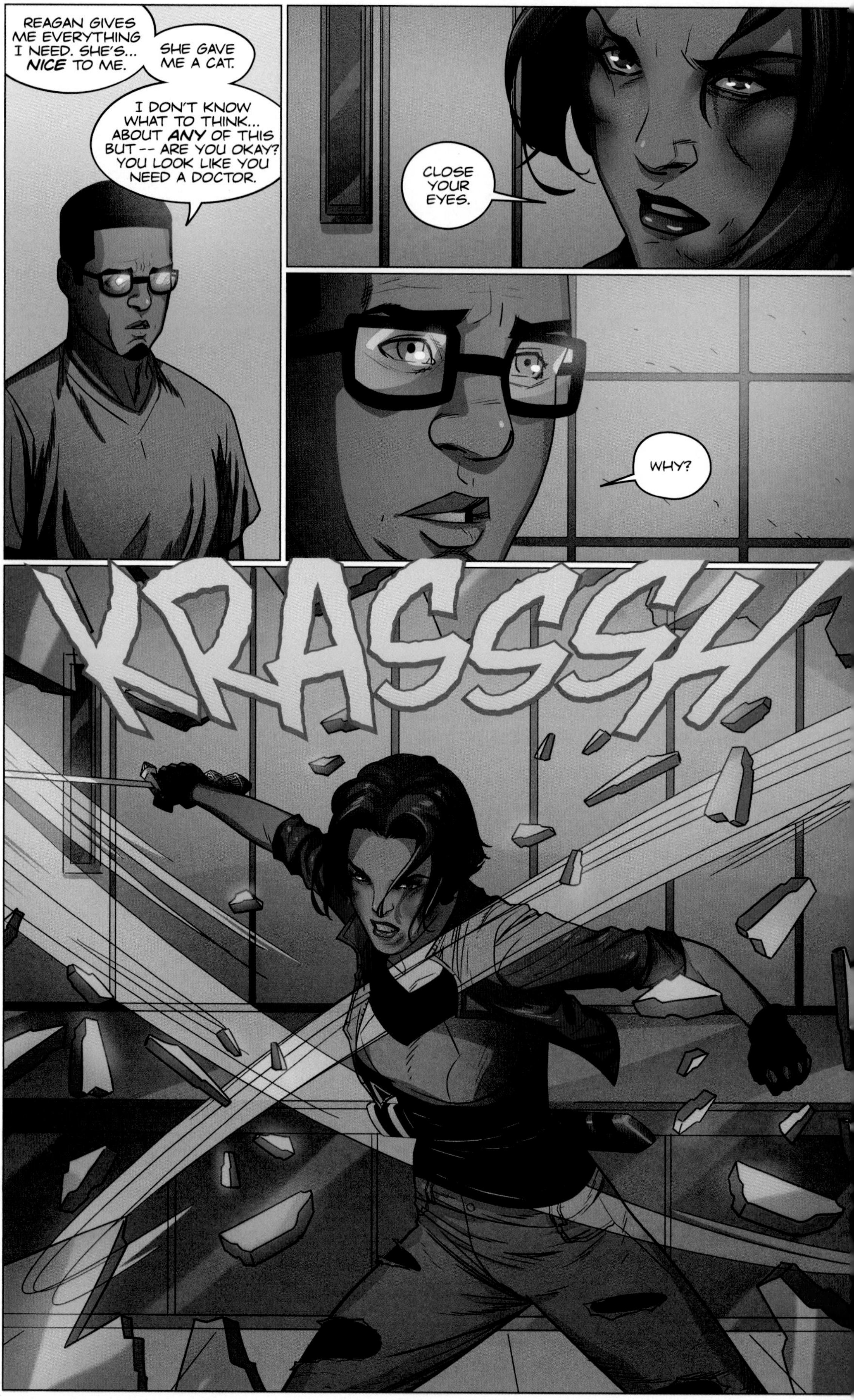
REAGAN GIVES ME EVERYTHING I NEED. SHE'S... NICE TO ME.
SHE GAVE ME A CAT.
I DON'T KNOW WHAT TO THINK... ABOUT ANY OF THIS BUT -- ARE YOU OKAY? YOU LOOK LIKE YOU NEED A DOCTOR.
CLOSE YOUR EYES.
WHY?
KRASSSH!

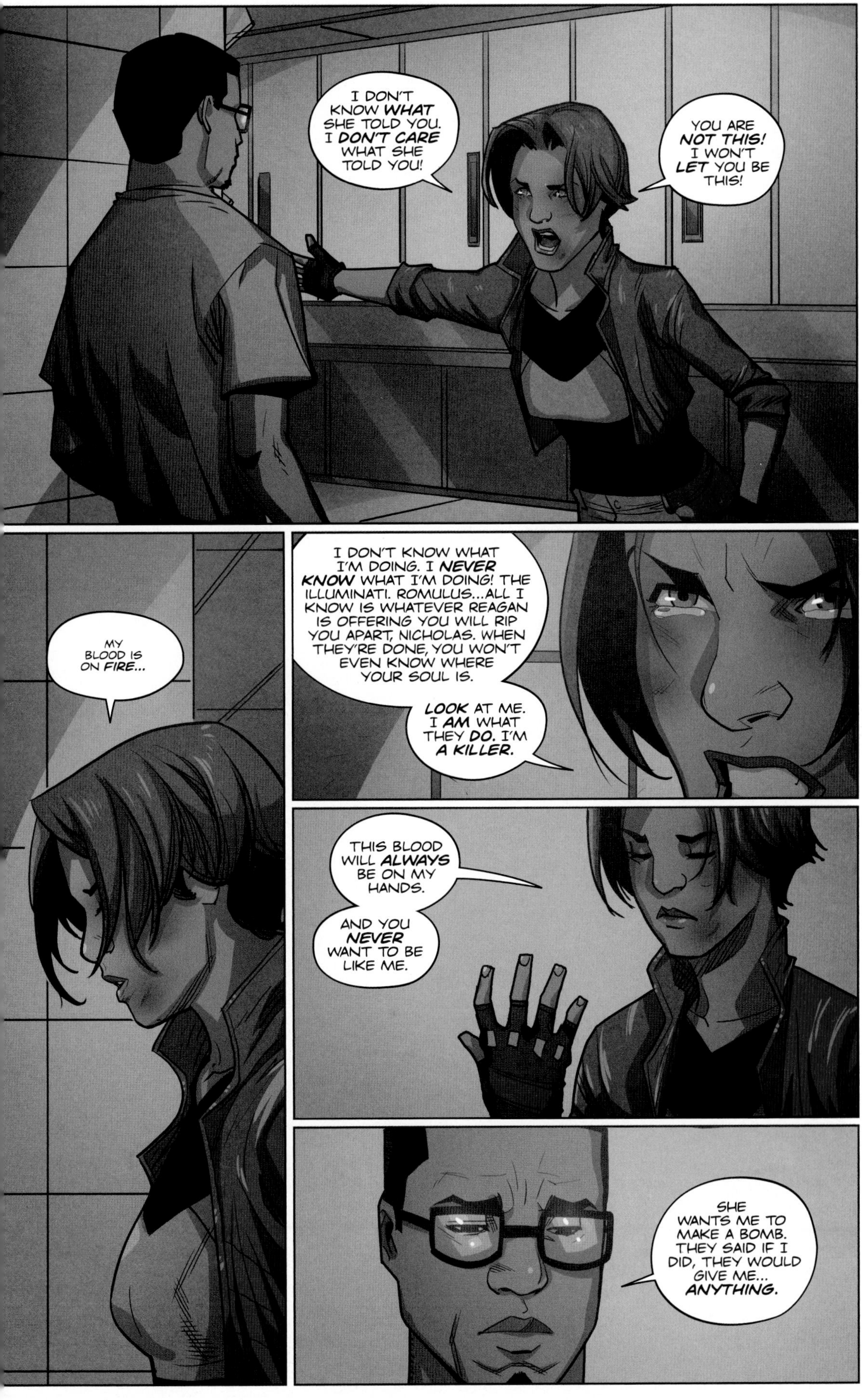
I DON'T KNOW WHAT SHE TOLD YOU. I DON'T CARE WHAT SHE TOLD YOU!
YOU ARE NOT THIS! I WON'T LET YOU BE THIS!
I DON'T KNOW WHAT I'M DOING. I NEVER KNOW WHAT I'M DOING! THE ILLUMINATI. ROMULUS...ALL I KNOW IS WHATEVER REAGAN IS OFFERING YOU WILL RIP YOU APART, NICHOLAS. WHEN THEY'RE DONE, YOU WON'T EVEN KNOW WHERE YOUR SOUL IS.
LOOK AT ME. I AM WHAT THEY DO. I'M A KILLER.
MY BLOOD IS ON FIRE...
THIS BLOOD WILL ALWAYS BE ON MY HANDS.
AND YOU NEVER WANT TO BE LIKE ME.
SHE WANTS ME TO MAKE A BOMB. THEY SAID IF I DID, THEY WOULD GIVE ME... ANYTHING.

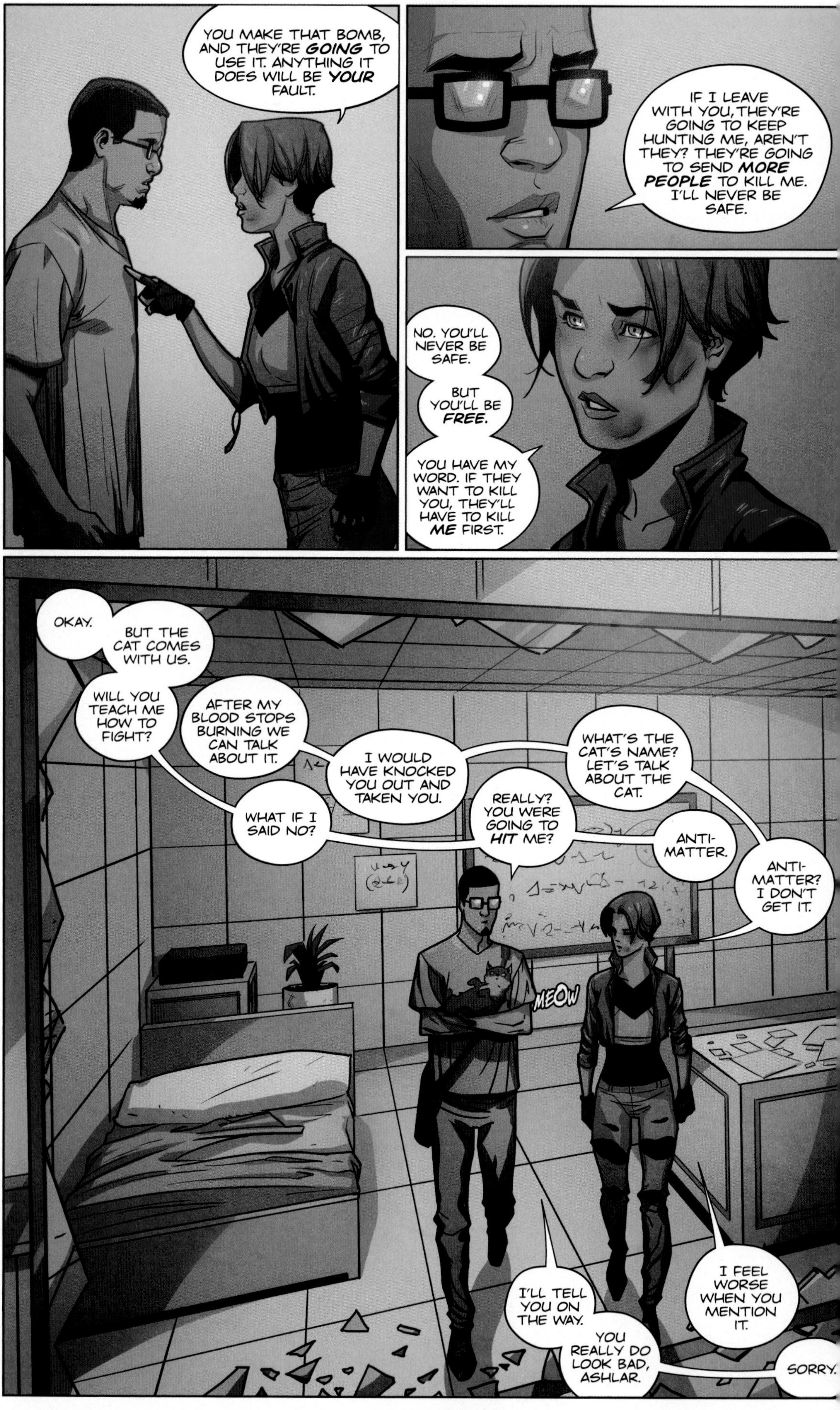
YOU MAKE THAT BOMB, AND THEY'RE **GOING** TO USE IT. ANYTHING IT DOES WILL BE **YOUR** FAULT.
IF I LEAVE WITH YOU, THEY'RE GOING TO KEEP HUNTING ME, AREN'T THEY? THEY'RE GOING TO SEND **MORE PEOPLE** TO KILL ME. I'LL NEVER BE SAFE.
NO. YOU'LL NEVER BE SAFE.
BUT YOU'LL BE **FREE.**
YOU HAVE MY WORD. IF THEY WANT TO KILL YOU, THEY'LL HAVE TO KILL **ME** FIRST.
OKAY.
BUT THE CAT COMES WITH US.
WILL YOU TEACH ME HOW TO FIGHT?
AFTER MY BLOOD STOPS BURNING WE CAN TALK ABOUT IT.
WHAT IF I SAID NO?
I WOULD HAVE KNOCKED YOU OUT AND TAKEN YOU.
REALLY? YOU WERE GOING TO **HIT** ME?
WHAT'S THE CAT'S NAME? LET'S TALK ABOUT THE CAT.
ANTI-MATTER.
ANTI-MATTER? I DON'T GET IT.
MEOW
I'LL TELL YOU ON THE WAY.
YOU REALLY DO LOOK BAD, ASHLAR.
I FEEL WORSE WHEN YOU MENTION IT.
SORRY.

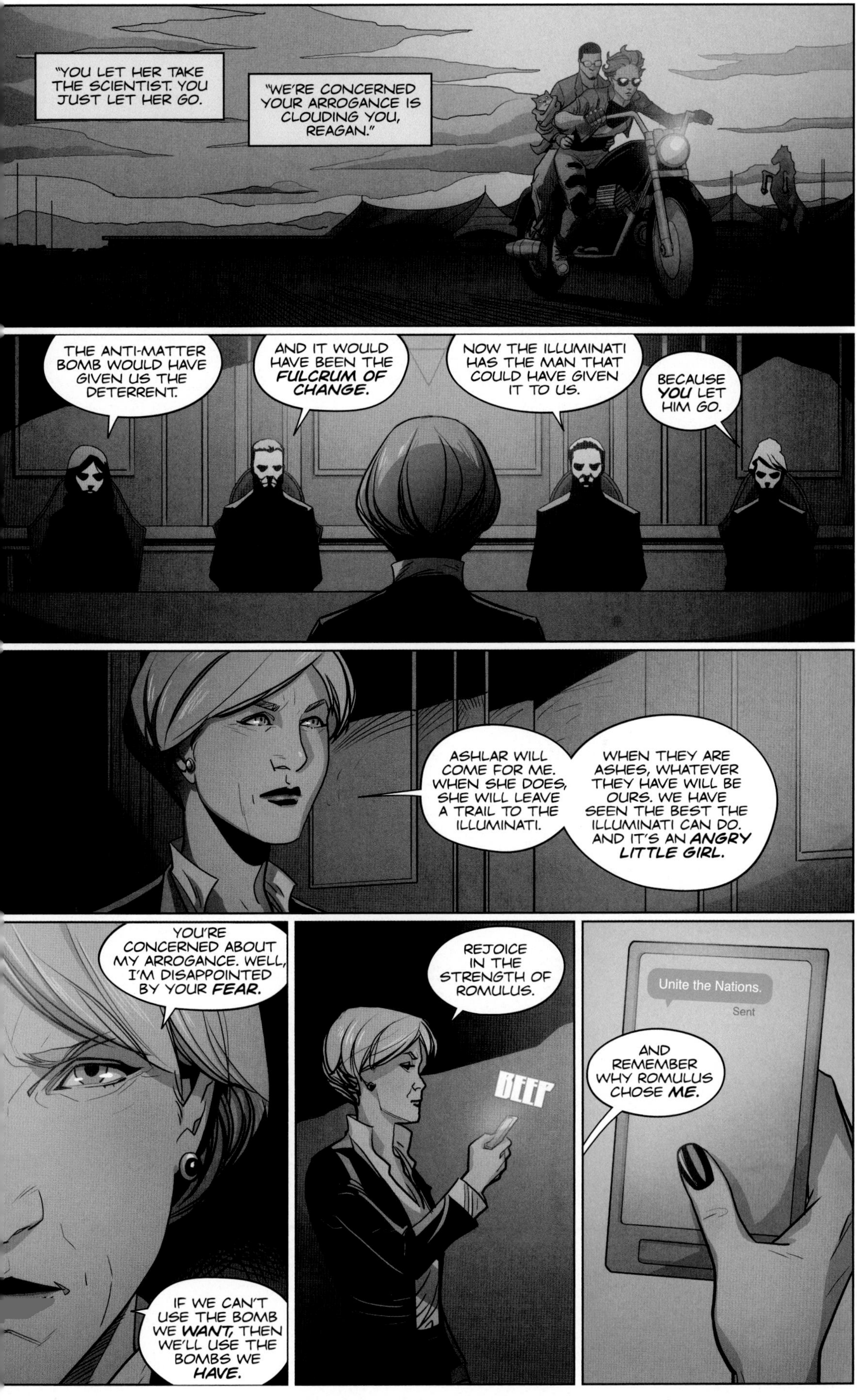
"YOU LET HER TAKE THE SCIENTIST. YOU JUST LET HER GO.
"WE'RE CONCERNED YOUR ARROGANCE IS CLOUDING YOU, REAGAN."
THE ANTI-MATTER BOMB WOULD HAVE GIVEN US THE DETERRENT.
AND IT WOULD HAVE BEEN THE FULCRUM OF CHANGE.
NOW THE ILLUMINATI HAS THE MAN THAT COULD HAVE GIVEN IT TO US.
BECAUSE YOU LET HIM GO.
ASHLAR WILL COME FOR ME. WHEN SHE DOES, SHE WILL LEAVE A TRAIL TO THE ILLUMINATI.
WHEN THEY ARE ASHES, WHATEVER THEY HAVE WILL BE OURS. WE HAVE SEEN THE BEST THE ILLUMINATI CAN DO. AND IT'S AN ANGRY LITTLE GIRL.
YOU'RE CONCERNED ABOUT MY ARROGANCE. WELL, I'M DISAPPOINTED BY YOUR FEAR.
IF WE CAN'T USE THE BOMB WE WANT, THEN WE'LL USE THE BOMBS WE HAVE.
REJOICE IN THE STRENGTH OF ROMULUS.
BEEP
Unite the Nations.
Sent
AND REMEMBER WHY ROMULUS CHOSE ME.

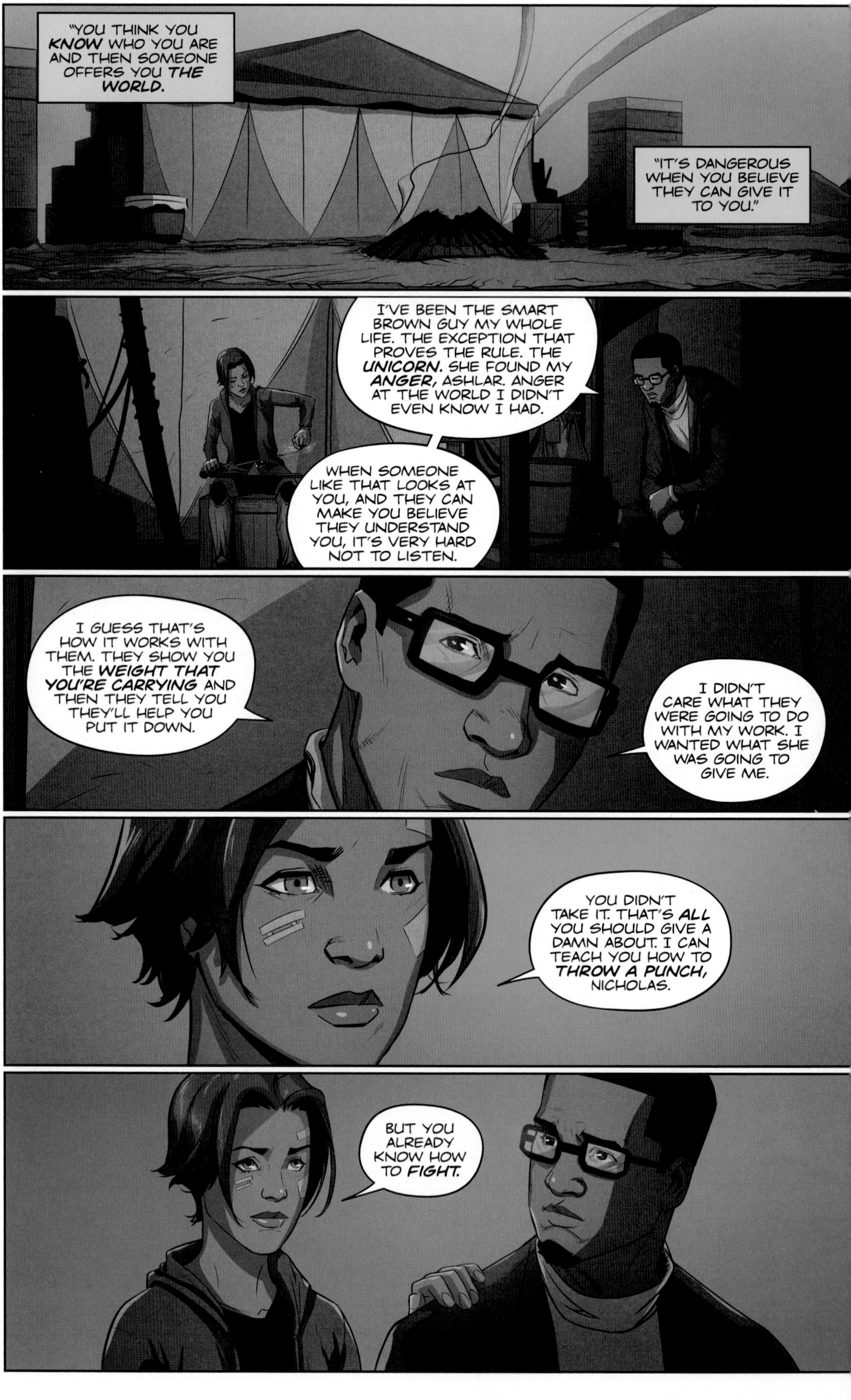
"YOU THINK YOU KNOW WHO YOU ARE AND THEN SOMEONE OFFERS YOU THE WORLD.
"IT'S DANGEROUS WHEN YOU BELIEVE THEY CAN GIVE IT TO YOU."
I'VE BEEN THE SMART BROWN GUY MY WHOLE LIFE. THE EXCEPTION THAT PROVES THE RULE. THE UNICORN. SHE FOUND MY ANGER, ASHLAR. ANGER AT THE WORLD I DIDN'T EVEN KNOW I HAD.
WHEN SOMEONE LIKE THAT LOOKS AT YOU, AND THEY CAN MAKE YOU BELIEVE THEY UNDERSTAND YOU, IT'S VERY HARD NOT TO LISTEN.
I GUESS THAT'S HOW IT WORKS WITH THEM. THEY SHOW YOU THE WEIGHT THAT YOU'RE CARRYING AND THEN THEY TELL YOU THEY'LL HELP YOU PUT IT DOWN.
I DIDN'T CARE WHAT THEY WERE GOING TO DO WITH MY WORK. I WANTED WHAT SHE WAS GOING TO GIVE ME.
YOU DIDN'T TAKE IT. THAT'S ALL YOU SHOULD GIVE A DAMN ABOUT. I CAN TEACH YOU HOW TO THROW A PUNCH, NICHOLAS.
BUT YOU ALREADY KNOW HOW TO FIGHT.

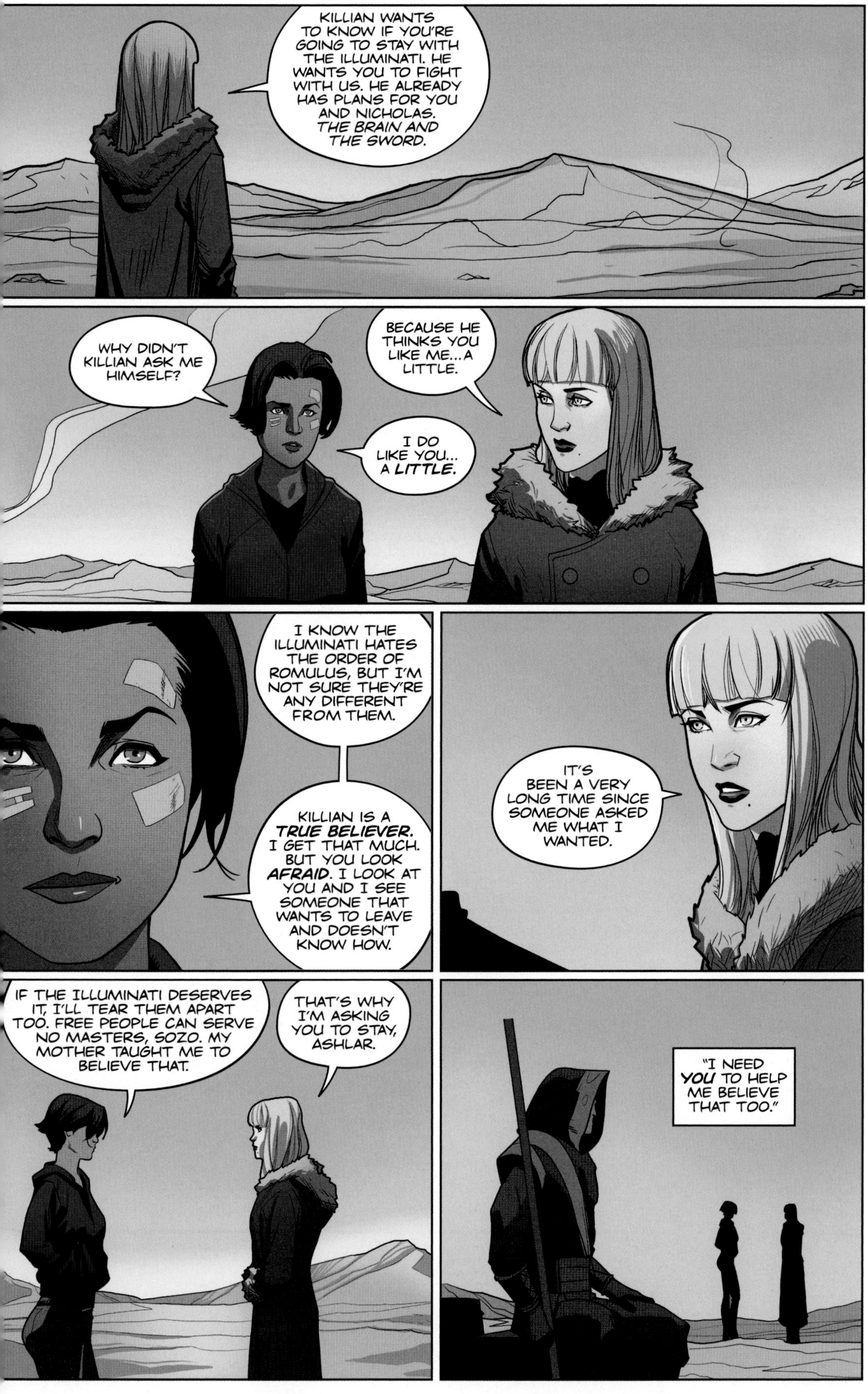
KILLIAN WANTS TO KNOW IF YOU'RE GOING TO STAY WITH THE ILLUMINATI. HE WANTS YOU TO FIGHT WITH US. HE ALREADY HAS PLANS FOR YOU AND NICHOLAS. *THE BRAIN AND THE SWORD.*
WHY DIDN'T KILLIAN ASK ME HIMSELF?
BECAUSE HE THINKS YOU LIKE ME...A LITTLE.
I DO LIKE YOU... A ***LITTLE.***
I KNOW THE ILLUMINATI HATES THE ORDER OF ROMULUS, BUT I'M NOT SURE THEY'RE ANY DIFFERENT FROM THEM.
KILLIAN IS A ***TRUE BELIEVER.*** I GET THAT MUCH. BUT YOU LOOK ***AFRAID.*** I LOOK AT YOU AND I SEE SOMEONE THAT WANTS TO LEAVE AND DOESN'T KNOW HOW.
IT'S BEEN A VERY LONG TIME SINCE SOMEONE ASKED ME WHAT I WANTED.
IF THE ILLUMINATI DESERVES IT, I'LL TEAR THEM APART TOO. FREE PEOPLE CAN SERVE NO MASTERS, SOZO. MY MOTHER TAUGHT ME TO BELIEVE THAT.
THAT'S WHY I'M ASKING YOU TO STAY, ASHLAR.
"I NEED ***YOU*** TO HELP ME BELIEVE THAT TOO."

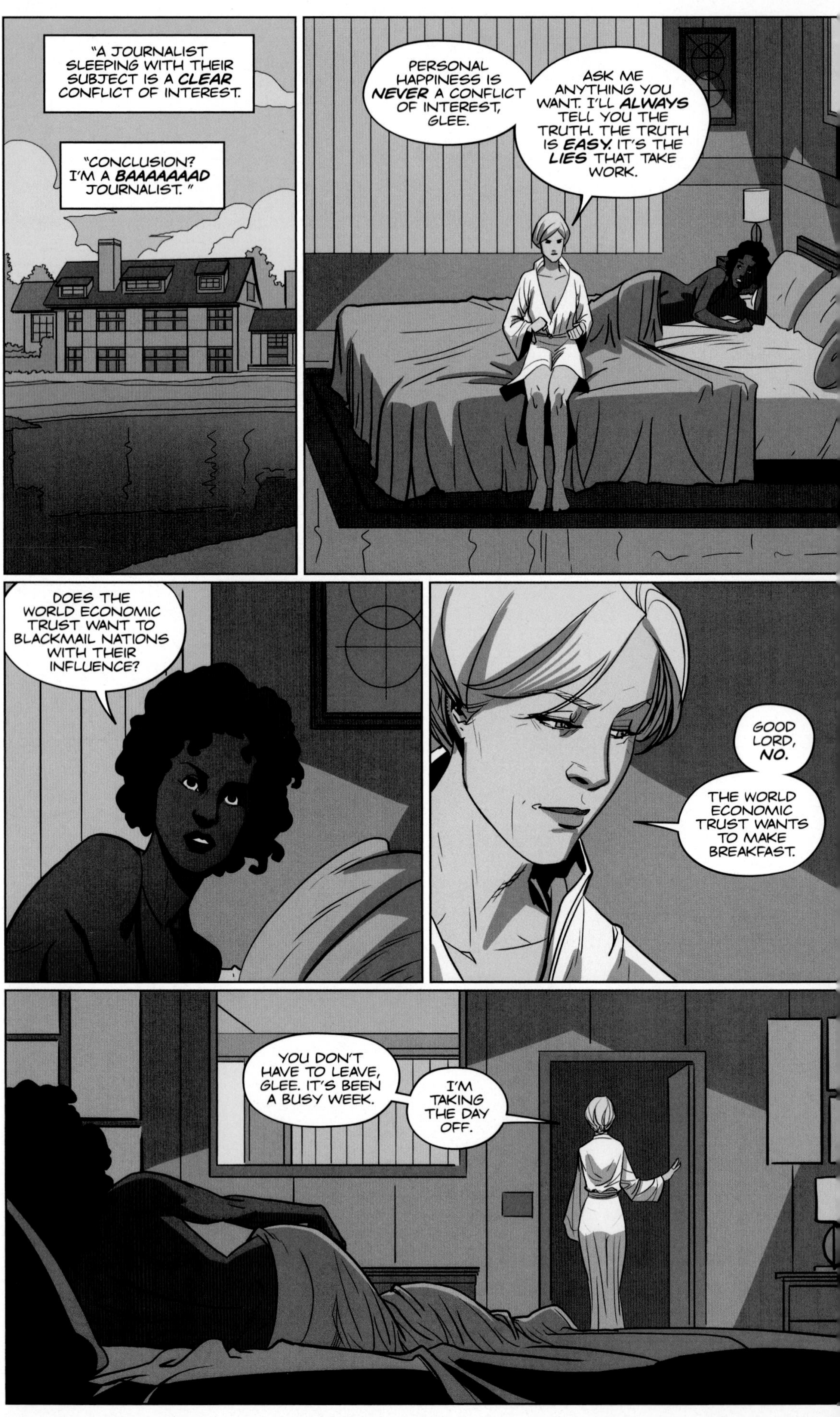
"A JOURNALIST SLEEPING WITH THEIR SUBJECT IS A CLEAR CONFLICT OF INTEREST.
"CONCLUSION? I'M A BAAAAAAAD JOURNALIST."
PERSONAL HAPPINESS IS NEVER A CONFLICT OF INTEREST, GLEE.
ASK ME ANYTHING YOU WANT. I'LL ALWAYS TELL YOU THE TRUTH. THE TRUTH IS EASY. IT'S THE LIES THAT TAKE WORK.
DOES THE WORLD ECONOMIC TRUST WANT TO BLACKMAIL NATIONS WITH THEIR INFLUENCE?
GOOD LORD, NO.
THE WORLD ECONOMIC TRUST WANTS TO MAKE BREAKFAST.
YOU DON'T HAVE TO LEAVE, GLEE. IT'S BEEN A BUSY WEEK.
I'M TAKING THE DAY OFF.

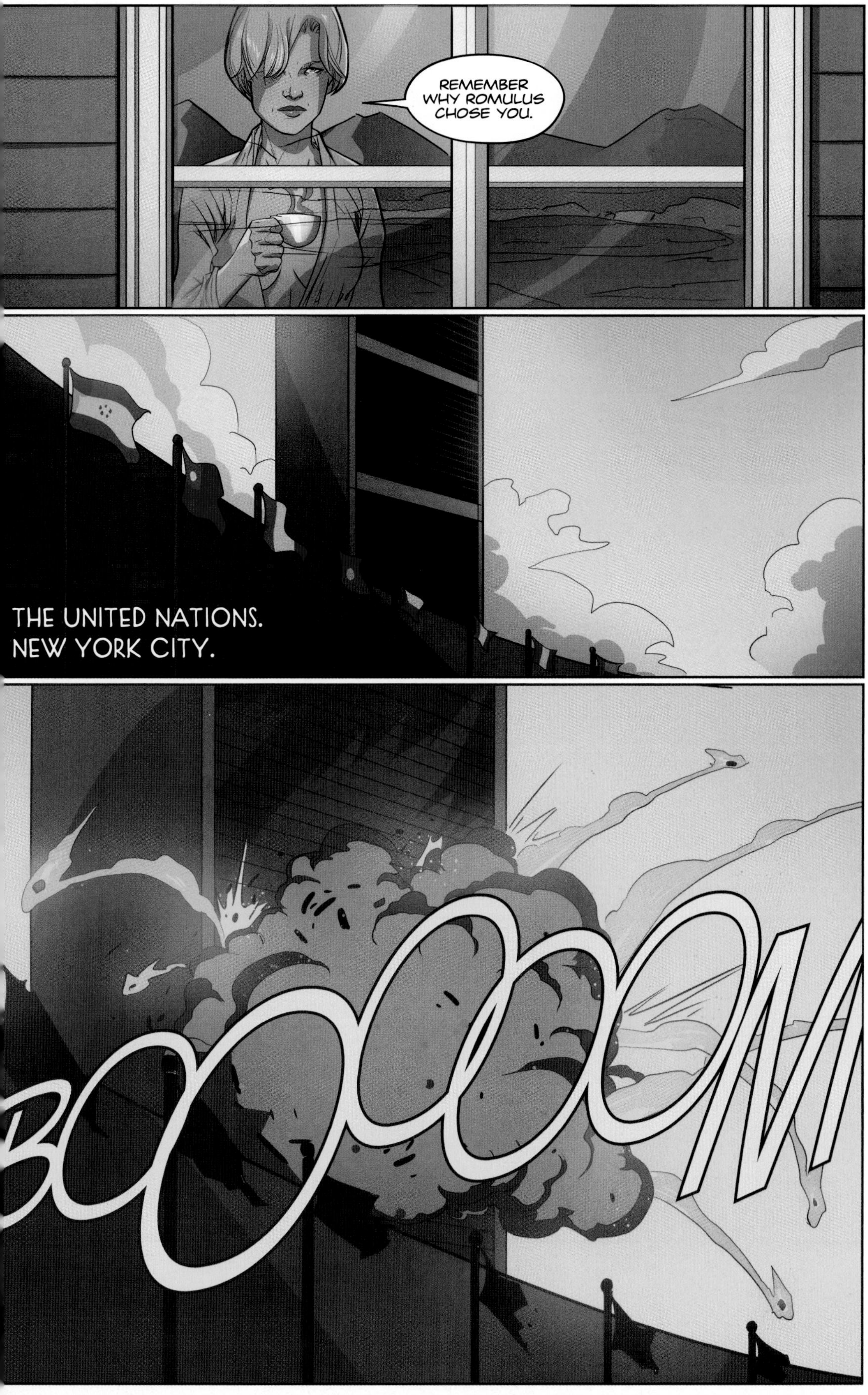
REMEMBER WHY ROMULUS CHOSE YOU.
THE UNITED NATIONS.
NEW YORK CITY.
BOOOOOM

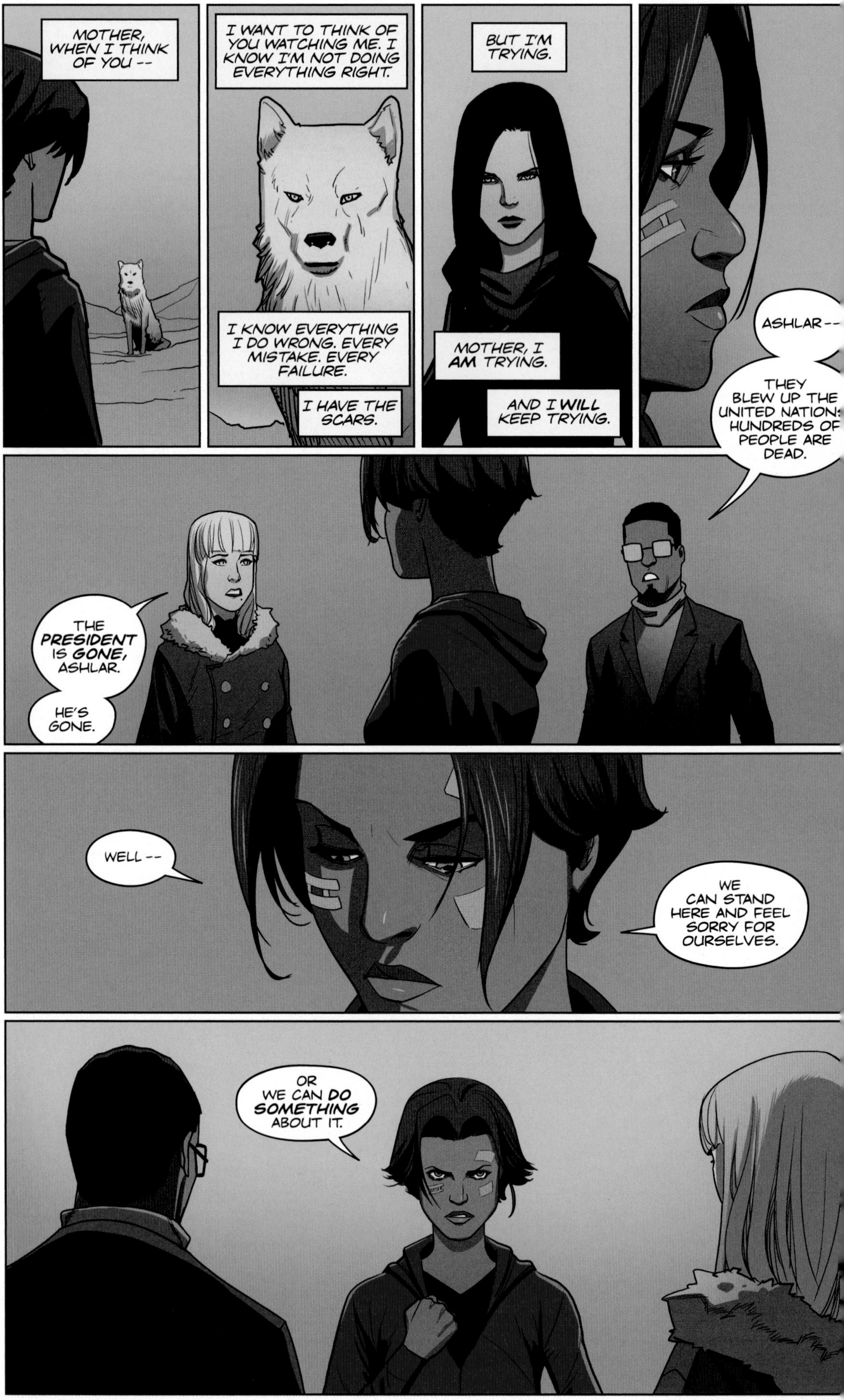

MOTHER, WHEN I THINK OF YOU --
I WANT TO THINK OF YOU WATCHING ME. I KNOW I'M NOT DOING EVERYTHING RIGHT.
I KNOW EVERYTHING I DO WRONG. EVERY MISTAKE. EVERY FAILURE.
I HAVE THE SCARS.
BUT I'M TRYING.
MOTHER, I AM TRYING.
AND I WILL KEEP TRYING.
ASHLAR --
THEY BLEW UP THE UNITED NATION
HUNDREDS OF PEOPLE ARE DEAD.
THE PRESIDENT IS GONE, ASHLAR.
HE'S GONE.
WELL --
WE CAN STAND HERE AND FEEL SORRY FOR OURSELVES.
OR WE CAN DO SOMETHING ABOUT IT.

CHAPTER FIVE:
EXTRAS

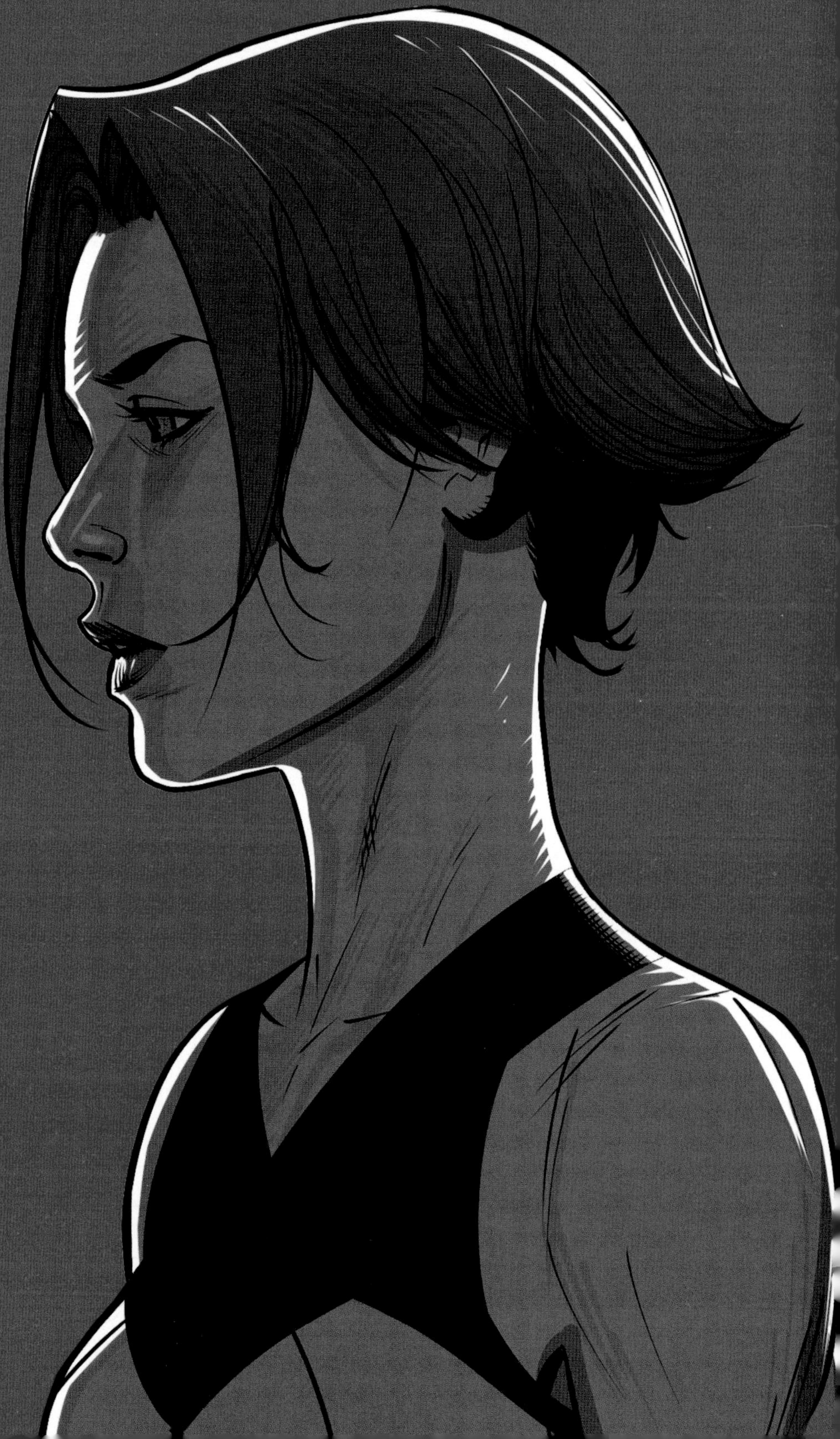

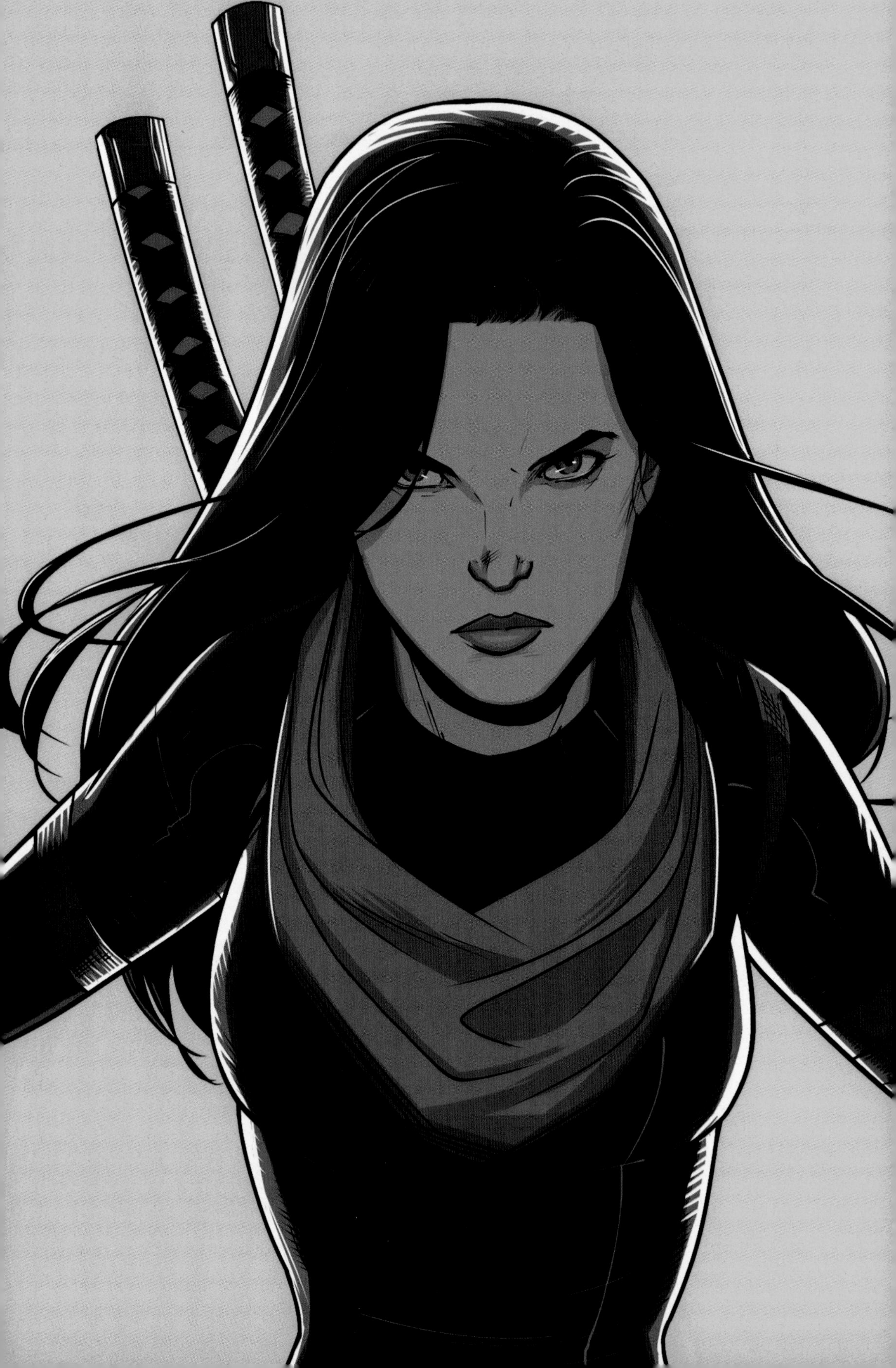

For Ashlar.

My daughter who is my vengeance,
vengeance that glows like forged
metal.

You are the bridge that joins
life,
with death,
and love.

I am your mother.
In your memory, shall I be
immortal.
In your hand lies my redemption.

And the fate of the world.

I am ashamed of what I have left
for you.
That I could not do more.
That I could not be more.

Close your eyes, my daughter.
Find me in the dark.
Howl for me, and I will be with
you.

I cannot tell you what I have see
in eternity,
but I can tell you what I imagin
it will show me.

I will see a world in balance,
where man is a tree that grows
towards the sun,
roots running deep,
watered by crystal rain.

Death will follow you.
Death wants you,
but She must wait.

The Last of the Wolves,
will find the throat of Romulus.
Your fangs will sink through its
armor.
Your tongue will drink of its
blood.

In my end,
your purpose is found.
Wrap your hands around Romulus,
hold it to the earth.

And if you must die,
if that is written in the Book of All
Fates,

Do not die alone.

Deny our enemy no cruelty.
For they will give you all that is
cruel.

Deny our enemy no anger.
For they will blanket you with rage.

Deny our enemy no fear
no pain
no murder.
For they have no limits to their evil.

I named you Ashlar,
for you are the strongest stone,
the base of the temple of truth.

Everything you need to destroy
Romulus,
you have already been given.

Find yourself.

I set us both free,
because I know you loved me.

I would live again.
To die again.

Because I love you.

Axis. Mater Lupus.

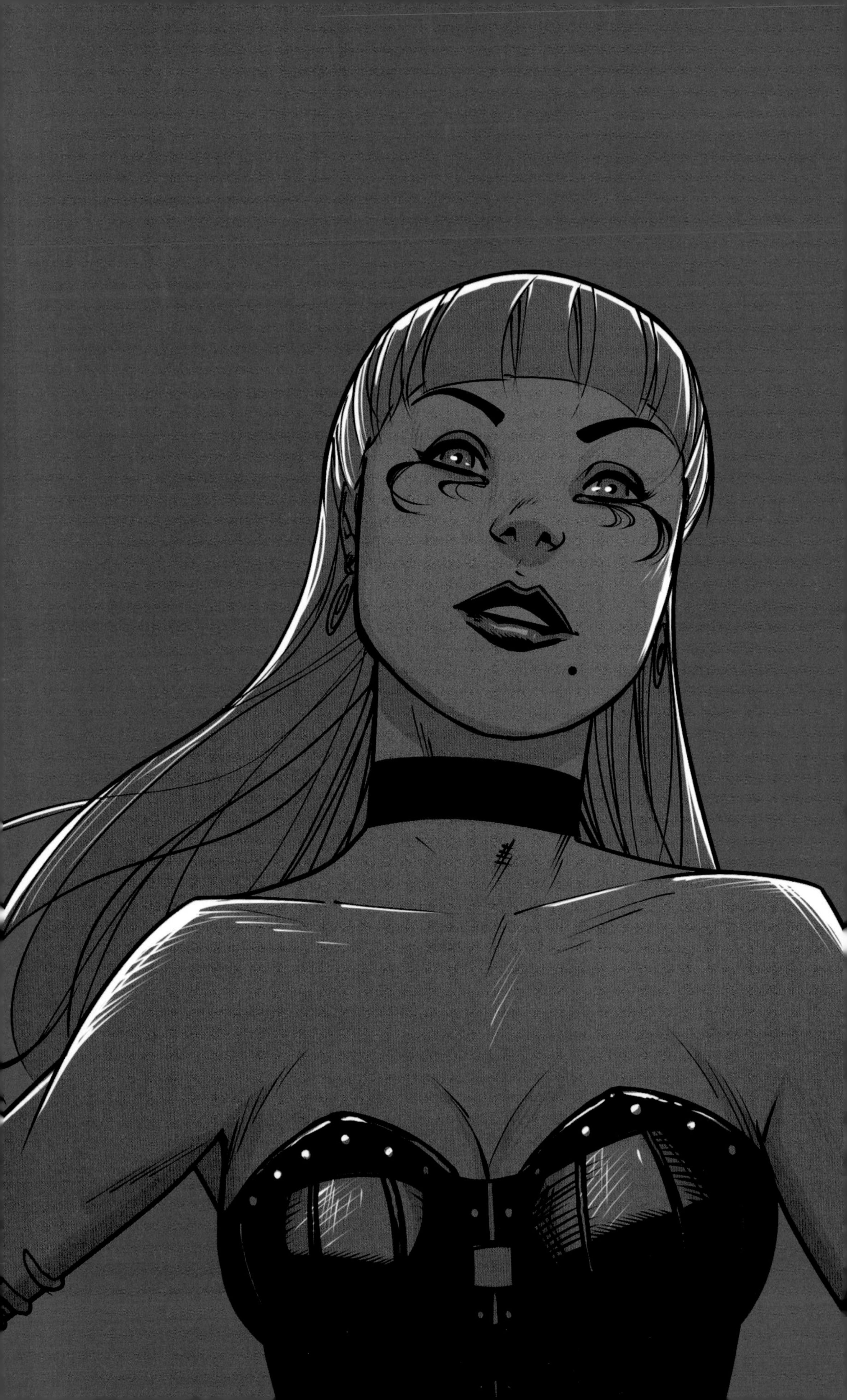

[redacted]

OP SECRET

November 21, 1963

EMORANDUM FOR
Robert Kennedy, Attorney General

UBJECT: Examination of Global Collusion affecting National Se-
urity.

obby,

always called you the alarmist, but after the incident in [redacted] I fear I have underestimated the weight of the sys-
em we wanted to change and that the forces working against us
re coordinated and well financed. Our father taught us to 'fear
hat power that we can't see' and I've never been as blind as I
m in the Oval Office.

'm still reeling from the conversation I had with Ms. [redacted] in Stockholm. Never have I seen a woman with so much
ealth consumed by so much fear.

s [redacted] was unmistakably specific about her warning, and
hile I am well protected I do have concerns about Jackie and
he children.

hen I return from Dallas, I want to personally interview Mr. [redacted] Mr [redacted] and both members of [redacted] with
ou present in the room.

nder no circumstance are Hoover and Johnson to be made aware of
hese inquires. Before this investigation becomes a matter of
olicy, it should remain between family.

/S/ John F. Kennedy

[redacted]

Homo Homini Lupus Est. Homo Homini Lupus Est.

SEVEN SPHERES

Force

War

Fury

Speed

Grace

Pain

Death

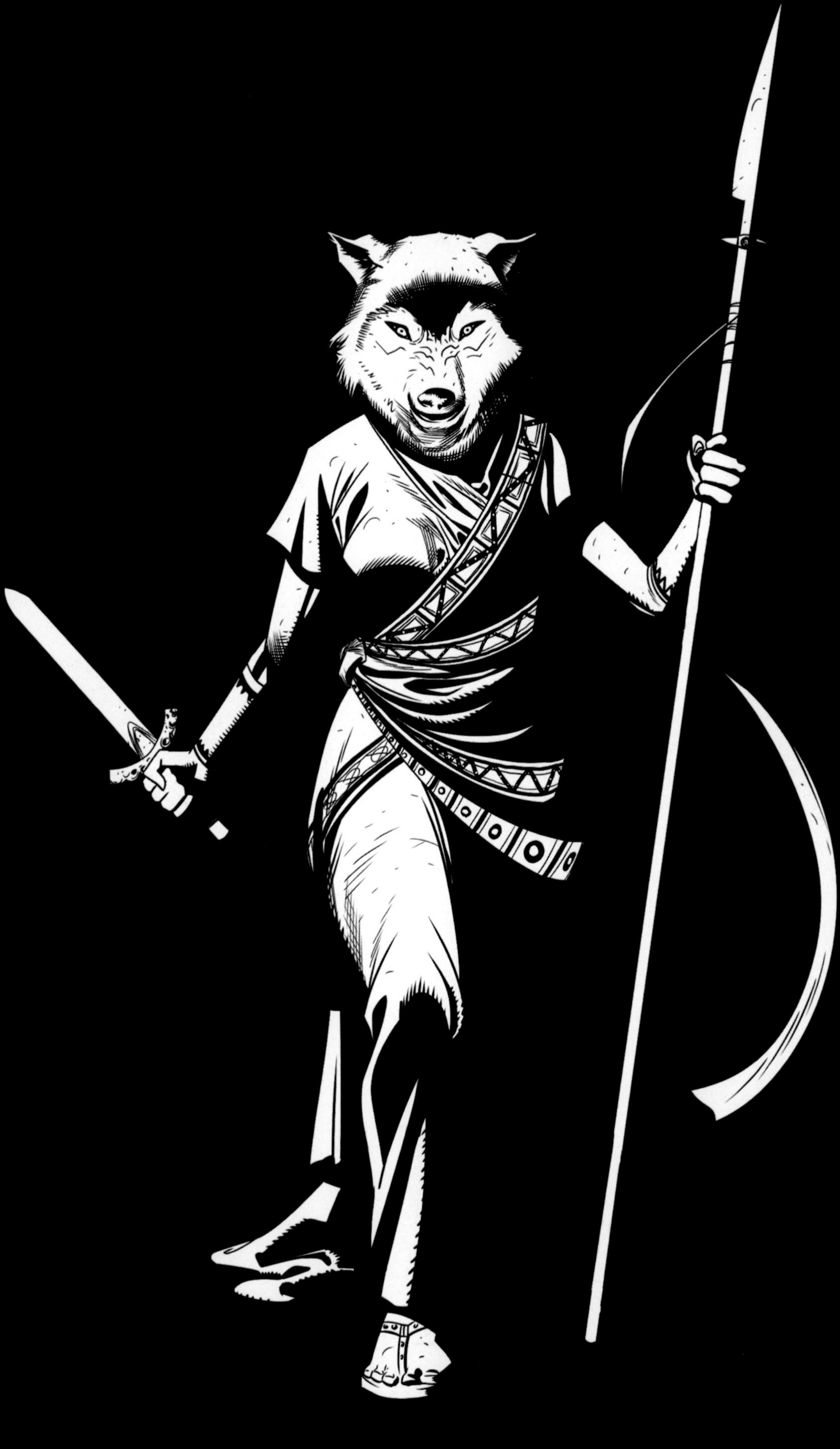

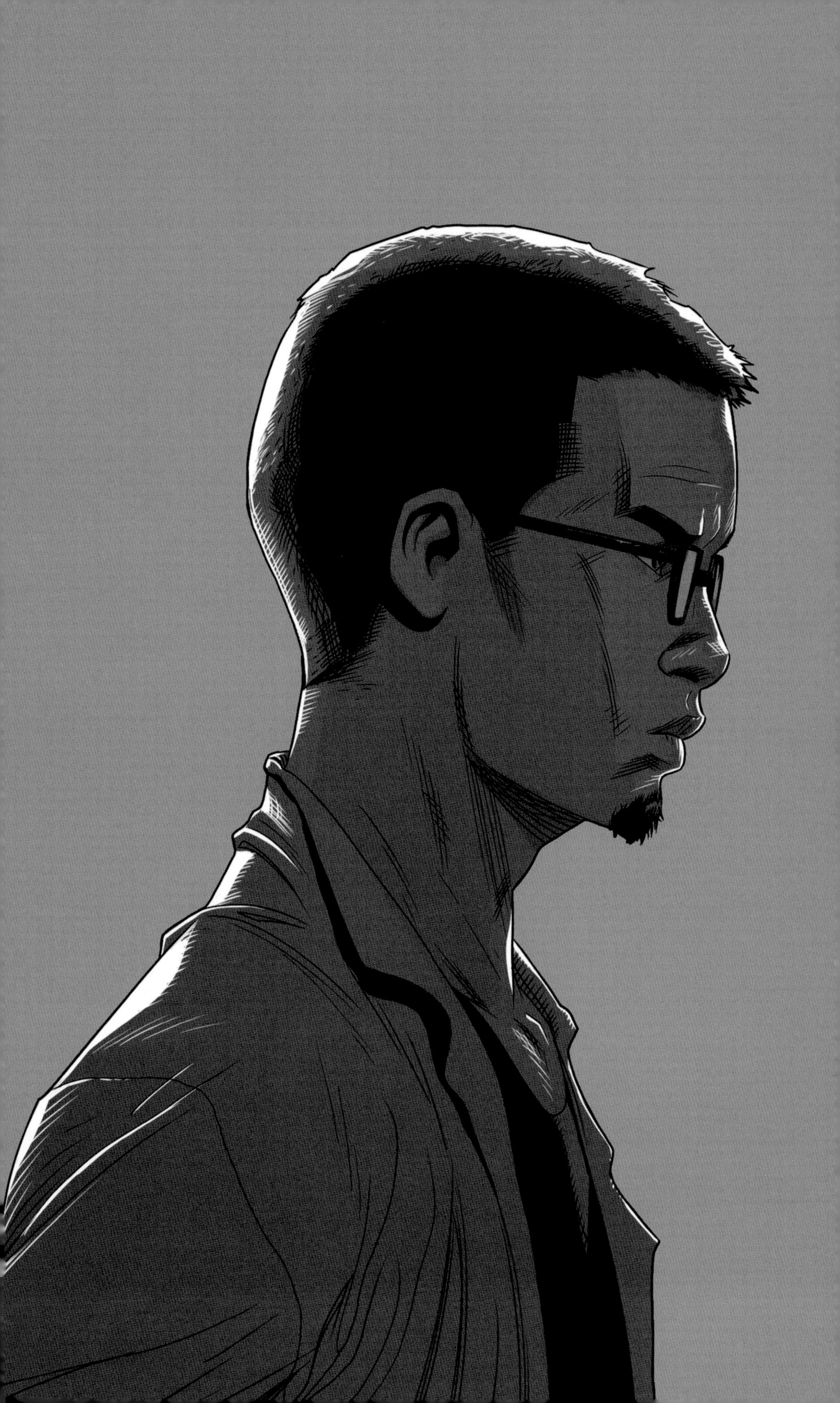

and the result is a life for women in the age of the double standard, of the mixed message, of the impossible task of emulating simultaneous fantasies of beauty, intelligence, subservience and vanity. One only need watch a single advertising block on any major television programme in my native country of Great Britain to see this propaganda in action. 85% of the products advertised to women, during the broadcast of media content aimed at women, are products concerning appearance. The cosmetic and weight loss industries have adverts in every single ad-buy cycle, with marketing statements designed to erode the physical confidence of the women who view them. The bulk of corporate messaging to women is: *You're not good enough. You're not pretty enough. You're not thin enough. Buy our products to fix the elements of yourself that are broken so you can have value in society.*

Conversely, men are given corporate advertising connected to empowerment products. Products offering financial independence, the power of consumer choice, affirmations of value and strength. Men are seen driving luxury cars, finding profit in judicious investments, seeking workplace promotion and dominating the financial independence of their households. Women are seen driving vehicles meant to carry children to school and extra-curricular activities, buying home cleaning products, battling weight gain and the natural process of aging. The assumption is that the average male consume is an ambitious individual who is looking for more foundational power in society, and that the average woman is concerned about how men judge her appearance. It's propaganda meant to influence the goals of women, steering them towards a solipsist obsession with superficial value and away from the pursuit of agency, knowledge and power.

n her seminal work, *The Destruction of Venus in the Age of Mars*, Dr. Helena Fabricant stated it simply: Girls are taught how to be princesses and men are taught how to become kings. There is no exaltation of the queen in modern society, no culture supporting a woman's right to rule a system. Womanhood itself is never the stated goal and in its place is the propagation of a perpetual girlhood, an inherent patriarchal definition of the feminine meant to continue the concepts of the subservient female always seeking validation through the eyes of male judgement.

Even women who successfully measure up to the near-impossible beauty and so-called grace standards society are destined to ultimately lose their sense of self when the power of their sexuality is deemed inherently destructive, dangerous, something to be tamed. The promiscuous man is worshipped by corporate dogma, valued for his ability to seduce and conquer. The promiscuous woman is deemed a slut, a whore, a harlot and made a villain to the sanctity of the societal contract. Simultaneously a woman is told her entire value lies in her ability to appeal to the sexual desires of men and that appealing too much to those desires makes her something to be feared and shunned and tamed. Be beautiful, but not too beautiful. Be sexy, but not too sexy. Be a lioness, but make certain you tell the world you are tame.

I have rejected this paradigm and witnessed first-hand the resistance every woman feels when they refuse to partake in a game they simply cannot win. The World Economic Trust that I have founded and all of its charitable efforts have continually been accused of corruption by forces in the media and the business community with no evidence of any wrongdoing and a willful denial of the positive effects of my work. This is not meant to be a defense of my career or my status, because neither requires defense.

I write this simply to highlight that even someone with the largesse of my platform is not exempt from the basic inequity at the heart of our historical definition of the feminine. In puritanical times, the woman who pursued knowledge and power and sought to share it with other women was targeted for destruction by the word witch

The word bitch has replaced that, but the effects are similar and the label is intended to yield the same result: passivity and subservience and a constant fear of burning at the stake. For me, it has been imperative that I stand firm in the face of that fire. I cast my power at the base of that fire with the mantra I use and share with the world:

I will not allow the patriarchy to determine what I want. I will determine desire for myself. I will not fear that desire.

I will explore it with reckless abandon. I will not be tamed. I will not be a princess. I will become a queen.

I will determine my own world, my own sphere of influence and I will not be ashamed of my own power.

I will rule.

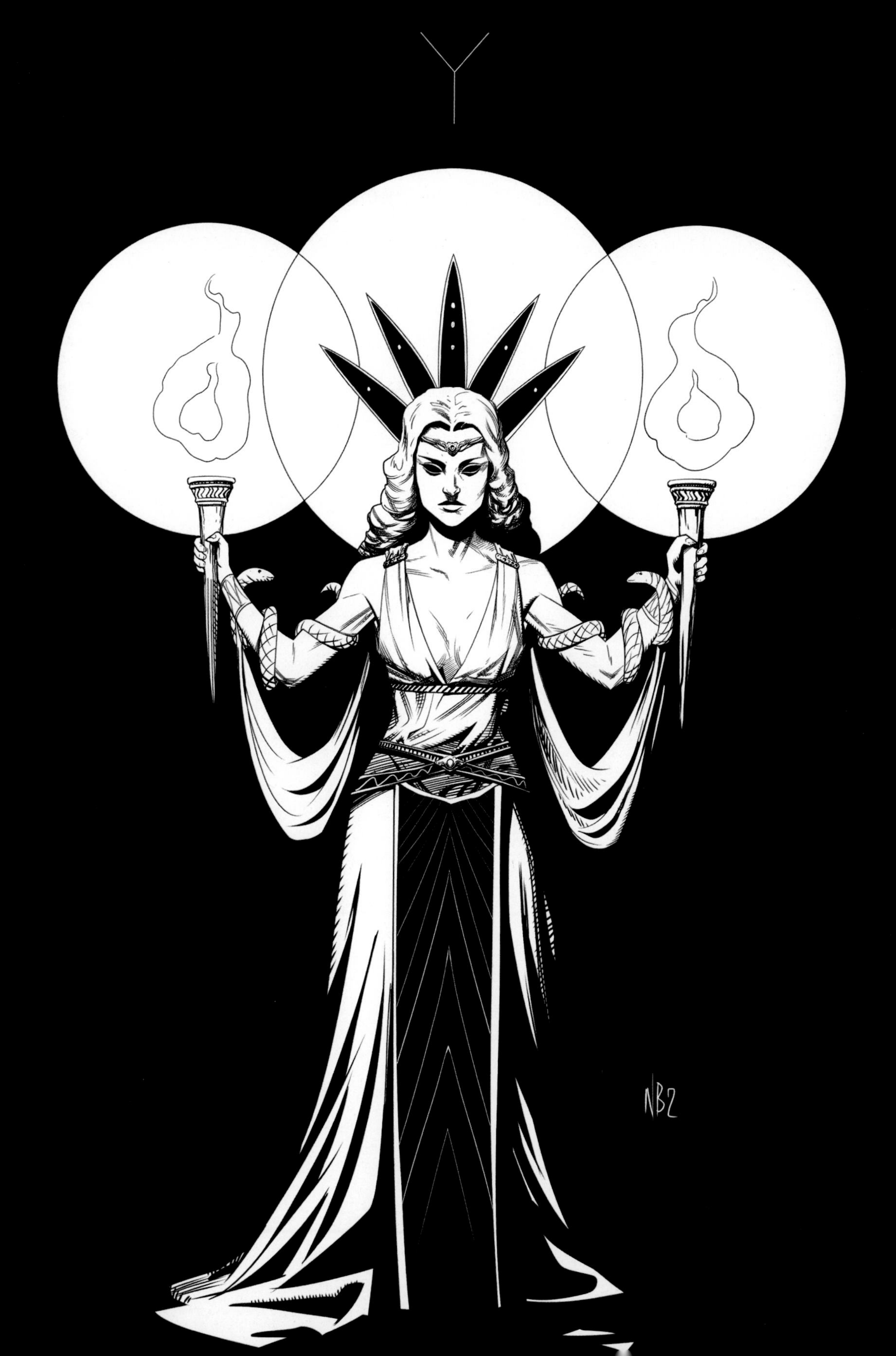

HAWKINS · HILL · SAEKI · VALENZA

GOLGOTHA

PREVIEW

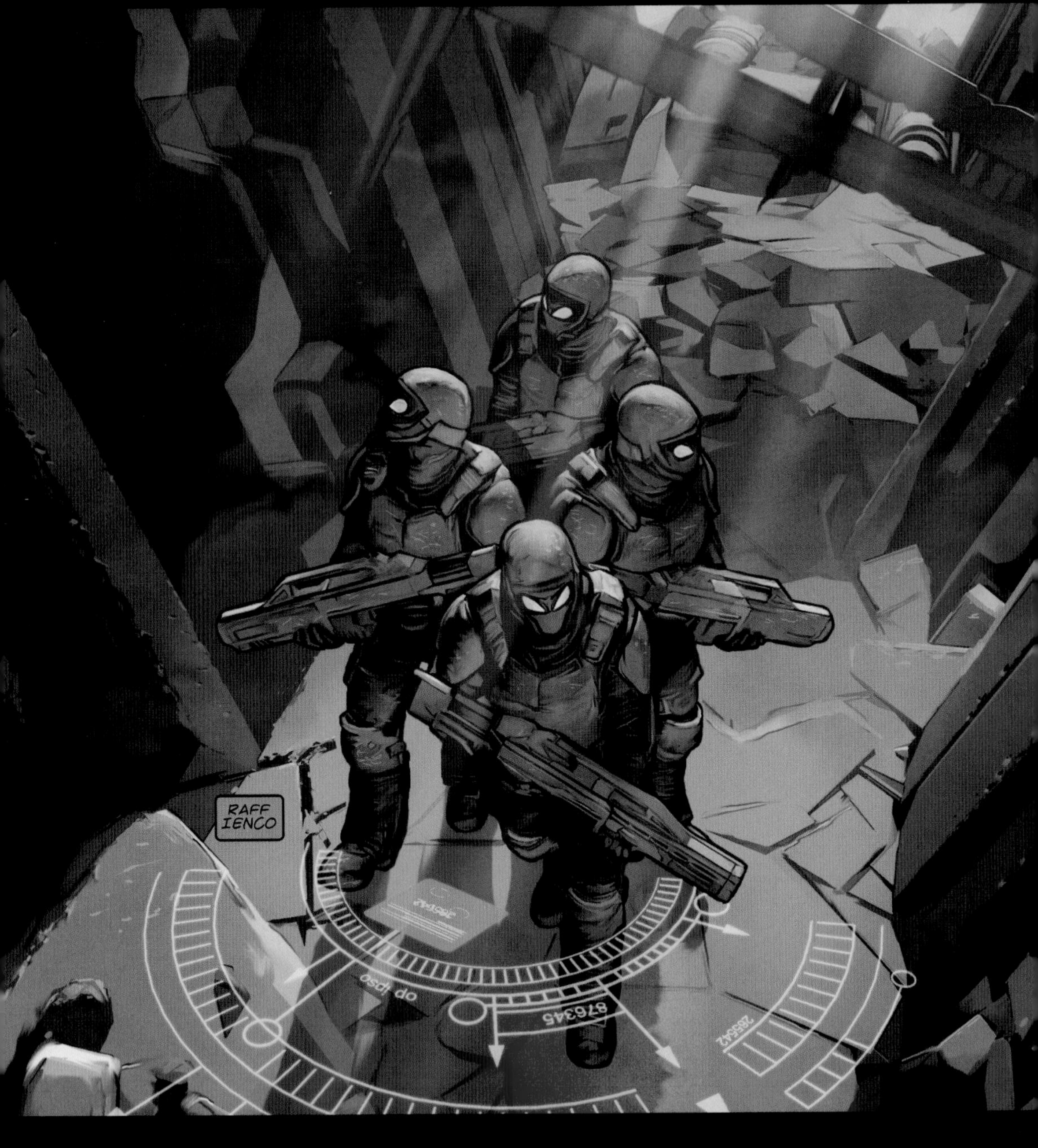
RAFF
IENCO
876345

IN STORES
OCTOBER
2017

MISSION STATEMENT

ISOCSS Golgotha.
Fleet number 18739840(09).
Modified Drawnheim MC-69B Taurus E-Class Vessel.

MISSION PARAMETERS:

Attempt to create the first human, mining colony beyond Earth.

DESTINATION: IAU-ACHILLES.

TIME TO DESTINATION: Est. 80 years.

ESSENTIAL CREW:

CARILLO, Anabelle.
(AEF. HUM-INT)

Born: **Chicago, Illinois.**

Decorated pilot in both sea and Earth Orbit operations.

Graduate of ISOC Naval Academy.

Unmarried. No children.

MEAD, Lancaster.
(Engineer)

Born: **San Diego, California.**

Graduate of MIT.

HIV Positive (Remission). Unmarried. No children.

ESSENTIAL CREW:

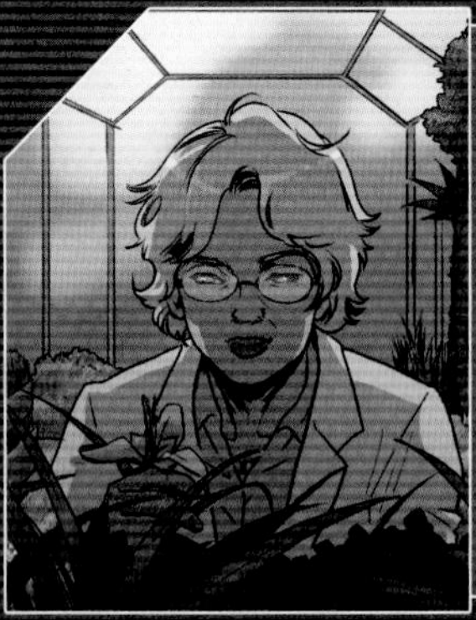

LIPPENCOTT, Charelene.
(PhD. Agrophysics)

Born: **Joplin, Missouri.**

Graduate Johns Hopkins (B.A. Applied Sciences), PhD Cornell University (Agrophysics).

Unmarried. No Children.

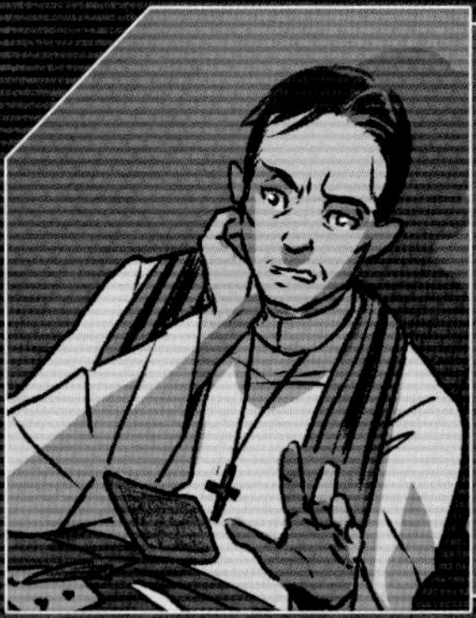

CHENG, David.
(Chaplain. AEF.)

Born: **New Orleans. Louisiana.** Base Chaplain, Flynn Air Force Base.

Graduate Saint Louis University (B.A. Religious Studies).

Widowed. Laura Cheng (Deceased). No Children.

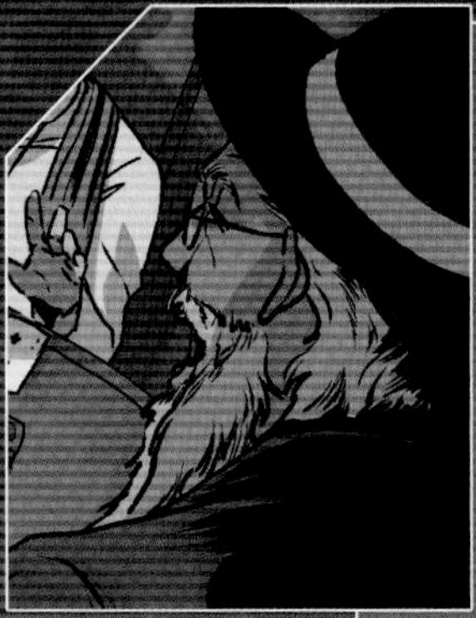

ROSENTHAL, Moshe.
(Rabbi. AEF.)

Born: **Haifa, Israel.** Dual Citizenship United States of America. Naturalized.

Graduate University of Haifa (B.A. Hebrew Literature and Language, Political Science).

Base Rabbi Rumsfeld Air Force Base.

Unmarried. No children.

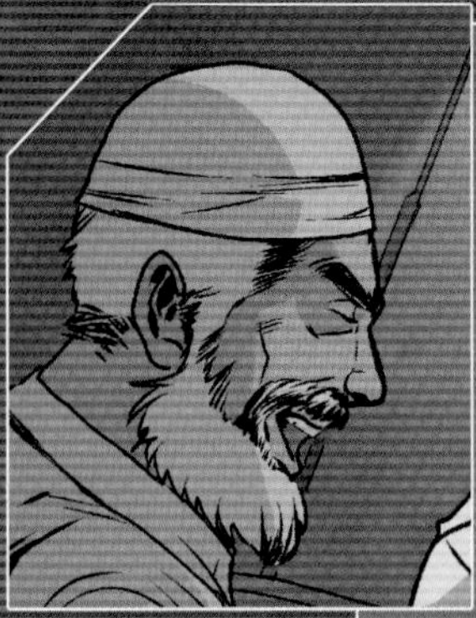

GAFANI, Abdul-Ghafaar.
(Imam. AEF.)

Born: **Istanbul, Turkey.** Dual-Citizenship-United States of America. Naturalized.

Graduate Harvard University (B.A. Philosophy). Founder North African Sunni Islam Mosque.

Served USMC, honorable discharge. Rank: Captain (declined).

Unmarried. No children.

ESSENTIAL CREW:

LAWTON, Michael.
(Cpt. 31st Special Forces Group. ISOC.)

Born: **Kansas City, Kansas.**

Graduated Wyandotte High School. No post graduate education.

Enlisted Marines. Served two tours Marine/Resource Coalition Conflict. Promoted to Special Forces.

Duty status: Active.

Married to Jennifer Lawton.
Expecting first child.

BARDOT, Cleménce.
(Applied Robotics. Kinematics. Control dynamics.)

Born: **Brooklyn, New York.**

Graduated Cornell University (B.A. Applied Robotics, M.S. Applied Robotics).

Winner Nobel Prize (Team Awarded).

Unmarried. No children.

CARPENTER, Jennifer.
(PhD. Xenobiologist.)

Born: **Los Angeles, California.**

Graduated UCLA (B.A. Biosafety) Graduated USC (PhD. Xenobiology).

Divorced. No children.

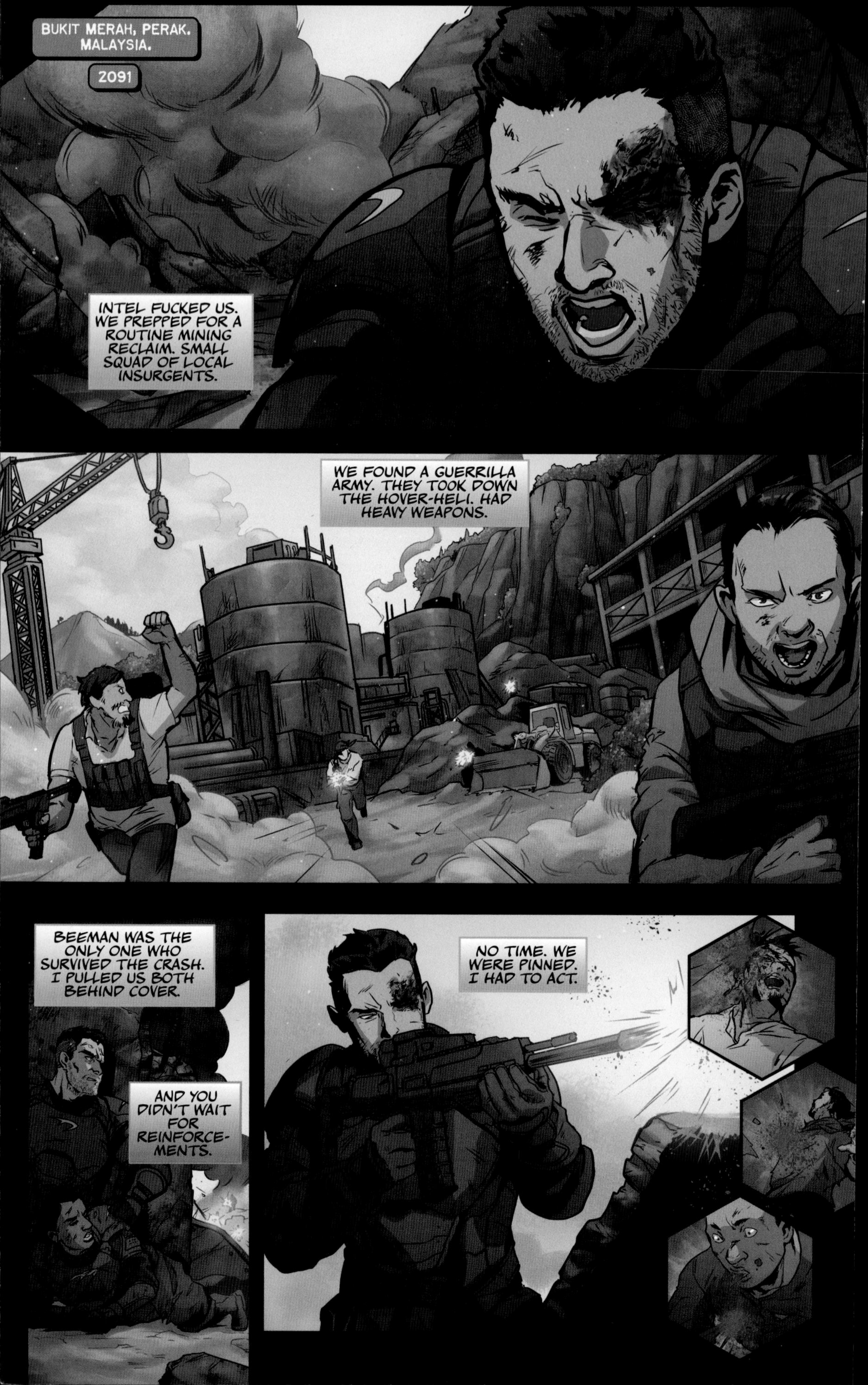
BUKIT MERAH, PERAK. MALAYSIA.
2091
INTEL FUCKED US. WE PREPPED FOR A ROUTINE MINING RECLAIM. SMALL SQUAD OF LOCAL INSURGENTS.
WE FOUND A GUERRILLA ARMY. THEY TOOK DOWN THE HOVER-HELI. HAD HEAVY WEAPONS.
BEEMAN WAS THE ONLY ONE WHO SURVIVED THE CRASH. I PULLED US BOTH BEHIND COVER.
AND YOU DIDN'T WAIT FOR REINFORCE-MENTS.
NO TIME. WE WERE PINNED. I HAD TO ACT.

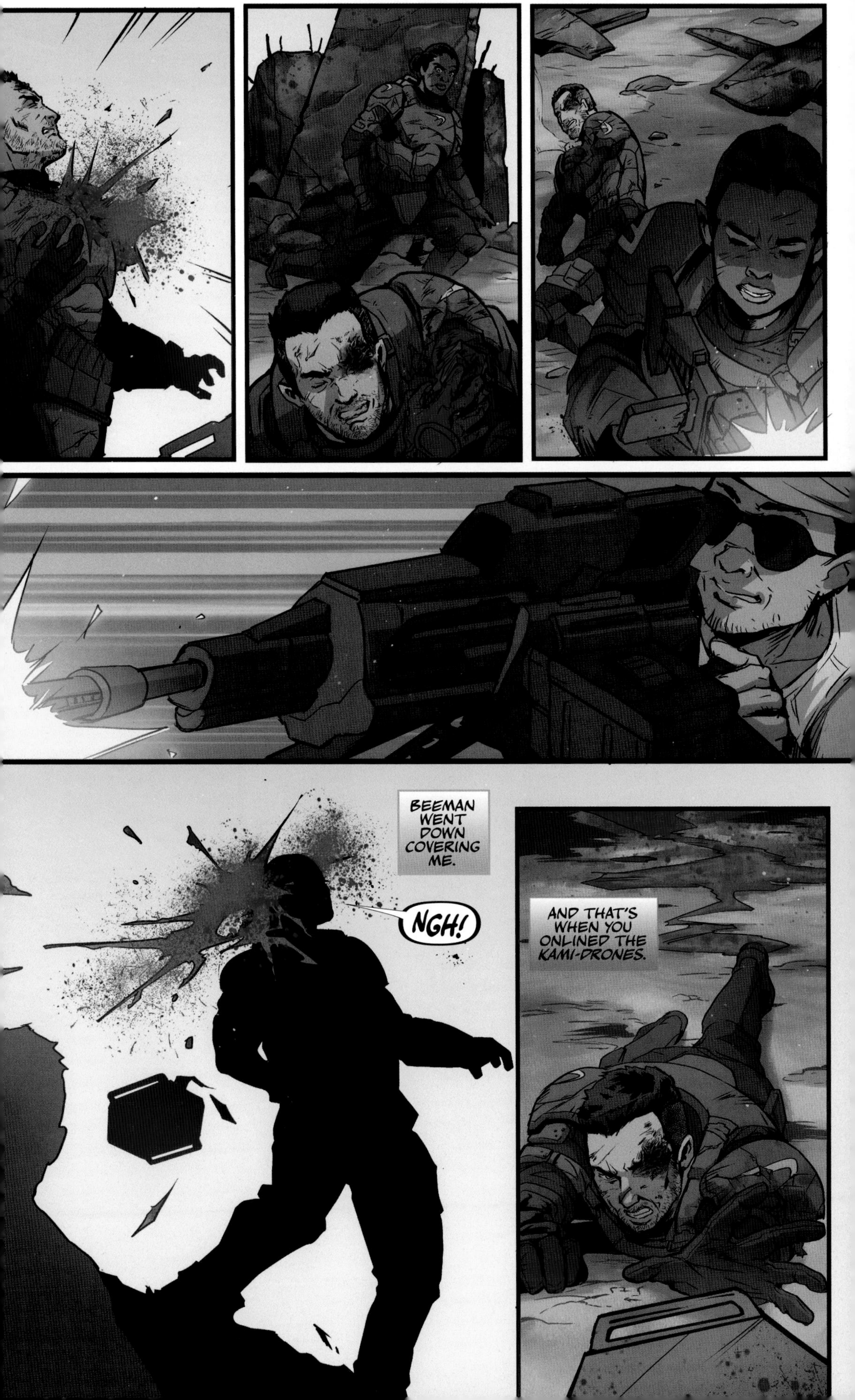
BEEMAN WENT DOWN COVERING ME.
NGH!
AND THAT'S WHEN YOU ONLINED THE KAMI-DRONES.

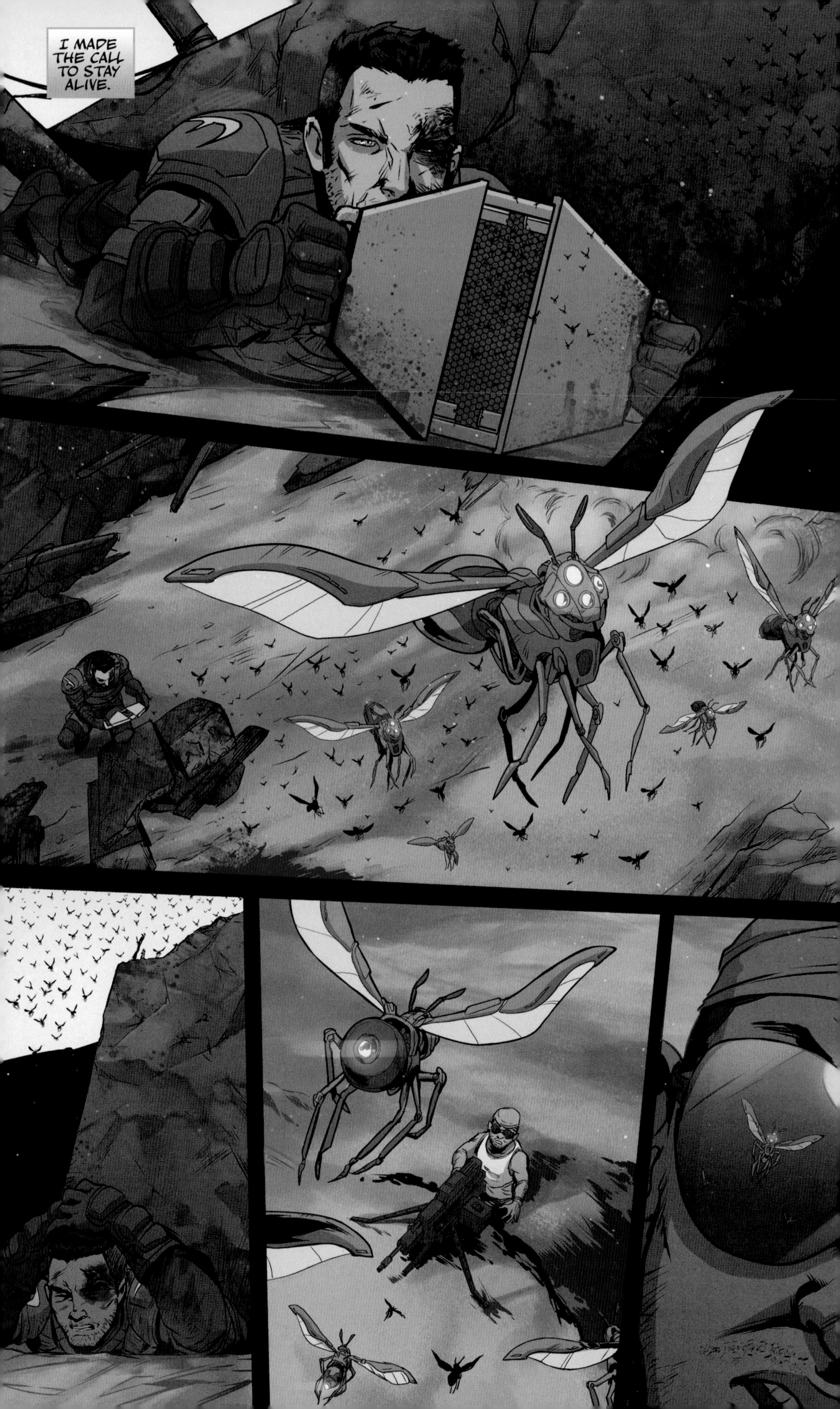
I MADE THE CALL TO STAY ALIVE.

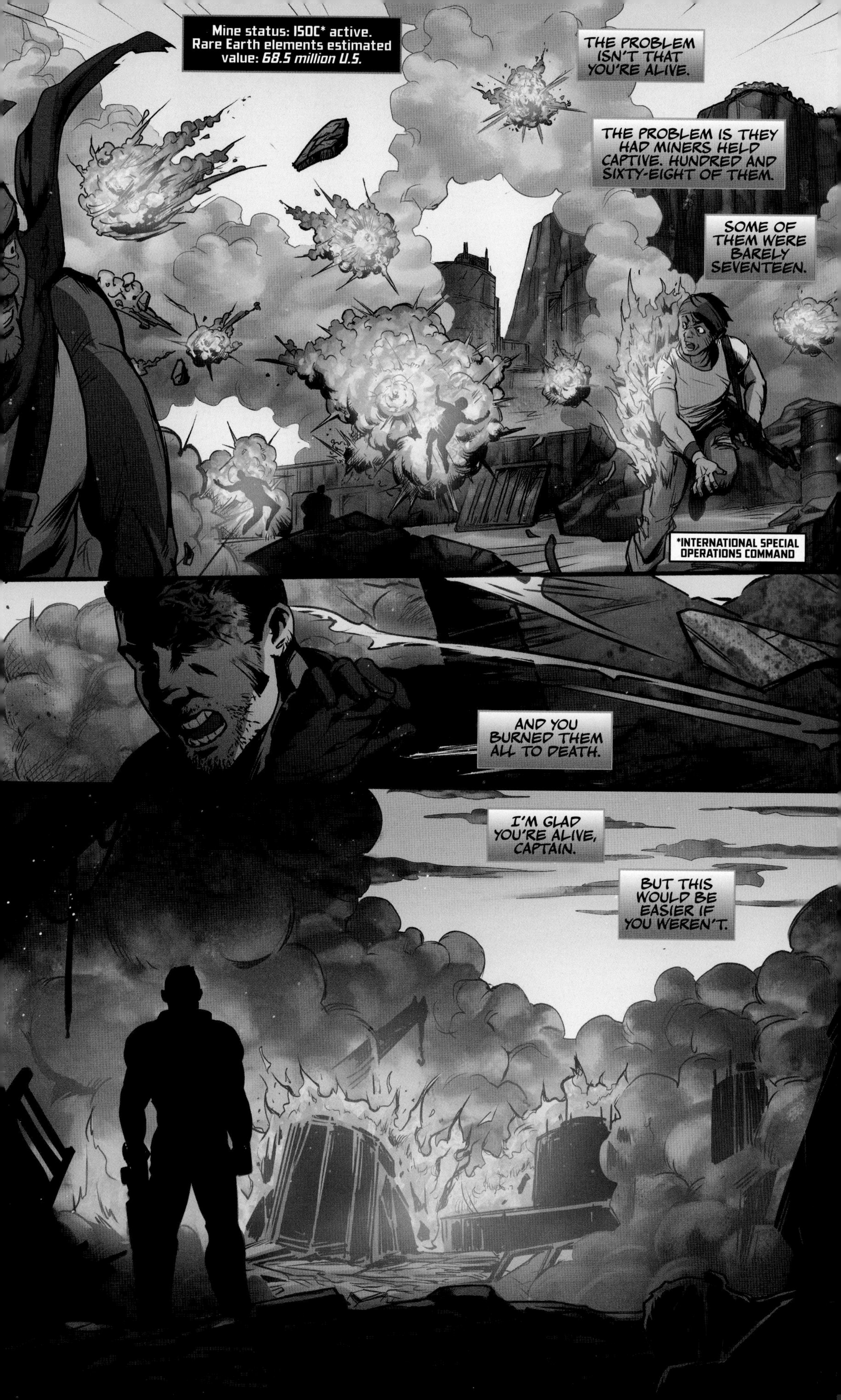
Mine status: ISOC* active.
Rare Earth elements estimated value: 68.5 million U.S.
THE PROBLEM ISN'T THAT YOU'RE ALIVE.
THE PROBLEM IS THEY HAD MINERS HELD CAPTIVE. HUNDRED AND SIXTY-EIGHT OF THEM.
SOME OF THEM WERE BARELY SEVENTEEN.
*INTERNATIONAL SPECIAL OPERATIONS COMMAND
AND YOU BURNED THEM ALL TO DEATH.
I'M GLAD YOU'RE ALIVE, CAPTAIN.
BUT THIS WOULD BE EASIER IF YOU WEREN'T.

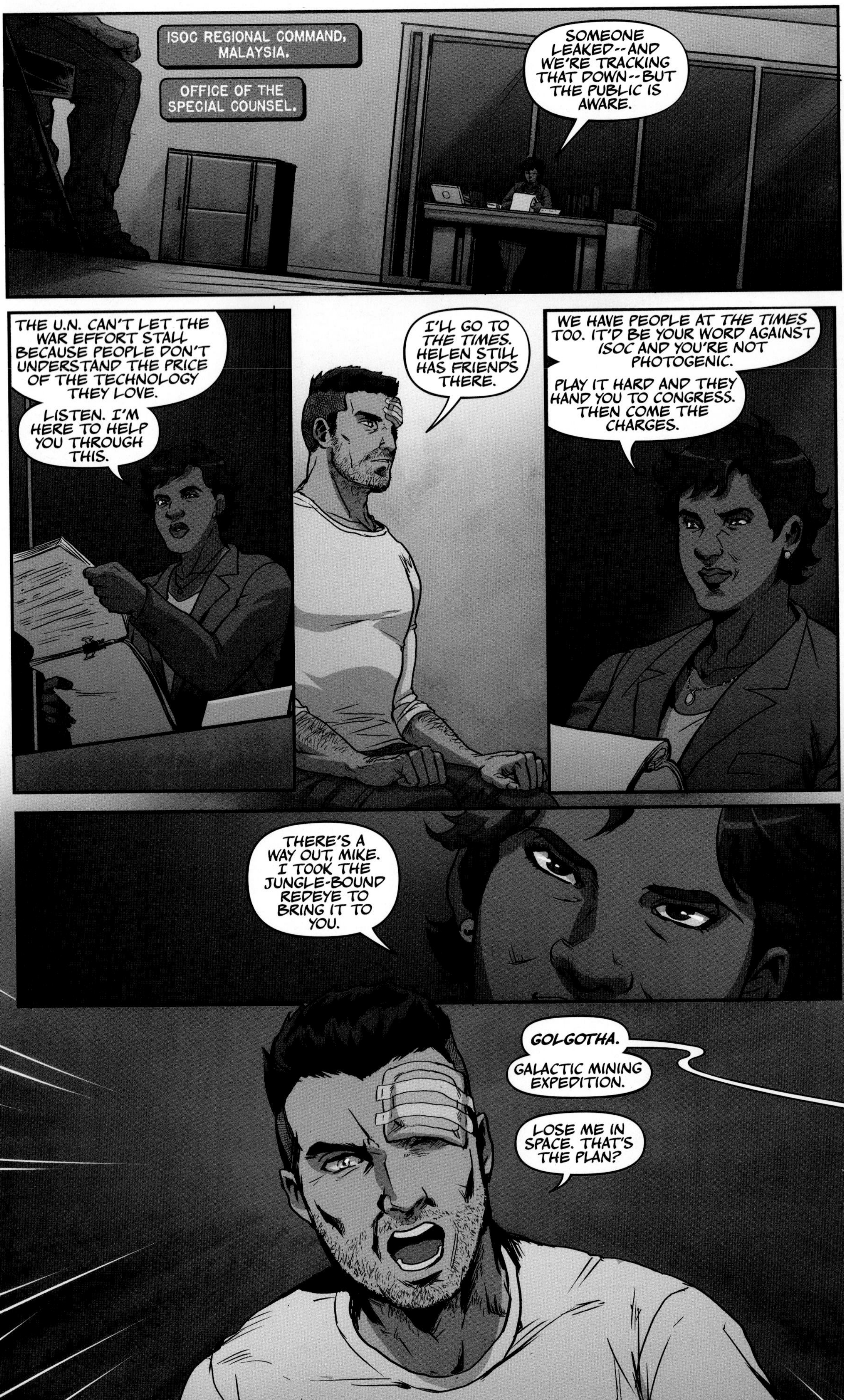
ISOC REGIONAL COMMAND, MALAYSIA.
OFFICE OF THE SPECIAL COUNSEL.
SOMEONE LEAKED--AND WE'RE TRACKING THAT DOWN--BUT THE PUBLIC IS AWARE.
THE U.N. CAN'T LET THE WAR EFFORT STALL BECAUSE PEOPLE DON'T UNDERSTAND THE PRICE OF THE TECHNOLOGY THEY LOVE.
LISTEN. I'M HERE TO HELP YOU THROUGH THIS.
I'LL GO TO THE TIMES. HELEN STILL HAS FRIENDS THERE.
WE HAVE PEOPLE AT THE TIMES TOO. IT'D BE YOUR WORD AGAINST ISOC AND YOU'RE NOT PHOTOGENIC.
PLAY IT HARD AND THEY HAND YOU TO CONGRESS. THEN COME THE CHARGES.
THERE'S A WAY OUT, MIKE. I TOOK THE JUNGLE-BOUND REDEYE TO BRING IT TO YOU.
GOLGOTHA.
GALACTIC MINING EXPEDITION.
LOSE ME IN SPACE. THAT'S THE PLAN?

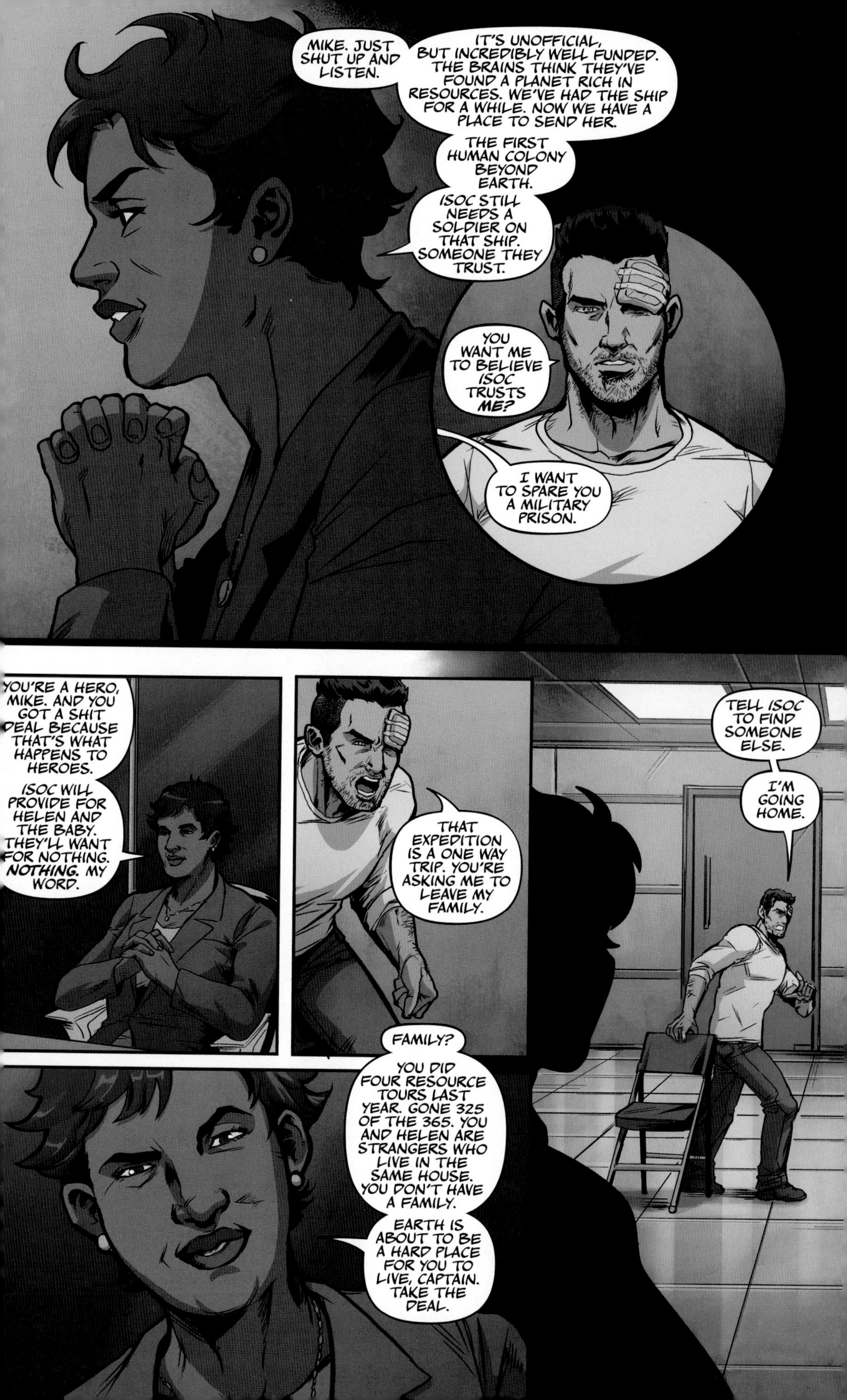
MIKE. JUST SHUT UP AND LISTEN.
IT'S UNOFFICIAL, BUT INCREDIBLY WELL FUNDED. THE BRAINS THINK THEY'VE FOUND A PLANET RICH IN RESOURCES. WE'VE HAD THE SHIP FOR A WHILE. NOW WE HAVE A PLACE TO SEND HER.
THE FIRST HUMAN COLONY BEYOND EARTH.
ISOC STILL NEEDS A SOLDIER ON THAT SHIP. SOMEONE THEY TRUST.
YOU WANT ME TO BELIEVE ISOC TRUSTS *ME?*
I WANT TO SPARE YOU A MILITARY PRISON.
YOU'RE A HERO, MIKE. AND YOU GOT A SHIT DEAL BECAUSE THAT'S WHAT HAPPENS TO HEROES.
ISOC WILL PROVIDE FOR HELEN AND THE BABY. THEY'LL WANT FOR NOTHING. *NOTHING.* MY WORD.
THAT EXPEDITION IS A ONE WAY TRIP. YOU'RE ASKING ME TO LEAVE MY FAMILY.
TELL ISOC TO FIND SOMEONE ELSE.
I'M GOING HOME.
FAMILY?
YOU DID FOUR RESOURCE TOURS LAST YEAR. GONE 325 OF THE 365. YOU AND HELEN ARE STRANGERS WHO LIVE IN THE SAME HOUSE. YOU DON'T HAVE A FAMILY.
EARTH IS ABOUT TO BE A HARD PLACE FOR YOU TO LIVE, CAPTAIN. TAKE THE DEAL.

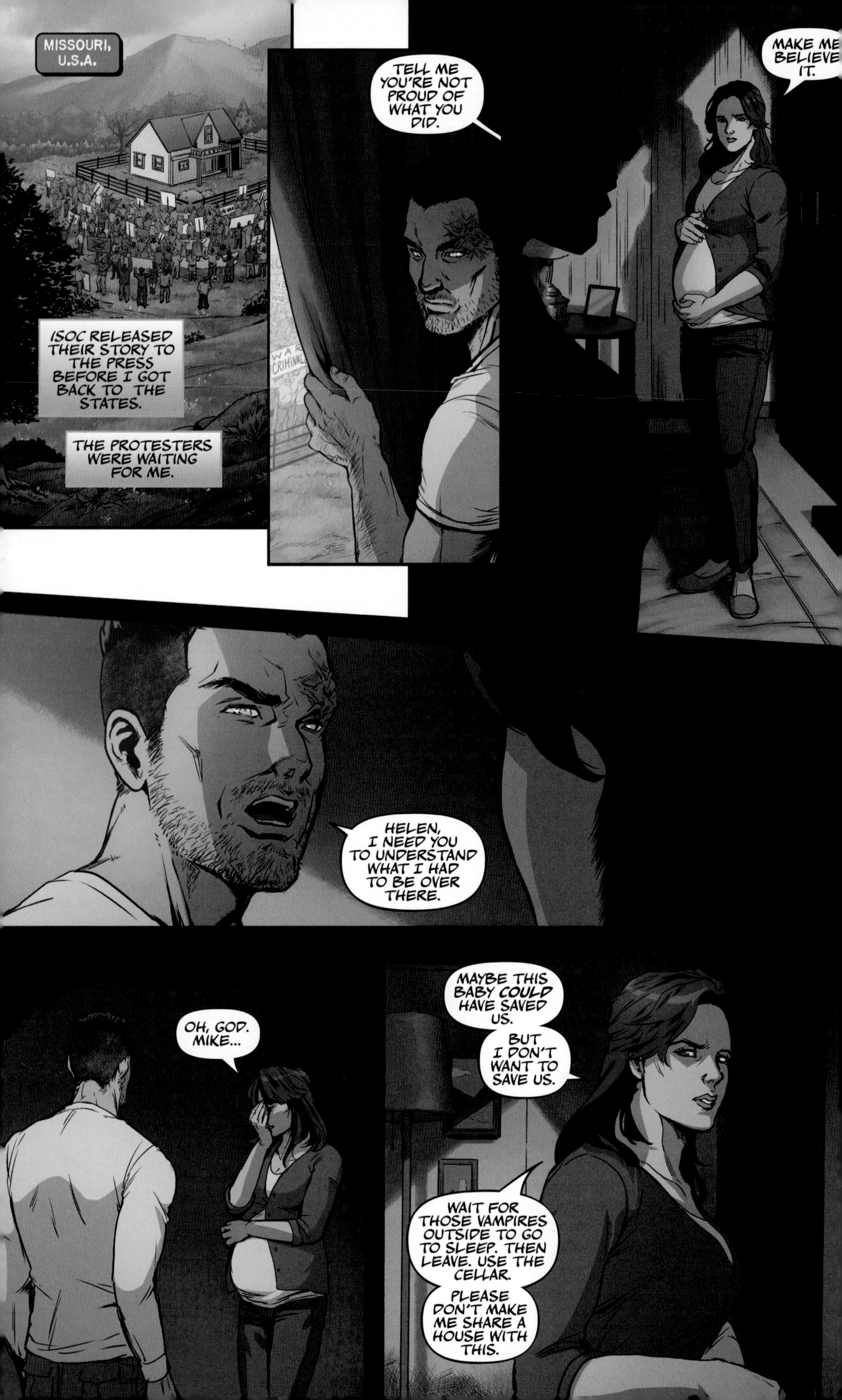
MISSOURI, U.S.A.
ISOC RELEASED THEIR STORY TO THE PRESS BEFORE I GOT BACK TO THE STATES.
THE PROTESTERS WERE WAITING FOR ME.
TELL ME YOU'RE NOT PROUD OF WHAT YOU DID.
MAKE ME BELIEVE IT.
HELEN, I NEED YOU TO UNDERSTAND WHAT I HAD TO BE OVER THERE.
OH, GOD. MIKE...
MAYBE THIS BABY COULD HAVE SAVED US.
BUT I DON'T WANT TO SAVE US.
WAIT FOR THOSE VAMPIRES OUTSIDE TO GO TO SLEEP. THEN LEAVE. USE THE CELLAR.
PLEASE DON'T MAKE ME SHARE A HOUSE WITH THIS.

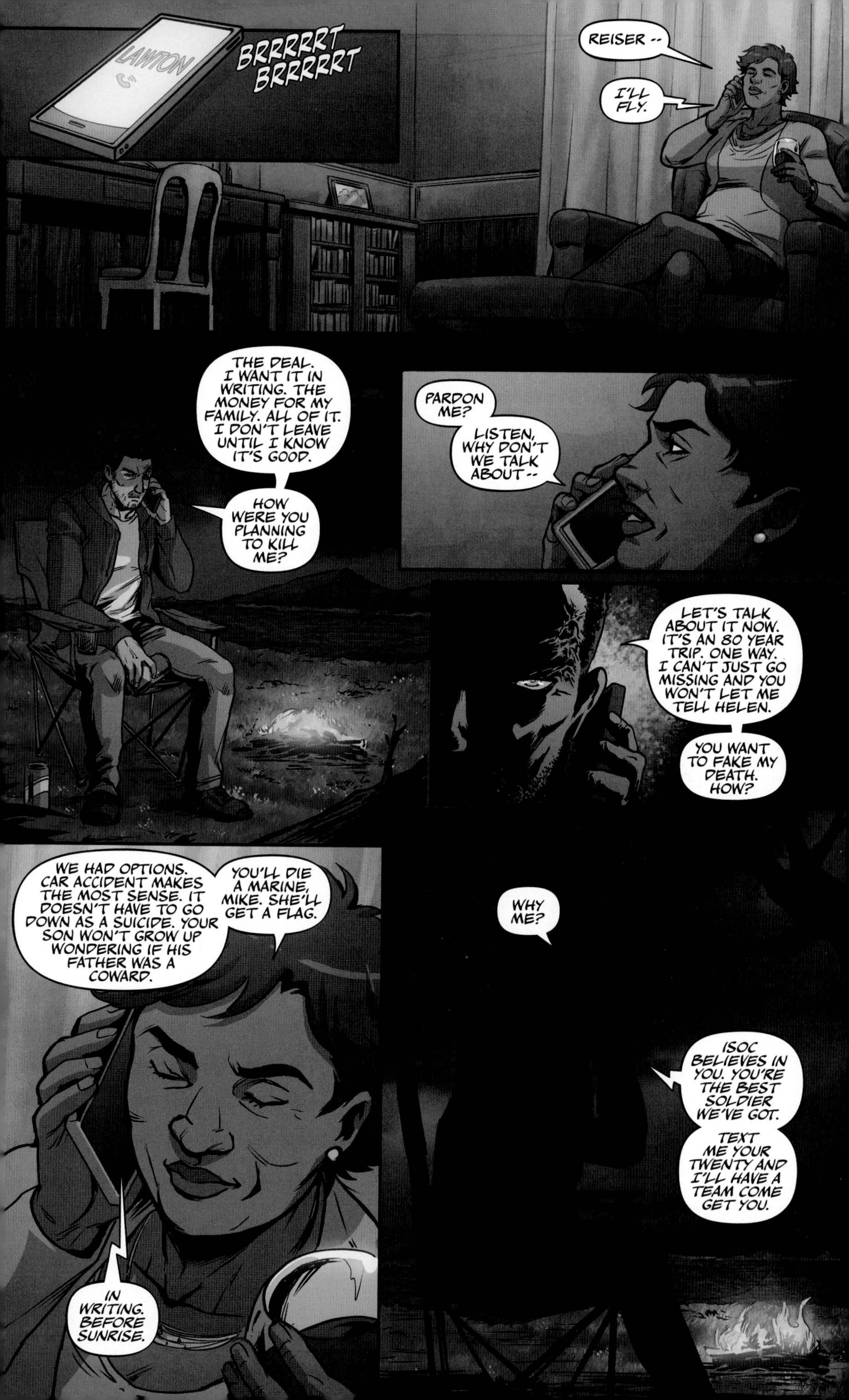
LAWTON
BRRRRRT BRRRRRT
REISER --
I'LL FLY.
THE DEAL. I WANT IT IN WRITING. THE MONEY FOR MY FAMILY. ALL OF IT. I DON'T LEAVE UNTIL I KNOW IT'S GOOD.
HOW WERE YOU PLANNING TO KILL ME?
PARDON ME?
LISTEN, WHY DON'T WE TALK ABOUT --
LET'S TALK ABOUT IT NOW. IT'S AN 80 YEAR TRIP. ONE WAY. I CAN'T JUST GO MISSING AND YOU WON'T LET ME TELL HELEN.
YOU WANT TO FAKE MY DEATH. HOW?
WE HAD OPTIONS. CAR ACCIDENT MAKES THE MOST SENSE. IT DOESN'T HAVE TO GO DOWN AS A SUICIDE. YOUR SON WON'T GROW UP WONDERING IF HIS FATHER WAS A COWARD.
YOU'LL DIE A MARINE, MIKE. SHE'LL GET A FLAG.
IN WRITING. BEFORE SUNRISE.
WHY ME?
ISOC BELIEVES IN YOU. YOU'RE THE BEST SOLDIER WE'VE GOT.
TEXT ME YOUR TWENTY AND I'LL HAVE A TEAM COME GET YOU.

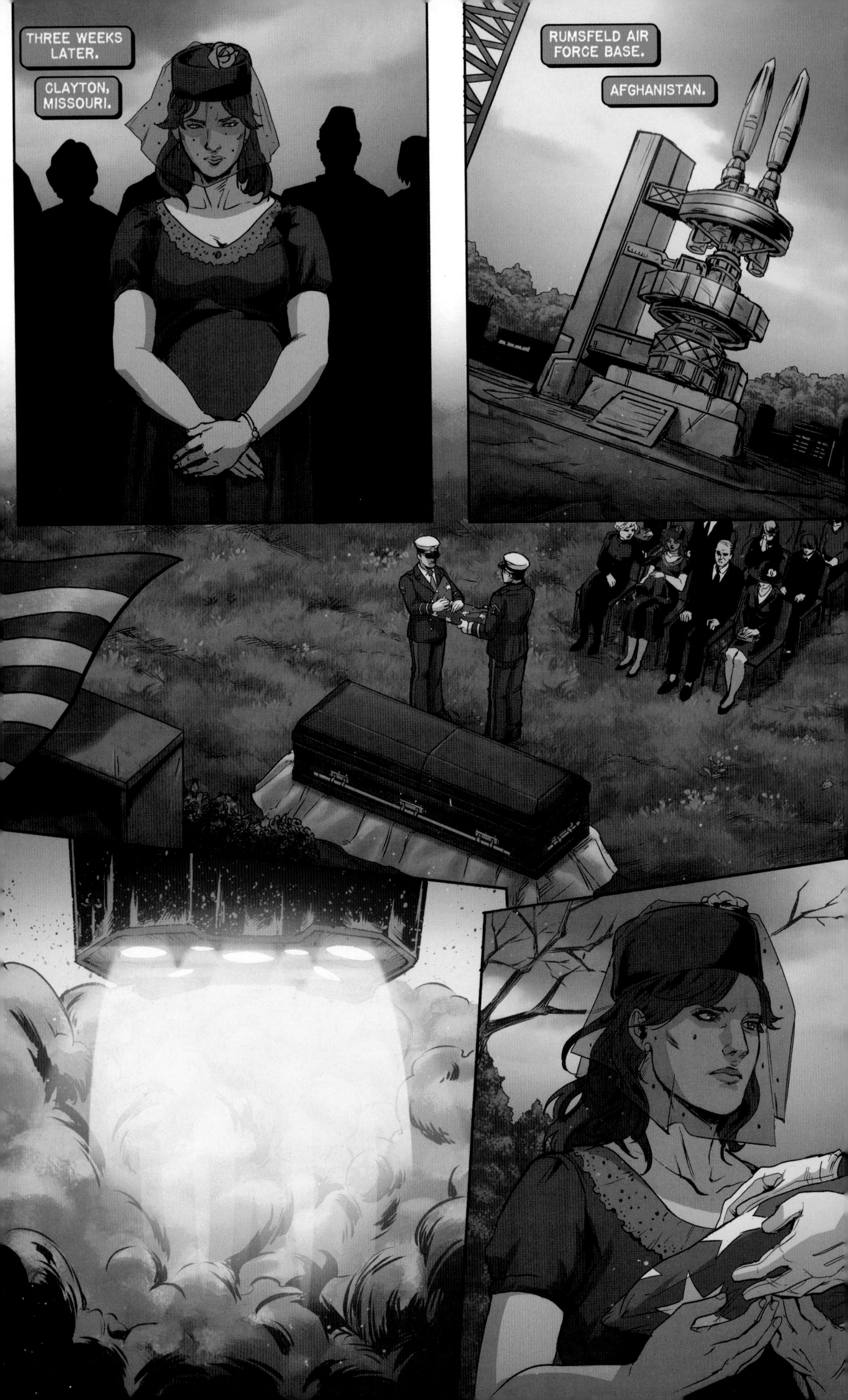
THREE WEEKS LATER.
CLAYTON, MISSOURI.
RUMSFELD AIR FORCE BASE.
AFGHANISTAN.

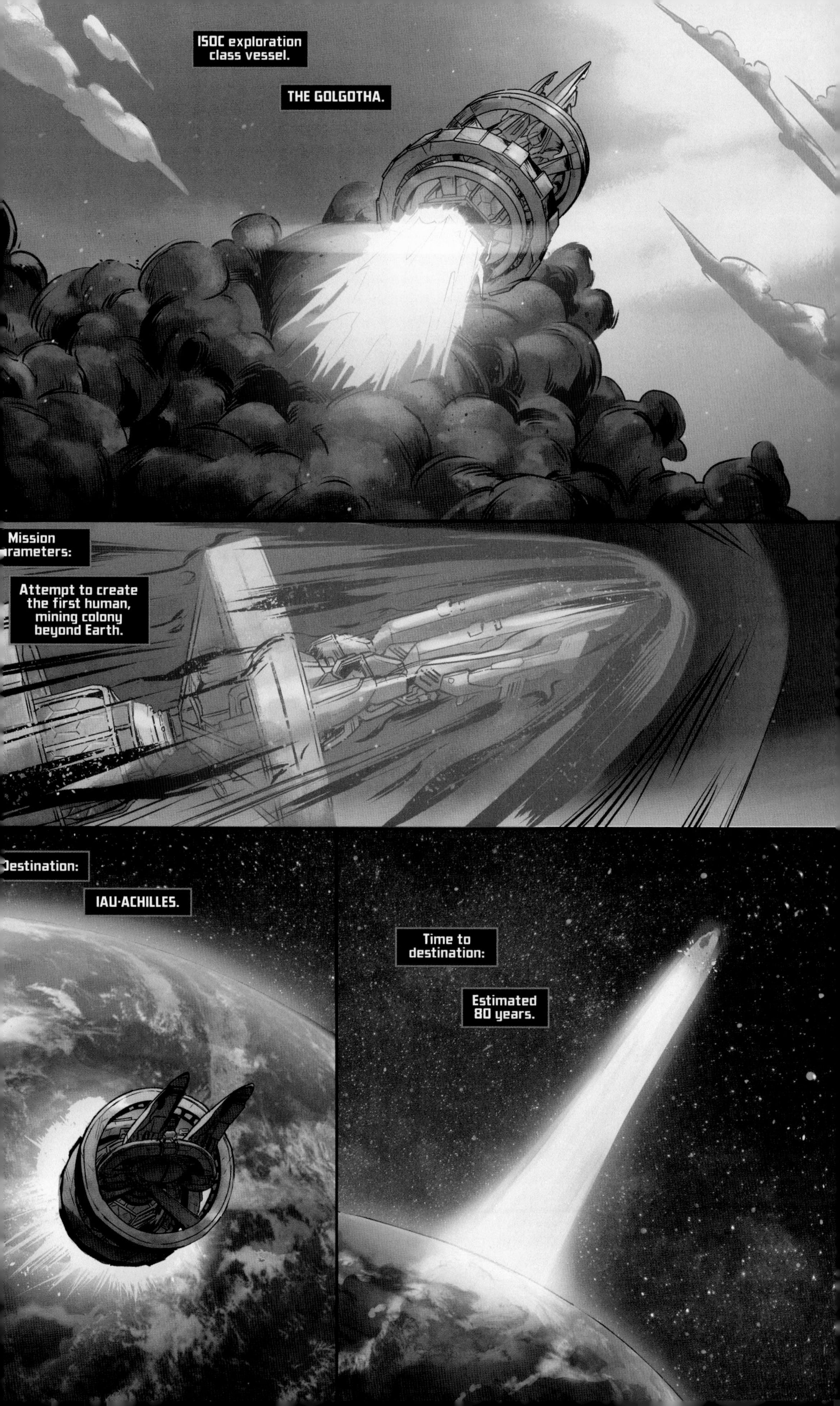
ISOC exploration class vessel.
THE GOLGOTHA.
Mission rameters:
Attempt to create the first human, mining colony beyond Earth.
Destination:
IAU-ACHILLES.
Time to destination:
Estimated 80 years.

Essential crew:

CARILLO, Anabelle. AEF. HUM-INT backup pilot to automated ship system.

MEAD, Lancaster. Engineer.

LIPPENCOTT, Charlene. PhD. Agrophysics.

GAFANI, Abdul-Ghafaar. Imam. AEF.

CHENG, David. Chaplain. AEF.

ROSENTHAL, Moshe. Rabbi. AEF.

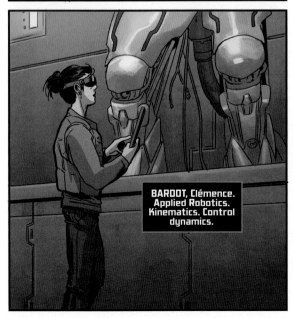

BARDOT, Clémence. Applied Robotics. Kinematics. Control dynamics.

LAWTON, Michael. Cpt. 31st Special Forces Group. ISOC.

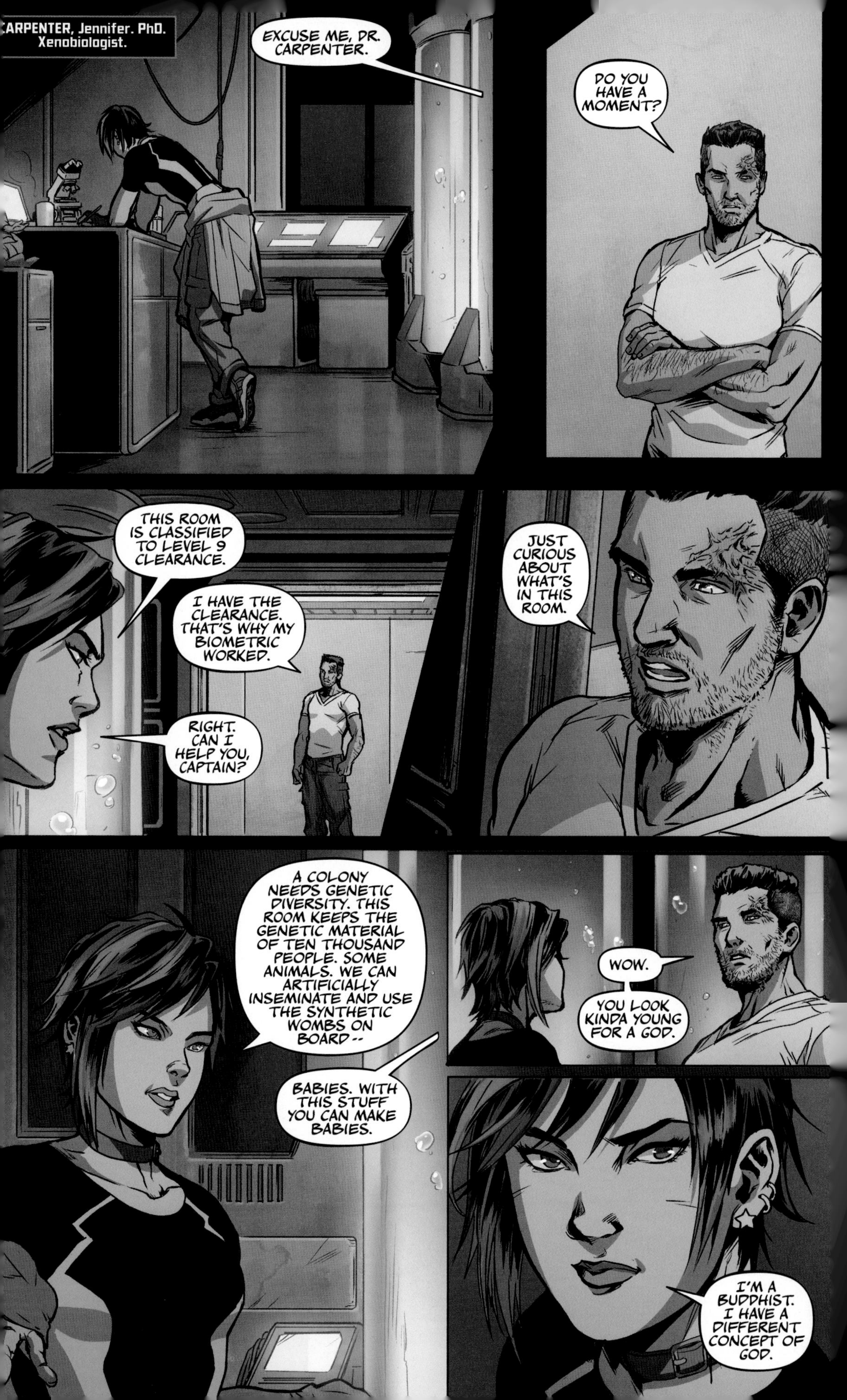
CARPENTER, Jennifer. PhD.
Xenobiologist.
EXCUSE ME, DR. CARPENTER.
DO YOU HAVE A MOMENT?
THIS ROOM IS CLASSIFIED TO LEVEL 9 CLEARANCE.
I HAVE THE CLEARANCE. THAT'S WHY MY BIOMETRIC WORKED.
RIGHT. CAN I HELP YOU, CAPTAIN?
JUST CURIOUS ABOUT WHAT'S IN THIS ROOM.
A COLONY NEEDS GENETIC DIVERSITY. THIS ROOM KEEPS THE GENETIC MATERIAL OF TEN THOUSAND PEOPLE. SOME ANIMALS. WE CAN ARTIFICIALLY INSEMINATE AND USE THE SYNTHETIC WOMBS ON BOARD--
BABIES. WITH THIS STUFF YOU CAN MAKE BABIES.
WOW.
YOU LOOK KINDA YOUNG FOR A GOD.
I'M A BUDDHIST. I HAVE A DIFFERENT CONCEPT OF GOD.

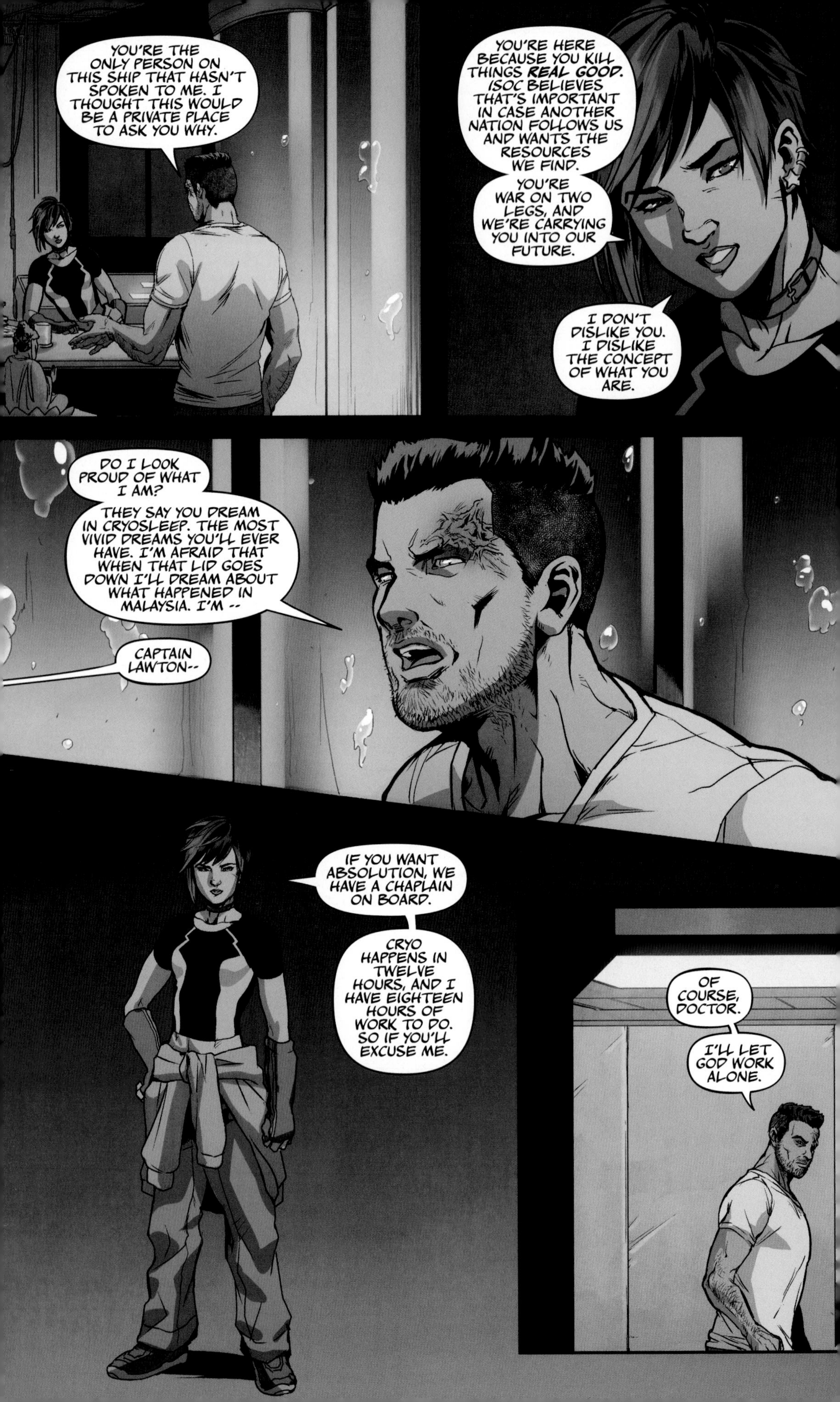
YOU'RE THE ONLY PERSON ON THIS SHIP THAT HASN'T SPOKEN TO ME. I THOUGHT THIS WOULD BE A PRIVATE PLACE TO ASK YOU WHY.
YOU'RE HERE BECAUSE YOU KILL THINGS REAL GOOD. ISOC BELIEVES THAT'S IMPORTANT IN CASE ANOTHER NATION FOLLOWS US AND WANTS THE RESOURCES WE FIND.
YOU'RE WAR ON TWO LEGS, AND WE'RE CARRYING YOU INTO OUR FUTURE.
I DON'T DISLIKE YOU. I DISLIKE THE CONCEPT OF WHAT YOU ARE.
DO I LOOK PROUD OF WHAT I AM?
THEY SAY YOU DREAM IN CRYOSLEEP. THE MOST VIVID DREAMS YOU'LL EVER HAVE. I'M AFRAID THAT WHEN THAT LID GOES DOWN I'LL DREAM ABOUT WHAT HAPPENED IN MALAYSIA. I'M --
CAPTAIN LAWTON--
IF YOU WANT ABSOLUTION, WE HAVE A CHAPLAIN ON BOARD.
CRYO HAPPENS IN TWELVE HOURS, AND I HAVE EIGHTEEN HOURS OF WORK TO DO. SO IF YOU'LL EXCUSE ME.
OF COURSE, DOCTOR.
I'LL LET GOD WORK ALONE.

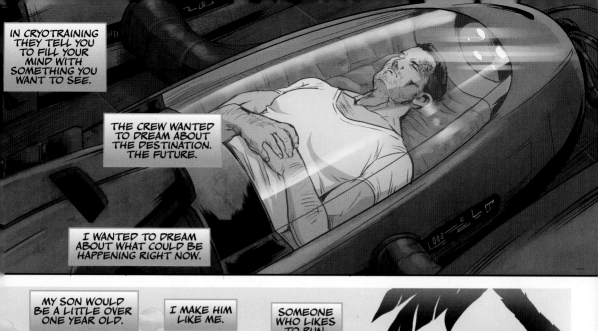

IN CRYOTRAINING THEY TELL YOU TO FILL YOUR MIND WITH SOMETHING YOU WANT TO SEE.

THE CREW WANTED TO DREAM ABOUT THE DESTINATION. THE FUTURE.

I WANTED TO DREAM ABOUT WHAT COULD BE HAPPENING RIGHT NOW.

MY SON WOULD BE A LITTLE OVER ONE YEAR OLD.

I MAKE HIM LIKE ME.

SOMEONE WHO LIKES TO RUN.

I MAKE THE GOVERNMENT MONEY ENOUGH FOR HELEN TO GET THAT BEACH HOUSE.

THE HOUSE I DIED TO GIVE HER.

I SEE THEM BETTER OFF WITHOUT ME.

I SEE THEM...

I SEE...

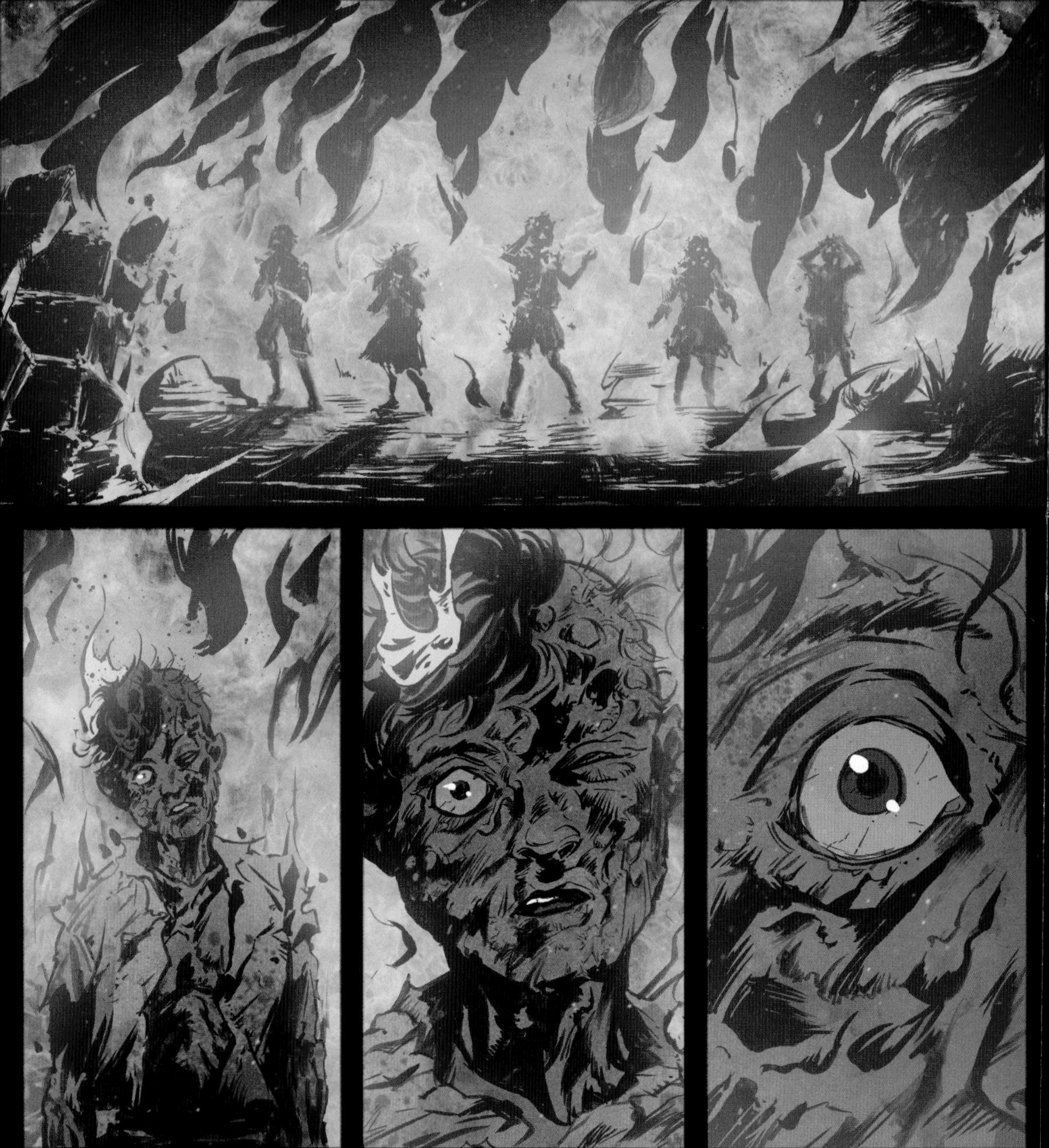

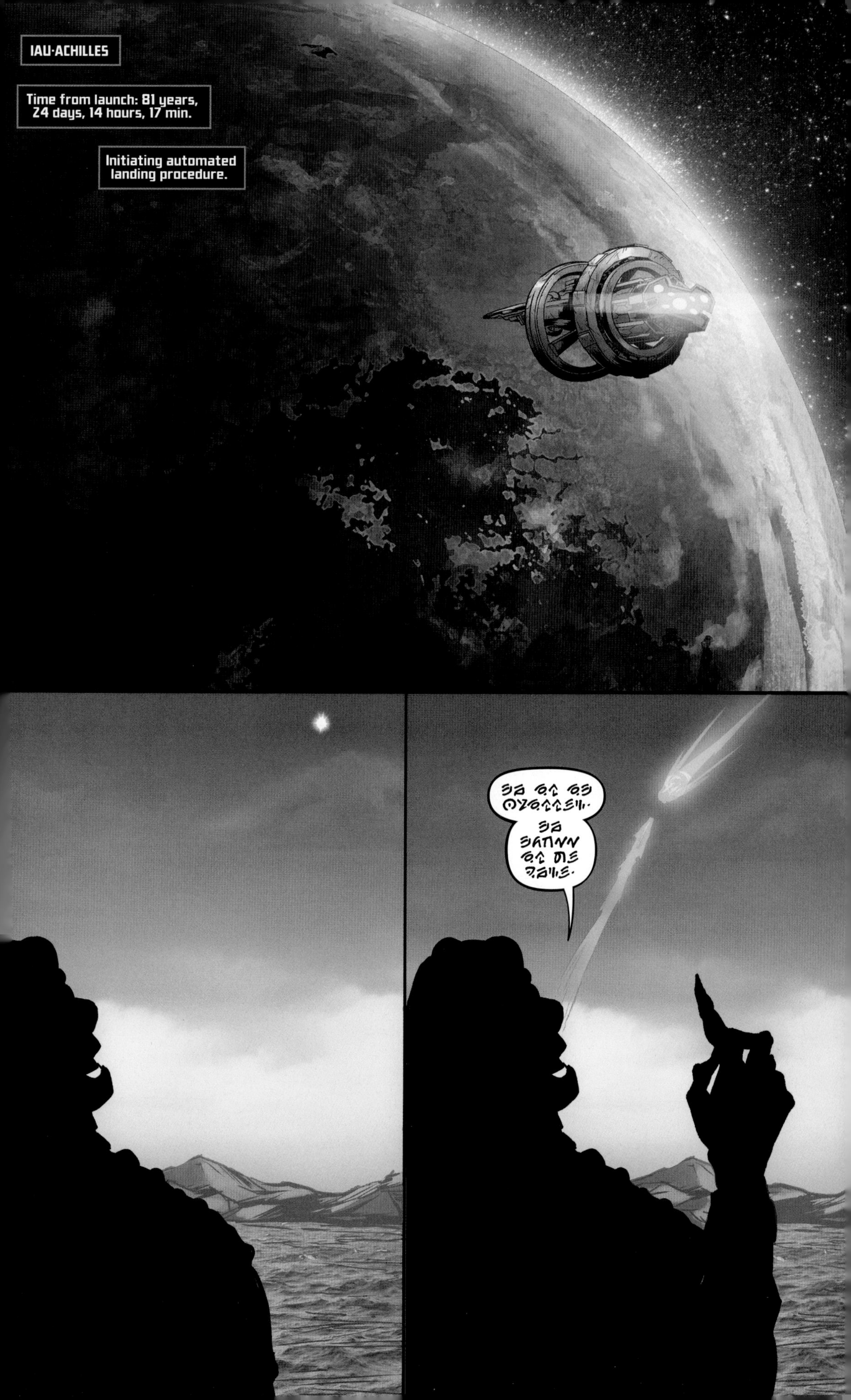
IAU-ACHILLES
Time from launch: 81 years, 24 days, 14 hours, 17 min.
Initiating automated landing procedure.

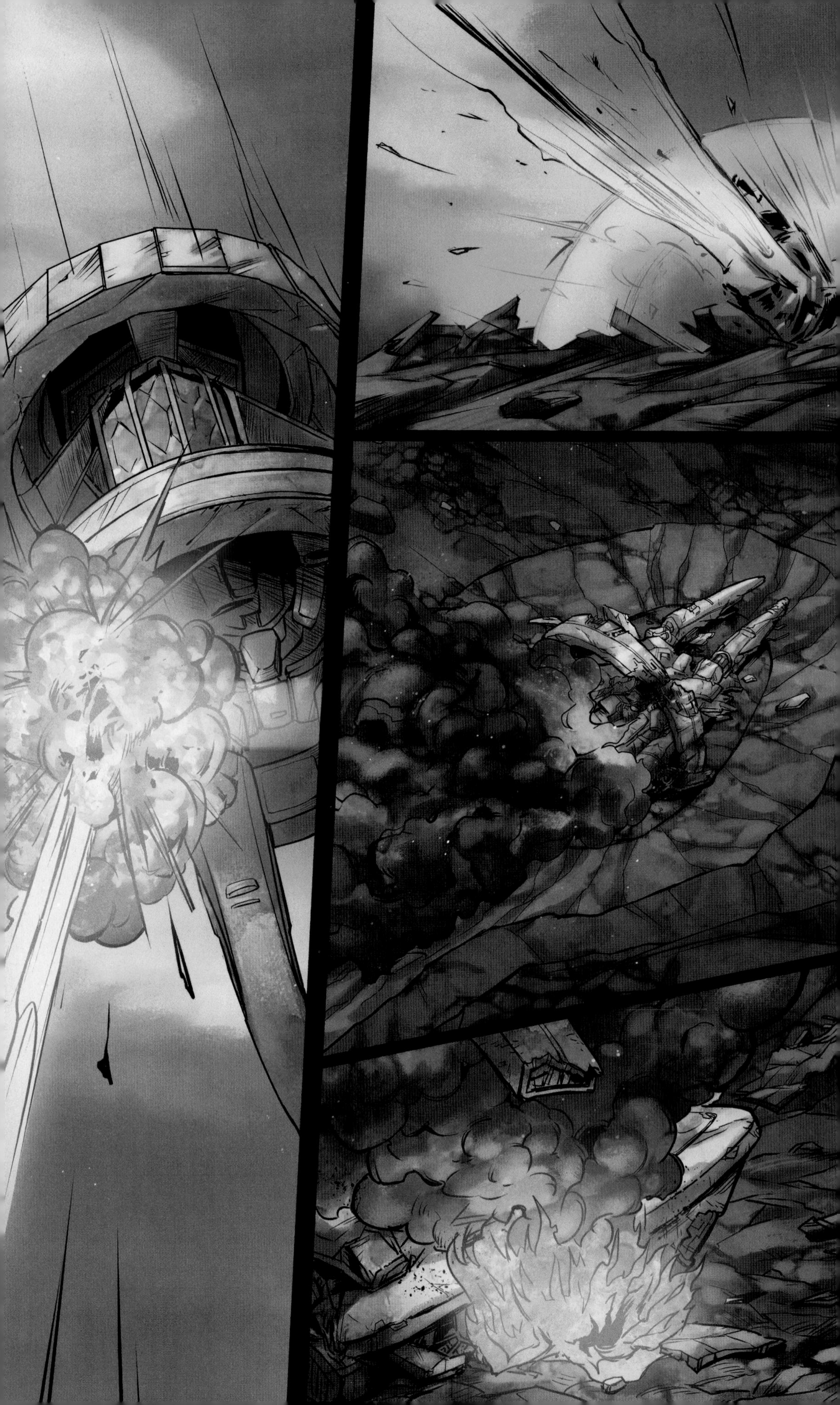

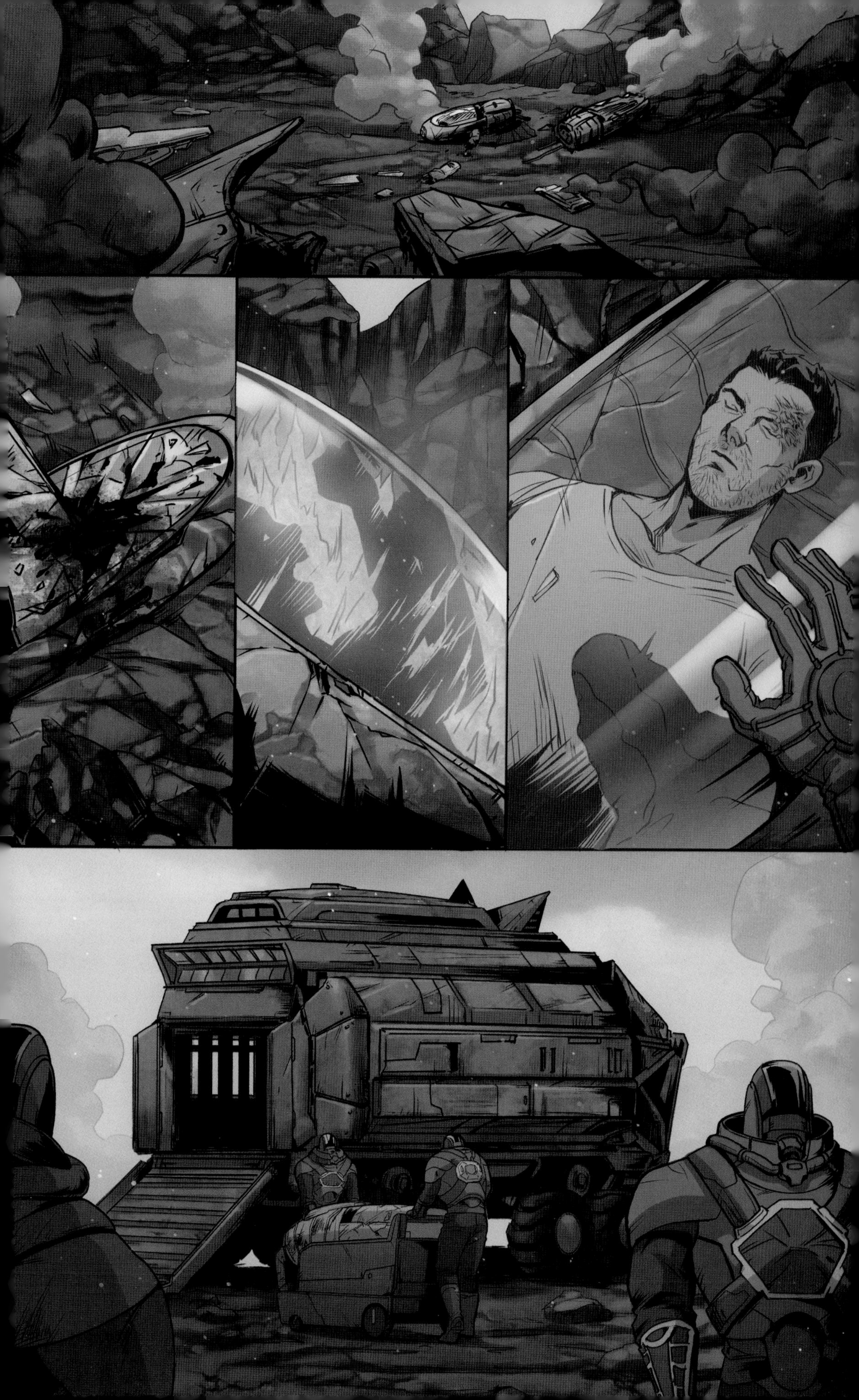

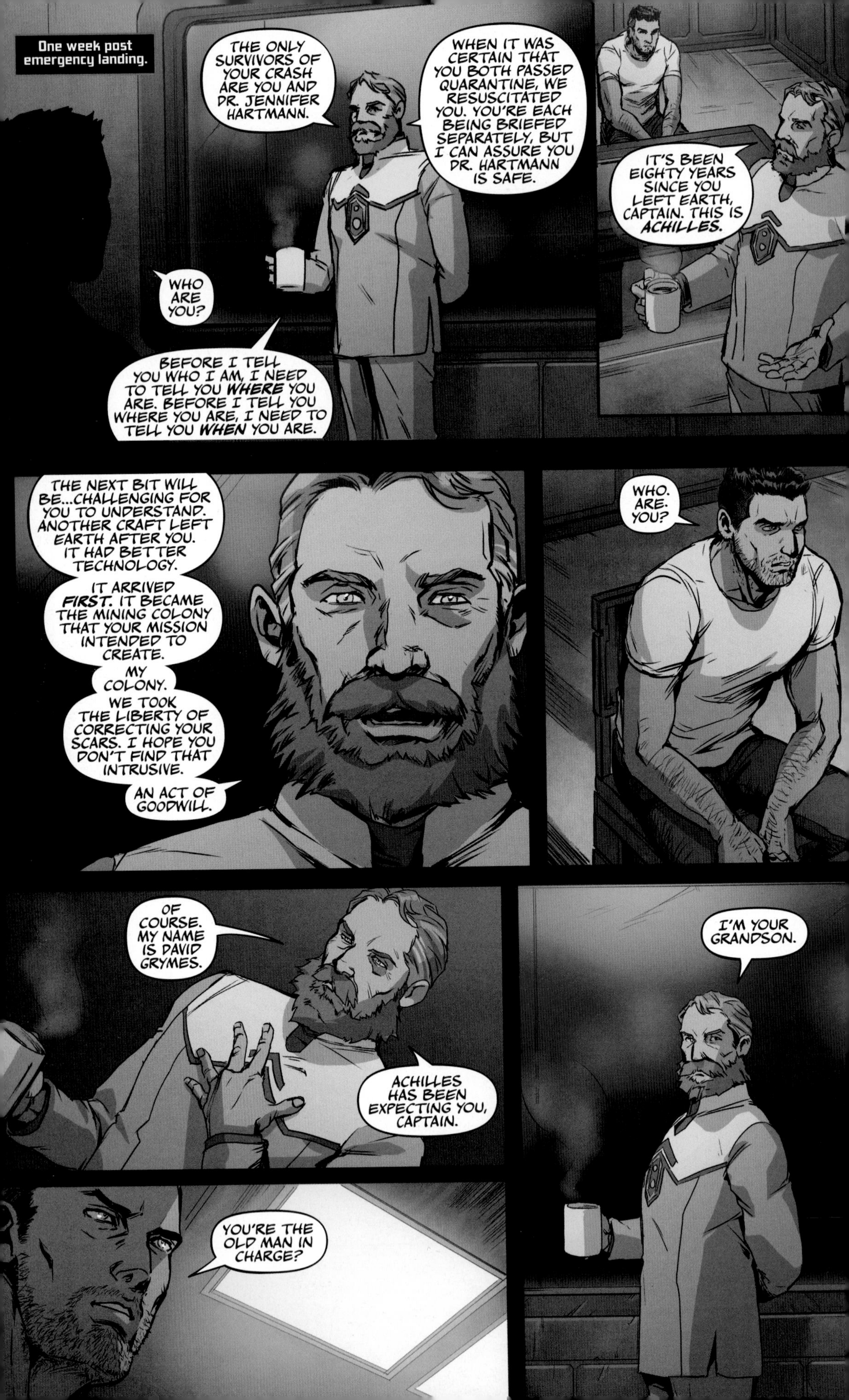
One week post emergency landing.
THE ONLY SURVIVORS OF YOUR CRASH ARE YOU AND DR. JENNIFER HARTMANN.
WHEN IT WAS CERTAIN THAT YOU BOTH PASSED QUARANTINE, WE RESUSCITATED YOU. YOU'RE EACH BEING BRIEFED SEPARATELY, BUT I CAN ASSURE YOU DR. HARTMANN IS SAFE.
WHO ARE YOU?
BEFORE I TELL YOU WHO I AM, I NEED TO TELL YOU WHERE YOU ARE. BEFORE I TELL YOU WHERE YOU ARE, I NEED TO TELL YOU WHEN YOU ARE.
IT'S BEEN EIGHTY YEARS SINCE YOU LEFT EARTH, CAPTAIN. THIS IS ACHILLES.
THE NEXT BIT WILL BE...CHALLENGING FOR YOU TO UNDERSTAND. ANOTHER CRAFT LEFT EARTH AFTER YOU. IT HAD BETTER TECHNOLOGY.
IT ARRIVED FIRST. IT BECAME THE MINING COLONY THAT YOUR MISSION INTENDED TO CREATE.
MY COLONY.
WE TOOK THE LIBERTY OF CORRECTING YOUR SCARS. I HOPE YOU DON'T FIND THAT INTRUSIVE.
AN ACT OF GOODWILL.
WHO. ARE. YOU?
OF COURSE. MY NAME IS DAVID GRYMES.
ACHILLES HAS BEEN EXPECTING YOU, CAPTAIN.
YOU'RE THE OLD MAN IN CHARGE?
I'M YOUR GRANDSON.

CHRIST...

THIS IS THE *ACHILLES COLONY.*

THE FIRST OF SEVEN HUMAN COLONIES IN THIS GALAXY.

I AM THE OLD MAN IN CHARGE.

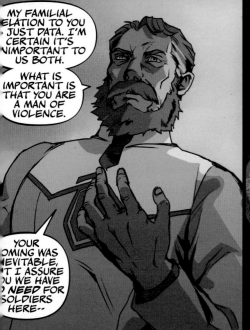

MY FAMILIAL RELATION TO YOU IS JUST DATA. I'M CERTAIN IT'S UNIMPORTANT TO US BOTH.

WHAT IS IMPORTANT IS THAT YOU ARE A MAN OF VIOLENCE.

YOUR COMING WAS INEVITABLE, BUT I ASSURE YOU WE HAVE NO NEED FOR SOLDIERS HERE--

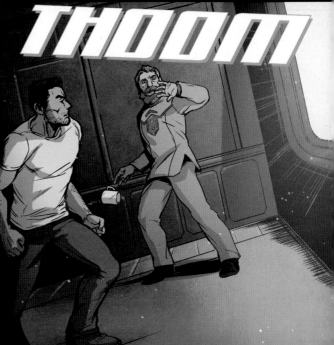

THOOM

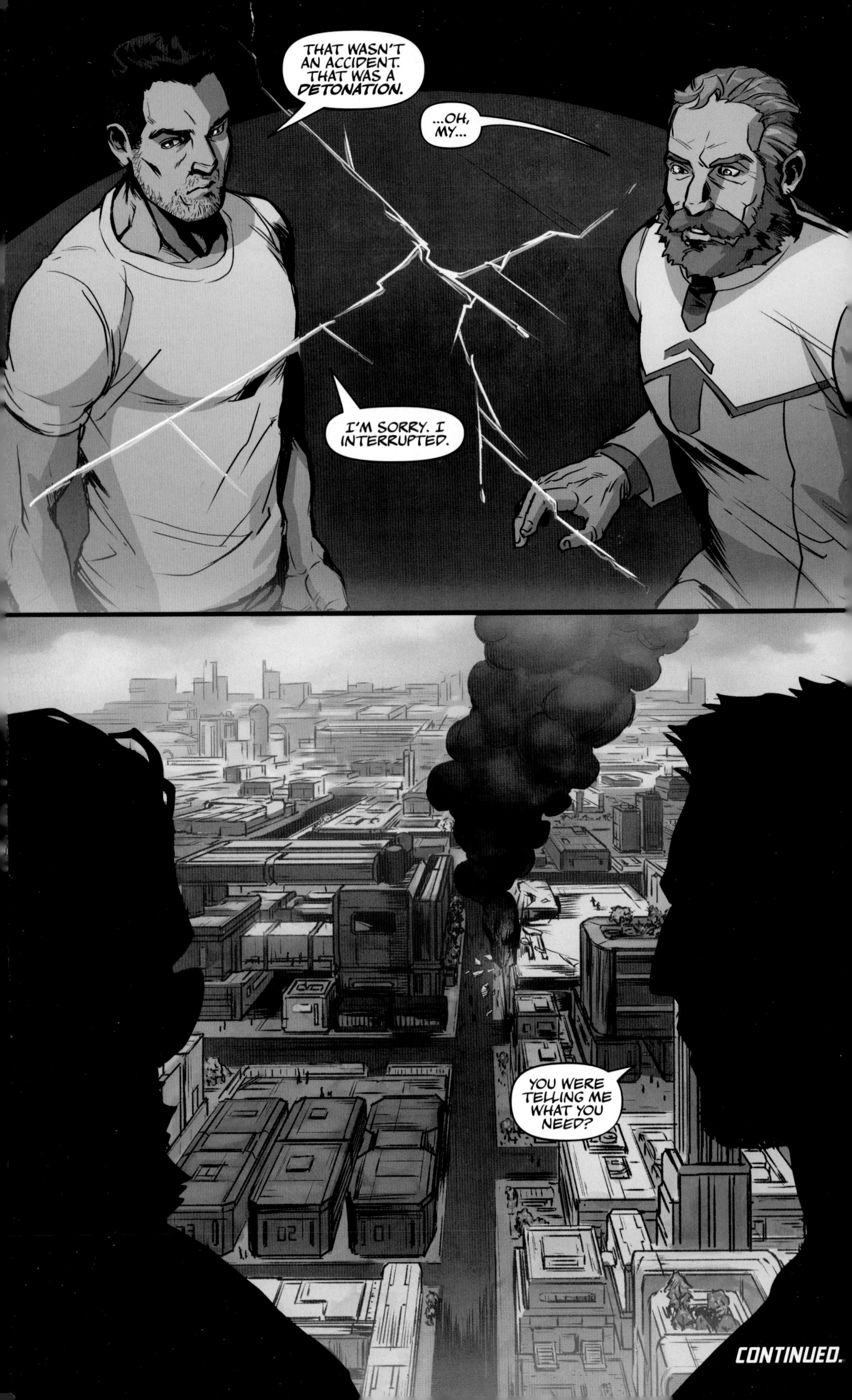
THAT WASN'T AN ACCIDENT. THAT WAS A DETONATION.
...OH, MY...
I'M SORRY. I INTERRUPTED.
YOU WERE TELLING ME WHAT YOU NEED?
CONTINUED.